BLOOD TIES

BLOOD TIES

LIN LE VERSHA

This edition produced in Great Britain in 2023

by Hobeck Books Limited, Unit 14, Sugnall Business Centre, Sugnall, Stafford, Staffordshire, ST21 6NF

www.hobeck.net

A CIP catalogue for this book is available from the British Library.

ISBN 978-1-915-817-603-7 (ebook)

ISBN 978-1-915-817-04-4 (pbk)

Cover design by Jayne Mapp Design

https://jaynemapp.wixsite.com

 Created with Vellum

ARE YOU A THRILLER SEEKER?

Hobeck Books is an independent publisher of crime, mystery, thriller and suspense and we have one aim – to bring you the books you want to read.

For more details about our books, our authors and our plans, the chance to enter competitions, plus to download *Crime Bites*, a free compilation of novellas and short stories by our authors sign up for our newsletter at **www.hobeck.net**.

You can also find us on Twitter **@hobeckbooks** or on Facebook **www.facebook.com/hobeckbooks10**.

HOBECK ADVANCED READER TEAM

Hobeck Books has a team of dedicated advanced readers who read our books before publication (not all of them, they choose which they would like to read). Here is what they said about the first Steph Grant Murder Mystery *Blood Notes*.

'...a crime story with a bit of a difference...'

'I loved this book, the story, the plot, everything.'

'The reader is immediately hooked.'

'A dark and intriguing thriller that will keep you guessing right to the end.'

For Freda

PROLOGUE

HE HEARD the door open and dived under the bed. He breathed in dust – tried to hold his breath. Sweeping his hands across the floor in front of his face, he made a fluff mountain, which he shoved away.

The dust was getting up his nose, and he was terrified of sneezing. He squeezed his nostrils together with his fingers. Counted to five. The tickle passed.

Just out of reach, in the gloom, he spotted the red tractor – he thought he'd lost it forever. The farmyard didn't work without it. In silent slow motion, he squirmed towards it on his tummy, stretched out and closed his fingers around it. He'd never thought to look there – all this time without it.

He heard the door click shut. He was facing the wrong way to see who it was, but the big blue shoes came into view and walked alongside the bed.

He held his breath. That was no good – wouldn't be able to do it for long enough. He gave up and went back to breathing. The sound as he let out his breath was too loud. If he could hear himself, they would too. Could they hear the throbbing inside his body?

'Morning. Another glorious day!'

The blue shoes went over to the wall with the long window – metal rings rattled along the pole. His eyes closed themselves as sudden bright sunshine flashed along the dark wood. Could they see him in the light? He held himself so stiff it hurt. The shoes were now close – with a teeny stretch, he could touch the brown bits stuck in the folds. Could it be dog poo? Yuk! He sniffed but couldn't smell anything.

'Now, let's make you more comfortable.'

A creak. Without warning, the light went out as a dark green cover dropped over the side of the bed. He was in a black cave. If he turned his head to the side and squashed it flat to the floor and peeped through the crack of light below the cloth, he could just see the feet out of his left eye. Blue shoes moved up the bed, towards the pillows. The creaks got louder. The bed juddered on its wheels. The mattress bounced and squeaked above him. It stopped. Silence.

The shoes turned the other way and disappeared. He heard the door open then shut with a tiny click. He lay still. As still as sleeping lions at parties. Counted to ten, five times. Nothing. Nothing from the bed.

He slid on his tummy towards the green cloth, lifted it up to make an opening in the cave and pulled himself up. Standing beside the bed, he stared at Ker-Bear, who lay still with his eyes closed. How could he fall asleep again when he'd only just woken up?

Slowly, he reached out and touched the arm that hung over the edge of the bed. Nothing. He wobbled it a little. Nothing. Then a little shake. Then harder. Nothing. Why wouldn't he wake up? Ker-Bear must be really, really tired. He gave up.

On tip toe, he crept in slow motion out of the room, closing the door behind him.

CHAPTER ONE

DEREK PEED on the legs of Henry VIII. 'Derek! Leave!' Steph plunged down to grab his collar and drag him away from the stone statue. 'Why does he always choose the most embarrassing places?'

'That's males, darling,' drawled Caroline.

Steph frowned at Marlene, Caroline's white fluffy cushion of a dog, who appeared to be smiling indulgently at the antics of Derek. Perfectly behaved, she trotted along at Caroline's feet, while Steph's dog frantically snuffled around, darting from smell to smell. Derek, a black and white collie cross, had been rescued by Steph when she moved to a flat with a garden in Oakwood two years earlier, and she was convinced his boisterous behaviour resulted from his deprived puppyhood.

'Oh look – there's Hale and Margaret with the picnic. How about that spot under the oak, out of the sun?' Caroline pointed to an enormous tree, about a hundred metres away on the edge of a wood. 'Must take care we don't exacerbate our wrinkles, darling.'

Steph waved at Hale and pointed to the oak tree. After

their walk through the park, the arboretum and down to the lake, he had offered to return to the car park with Margaret to collect the picnics; having deciphered Steph's semaphore, he changed direction and the four of them arrived together. Two plaid rugs, four directors' chairs and a large bowl of water were quickly arranged under the dense canopy of the oak tree.

They sat facing Glebe Hall, which glowed in the May sunshine. Picnics at their feet, Steph smiled at the contrast that summed up the couples so well. The picnic that she and Hale had brought comprised a selection of wobbly silver foil packets shoved into a lifelong supermarket bag, supplemented by a few purchases from Morton's, the local deli, while Caroline and Margaret's picnic was elegantly arranged in a well-used wicker basket.

'Didn't realise it was going to be so hot when we left.' Hale took off his Panama hat and fanned his face. Sheepishly, he grinned back at Steph, acknowledging that she'd been right about the heat and the hat.

This May Day weekend had taken them by surprise; it felt more like high summer. Caroline had phoned early that morning and suggested the walk and picnic. For once, Detective Chief Inspector Hale had a weekend off, so Steph accepted for them both. He got on well with Caroline and her partner Margaret, so didn't complain when his plan of total collapse in front of the football on TV was disrupted.

Marlene, in superior pose, sat quietly beside Caroline, observing the ant people walking around the gardens of the Tudor mansion. Derek, however, rolled around the red and green tartan blanket, legs in the air, destroying the elegant art installation Caroline had created, which could be entitled *A Summer Picnic*.

'Derek, come!' Steph used her dog trainer voice. Her dog,

who had refused all attempts to be trained, pulled at the corner of the rug, then crouched, looking as if he was going to drag it away. Steph delved into her picnic bag and pulled out a large section of marrow bone filled with minced chicken. 'Bone, Derek, bone!'

At the magic word, Derek swivelled to his feet, leaped across the crumpled pile of plaid and sat, hypnotised by the bone in front of his nose. He made a small whine. Taking it in his mouth, he trotted off to the edge of the group and, with his tail helicoptering, started the long job of licking out the chicken mush.

'Amazing trick, teaching him to talk – shame about the rest of the training!' Hale, who got up to straighten the rug, moved out of Steph's glare. 'Just look at Marlene, perfectly behaved and without a bone.' He grinned back at her; she stuck her tongue out at him.

'Poor love, had a deprived puppyhood!' Caroline surveyed Derek sympathetically and they all laughed at Steph's well-worn phrase.

Steph joined in, pleased to spend time with her favourite people. 'Shall we have lunch?'

'Good idea.' Margaret fiddled with the tan leather straps on their basket. Caroline watched for a moment and, without saying a word, leaned forward and undid them for her. Margaret had been diagnosed with Parkinson's two years earlier and refused to let it interfere with her life, but it did. She was doing well and was fiercely independent, but even she had to admit that her dexterity was blunting and her movements were less sure.

Caroline and Margaret had been partners for over thirty years and appeared to have a very happy marriage for such different people. Caroline, tall, fly-away long grey curls and a wardrobe of dramatic, floaty dresses and vibrant scarves was the polar opposite to the solid Margaret in her sensible brown brogues, country woman tweed skirts and Barbour jackets.

Heads down, digging in bags and baskets, they were startled by a voice. 'Hello, how lovely to see you here.'

'Bella!' Caroline and Steph spoke together as they recognised the tall, dark-haired girl standing at the edge of the rug, patting Derek. Caroline continued, 'Of course, you live here!'

'Yes, it's all hands on deck on Open Day and the sunshine has tempted so many people here. Great to see you both – must dash – on car park duty next. Enjoy your day!'

As she walked away towards the entrance, Hale said, 'Who was that?'

'Bella,' Caroline and Steph chorused.

'One of your students, by any chance?'

Caroline smiled. 'You must be a detective! Year 13, just about to take her A Levels – she's actually my god daughter and in my Art set—'

'Aren't they all?' Hale laughed at Caroline, the popular Head of Art at Oakwood Sixth Form College. He turned to Steph. 'You know her too, then?'

Before Steph could answer, Caroline butted in, 'I'd give a pound for any student that Steph doesn't know.'

'You wouldn't have to give much!' laughed Margaret. 'She knows them all!'

It was unusual for Margaret to make personal comments, so Steph took it as a compliment. She had worked at the college for almost two years as the receptionist and Principal's PA and loved being with the students and staff – particularly Caroline.

'I'm starving! Time for the picnic, darlings,' Caroline handed out plates and paper napkins to them before inspecting the open basket and the contents of the silver packages. Luckily, Morton's was open on a Sunday and sold delicious food, just right to add to what was lurking at the bottom of Steph's fridge.

'Oh, lovely! Morton's pork pie!' Margaret reached for a segment.

'Yummy! Can't beat them – a real taste of Suffolk!' Caroline handed the plate to Steph. 'What a treat this is to sit in the sun—'

'—and sip Prosecco!' Hale poured the fizz into four plastic flutes and handed them around. The Prosecco was cool, the chat stimulating and the laughter contagious.

After lunch, they sat back, contentedly observing the other visitors to the Glebe Hall Open Day. Steph had always admired the high brick walls as she drove from Oakwood to Southwold for her regular Derek walks on the beach. The locals called them the crinkley-crankley walls, as the bricks undulated in semi-circular waves, hiding the mansion from prying eyes until the walls reached a dense wood by the main road. So unnecessary, but attractive and presumably built when labour was cheap. She had often wondered what the walls protected and now she could see the most elegant red brick Tudor house with a broad central section and two wings jutting out on either side. Beautifully proportioned – the skyline was peppered with curly chimneys behind the crenelated top of the walls.

'Imagine living there when it was first built.' Steph scrunched up the silver foil and shoved it in her bag before Derek ate it. She needn't have worried; he was fully engaged licking out the inside of the bone.

'Just imagine it! Freezing cold in winter, flea bites from the straw on the floor, no antibiotics so a bad tooth could kill you, and living on soggy turnips for months when the larder's empty.' Hale fished out a stray piece of foil blown under his chair.

'There speaks the last of the romantics.' Caroline smiled at him.

'Hale, as usual, talks sense.' Margaret prodded Caroline clearly concerned that she might have upset Hale.

'I wonder what it's like inside.' Steph finished packing up the rest of the food.

'Much of it a modern version of a National Trust house, but with a few original parts. Why don't you go and see? Margaret and I are happy to stay here in the sunshine with the hounds.' Caroline patted her 'hound' Marlene, as if to re-assure her she was going nowhere. Had Marlene appeared to look worried for a moment? Surely not.

'That doesn't sound fair,' Steph protested.

'No, it's fine. Margaret and I have known the Percys for years – been there masses of times for suppers when Margaret gave recitals on their grand piano.'

Margaret, a music teacher at the college, had been a well-known pianist locally and given many concerts before her hands became unreliable.

'If you're sure?' Steph hoped they were. It was rare to have whole days with Hale, and she valued any time they had alone together.

'Absolutely. Off you trot. We're happy dog-sitting.' Caroline waved towards the house. 'I may even get my sketchbook out.'

Getting up before they changed their minds, Steph and Hale strode across the billiard table lawn towards the mansion, glowing red in the sunshine.

CHAPTER TWO

Having paid their entry fee and joined about twenty others inside the grand entrance hall, they waited obediently for their guide. The white marble floors, walls and grand staircase – this one would certainly be described as sweeping – created an impressive atmosphere of generations of solid wealth.

'You'd think it would be cold, wouldn't you? But strangely, it works.' Steph leaned in to Hale and muttered in his ear. As in church, this house demanded lowered voices.

'Hardly authentic, though, is it? How many Tudor houses imported Italian marble? Originally they used wood.' Hale's voice at normal volume rang out across the hall.

'Quite correct, sir.' The buzz of whispered exchanges in the crowd stopped. 'It was wood until the fire in the early seventeenth century destroyed the original entrance hall – this was re-built by one of my ancestors.' The perfect received pronunciation, encased in a deep voice, belonged to a tall man standing on the first step of the staircase.

Steph was pleased to see that he fitted in perfectly with her image of a country aristocrat – red trousers, arty silk embroidered waistcoat, open-necked shirt topped by a well-sculpted face and particularly full lips. His dark hair shot with grey, deep smile and frown lines added to his charm somehow, rather than making him look old. Fanciable? Well, he certainly fancied himself from the way he was posing! He opened his arms in a wide greeting, enfolding the entire group – a feature Steph was taught on the 'How to Give a Presentation' course in her former career as a police officer. Professional polish too, then.

She felt Hale stiffen beside her. This man, who introduced himself as Hector Percy and the owner of Glebe Hall, was clearly getting up Hale's nose.

'Welcome to Glebe Hall, which has been in my family since 1532, when it was gifted by Henry VIII—'

'He means his family grabbed it off some poor man who was executed,' Hale hissed.

'—following my ancestor's heroic action in putting down a plot to kill the king.'

'Ahhs!' and intakes of breath wafted through the group.

'Told you so.' Hale nudged her and grinned.

'Shhh!'

'Over that fireplace,' heads swivelled as one to the right, 'you will see his portrait. Notice the typical Tudor ruff above his jewelled jerkin and the house behind him. At that stage it was a three-storey house with no wings. The east and west wings were added by his great grandson when the house was repaired after the fire. That was when they had the money and labour to build something so grand.'

'He escaped the fire then?' Hale couldn't keep quiet, could he?

'Luckily, he did. His portrait was hung upstairs and wasn't damaged by the smoke or fire.' The man gave Hale a polite smile. 'Now follow me through to the formal dining room...'

The tour took in the ground floor sitting and dining rooms, displaying solid dark oak furniture polished over several hundred years, then upstairs to a Tudor bedroom with an uncomfortable-looking four poster bed, covered with a beautifully preserved embroidered crewelwork counterpane. They returned to the ground floor and blinked as they entered a sunlit modern conference room to the right of the entrance hall. Hector Percy indicated that they should sit in the rows of comfortable navy leather chairs.

'I hope you enjoyed the Tudor world we have worked hard to retain. Now we would like to introduce you to our twenty-first century use of the house, in which we invite you to share.'

Electric blinds smoothly blocked out the light from the line of long windows. A screen appeared from a slot in the ceiling and a projector played a ten-minute film, showing all the opportunities they could enjoy at Glebe Hall. Besides weddings, memorable parties for that special birthday or sensitive farewells to a loved one, they could attend a monthly cinema club, regular yoga and meditation sessions and workshops on how to design and print textiles or learn to cook, under the eye of the Michelin chef who designed the Glebe Hall pop-up restaurant meals. The film closed with an impressive drone shot of the hall, showing its extensive grounds, and a final image of their host looking pensive and aristocratic in front of his birthright.

As they left the presentation, they were handed glossy packs by a tall, executive-looking man in designer jeans and pale blue shirt who, with a professional smile, shook Hale's hand. He reminded Steph of one of those men on afternoon TV adverts who offer reliable investment advice or funeral plans – silver haired, charming and middle-aged fit. Close up, his well-groomed elegance was flawed by a peppering of pock-marks on his cheeks and chin, which told of teenage acne. 'Jon Henderson, Marketing Director. Lovely to see you both, do come again or join one of our courses. My card—'

Hector appeared and, patting him on the back, took the packs from him to give to the line of potential customers, who were no doubt waiting for a chance to speak to the lord of the manor. The Jon man stood back, putting his cards back in his pocket.

'Thank you.' Hale reached out to him.

Surprised, Jon handed Hale one of his cards and smiled. 'Hope to see you again.'

Hale nodded but said nothing until he was out of earshot and halfway towards Caroline and Margaret, then he burst out laughing. 'What a con! They get us to pay to see a few rooms and then try to get us to join their exclusive cult.'

'Don't be ridiculous. It's not a cult. What makes you think that, anyway?'

'Classical techniques of grooming. Make you feel part of the tribe in a positive environment and tempt you in, to find a greater meaning in your life. Yoga, meditation – that's the tip of the financial iceberg you'll be contributing to.'

'A conference centre and facilities like these could add a great deal to the local community and—'

'—and to that man's bank balance. That Hector chap is so up himself. I felt sorry for his sidekick. That was so rude.'

'It must cost a lot to keep this place going.'

'Maybe they should demolish it and build homes for the homeless around here.'

She had some sympathy with his view; after all, it was an enormous house surrounded by a massive plot of land for so few people, but she presumed they employed a large band of local people to keep it all running.

They reached Caroline, who waved at them, and Margaret, who appeared to have nodded off. Derek saw Steph out of the corner of his eye and half jumped up to greet her, then slumped down again to finish his bone. So much for his priorities!

'Coffee? And one of these wonderful chocolates your gorgeous man brought along for us?' Caroline passed the flask and mugs, while Margaret, now awake, opened the large box of Morton's champagne truffles, which she held out to them.

'So, did you enjoy your trip into the world of the Percys?' Caroline had a smile that suggested she already knew the answer.

'Hale has gone all peasants' revolt and, as an additional crime against them, thinks they're running a cult.' Sipping the nutty coffee, Steph grinned at Hale over the rim of her mug.

'You know them, you say?' Hale was intrigued.

'Come on, have another. We need to eat them before they melt – well, that's my excuse, anyway.' Caroline passed them the tray of chocolates. 'Yes – known them for yonks. Used to go with Hector and Esme, his wife, to hunt balls and, you know, the usual stuff one did. Also got to know Madeline and Jon Henderson when they moved here – that's how I became Bella's godmother – great pals we were.'

'Bella said they lived here. Where?' Steph popped another chocolate-dusted truffle in her mouth, trying hard to find the champagne.

'Hector inherited the house and came up with a creative way of affording to stay here.'

Hale grunted. 'Don't tell me they were short of money with that pile!'

15

'Actually, they were. Death duties were crippling, and when Hector took over, he discovered nothing had been done to it for years – needed a fortune spending on it.'

Caroline reached down and poured another coffee and passed the flask to Hale. 'Well, in the late nineties, he invited two of his university pals to come and live with them for an injection of cash, presumably from their house sales. You see the side wings—' She pointed at the east and west sides of the house jutting out from the central spine. 'Well, each couple owns a wing for their private space – Bella lives in the east wing with her parents. Hector and Esme kept that central section. They all contribute equally to the housekeeper, cook, gardener and all the other staff.'

'Wow! That sounds like paradise! To live in this beautiful place and have all the daily grind taken away – living the dream.' Steph knew she sounded envious as she recalled the challenge of holding down a demanding job and trying her best to be a domestic goddess. 'To think of coming home and finding someone else has done the cleaning, shopping and cooking. Actually, that wasn't so bad, it was deciding what to cook I found difficult. Every night I'd stand for ages peering into the freezer for inspiration, and as for the ironing...'

Hale smiled across at her. 'Well, you obviously succeeded. I noticed none of that at work. You did a great job and Mike was always so positive about how wonderfully you balanced work and home.'

She felt the blood rushing to her cheeks. Hale was such a lovely man, making her feel good about herself – she was so lucky to have him. Sexy too. When she and Mike had moved from the Met to the Suffolk police, Philip Hale, always known for some bizarre reason as Hale, had been her boss for twelve years. After Mike's heart attack and her retirement from the police, she'd thought that was it – a lonely widow with her rescued dog, until Hale arrived at the college to investigate the murder of a student. A tragic way to re-kindle their relationship, but the start of the next exciting stage of her life.

Caroline reached out and touched Margaret's hand. 'Come on, my love, I think it's time to go. The sun is running out of heat, and I've got some sketch books to mark.'

With that, they collected the detritus of the picnic and wandered back to the car park. As they were packing the bags into the car, Steph turned to look at Glebe Hall, silhouetted against the sun. 'Maybe I will come back for a yoga course or learn to cook properly – you could always come with me.'

'Look! Quick! Look at that! Over there!' Hale pointed at the house. Alarmed, she swivelled round to see the emergency. 'Is that a pig flying over that roof?'

CHAPTER THREE

ESME GAVE up trying to chase sleep and slipped out of bed. She picked up her phone to check the time; 2.17 flashed at the top of the screen. What was it – over three hours since she came to bed? Grabbing her dressing gown from the bottom of the bed, she pressed the phone torch app, hiding the light from Hector with her hand, and slipped her feet into her Ugg boots.

Using the sharp beam to guide her, she crept out of the bedroom, across the landing and down the wide, marble stairs to the kitchen, where at last she turned on the light. The eco bulb emitted a slight glow as it slowly woke up. The hall light was always left on, but each night Hector did the rounds of the ground floor of their portion of the house, checking all the windows and doors were locked and turning off all the room lights.

In the enormous kitchen she pulled up her chair by the constantly warm Aga, removed Middleton from her favourite squishy-cushioned chair, carried him across to his basket opposite, then sat down. Her elegant tiger-striped ginger cat meowed angrily, apparently indignant at being disturbed, but trod himself a new nest and soon settled down.

All signs of the Open Day and supper had been cleared away, but a few biscuit tins were piled up at the end of the long scrubbed pine table, and she padded across to see what was in them. Scones! Brilliant! Maybe a scone with a cup of chamomile tea would help her sleep.

She'd hardly touched a thing at supper, as the post-mortem of the Open Day dominated the chat. The six of them always filleted the day and worked out how much new income might result, but this time it was just her, Hector, Madeline and Jon Henderson who shared venison stew and roasted vegetables then the local Baron Bigod cheese, left over from the stall. Luke and Zac had made their excuses and said they both had to be up early for work the next day, so needed to prepare. They'd never done that before. Maybe Hector was right – they were thinking of leaving.

Hector was obsessed. Obsessed with Glebe Hall, obsessed with his inheritance and obsessed with who would take it on after him. Every day he would frown, stride around, then come to see her to worry, reciting the same script. Recently she'd found that even her deepest meditation hadn't restored her calm. She suspected he was right; they had created the perfect existence for themselves and their friends and now, after fifteen years, the arrangement was crumbling. If it did, his life would be over as far as he was concerned, for they could no longer afford to live at Glebe Hall.

Imagine it being turned into a conference centre by the people who hired the facilities for their team building and leadership programmes. Or worse? Perhaps it would be taken over by the Outward Bound Crew, who would build more zip wires, survival stick houses and bonfires in the woods, or the Glam-

Glampers who would erect more yurts and shepherds' huts for Londoners to breathe the air while visiting Latitude, the music festival down the road.

Would any of these things be so bad? They could still live in the house, couldn't they? No, Hector thought it would be sacrilege. And she didn't dare think of the residential nursing home that many houses their size became. The tea was comforting, and the scone stopped her stomach rumbling. What was wrong with her? What was happening to Hector and their marriage?

Today had been their twenty-fifth wedding anniversary. Most people she knew had a party or went on an exotic holiday to celebrate their love. Or was it their stickability? And what did she and Hector do? Host another Open Day, hoping to attract more people to use their conference facilities and workshops.

Madeline, as usual, had done the best out of the day with her Free School. Strange name for something you paid for. She and Hector had set it up seven years ago, and it was doing very well – not only financially but also raising the reputation of the Hall in the area, and the kids she taught appeared to do brilliantly compared with other local schools.

Hector and Madeline always got on so well – sparked ideas off each other and seemed to be on the same wavelength somehow. He called her 'My Maddy' after some pop star he'd once fancied. Was Hector— What was that noise?

She wasn't imagining it – a noise in the hall. Was that the front door clicking shut? Could the wind have blown it open? No, Hector always checked. She held her breath. Listened hard. A scraping – someone walked into the large table in the centre of the entrance hall. Who was there? Footsteps, soft steps on tip toe came towards the kitchen door. As quietly as possible, Esme grabbed a knife from the block, flattened herself against the wall behind the door and held her breath.

Another scrape – a chair? Surely a burglar wouldn't make so much noise? She peeped through the crack of the door but couldn't see anything in the dull overhead light. The steps came closer until a dark figure strode, or rather staggered, across the kitchen and opened the fridge door, which lit up his face – Jack!

Just as he was slurping from a carton of orange juice, she came up behind him.

'What the hell are you doing coming home at this time and where have you been?'

He swung around and she was smothered by boozy breath, forcing her to turn her face away in disgust. His clothes stank of cigarette smoke. Or was it... Surely not?

'Mumsy – could say same t'you – think I've had – better time than you!' He giggled loudly.

'Jack! Do you know the time?'

'Time to dance?'

He pulled her close to him and, holding her hand out, attempted a clumsy waltz around the table and stepped on her toes.

'Ow! Jack! Stop!'

As he tripped over his feet, Esme held onto the table and Jack went over her legs, sprawling across the floor. 'Ouch!'

He saw the knife she'd dropped in the mad dance, picked it up and knelt, hands outstretched, beseeching her dramatically 'Don't stab me, Mumsy – not good – don't kill me.' He assumed a woeful expression, apparently trying to look like an appealing child or spaniel in need of affection. He failed.

She took the knife from him and put it on the table behind

her. 'Jack, you're wrecked and not only on booze from the smell of you—'

'Could be right – yes, Mumsy right – always right—' He was getting louder.

As she helped him clamber to his feet, Esme shook him, thrust him backwards into her chair, then hissed, 'Will you shut up? You'll wake your father.'

'Oh no! Not Father! Lord and master!' His voice became a stage whisper. 'Shouldn't upset Daddy, should we, Mumsy?'

'Jack – you have college in a few hours. Days away from your A Levels and you get yourself in this state. Where have you been?'

'Out. Had fun – don't do fun, do you?' He stretched for the orange juice carton she'd put on the table and glugged at it. Trickles of juice ran down his chin onto his shirt, which was spattered with dark spots. Blood? Yes, blood. It must have come from his nose, now slightly out of shape, with crusty bits of blood stuck under each nostril.

'Have you been in a fight?'

'Fell over – head hurts – need cuddles, Mumsy.'

'That's the last thing you need. Now, drink some water and go up to bed. I'll wake you at eight and give you a lift to college. You'd better be fit to go.'

She helped him stand; he wobbled as his feet went in different directions as she tried to keep him upright while pushing him towards the stairs. Supposing they got halfway up, and he slipped down the marble? A solution or another problem? At least she wouldn't have to listen to Hector banging on any more about what a disappointment her son was. Horrified she could think such a dreadful thing, she struggled to help Jack up the slippery steps and told herself she loved him but wished he'd stop behaving like this – it was becoming a habit.

'That's right. Lift your left knee and then the other one – good boy. Twelve, thirteen, fourteen – that's right, well done.' Her voice transformed to the one she'd used to teach him to count as they climbed the stairs each day when he was little. Now, taller than she was, his weight hurt her back, and drunk, he was a total nightmare. She'd kept from Hector how many times she'd had to do this. 'That's right – just two more. Now shhh! We'll creep past Mummy's bedroom door to yours.'

'Sssssshh!' Jack tried to put his right index finger up to his mouth, missed and hit his ear, then frowned at his uncontrollable finger accusingly and hissed more. The loud hissing noise was enough to wake Hector, but she left it. Better than arguing with him again. Anyway, Hector wouldn't wake after the two bottles of Lafitte from his father's cellar he always opened to celebrate an Open Day. How many more Open Days would that cellar support?

Turning the knob on his bedroom door, she dragged Jack to his bed, as he appeared to be falling asleep on his feet. Deciding not to undress him, she took off his muddy shoes and covered him with the duvet. Looking back at him, her beautiful boy was still in there somewhere.

She crept out of his room to her own, ignoring the lights she'd left on downstairs, and slipped under the covers beside a snoring Hector. At least he hadn't been disturbed, which was a bonus. How would she explain the broken nose? Rugby? He approved of rugby. Would he notice anyway? She turned her back to him, tugged at the duvet he'd claimed, shut her eyes and breathed in deep and slow, trying to find some sleep before the relentless week started again.

CHAPTER FOUR

THE DOOR FLEW OPEN, followed by a crash. Steph jumped at the unexpected intrusion, only to see Hale sprawled across the floor.

'Bloody Hell! What's that doing there?' As he pulled himself up, he gave a killer glare at the parcel he'd tripped over.

'I'm so sorry! Are you all right?' She gave him her hand and helped him up. 'Sorry. Just brought it in and had to feed Derek. Didn't know you'd be home this early.'

Hale took off his tie and headed towards the bedroom to get changed. 'All the criminals in East Suffolk must be on holiday. Spent the afternoon working through the paper mountain I've been ignoring for weeks – I'm all in.' He started unbuttoning his shirt. What was coming next? 'Thought we could go down to The Harbour Inn for an early supper and walk the mutt by the sea.'

Recently, Hale had been referring to Derek as 'the mutt' and Steph assumed it was his way of adopting Derek too. 'Great! I'll get my trainers.'

Oakwood was basking in an early summer. The pavement

tables outside restaurants on the High Street were packed and the front garden of The Leg of Mutton and Cauliflower was crammed with smiling, chatty people. Chairs had been placed in the front gardens of the Victorian terraces to catch the sun, and neighbours chatted over the hedges. It felt like a holiday had landed.

As they drove towards Southwold, the sun flickered through the trees, showcasing the fluorescent green leaves of spring. Her hand on Hale's thigh, she felt content. Yes, that was the word, content – not the riotous extremes of early love affairs but the comfortable, secure love of a settled long-term relationship. And he was so sexy.

In his early fifties, Hale had avoided the sagging stomachs of so many men his age and was fit. Although his smile lines were getting deeper, his high cheekbones defined his face, and she loved staring into his grey-blue eyes. Yes, she was a lucky woman!

'What are you grinning at?' He placed his hand on hers and squeezed it gently. A muntjac deer ran out of Glebe Hall gates, skittered across the road in front of them and Hale slewed to avoid it. 'Serves me right for not concentrating!'

Steph followed the path of the deer, soon lost in the shadows of the dense undergrowth of the wood to her left. 'Funny, that crinkley-crankley wall suddenly stopping there.'

'They sliced it when they built a road through the wood – see? It continues on the other side of the road – same trees.'

'Not just a pretty face, are you?'

'Second word's off!'

Searching once again in the wood for the deer, she saw a gigantic cloud of black smoke billowing up from behind the trees. 'A fire! Look! Over there – looks serious.'

Hale swivelled his head. 'You're right. They'll need help.'

Swerving the car in a U-turn at the entrance to a minor road, Hale put his foot down and drove back a few hundred metres to the Glebe Hall gates, which were wide open. An anxious-looking man in brown overalls was waving at them.

'Police,' Hale shouted through his open window.

'Follow the road, turn right at the house, past the barns and you'll see it. Waiting for the fire engine and ambulance.' Panic oozed out of every word, and the man, a gardener by the look of it, was desperate. It must be grim.

Metal pressed to the floor, Hale sped through the deserted grounds, past the barns. Then they saw it. Clouds of dense black smoke rose above the trees in the woods beyond and filled the sky. That was some fire! Parking beside a couple of quad bikes, they ran through the clearing towards the smoke. Flames leaped high from a car engulfed in vicious orange flames, giving out a massive heat.

'Get back, now! Get back!' Hale screamed at the two men hovering at the side of the blazing car. Gesturing at Steph to stop where she was, Hale ran, grabbed the man nearer to him, and pulled him away. 'It'll explode. Move!' The man staggered backwards, hypnotised by the flames until he reached Steph. He reeked of smoke. His face was black except for the clear tracks made by tears; the snot coming from his nose dripped, unnoticed.

'Are you hurt?' Steph scanned him quickly and checked he wasn't injured or burnt.

'Not me – Madeline – there!' His horrified face told the story. They stood, stunned, watching the flames eat the car. The air was full of black specks, and Steph was relieved that the overpowering smell of petrol and burnt rubber swamped the other smell she knew would be coming from what was in the front seat. She only hoped it had been quick.

Regular gunshot sounds came from the car as tyres, glass and electrics exploded. At each bang, a little puff of grey punctuated the solid black smoke. The fire appeared to be getting stronger, the black smoke thicker. Where was that fire engine?

As he was dragged away by Hale, the second man flailed at him, squirming, trying to loosen Hale's tight grip on the back of his shirt. 'Madeline – she's there. Let me go! Let go!'

Hale was too strong for him and at last he gave in. Clearly, Hale didn't trust him, as he propelled the man behind the trunk of the gigantic oak tree, holding onto the back of his shirt, which once had been white but was now torn and streaked with black sooty stains. An ear-splitting bang echoed through the wood as the petrol tank exploded and a fireball erupted into the sky. Turning their faces from the intense heat, they shielded their heads as they were showered with ash and bits of stuff no longer recognisable as belonging to a car.

At last, Hale released the man's shirt, and he collapsed to his knees, howling and screaming up at Hale. 'Madeline! She's in there! You stopped me! Madeline!'

The blobs of raw flesh he held up no longer resembled hands, while his arms were blistered with chunks of the skin grated and bleeding, and his white shirtsleeves had melted up to the elbow, the ragged edges now brown and singed. He sobbed hysterically.

A blue light flashed up behind them. At last, the ambulance. A paramedic, bag in hand, leaped out of the cab. His eyes darted over the four, appraising the situation, and identified the man on the ground beside Hale as needing urgent treatment. 'What's your name?'

The man mumbled, 'Jon'

'Right, Jon, we'll sort you out in the ambulance and then get you off to hospital.' He helped him to stand and, with his arm on Jon's shoulder, guided him gently to the back of the ambulance.

Shocked, Steph recognised the voice first and realised the badly burnt Jon was the immaculately dressed man handing out the information packs to them at the Open Day. Then he'd not had a grey hair out of place; now he was a total mess.

'Right, let's take a look at the rest of you.' After opening the back door of the ambulance for his colleague, the ambulance driver jogged towards them and faced the man Hale had rescued first. 'Any other burns? Did you breathe in the smoke?' The man collapsed by the tree shook his head. 'Good. I'll check your breathing. At least out here and with a car – less smoke damage – not like indoors.'

Hale and Steph stood back so the paramedic could examine the man, who appeared to be having problems standing. Having listened to him breathing, the paramedic nodded, picked up the man's hands, turned them over, examined them, then swept his eyes over the rest of his body, before turning to Steph and Hale. 'You two OK?'

Hale nodded. 'Yeah, fine, thanks.'

'He looks as if he got away with it. Shocked, naturally.'

'Thanks. I'm Chief Inspector Hale, Suffolk police.' Hale stepped forward, clearly wanting to talk. 'Just happened to be driving past—' His words were drowned out by the screaming siren of a fire engine which skidded to a halt alongside the burning car. Firemen appeared from all around the engine, and dashed into action, dragging out the heavy flat hoses over their shoulders and pointing nozzles at the car, waiting for the water to bombard the flames, which, having consumed anything they could, were dying down.

A loud hiss filled the wood as the water evaporated on contact with the searing hot metal, followed by clouds of white smoke, then the black carcass of the car slumped as the last flickers were extinguished. Steph turned away, so she didn't have to see what was inside the car.

'Right, I've done what I can to his hands. We need to get going.' The first paramedic shouted over, returning to the cab, clearly anxious to get Jon to the hospital. The driver paused and indicated that Hale and Steph should walk a few yards away with him. 'He's shocked.' He nodded at the man, now with his eyes closed, sitting on the ground, slumped against the tree. 'You know what to do. If you get worried, give us a call or take him to A&E. Make sure someone stays with him.'

'Will do and thanks.' They watched as the ambulance backed onto the road through the trees and sped off, the blue light thrown back by the white trunks of the silver birches.

The fire now out, one of the fire crew came towards them. 'Hale, a bit below your rank, this?'

'Hi Ben. Happened to be passing. Ah! Here come the troops.' Two police cars had joined the growing line of cars at the edge of the clearing and four uniformed police officers strode towards them – two men and two women. They look surprised when they recognised Hale.

Hale, the police officers and the fireman formed a huddle out of Steph's earshot and talked in low voices. Steph returned to the dazed man sitting against the trunk of the tree, who stared at nothing in the distance. She knew he wouldn't be able to take anything in, so crouched down beside him and held onto his elbow, just to let him know she was there.

Hale was obviously briefing the group of officers and giving them instructions. Two returned to their car, presumably to call for the SOCO team, while the others went towards the black outline of the car.

Ben took off his helmet and wiped the sweat off his face,

obviously waiting until Hale had finished and they were alone, then waved at the car and appeared to be explaining something. As he finished talking to Hale and strode back to the car skeleton, his voice carried. '...let you know.'

'Right, that's all the arrangements made. We need to get him back to the house and quick.' Hale gently touched the man's shoulder. 'Mr Percy.' He stooped to make it easier to look into the trembling man's eyes, which squinted open. 'Mr Percy, we'll drive you back to the Hall. Can you get up?'

Surprised, Steph scrutinised the man, now hunched on the ground, arms across his body, shivering. Of course! It was Hector Percy. In his bedraggled state and without his professional sheen, she hadn't recognised him. They helped him to his feet. Hale took off his jacket, put it around Hector's shoulders, and guided him through the trees to the car, urging him on in a calm 'it will be all right' voice.

CHAPTER FIVE

An ancient heart-shaped handle, fixed to a wrought iron rod, hung alongside the heavy weathered oak door, disappearing through a hole in the bricks beside it. Steph tugged at it but heard nothing, assuming it was ringing somewhere in the bowels of the house. Would it wiggle one of those little panels in the servants' hall, like in *Downton Abbey*?

The door was opened by an elegant blond woman in smart casual clothes – a gold horsey-design Hermes scarf artfully arranged around her neck. Smiling, she looked at Steph, 'Hello. May I help you?'

Before Steph answered, Hale arrived beside her with Hector, half conscious, draped over his shoulders.

'Good heavens, Hector! Whatever has happened? Come in!'

Almost running through the hallway in front of them, she opened a door on her left.

'Bring him through here.' She nodded towards a sofa by an enormous stone fireplace. 'Yes, on that one would be best.'

Hale helped Hector to climb on the brown leather

Chesterfield, where he lay hunched up, still shaking. 'He's had quite a shock and needs to rest, but some sweet tea would help.'

'Sweet tea, you say?' The woman pulled two throws off the other sofas, which formed three sides of a square in front of the fireplace, and tucked them around him.

'That will help. If you show me the way to the kitchen, I can go?' Hale half stood up. Steph knew this was a Hale ruse to have a nose around.

'No, please stay with him. Won't be a minute.'

As she dashed out of the room, Hector opened his eyes. A puzzled look passed across his face as if he was trying to work out who they were. 'That should never... never have happened. Should have stopped it.'

'Sorry, what was that?' Hale moved in closer so he could hear the near whisper, but Hector closed his eyes again and his head flopped back onto the cushion Steph had put there.

'Did you catch that?' Hale hissed. She shook her head. She wasn't sure.

Hector's eyes closed, and he cocooned himself deeper into the blankets. Steph admired the gigantic sitting room, which, despite the predominantly brown antique furniture, glowed in late sunlight. The peach walls gave an effective back-drop to the masses of pictures that created an art gallery through the ages.

Traditional oils of Constable-type landscapes in large gilt frames hung beside early twentieth century family portraits and on the wall by the door, a full set of ten hunting and shooting watercolours that appeared to come from the eighteen hundreds. In the backgrounds of four of them, she recognised Glebe Hall. Either side of the imposing stone fireplace, blackened with years of wood fires in the wrought iron basket, were two dramatic David Hockney oils. The eclectic nature of the collection worked well and was evidence that the Percys certainly had good taste and the money to indulge it.

A fluttering to her left made Steph aware of the woman returning with a tray loaded with mugs and pots and cleared a space for it on the low table in front of the sofa. The woman perched beside Hector, helped him to sit up and reached for a mug filled to the brim. 'Here, darling, sip this.' She looked across at Hale. 'Hope coffee's all right – he hates tea.'

Hector, finding it difficult to drink half lying down, pulled himself upright beside her and she held the mug to his lips. After a couple of sips, he took the mug and could drink it by himself while she arranged the throw around his shoulders.

'Sorry, how rude of me! I'm Esme Percy, Hector's wife, and you are...?'

'Chief Inspector Hale, Suffolk police and this is Steph Grant.'

A look of alarm swamped Esme's face. 'Good heavens, what has Hector done to involve the police? Sorry, no – I'm forgetting myself. There's coffee or tea on that tray in the pots. Please help yourselves. You look as if you need it. Now what were you saying?' All this in a mad torrent of words. Steph moved to the tray and noticed the woman staring hard at her.

'Steph Grant... I'm sure we've met before – don't tell me – I know! It was the college – you were there when I brought Jack up for his interview.' She checked that Hector was drinking his coffee before examining Steph once more.

'Oh! Jack! Yes, of course!' At that moment, on the sideboard Steph noticed a photo of a student she'd seen around college – a mini version of Hector. 'Always talking about his horse.'

'That's Jack! But what am I going on about when – sorry, Chief Inspector, please tell me what Hector has done?'

'Nothing, as far as I know.' Having helped himself to tea, he sat down beside Steph on the identical sofa opposite. 'We were on our way to Southwold, when we saw the smoke of a massive fire in your grounds, and I found a car ablaze with your husband and another man trying to—'

'Rescue Madeline.' Hector's voice had the same depth they'd heard in his presentation, but now it sounded hoarse and worn out. Steph noticed Hale frowning as he watched the exchange between Hector and Esme.

'Madeline?'

'The car caught fire.'

'Madeline? Where?'

'Badgers' Wood.' Hector pulled the fawn cashmere throws further up his body. He trembled again.

'What on earth was she doing in a car in the wood?'

Hector sighed and handed her the mug. Esme raised her eyebrow.

'No more. That's fine.' He raised his voice a little. 'I feel so much better. Thank you for your help.' Hector pushed the top throw away onto the floor and stared at Hale as if, having brought him home, he was now being dismissed. Hale acknowledged the comment with a polite incline of his head but remained seated and waited.

'Go on – you were saying.' Esme put the mug on the table, bending down to pick up the throw at the same time as prompting Hector.

'Jon phoned late afternoon, not sure when – Madeline had been drinking and was rowing with him. Didn't say why. She'd driven off in her car – she was too drunk.' He swallowed, then cleared his throat several times, as if trying to free his voice. 'Another, Esme.'

Esme got up and poured out the coffee, stirring in two

loaded teaspoons of sugar, then handed the mug to Hector, who sipped at it before lowering it. 'Grabbed the quad bikes; Jon got ahead on his. I followed him to Badgers' Wood. She'd gone off the road, hit a tree – the car was on fire. The flames were—'

His husky voice gave out; he gulped more coffee, then let the mug rest on his leg, his head down. 'The flames... so hot... we tried... door wouldn't open.' He took another sip of coffee and stared ahead. 'Jon wouldn't give up; he kept going back – it wouldn't open – he was badly burnt – went to hospital in the ambulance – his hands were so badly burnt, it was horrible.'

'Oh my God, that's terrible! Oh, no! Poor Madeline! How dreadful.' Esme, now pale and tearful as the story seeped in, reached out and touched Hector, who sat forlorn and diminished. No longer the confident business executive, but a man hollowed out by the tragedy he had observed.

'Where's Madeline now?'

'What? You don't – nothing left. Fire was so fierce – there's nothing left.'

She took the mug from him, and his head fell into his hands.

Hale stood 'You heard nothing, Mrs Percy?'

'No. Running a yoga class in the studio – the barn at the opposite side of the estate to Badgers Wood.'

'Thank you for the tea. We'll leave you in peace. You should stay with Mr Percy for the next twenty-four hours, at least.' He put his and Steph's mugs back on the tray. 'If you have any concerns, phone for an ambulance. He's been through a traumatic experience, and it may take time for him to process it.'

Esme straightened her scarf, stood and, after turning to

check Hector was no worse, showed them to the front door. 'Thank you so much for your help, Chief Inspector.'

At the door, Hale shook hands. 'You're welcome. The Fire Investigation Officer and members of the local forensic team will be around the site for a day or so and we'll need a statement from Mr Percy and Jon...?'

'Henderson, Jon Henderson. Thank you once again.' She pushed the heavy door shut.

Derek, clearly pleased to see them, bounced around in the back as they climbed into the car. About to turn on the ignition, Hale paused. 'So much for my evening off! I was really looking forward to that drink and a walk.'

'Too late now.' She sniffed the sleeve of her blouse and wrinkled her nose at the acrid smoke smell. 'I need a shower.'

'We could get a take-away curry!'

He started the engine, and they drove around the house and out of the filigree wrought iron gates.

'She did say Henderson, didn't she?'

'Yes, why?' Hale turned left onto the main road.

'I'm sure that's Bella's surname.'

'The girl we met at the picnic?'

'Yes, Caroline said she lived in the east wing, remember? It sounds as if it could be her mother in that car. Poor girl!'

Subdued, they drove back into Oakwood.

'Anyway, what were you and Ben talking about?'

Hale sighed. 'Life's never simple, is it? He's convinced petrol was used as an accelerant – all around the car apparently.'

'You mean the fire was started deliberately?'

'That's exactly what it means.'

CHAPTER SIX

Esme shut the door behind the policeman and the woman from college and stood with her back to it breathing deep, slow breaths. What a shock! Should she phone Caroline to tell her? Ages since they'd spoken – they'd been great friends once, but while Madeline had stayed close to Caroline, she'd drifted away.

Shutting the sitting-room door, she sat on the sofa opposite Hector, who was still trembling, and examined him. He didn't appear to be injured, just extremely shaken.

'You look so shocked. Can I get you anything else?'

Hector raised his head. 'No, thanks. Just be here.'

Surprised to see him so wobbly, she moved across and put her arm around him, and his head immediately flopped onto her shoulder. A few minutes later, she slid her head forward to look at his face. Had he fallen asleep?

'Shall I help you up to bed or would you like to lie down here?'

'No, I'll be fine. Just need to get over the shock. I'll sit here with you.'

They sat in silence. He reached for her hand and held onto it, hard. 'Picture of that car – can't get it out of my head. I close my eyes and all I see are flames. So high – so hot. Couldn't believe how quick.'

'What happened?'

He pulled away and looked at her. 'I told you when that policeman was here.'

She also pulled away slightly so she could see the whole of his face. 'I heard what you told them. But they think there's something more.'

'Something more? Whatever can you mean?' Evidently, her gaze had penetrated his guard; he dropped his head again.

'More than what you told them.'

'I told him what happened, and that's all there is.' His voice showed he was finished, and she shouldn't pry further.

She felt uncomfortable confronting him but did it anyway, convinced there was more. 'You were shocked so may not have noticed, but I could see that policeman's body language and I felt there was something... something he wasn't saying.'

Hector frowned and threw off the final blanket. 'That's ridiculous. You're always trying to read more into situations than is actually there. Nothing is simple for you, is it? It has to be a drama – no, a five-act play! If they knew something, they'd tell us.'

'Not if it was to do with you, they wouldn't.'

'I've told you.' Despite his hoarse voice, he managed to raise it. 'There is nothing more to say. I don't care how he looked; there is nothing else to say – do you hear me?'

In one way Esme was pleased he was getting back to normal and not the dependent child-man he'd been for the last half hour, but for a while she'd enjoyed feeling needed. 'That's fine, then.'

Further discussion was stopped when the door slammed open and Jack bounced in, threw his bag on the floor, jumped over the back of the Chesterfield opposite and stared at them. 'What's the fire engine doing in the woods and why are they poking about in the bushes there?'

'They're doing what?' Esme demanded, giving an 'I told you so' glance at Hector.

'A fire truck is squirting water all over a burnt-out car and the ground around it and about six men with long sticks are poking about the bushes a long way from the car. What are they looking for and whose car was it?'

Hector's head had gone down again, and it was obvious he had no intention of answering Jack's questions, so Esme replied. 'Your father and Jon found Madeline had crashed her car, which burst into flames and she couldn't get out. Jon's in hospital – he burnt his hands trying to rescue her.'

'Madeline? Couldn't get out? You mean... she's...'

'Yes. She's dead. In the car.'

'Fuck! That's terrible! I feel sick at the thought of it! Horrific! Does Bella know?'

Esme stood. 'Oh! Bella! There'll be no one there to tell her! I'll go round at once.'

'I'll come too.'

Esme held out her hand as she moved to the door. 'No, you stay here with your father. He's not to be left alone. He's in shock.'

She shut the door firmly behind her. The clack of her heels echoed through the marble entrance hall until she reached the carpeted corridor, lined with oil paintings and portraits in dull gold frames, and arrived at the new oak door at the end. She pressed a bell and could hear ringing inside.

Within seconds, Bella opened the door. 'Esme! Mum and

Dad aren't here – they must have gone shopping. Shall I tell them you called?'

'No, darling. Let's go inside and sit down, shall we?'

CHAPTER SEVEN

'I'm so sorry you and Hale were involved in poor Madeline's death at Glebe Hall yesterday. It must've been appalling,' Caroline whispered as she leaned over the Reception desk. 'I can't believe it. I only saw her last week.'

'Sorry?' Steph suddenly concentrated on straightening the visitors' book to avoid Caroline's penetrating laser eyes.

'Don't go all discreet, darling. Esme Percy phoned me and it's all over social media, you know.' Caroline scrambled around in her red leather bucket bag and fished out her phone. 'Look, here it is!' She fiddled with the screen, then handed it over to Steph.

A tweet on the Glebe Hall site announced the death, too soon, of Madeline Henderson in a dreadful accident – may she rest in peace. Steph closed her mouth, which she couldn't recall opening, and, handing back the phone, looked across at Caroline.

'Golly, that was quick!' she heard herself exclaiming, amazed at the speed that everyone knew everything now.

'Can't keep anything quiet now, can you? I was devastated when I heard.' Caroline sighed. 'Been friends for yonks. What a tragedy – such a talented woman.'

'Yes, it was grim.'

'Poor Madeline. What happened? Esme was almost hysterical on the phone and made little sense.'

Steph sighed and assumed as it was going to come out anyway, she might as well reveal to her friend as much as would be out there within hours.

'We were on our way to Southwold to walk Derek about seven, and, as we passed the Hall, we saw masses of smoke and found a car on fire. Apparently, Madeline was in it and her husband was distraught that he hadn't been able to rescue her. He went to hospital with burns to his hands and we took a shocked Hector home.'

Caroline's face paled. There was a moment of silence, in which Caroline appeared to be imagining the scene and Steph re-lived it.

'How awful for you, too. Are you OK?' Caroline reached across and touched Steph's arm. 'And horrendous for Bella and that sweet man, her father, Jon. What must they be going through?' She shook her head. 'I can't believe it! What an appalling way to die.'

'Horrible.'

'Madeline was a truly remarkable woman – so beautiful, so alive, and a brilliant teacher now... How dreadful for Bella... and just before her A Levels. I must apply for special consideration with the exam board. Did you see her?'

'No, only her father and the Percys.'

'Darling, how grim for you, and Hale, too.'

'Yeah, not easy.'

The sliding door on the glass box that was the college's Reception swooshed open and Peter Bryant, the Principal, bounced in. 'Morning, Steph, Caroline. What a glorious morning! It always does this just before exams, doesn't it? Tempts the students away from revision, but it's such a welcome change.' With that, he breezed off into his office through the door at the end of the long Reception desk.

Caroline raised her eyebrow. 'He's not heard, then.'

'No, doesn't look like it. I'll make him some coffee and tell him.'

Steph moved down the desk, about to go up the corridor to the small kitchen where the coffee machine lived, when the door opened to reveal a man whom Caroline rushed up to and hugged.

'Zac! What are you doing here? I was going to cover your textile group!'

When she released him, Steph recognised the part-time textiles teacher who worked in Caroline's department. He looked pale and exhausted. 'Couldn't let them down so close to their assessment. I'll be fine.' With a nod to Steph, he left Reception and climbed the stairs to Caroline's empire.

'You know who that is?'

Steph was puzzled by the question. She knew he was very part-time and came in one or, at most, two days a week.

'Zac lives at Glebe Hall with his partner, Luke. They own the wing on the right – the west wing. Lived there for about fifteen years.'

Once again Steph marvelled at the extent of Caroline's local knowledge, but then she'd lived in Oakwood for ever and she'd known the Percys and Hendersons for years.

'A brilliant designer; used to work for Liberty. Our students adore him, and they always get top grades. Must go – he may need to talk.'

People found it easy to talk to Caroline, and she also knew how to keep secrets. Apparently, she'd kept her relationship with Margaret secret for years. Steph watched her float off upstairs, her vibrant electric-blue linen dress perfect as usual, but out of joint with the sadness and tragedy they'd been discussing.

Over coffee, she told Peter all she knew about the fire at the Hall. His cheerful mood dissipated and he shared her deep shock at the story and the impact on Bella.

'Caroline said she'd organise special consideration for Bella's exams, but I suspect at the moment that's the least of her worries.'

Peter went over to his desk to look at Bella's timetable. Perfectly groomed, his rugby player build and good looks made him popular with the female parents, many of whom wondered why he didn't get married again. At Steph's news, he looked deflated and older, the lines around his eyes showing up in the light from the window. He looked up at her. 'Art, English and History and hoping to go to King's College, London.' Plonking himself back down by the low table, he reached out for his cup, which Steph noticed was empty.

'Another?'

'Please.'

She gave them both refills, and they sat silently, sharing the awfulness of Madeline's death. Steph sneaked a glance at her watch – eight thirty. She needed to get back to Reception at the peak of the morning rush.

'Yes, you get on. Please send Bella some flowers from me and all the staff. Poor girl, how devastating and in such dreadful circumstances.'

Steph took the cups with her and, as she closed his door, tried to look as normal as possible to the hordes of chatty students and members of staff piling though the door on their way to their lessons or to grab a quick drink in the canteen or the common room. She loved her job; she felt rooted in the family culture of the college and knew that, once the news percolated down, they would all share in the sadness of one of their students. They were only there for the two years of their A Levels, but Oakwood College was a very special place.

After a morning of routine admin, she was surprised to hear raised voices from Peter's room. She had seen Paul Field, the Vice Principal, go in about ten minutes earlier. Although she was Peter's PA, he never checked with her, a lowly member of the admin staff, whether Peter was free, but thought it was his right to walk in on whatever Peter was doing. Apparently, he'd applied for the Principal's job, assumed it was his and hadn't forgiven Peter, an outsider, for beating him to it. Now the college he thought he managed no longer existed. Peter was so patient with him.

Her phone rang. It was Peter asking her to step into his office.

As she entered, she was hit by the solid tension between the two men – Peter frowning at his desk, Paul Field standing over him, his red face matching his tie and the floppy silk pocket handkerchief he always wore. Irritated, Peter thrust his chair back, got up from his desk and sat down in one of the red leather chairs around the coffee table, gesturing for Steph to join him in the one opposite.

Paul Field hovered on the edge, evidently not wishing to lose the advantage of his height – all five feet seven inches of it. Waiting, Peter smiled up at him, until at last Paul Field gave in and joined them. As he sat, he made fussy minor adjustments to the knife-edged fold on his trousers and unbuttoned his jacket to display its red silk lining.

Peter turned to Steph. 'Steph, we'd like the benefit of your experience on an issue that has arisen.'

Paul Field looked as if the benefit of her experience was the last thing he wanted. Peter ignored his sneer. 'The student council has asked that we have sessions on consent in the General Studies programme. They say they know all about contraception and drugs—'

'I bet they do.' Paul Field couldn't resist it, could he?

'—and it's the more subtle aspect of sexual relationships they would like to discuss and about which they have concerns.'

'That has nothing to do with us,' countered Paul Field. 'We should be educating them for university and getting them good A Level grades – that's our job, not interfering in their lives outside college.'

Peter gave Steph an encouraging look, so she waded in. 'But it is our job to prepare them for their lives outside college and the world in which they'll live. Surely, we have a duty to prepare them for their futures, and understanding the need for consent is vital if they're to respect one another.'

Paul Field bristled. 'In my day, girls didn't go out, get blind drunk, then blame the boys when they woke up the next morning regretting what they'd done the night before.'

'So, it's the girls' fault that boys take advantage of them?' Steph could feel her temper rising at this silly man's outdated prejudice. 'They ask for it, in other words?'

'That's beside the point.'

'What is the point, then?'

He appeared affronted by her challenge, pulled himself up in his chair and spoke as if to a particularly dense student. 'The point is, we are a place of learning – academic learning, not the social services.'

'But the students have asked for this. Shouldn't we respond?'

'We? Who is "we", Mrs Grant? I haven't noticed you in the classroom dealing with these issues.' His piggy eyes flashed at her, daring her to reply, and as he shook his head, a lock of his careful comb-over came adrift and hung to the side of his forehead. It caught the light and emphasised its flat, dyed colour.

'Paul, that is totally unacceptable!' Peter drilled into Paul Field with his eyes, and the Vice Prinicpal had the grace to lower his first. 'Steph, if we covered consent, do you think our students might avoid getting into some of the dreadful situations you've had to sort out in your previous life?'

'Absolutely. I'm sure it would help. To give our students the opportunity to explore the issue in a safe environment before they end up crossing the line could save some of them from the courts, criminal convictions and ruining their lives.'

'You're being a little overdramatic, aren't you?' Paul Field sneered across at her, pushing the stray lock back in place.

Should she ignore him or hit him? He really was a pompous little man.

'That settles it – I've heard enough,' said Peter. Steph, please contact the local victims' support charity to get someone in to run a series of sessions on consent. We'll pay them, of course.'

'Yes, I'll do it immediately.' As she lifted herself up to leave, Paul Field threw her a death stare, shot out of his chair and left Peter's office, slamming the door behind him. A whiff of his old-fashioned spicy after shave remained.

Peter sighed. 'Sorry Steph. If I'd thought it would go like that, I wouldn't have involved you.'

'That's fine. Been through much worse. I think it's a good thing to do, especially since the students have asked for it.'

'Good. See you later.'

As Steph returned to Reception to make the phone call, she had no way of knowing how the college was about to be invaded by the fallout from this very issue.

CHAPTER EIGHT

'Aren't you pleased you came to live here? Just look at that amazing view, darling.'

Steph scanned the clear azure sky above a flat sea, the calmest she'd ever seen. Hardly moving, it made the tiniest murmur as it folded over to dribble between the pebbles. Derek made perfect chevrons through the glassy surface, as he swam after the ball Caroline had chucked far out for him to retrieve. As usual, she'd dressed for the part in a Breton blue striped pullover and jeans, her hair tied back with a sea green scarf.

No rip tide to sweep him away today or even waves to smash through, but with his head high Derek swam towards the ball, snapping it in his jaws before turning and doggy paddling back to shore. Marlene sat well out of reach of the salt water, imperiously surveying the soggy Derek as he climbed back on dry land. He dropped the ball at Caroline's feet, shook a glittering fountain of droplets, then sat, waiting patiently for her to throw the ball once again.

She did, then stepped closer to Steph as they watched Derek take another marathon swim along the sparkling path of the sun. 'Just breathe in that smell – what is it, ozone? Whatever it is, makes me glad to be alive! We're so lucky, aren't we?'

'Yes, we are.' Steph enjoyed the moment of calm contentment and shared Caroline's appreciation of this special place. She gazed back at Southwold, huddled around the tall white lighthouse growing out of the houses in the surrounding streets. The row of solid Edwardian houses along the top of the cliff led down to the pier with its arty slot machines, grey zinc water clock and bronze metal labels coating the handrails, celebrating the loves and lives of those who had stepped above the sea on their seaside holidays. Yes, Caroline was right. This was a special place.

'Shall we go for a drink at The Sail Loft? We're almost there.' Caroline grinned at her.

'Isn't it a bit early?'

'Come on, it's Saturday and the sun will have gone down over the yard arm somewhere in the world.'

'OK, yes let's.'

'We should make the most of this weather while it lasts.'

They sat on benches looking over the marshland and Steph smiled at the sun glinting on the dyke and turning the reeds into a deep gold. Their dogs lay curled up beside them. 'What a view – you should paint that.'

'Never as good as real life, darling – can look awfully chocolate boxy.' Caroline moved a little closer and leaned her elbows on the table. 'I have something I need to tell you.' She turned her head to make sure no one was close enough to hear what she was about to say.

'Oh! Should I be worried?' Steph felt alarmed, as Caroline looked so serious. Was Margaret worse? 'Is it Margaret?'

'No.' Caroline patted Steph's arm. 'It's me who should be

worried, I suspect. Well, here goes! I've got a student living with me.'

'What? "Living with you" – what do you mean?'

'What I say. I'm offering sanctuary to a student.'

'Sanctuary! Who?'

Caroline sipped her white wine spritzer. Was she relishing the tension she was creating, or was she really worried? 'Bella, from Glebe Hall.'

'Bella?'

'Yes.'

'But she's just lost her mother.'

Caroline sighed. 'Yes, she has, but it's more complicated than that. She's devastated, but that's not it. Well – I suppose it's part of it. She says she has to get away for her own safety and won't go back.'

'What does "her own safety" mean? Who's threatening her?'

'She won't say. Says she can't yet.'

Steph drank her cider, waiting for more information from Caroline. She was a brilliant teacher, one of the most popular members of staff, and all the students loved her, but she assumed rules and regulations applied to other people, not her. Now what had she done?

'She turned up at my house last night in a dreadful state. We sat her down, and although she was almost incoherent, what she said made me believe this is serious.'

Steph knew Caroline loved a drama and often embroidered reality to give it a little more colour, but this was bizarre, even for her. 'What did she say?'

'She's obviously grieving and in deep shock from the death of her mother, but she said she was in danger if she stayed at

Glebe Hall. She said if I won't let her stay, she'll go to London and won't sit her A Levels. She'll ruin her life!'

'That sounds a little dramatic. Wouldn't she give you a clue?'

'No. In between her tears, we got her to eat little and put her to bed. After a long sleep, she was slightly calmer this morning, and she's been working with me at home all day, but she's in a dreadful state.'

'Does her father know she's with you?'

'Don't think so... No, I'm sure he doesn't' She dipped her finger in her glass and jiggled one of the ice cubes before giving Steph a knowing look. 'I suspect he's the problem!'

Why did Caroline get herself in these messes? She knew why. Caroline had the most enormous heart and anyone in trouble found it easy to talk to her, getting a good hearing and massive support. It was one thing listening to a student, but to let her move in was pretty risky.

Steph realised Caroline was waiting for her reaction, probably her approval. She took a deep breath. 'You're right – if Bella's in danger, we have a responsibility to safeguard her, but we don't want her father to report her as a missing person. Perhaps she should send him a text saying she's safe?'

'I'll talk to her and see what she says.'

'And what about Peter? Have you told him?'

Caroline sat up straight. 'No. Why should I?'

'What? You must tell him – she's one of his students and you're a member of his staff. He must know. It's a safeguarding issue.'

'Oh, I'll let him know first thing on Monday.' Caroline appeared irritated that Steph was challenging her. 'Anyway, what's wrong with helping a student in trouble? She's eighteen, a young adult who can choose for herself where she lives.'

Caroline took another sip of her spritzer, evidently thinking up further arguments to support her case. 'Bella's lost her mother in the most appalling accident, and she feels her life is at risk if she stays in her home. I am safeguarding her. And anyway, she's my god-daughter.'

'But she's still a student. You must tell Peter.'

Caroline shook her head, staring Steph down. '*I said, I'll tell him first thing on Monday.*' Her voice rose, each word enunciated sharply, then she looked around, presumably to see if anyone had heard her outburst. No one seemed to be interested in them. She leaned in closer to Steph and lowered her voice.

'Look, I know what I've done is a little – shall we say unorthodox – but I do know Bella and her family well and she was in a dreadful state. You should have seen her, Steph. There's nothing of her, but after Madeline – well, she's not been eating at all; she can't stop crying and can't begin to think of a future without her mother.'

Caroline should have been a politician or a diplomat – she could persuade the most intransigent person to see her point of view. Steph felt conflicted between the rules, which she knew should be followed, and the loving response Caroline was displaying to this girl who was suffering in the most tragic circumstances.

'Imagine being eighteen and your mother dying, then add the horrendous way it happened. It's a wonder she's not going mad. I think she's coping well but needs to be away from whatever's scaring her and to be safe and cared for. I can do that. Is it so wrong?'

'No, of course it isn't, but you have to be so careful...'

'I do know that—' The smell of the burgers being carried to the next table wafted over them. Caroline waited until the waitress had returned to the restaurant, then leaned further in, her voice now soft. 'But I was hoping Hale would see Jon Henderson.'

'What? Why should he get involved in your mess?'

Derek leaped up as a standard brown poodle appeared under the table, both wanting a jolly good sniff. Its owner, an enormous man in a boiler suit with a plumbing company's logo on the breast pocket, rushed across and grabbed its collar. 'It's OK – he's really friendly – loves other dogs!'

The friendly dog bared his teeth menacingly, growled at Derek and Marlene then crouched down low, ready to pounce. His owner grabbed his collar and dragged the reluctant dog away, his paws leaving tracks in the gravel, then fixed his lead under the legs of the bench. Threat over, Derek settled down and Marlene jumped up on the bench beside Caroline.

Steph patted Derek. 'Good boy!' She gave her attention to Caroline. 'And exactly why should Hale be involved?'

'Well, according to Bella, he's already involved. Apparently, Hale arrived there yesterday when she was in the middle of a row with her father, and that was when she walked out – literally walked out with nothing, not even a toothbrush. She was so scared.'

Steph said nothing.

'All I'm asking is that Hale goes back to talk to Jon Henderson and find out what has led Bella to seek sanctuary with me – it may be illegal what's going on there.'

CHAPTER NINE

'She's done what? I can't believe that woman sometimes!' Exasperated, after Steph had told him Caroline's news over supper, Hale ran his fingers through his hair, always a sign of his frustration. 'And she expects me to talk to Bella's father?'

'Hey! Don't shoot the messenger! It's not my fault and you have to admit, an awful lot seems to be going on at Glebe Hall recently. Maybe this is linked to the fire and the death of her mother.'

'OK, I suggest we start by visiting Bella and hearing her side of the story first.'

Without waiting for him to change his mind, Steph phoned Caroline and asked if they could visit Bella. There was a long pause, followed by some mumbling in the background, which Steph couldn't hear. At last, Caroline came on again and said she'd phone back.

Hale raised his left eyebrow and gave Steph a knowing look.

'Don't say anything!' She cleared the table while he filled the dishwasher and switched it on. It appeared that Bella didn't want to see them, so they settled down in front of the spy series they were watching.

Steph had banned police dramas as Hale was always huffing and getting cross, claiming that in real life it could never happen. In the middle of a tense pursuit scene, the phone rang; it was Caroline telling her that Bella had agreed to see them both, but they needed to know that she was fragile. A little vexed that Caroline didn't credit her with an awareness of the sensitivity needed, Steph reached for Derek's lead.

'You're not taking the mutt?'

'Why not? He enjoys seeing Marlene, don't you Derek?'

'Seriously? All they ever do is hump each other—' Halfway to the door, Hale ground to a halt as Steph glared at him. 'Fine, bring him then.' He led the way out to the car.

Caroline's house, as usual, resembled a glamorous feature in an interior design magazine. Steph assumed she'd cleared away supper, as they were sitting in the conservatory at the back of the Victorian cottage overlooking the common. A tray of coffee and biscuits arranged on the table in front of the matching Lloyd Loom basket-weave chairs would have made the perfect photograph.

As they arrived, Margaret pulled herself up, picking up her coffee mug. 'Good to see you, Steph, Hale, and thanks for a lovely picnic. I'll leave you to it, then. I've got some compositions to mark for my music set.' With that, she walked back into the house, and they heard her climbing the stairs to her study.

Caroline had been right. Bella looked grim. Puffy eyed, pale, her dark hair pulled back in a tortoiseshell comb, she was painfully thin and sat beside Caroline sipping coffee and peering at them above the rim of her mug, her black voluminous top and leggings highlighting her grief. The confident girl from a few days ago had gone – she appeared to have shrunk and looked about twelve.

'Bella, we are so sorry about your mother. You must be having a dreadful time.' Steph sat opposite her, next to Hale on the small sofa.

'Thank you.' Bella's voice was just above a whisper. 'Thank you for all you did to help at the – the car. Dad said you stopped him from being burnt worse.'

Caroline touched Bella's arm, smiling at Hale. 'He's one of the good chaps and will help if he can.'

Caroline's comment had clearly made Hale feel concerned, as he frowned, then shook his head and smiled at Bella. 'Caroline's being very kind. I'd like to do whatever I can to help you. If you feel up to it, why don't you tell me what's been going on?'

'Would you like me to go?' Caroline turned to Bella.

'No, Caroline, stay, please.' Her hand went out, as if to stop her moving; Caroline smiled at her. Evidently re-assured, Bella sat back in her seat, looking a little relieved.

Caroline poured coffee, handed them mugs and sat beside Bella, cradling her hand. They both looked expectantly at Hale.

'Over to you, Bella. Do you think you can tell us what's been happening?' Hale sounded and looked relaxed. Steph was proud of him and admired how he coped so well with whatever was thrown at him.

After a long pause, the strength of Bella's determined voice took Steph by surprise. 'I'm not going back to that place or to my father. I want to make that clear from the start.'

'Right.' Hale held up his hand in agreement. 'OK. Tell me what happened.'

They gave Bella space until she was ready to talk. She was

obviously finding this difficult and looked as if she would burst into tears at any moment. Although she knew Caroline should have handled it differently, Steph could see why she'd taken Bella in – she desperately needed love and care.

'I'm not sure where to start. For some days or even weeks before that day, Mum was strange, not herself. She spent a lot of time alone, went for long walks and always looked sad – as if she was worrying about something. Before, she'd always been so happy and bouncy...' Her voice quivered and she took a sip of coffee.

Hale smiled at her. 'You're doing great. Don't rush.'

'Well, the day before the fire, she and Dad had the most terrible row. I think I must have come home at the end of it, but I could tell it had been going on for ages. They thought I couldn't hear upstairs in my bedroom.'

She dabbed at her eyes and blew her nose, clearly trying to keep herself under control, but despite her effort, tears trickled down her cheeks. She wiped them away with the back of her hand.

'Do you know what they were arguing about?'

'It was difficult to hear the words, but "Hector" and I think "Hall" got shouted a lot. Then it went quiet. Dad slept in the guest room that night.' She paused and took a sip of coffee.

'Go on, you're doing well.' Hale smiled encouragingly.

'The next day I went to college as usual, and when I got home – home late – too late – it was all over. Dad was in hospital and Mum had – she'd – she'd gone.'

'You weren't there at all that day?'

'No. If only I'd come home at the normal time and not gone round to see Graham—'

'Graham?'

'My boyfriend. In the year above me at college. He's a real

genius at history, and it helps to make revision notes together.'
Hale's nod prompted her to continue. 'If I'd gone home, she
may be... perhaps I could have stopped her, and she'd be here –
not – not in that car—' Her head went down. Her tears dripped
onto her lap and she tried to stifle a sob.

Steph felt the girl's anguish. 'You can't blame yourself,
Bella. Even if you'd been there, you may not have been able to
stop it.'

Bella turned to Steph. 'But you don't understand. I could
have. That's exactly what I could have done.' She blew her
nose and scrubbed at her eyes with a tissue Caroline handed to
her. 'I could have stopped it all.'

'How?'

'She would have listened to me. She'd been angry with Dad
for days and kept – I don't know – kept sort of running away
from him. If I'd been there that afternoon, she'd have run to me
instead.'

The awfulness of Madeline's death and the way it was
tearing her daughter apart in front of them clearly made them
all feel totally helpless. What could they say to make her feel
better? Should they even try?

Bella sat up straight, her eyes now fixed on Hale. 'And they
keep saying Mum was drunk – she can't have been drunk.
They're lying. I know they are.'

'What makes you think that?' Hale's gentle voice reflected
his concern.

'You see, her father was an alcoholic and Mum hardly ever
drank. An occasional glass of Prosecco – but that was it,
perhaps a glass of wine when we ate out. She knew what it
could do. She lived with it and hated it when she was growing
up.'

'I see.' Hale nodded but appeared puzzled.

'I told Dad and Hector that and he said I was wrong, that I wasn't there so I wouldn't know – I hadn't seen her. And then Hector left and Dad and me – we had the most enormous row.'

'About?'

Bella lowered her head and bit her bottom lip as if weighing up her next move. 'I can't tell you – not yet – but I felt threatened – yes, that's it – threatened. I don't feel safe there anymore.'

'Because of something your father said or did?'

She stopped again, then blurted out, 'Yes, but not just him the whole place. All of them. I can't stay there; I'm not going back, and I'm scared.' She gave Hale a determined look. 'If you hadn't come at that moment, I don't think I'd have got away.'

CHAPTER TEN

SOMEONE WAS KICKING hard on the dining room door; Esme ran to open it and Jon stumbled in. 'Bella's still not come back. That's all weekend.'

'Have you eaten?'

'Too worried, but thanks.'

His hands, swathed in bandages, would make it difficult for him to do anything, even eat. His thumb and fingers on his left hand poked through the tight strips covering up his burns and she assumed he tried to turn the doorknob but couldn't get a grip on it, so resorted to kicking the door.

She glanced at his face. Dark shadows beneath his eyes and an untidy grey stubble didn't suit him. So different to the usual immaculate, well-dressed Jon. He really wasn't coping at all, was he?

Hector was sitting at the head of the table eating scrambled eggs, bacon and toast, the *Telegraph* propped on the salt and pepper pots. 'Have you seen what these pathetic idiots are saying now, trying to stop that nuclear power station being built at Sizewell?' He slapped the paper against the table.

'Bugger up the wildlife at Minsmere bird sanctuary! Total rubbish. We should produce more of our own energy, not rely on foreigners – what morons, worrying about a few birds. Esme – get Jon breakfast, will you?'

Jon nudged a chair out with his foot and sat at the polished mahogany table.

Hector looked up from his paper. 'Coffee?'

'Please.'

'He'll need a cup, too.'

Esme paused in the doorway, looking back at Jon, shocked at the dramatic change in him over a few days. At university he'd always been the best looking and sharpest dresser of the three friends – they'd pulled his leg about his habit of ironing a crease in his jeans. He always appeared immaculate, even in casual clothes, which hung well on his tall, thin frame. She'd never seen him like this before – the man sitting at the table was unrecognisable with his dirty blue shirt and stained beige chinos and he needed a shower.

Hector folded his paper and glared at her. 'Well, we haven't got all day.'

Esme retreated to the kitchen, leaving her own breakfast to go cold. She shrugged her shoulders – she could always grab something later. In the kitchen, the housekeeper was washing up after last night's supper.

'Liz, could you bring another breakfast into the dining room for Jon, please?'

Pulling off her yellow rubber gloves, Liz laid them over the edge of the butler sink. 'Scrambled eggs and toast? Bacon?'

'Please. All of it. Poor man looks famished. I should have thought earlier, but I'll make sure he eats all his meals with us from now on, so make enough for him too, please.' She took two cups and saucers off the pine dresser built into the wall of the kitchen. 'Oh, and another pot of coffee. Thanks.'

Carrying the cups, she returned to the dining room, noting that the door had been closed, presumably by Hector. She opened it and walked into a moment's silence, then Hector said in a loud voice, 'As I was saying, I'll contact the Environment Agency about Sizewell — knew James Tredegar at school. He's got clout.'

Jon didn't answer. She went to the sideboard and poured Jon a cup of coffee from the jug on the hotplate. 'You don't take milk or sugar, do you, Jon?'

'No. Just as it comes.'

She placed the cup on his left side and a bowl of muesli and milk beside it so he could use his working hand. 'Cooked breakfast is on its way. You look as if you need it. I'm sorry, we should have invited you earlier.'

'Not been up to eating much. You know, picking at things in the fridge. I've been fine.' He didn't look fine at all.

Esme returned to her seat. 'What were you saying about Bella? She isn't at home?'

Jon's eyes met Hector's, and she was sure he shook his head slightly. 'After her mother – you know, she was so upset – I accepted she'd want to be with friends, but I – er – I assumed she'd be home by now. It's been the whole weekend, and she's not back this morning.' He sniffed and wiped his eyes with his bandaged hand. 'Sorry... I'm a little worried, that's all.'

'More than a little, I'd say. We would be too.' Esme frowned. 'Not like Bella, is it? Such a sensible girl.'

What had gone on between them? His overlong explanation sounded like a guilty child. And what did Hector know about it? She knew him well enough to be sure he wasn't telling her everything. The door crashed open, and Jack lumbered towards the table, then veered away to the sideboard and picked up the coffeepot. He was wearing his morning face and not a lot else.

Esme tutted. 'Honestly Jack, appearing for breakfast in your boxers! Get back to your room and put on some clothes, wash your face, and brush your hair. I'll ask Liz to bring you breakfast.'

'Don't worry. I'll tell her on my way up. In a hurry. I'm late' Coffee cup in hand, he failed to notice the slop that overflowed the edge of the cup and left a small puddle on the polished oak floor.

'Get dressed and I'll drive you in.' Esme shook her head as Jack left. 'Hector, I'll need to buy some petrol.'

'I'll get some cash from the safe in the study and don't forget the receipt this time.' Hector frowned and stared ahead.

Esme smiled at Jon and raised her eyebrows. 'Kids! You don't think when they're cute babies that they'll grow into terrible teenagers, do you?'

'Bella's such a good girl, but she's been so upset by her mother's... er... Madeleine's... er... Not coping at all... well, she wouldn't, would she? They were so close.'

'Is there anything I can do?'

'No. But thanks, she—'

'—probably stayed with a friend. You know what women are like. They need other women at times like this. They talk, we act.' Hector's breezy tone was at odds with Jon's concerned face. What was Jon going on to say? Hector always dominated. 'She'll come running back after college. Should be comforting her father, not swanning off with her friends.'

'But Hector—'

'But nothing, Esme. We all have to deny our own feelings and get on with our duty at times like this. Family comes first.'

Hector's voice was louder and, recognising the signs, Esme knew better than to argue.

'Have you phoned her friends?' Esme picked up Hector's empty cereal bowl and put it on the sideboard.

'Er... Not yet. Thought she'd be back by now.'

Why hadn't he phoned her friends after the first night she'd been missing? Surely that would be the first thing to do? He was falling apart and no wonder after what he'd been through. She returned to her seat and took a mouthful of cold coffee.

The phone in Jon's pocket beeped. He fumbled it out and laid it on the table, pushing it against a glass bowl of pink roses to keep it still, and scrolled up to see what had arrived.

'It's from Bella!' He read it, then his shoulders slumped, and he appeared grief-stricken, not relieved. Esme wondered what was in the text. They both stared at him. He was transfixed by the phone, but still said nothing.

'She's let you know where she is, then? Good of her!' Hector's knife and fork clattered to his plate. Trust Hector.

Jon fumbled as he scrolled back up and re-read the text. 'I suppose I should stop worrying but—'

'Is she with a friend?' Esme brought the coffeepot over to Jon to re-fill his cup. 'I could always drive you there.'

'No.' Defeated and subdued, it was difficult to hear him. 'She's staying a few days with one of her teachers – Caroline, her art teacher.' Jon appeared thoroughly miserable – he must have hoped the text was to announce she was coming home.

Hearing this news, Hector frowned and Esme, dreading the threatened outburst, tried to lighten the tone. 'Oh, Caroline Jones? She'll be fine with her. Bella's godmother – great friends with Madeline and me, way before Bella was born—'

'What rubbish are you coming out with now? That woman

has no right to keep Bella from her father. She should be here where she belongs.'

Esme moved around the table to top-up Hector's cup. He put his hand on top of it – good job she was slow in pouring. 'What's wrong with Caroline suddenly? I thought you liked her?' Once again Esme resumed her seat but gave up on the coffee.

'Arty-farty woman who thinks she's better than she is. Wouldn't have stayed in Oakwood if she was any good. Only a tin-pot teacher in a small college. Anyone would think she was running the Royal Academy up there, not a few A Levels. And she's... you know...'

'Gay? Surely, you're not holding that against her, Hector? She's lived with Margaret for... what? ... must be well over twenty years. As much a marriage as ours.'

'Hmph!' Hector held up his empty cup. Once again, Esme trekked over to the sideboard and picked up the pot to hear Hector in decision mode. 'No Jon, it's wrong and unprofessional to use a power relationship to groom your daughter. She holds those students in her sway. It's not bloody well good enough, we'll—'

Liz entered, carrying a tray with Jon's breakfast and more coffee.

'Thank you, Liz.' Esme smiled at her.

'Shut the door on your way out, will you?' When Hector was sure the door was firmly shut, he continued. 'As I was saying, you get that down you and we'll go into that college and tell that Principal his fortune—'

Esme dreaded the scene he would make at the college, and from the look on Jon's face, he wasn't exactly enthusiastic about going either.

'Wouldn't it be better if I went to see Caroline to talk to her and Bella quietly and find out what's wrong and persuade her to come home?' Esme took the salt and pepper over to Jon's side of the table.

'Stupid idea. No, we need to take this to the top – always works best. This is unprofessional behaviour and I mean to sort it out.' He folded his newspaper. 'No hurry, Jon. Take your time, old man. You look as if you need that.'

They both watched as a depressed Jon chased lumps of scrambled egg around his plate, eventually trapping a forkful against a piece of toast, strategically placed at the edge of his plate. No one spoke. Esme tried a mouthful of her cold eggs and soggy toast but gave up. She had lost her appetite.

CHAPTER ELEVEN

WHAT STARTED AS A QUIET, routine morning for Steph suddenly deteriorated into chaos as two men stormed into Reception.

'I demand the see the Principal, *now!*' Hector Percy, reeking of some expensive cologne and wearing his lord of the manor suit of pink trousers, waistcoat and blazer, towered over her. In that one sentence, Steph could feel the force of the threat that had pushed Bella away.

Close behind, in Hector's shadow, stood Jon Henderson, his hands smothered in bandages. Unlike the dapper Hector, Jon was a wreck of a man – his un-ironed pale blue shirt and beige chinos a world away from the smart, elegant man at the Open Day. His silver hair needed a comb, and his deep brown eyes were sunk and surrounded by dark shadows. Steph felt so sorry for him.

Neither of them appeared to recognise her from the fire. Calling on her assertiveness training, she slowly raised her head, smiled, and said in a quiet voice, 'Good morning, Mr Percy, Mr Henderson. If you would like to wait over there, I will see if Mr Bryant is free.' She nodded towards the black leather sofas at the far end of Reception and came around the end of the long desk, blocking their way to Peter's door.

A slight frown registered Hector's surprise at her knowing their names. Jon started towards the waiting area, but seeing that Hector hadn't moved, returned to stand beside him. Hector appeared to have decided he was staying put, as he grasped the edge of the desk with both hands.

Before he could speak, she smiled again. 'Please wait over there.' She gestured to the sofas beside the sliding doors. 'I'll see if Mr Bryant is free.' This time it was her 'don't mess with me' voice – still calm, but they got the message and obeyed her.

Relieved, she knocked and walked into Peter's office, which, unlike the Reception glass box stuck onto the old building, was like stepping back into the nineteen thirties, when the college was built. Oak panels, copper hood over the fireplace and button-back leather chairs around a low oak table created an impression of calm academia.

'Mr Percy and Mr Henderson are in Reception and would like to see you.'

'Do you know what it's about?' Peter continued typing on his desk computer, where he appeared to be answering emails.

'I think so. Bella Henderson has fled Glebe Hall and gone to stay with Caroline Jones as she fears for her safety.'

'What!' His head jerked up. 'Caroline? How long?'

'I found out on Saturday, but Bella arrived at Caroline's on Friday night, apparently.'

'And you were intending to tell me this, when?'

'As soon as the morning rush was over. Caroline's got an appointment to see you at nine o'clock as soon as she's settled her class.' The knot in her stomach tightened.

Peter grabbed his jacket from the back of his chair and

pulled it on, moving towards her. 'It would have been helpful to have more than ten seconds to consider my reaction.'

'Sorry Peter, but you'd only just arrived, and I didn't know they'd show up in college.'

'Right, wheel them in – oh, and stay too, will you? If this gets nasty, I'll need a witness.'

Feeling embarrassed and a little annoyed that once again she was taking the flak for being the messenger, Steph went over to the two men and ushered them into Peter's office.

'Good morning, Mr Henderson, Mr Percy.' Peter shook hands with them both. They sat; Hector's laser eyes fixed on Peter's face. 'Mrs Grant will remain to take notes.' Not a request, an order. Relieved that she'd picked up her notebook and pen from her desk as she walked behind the men and for once had got something right, she joined them sitting around the low table.

'How may I help you?' Peter smiled at the two serious-looking men as if they had come for a social chat.

'You obviously don't know that one of your teachers has kidnapped Bella Henderson.' Hector deliberately and carefully enunciated each word of his rehearsed opening line to create the maximum dramatic effect. Jon lowered his head, but Steph could see a blush creeping up his face.

Ignoring Hector, Peter turned to Jon. 'First of all, Mr Henderson, may I again express my deepest sympathy for your loss? Your wife was a local legend – a brilliant teacher – and she'll be greatly missed.'

Jon Henderson tried to smile at Peter and mumbled, 'Thank you.'

Peter, it appeared, hadn't given the correct response, so Hector continued. 'Bella has just lost her mother in the most tragic circumstances and hasn't coped at all well with the loss.

She is a vulnerable child, open to exploitation.' He cleared his throat. 'On Friday evening, after a hysterical outburst, Bella left Glebe Hall and went to stay with one of your teachers, the Head of the Art Department.'

Peter frowned, head on one side. 'Let me get this straight. You're telling me that your eighteen-year-old daughter,' directing his gaze at Jon, 'left her home and went of her own accord to stay with Miss Jones over the weekend? I wouldn't call that kidnap.'

Despite Peter's stare, Jon didn't open his mouth, but the voice came from Hector. 'Of course we're not suggesting Miss Jones came to the Hall and drove off into the night with Bella, who, incidentally, now refuses to come home.'

'You've spoken to Miss Jones?' Once again, Peter directed his question at Jon.

'No, but Bella has been in contact with her father by text, and told him she's no intention of coming home and Miss Jones is happy for her to stay as long as she wants.' Hector appeared to be getting annoyed that he was talking to the side of Peter's face.

Before Peter could reply, Hector sat forward, drilling him with a vicious look. 'I'm horrified by your reaction, Principal! This is an illegal act. An abuse of a power relationship between a teacher and a student.'

Peter, raising an eyebrow, turned to Hector. 'I can assure you that Miss Jones, one of our longest serving teachers, has excellent relationships with her students and would never abuse her position or groom any of her students.' He stood. 'Thank you for the information you've provided. I can assure you my priority is the safety of my students and my staff. If I find any issue that needs further investigation, I will take the appropriate action.'

With an angry red face, Hector stood to face Peter, who appeared to be unperturbed by Hector's outrage. 'Appropriate action? I can assure you, Principal, that we shall inform the appropriate authorities. The Chief Constable is a personal friend, as is the chairman of the Suffolk Education Committee – let's see what they think of your appropriate action, shall we?' A small fleck of saliva landed on Peter's shirt as Hector stressed his consonants. They had both seen it but ignored it.

Hector pulled himself up even taller. 'And then, there's the Department for Education and Ofsted. I wonder how they will judge your cavalier behaviour towards the morals of your teachers and how they break their professional code of practice. You'll be hearing from us.' With that, he turned, grabbed at the handle, pulled the door wide open and stormed out, with Jon, looking embarrassed, following him.

Steph saw them out of the office and watched as they were forced to stop at the automatic sliding doors. Hector, obviously annoyed at having to wait for them to open, tutted before striding out into the car park. Jon, who had not said a word, shuffled out after Hector.

She returned to a grumpy-looking Peter. 'Great start to the morning! Now let's see what Caroline has to say.'

CHAPTER TWELVE

As SHE LEFT Peter's office, Steph bumped into Caroline, who grinned at her and winked, while making a graceful arm movement, letting Steph go back in first.

'Thanks a lot!' Steph mouthed to her as she returned to her seat.

The two women sat in silence waiting for Peter, who appeared to be in no rush to join them but completed something he was typing at his desk. Steph couldn't help but admire Peter's creation of tension, presumably developed over years of reprimanding guilty students. At last, he sat down opposite Caroline.

'Well, Caroline?'

'On Friday night, Bella Henderson, my god-daughter, and whose mother I have known for years before she was born, turned up at my house in the most dreadful state. She said she felt threatened, was in danger and begged me to let her stay.'

Impressed by Caroline's calm, articulate account, Steph glanced at Peter, who was listening attentively, but said nothing.

'Obviously, I tried my best to persuade her to go home. I offered to go with her and talk to Jon, her father, but she was terrified.'

Caroline appeared to waver a little under Peter's steady gaze and her words tumbled out. 'I've never seen her like that before – she was hysterical and said if I didn't let her stay, she'd go to London and not take her exams and live on the streets rather than go home. So, I let her stay.'

At last, he spoke. 'Where is Bella now?'

'At home, working on her art course work. Margaret's there – it's her day off.'

'So, let me get this right, Caroline.' He had that slow, reasonable tone, which always meant trouble. 'She's been with you for an entire weekend, and it didn't occur to you to tell me?' Peter paused. 'To phone me?'

For the first time ever, Steph saw Caroline looking uncomfortable, and she squirmed in her seat. Evidently, she knew she'd stepped over the line and didn't reply, but stared out of the window, distracted by some students laughing in the car park. Steph could see that Peter was becoming impatient and hoped this would not be another Paul Field dressing down. She had become good friends with Caroline and didn't want this to spoil it.

Peter waited until he had Caroline's full attention. 'You know as well as I do how dramatic students of this age can be. Once, when I was a Vice Principal, I had to find a bed for a student who claimed he'd been thrown out by his mother for leaving a sock on the floor. Of course, his mother's version was very different. Eventually, we got him back home with promises to improve his unacceptable behaviour, which believe me was much worse than an abandoned sock!'

Although he'd obviously finished his story, Steph knew not to interrupt, and hoped Caroline had picked up the same message. Luckily, she had, as she said nothing.

Peter dropped the pen he'd been holding on the table. 'I suspect Bella's is a case like that. She's in the depths of grief, having lost her mother in the most appalling circumstances, but she can only see it from her point of view at the moment.'

A car revved up and squealed out of the car park, making Peter wince.

At last Caroline spoke. 'You're right, she's devastated by her mother's death, but Bella is a sensible girl and when she says she's terrified to go home and fears for her safety, I believe her.'

'Has she told you why?'

'No. She won't say. Just that she's in real danger if she goes home.' Caroline shook her head and sighed. 'I really believe Bella's threatened – it's so unlike her. She's in a dreadful state.'

Peter appeared to be convinced by Caroline's concern and, for a few moments, was evidently considering his next step. 'Steph, I wonder if Hale should be involved, maybe—'

'He didn't know what to do either when—' Caroline clammed up and pulled a face at Steph when she realised what she'd said.

Immediately suspicious, Peter rounded on Steph. 'Oh, so Hale is already involved, is he? I hope this isn't going to be another instance of you and him keeping me out of the loop when it involves one of my students?'

Steph swallowed to relieve her dry mouth as her nerves kicked in. Trust Caroline to resurrect the tension between Peter and Hale – she'd worked hard to re-assure Peter of her loyalty and convince him he'd be fully involved after their last run-in. 'He's investigating the fire that killed Bella's mother and thought Bella might have run away because of something to do with that. He could get no further information from her, either.' It was best to come clean, and it was almost the truth – he had got nowhere.

'Well, you'd better warn him to be ready for an approach by the Chief Constable, and I'll wait for the local authority or even the Department of Education to contact me. It seems Hector Percy has friends in high places!'

'That proves it!' Caroline slapped her hand on the arm of the chair to make her point. 'If he's willing to go to those people, Bella's right – there must be something going on. Typical of him!'

'Typical? Why?'

'Hector and Esme, his wife, have always moved in county circles. He knows anyone worth knowing and will pull any strings to get what he wants.'

'You know him well, then?'

'Used to. Not so much recently. Just the usual cocktail and dinner parties at the Hall, you know the sort of thing.'

Peter's face suggested he didn't know the sort of thing at all. Picking up the pen from the table, he tapped it against his knee and appeared to be thinking. 'Well, we are where we are!'

Caroline appeared puzzled at this meaningless pronouncement.

With a sudden burst of energy, he stood up. 'I suggest Bella stays with you for the moment. If she tells you what's scared her, I expect you to tell me immediately so we can decide what to do. She's over eighteen and we want her to take her exams; meanwhile, I'll see if I can calm down the great and good.'

He walked towards his desk, then paused, apparently hit by a thought, and turned back to Caroline. 'This is a safeguarding issue, and as well as ensuring Bella's safety, I have a duty to safeguard you from any malicious accusations. I will speak to Social Services and clear it with them and get back to you. Thank you both.' Finally, he moved to sit at his desk, a sure sign he was dismissing them.

CHAPTER THIRTEEN

'IF YOU'RE COMING, come on. Hurry up.' Coat on, Hale waited impatiently by the front door.

'Are you sure I should come?' Steph pulled on her beige jacket. The heatwave had disappeared and the torrential rain and iron-grey skies had thrown the clock back to winter and now demanded extra layers. She shivered, hardly believing they had sheltered from the sun only a few days ago.

'Of course, you should be coming. I told you that I've reinstated you as a Civilian Investigator for the case and HR has approved it, so all you need do is sign the paperwork. They think that you'll be a valuable asset as you were there at the start of all this and as you know Bella at college.'

'I see.' Steph had been employed as a part-time Civilian Investigator on a couple of Hale's cases and had relished the role of working in the college while employing skills acquired over years in the police. 'And you've discussed this with Peter?'

'Of course.'

She thought back to the last case when she'd been caught in the middle, her loyalty split between the two men.

'Really?'

'Yes, really.' The irritation in his voice was no longer hidden.

'Right, well, if we can have the same rules as last time. Anything that affects his students or the college, he has a right to know and I can brief him.'

'Fine – as long as we decide what it is first.'

'Deal.'

'Glad that's sorted. Now come on!'

They splashed through the large puddles flooding the road as they drove through the elegant gates of Glebe Hall. After such a long period of drought, the stair-rod rain puddled on the surface of the concrete soil. Pulling up outside the main doors of the Hall, they dashed out of the car to the shelter of the pillaried porch and Hale tugged at the bell.

Esme opened the door. 'Hello. Is this something to do with Bella?'

'Could we have a chat with you and your husband, please?'

'Of course. Come through, you know the way. I'll get Hector.'

Once again, they found themselves in the enormous peach-coloured sitting room with floor-to-ceiling windows that over-looked the fluorescent green park. Over the last two days, the rain had made the lawn an even brighter green than when they were last there. The landscaping, according to Caroline the creation of Capability Brown, made a perfect picture of mature oak trees, leading down a gentle slope to the mile-long lake.

Their quiet appreciation of the view was interrupted by an energetic Hector, in navy track suit bottoms and white polo shirt, who bounced in, having appeared to have come from doing some exercise, presumably in a gym. Steph was struck again by his classic good looks now that he wasn't being aggressive and overbearing, but polite and controlled in his own kingdom.

'Hello again, Chief Inspector and, er... Mrs Grant.'

Hale took the lead, answering the unasked question. 'Mrs Grant is here in her capacity as a Civilian Investigator. She was in the force for thirty years before her change of career and we use her regularly to help us in specific cases when we're short of manpower.'

'I see. No doubt you're here to talk about Bella.' Not a question, but a demand from a man used to getting his own way.

Hale matched him. 'No, it's about the fire in which Madeline Henderson's body was found. We are now treating her death as suspicious.'

'What do you mean? Suspicious?' Esme interrupted.

Hector's head snapped round, and he glared at her. 'Perhaps our visitors would like some refreshment.'

'That's very kind, but no, thank you.'

After Hale's polite refusal, Esme resumed her seat while an irate Hector sighed. He appeared to find Hale's reappearance and questions annoying and unnecessary – an impression apparently picked up by Hale, who persisted. 'When we last met, Mr Percy, you were in no state to describe exactly the events of that day and now, with the benefit of hindsight, I would like you to tell me again what happened. From the beginning, please.'

'But you know all that.'

'Humour me. We were all in a state of shock having come from the fire.'

Once again, Hector sighed. He paused, and for a moment Steph thought he was going to refuse, but, after another dramatic sigh, he gave in. 'Very well, if I must. That afternoon I received a phone call from Jon, who was upset as he'd had a row with Madeline over something—'

'Do you know what?'

'No idea. You'll have to ask Jon.'

'We will. Please go on.'

Hector grimaced at Hale, presumably because he had dared to interrupt. 'Jon was in a terrible state. He said Madeline had driven off, and he was convinced she was too drunk to drive. We went after her on our quad bikes. There was the most enormous crash, and we saw the smoke. She'd crashed into a tree.'

'Really?' Hale frowned. 'When we got there, the car wasn't wrapped around a tree. It was in a clearing.'

'It must have ricocheted off one then!' The old Hector returned as his voice got louder and he appeared to resent Hale having the audacity to challenge him. 'All I know is that when Jon and I got there, the car was on fire with Madeline inside. We tried but couldn't get her out. You saw the state of Jon's hands. Then you arrived, and the rest you know.'

There was a moment of silence as a picture of that blazing inferno pushed its way into their minds, broken by Hale's next question. 'And can you explain how petrol was found all around the area of the car?'

'Sorry?' Hector frowned.

'The Fire Investigation Officer found petrol all around the car.'

Hector shook his head, apparently in disbelief at Hale's stupidity. 'You were there. The petrol came from the petrol tank when it exploded, obviously.'

Hale continued to hold Hector in his steady gaze. 'No. The fire had been started using an accelerant, petrol in this case.'

Esme gasped. 'You're saying someone deliberately set the car on fire with Madeline in it?'

'Well, it certainly wasn't me and I'm sure it wasn't Jon.' Hector retorted quickly, giving Esme an evil glance, clearly shutting her up once again.

'How do you know it wasn't Jon?' Hale got in quickly.

Hector cleared his throat and stared out of the window towards Badgers' Wood before responding. 'He... er... Well, I arrived soon after him... but he... I mean, Jon would never do anything to hurt Madeline—'

'What an appalling thing to suggest!' Esme, now pale, put her hand in front of her mouth as the idea planted by Hale appeared to take hold. Her eyes filled.

'Now look here, Chief Inspector, you have no right coming here and upsetting my wife like this. I've told you all I know and been as helpful as I can. This is a tragedy that will haunt us all for ever.'

Hector stood, clearly deciding the discussion was over. 'Unless you have firm evidence that implicates me or my wife, I suggest you leave and talk to Jon Henderson, who may be of further help to you. This involves his family, after all.'

Hale and Steph rose and left the sitting room, followed by Hector, who saw them to the front door, which closed behind them with a resounding clunk.

Steph buttoned up her jacket before stepping out into the rain. 'I'd say that friendship's going to be pretty strained. Let's see what Jon says.'

CHAPTER FOURTEEN

A MODERN, smaller version of the Percys' bellpull hung beside a door that had replaced one of the long windows at the tip of the east wing. Hale had hardly touched it when Jon opened the door.

'Chief Inspector Hale, Mrs Grant.' His paws nudged his mobile on the hall table, stopping it from falling off the edge.

'You'll know why we're here.' Hale nodded towards the phone. 'Perhaps we could have a chat?' Hale glanced behind Jon at the long hall with four doors leading from it.

'Of course. Come through to the sitting room.'

He led them through the second door on the right and they entered a smaller and more modern version of the Percys' sitting room – cream carpet, natural linen chairs and sofa, punctuated with vibrant blue and green silk cushions. The gold frame on the most enormous glass coffee table in the centre of a modern abstract carpet glinted in the light from the long windows. There were fewer pictures than the Percys had, but they were more modern abstracts, beautifully hung to make the most of each of them.

But this was a very different room to that of the Percys. Papers, magazines and unopened letters were piled on or under or behind most chairs; empty wine bottles, dirty glasses and a few mugs littered the stone hearth and the curtains at three of the windows were not tied back in artistic swags but thrown open. Closer to the lake, the view through the windows onto the picture book park became sharper and more impressive.

Jon noticed them looking out at the landscape. 'Amazing, isn't it?' He walked with them over to the floor to ceiling window, where they stood admiring the perfect pastoral view. 'Capability Brown knew what he was doing. In the original house this would have been the morning room – catches the sun most of the day. The original ladies of the manor would have used it as their sitting room – writing their letters, reading, and giving orders for dinner to the housekeeper.'

Steph turned from the perfectly ordered landscape back to a room in chaos.

Evidently, Jon became aware of her survey. 'Sorry about the mess. Haven't felt like doing anything since Madeline... and then Bella... I'm sure you can understand... and with these—' He held out his hands bound with boxing glove size bandages. 'It's not easy.'

'May I help?' Steph lifted a pile of papers off an armchair and took them across to a glass-topped table in the bay window, adding them to the mass of documents and files already there. She noticed a document headed *The Last Will and Testament* – presumably Madeline's, but she couldn't see what it said.

Beside it were two photographs in identical silver frames. One of Madeline and Jon in their wedding finery in front of a Gothic arch, presumably the church where they married. It was the first time Steph had seen Madeline, and she was stunning; long blonde curls artfully framed her delicate face, with enormous eyes and a wide smile – a tall perfect bride in her lacy wedding dress. She could have been a model. Come to that, so could the man who had his arm around her shoulder. Jon was about four inches taller than her, with deep red chestnut hair and intelligent brown eyes – happiness radiated out from this charmed couple.

The second photo showed them at another, more recent celebration – a wedding anniversary? Again, they presented as the perfect middle-aged couple but more subdued somehow. With broad smiles for the camera they looked happy and content, but there was something – a distancing, perhaps?

Despite his grey hair, Jon had aged well, and the remnants of his teenage acne didn't show up on the photos – he resembled the archetypal silver fox Steph had met on the Open Day. Confident, elegant, and so fanciable – if anything, age had made him more so – and, from the intense look in his dark brown eyes, he still adored his Madeline. She appeared little older than on her wedding day, all those years ago. Few wrinkles, the same curls worn a few inches shorter, cupid bow lips that Bella had inherited, and wide blue-grey eyes posed for the camera, but Steph sensed something had changed.

'Madeline was beautiful, wasn't she?' She heard herself blurting it out and turned to see a crestfallen Jon. 'I'm so sorry—'

'No. I'm pleased you've seen her as she was, not...'

'She was lovely.' Steph sat in the armchair she'd just cleared.

Jon scanned the room as if seeing it for the first time. 'The housekeeper said she'll come in later and do a clear up. I certainly need it, don't I?' He smiled, sheepishly.

He had deteriorated further since she'd seen him at college.

He had aged about five years and the smart executive in the photo frame had been replaced by a ragbag of a man, and a rather smelly one at that. Steph wondered when he'd last showered, but immediately felt mean when she saw the grubby bandaged hands resting on his lap.

Hale cleared a seat on the matching small sofa, while Jon had settled in what she presumed was his favourite chair beside the fireplace. The ash from a wrought iron log fire basket was waiting to be removed and appeared to comprise log shapes but also quite a lot of paper. What had he been burning? It must have been such an effort with his hands like that.

On a glass table beside Jon's chair, a large plastic beaker, about a third full of brandy or whisky, tottered close to the edge. Steph could smell the tang of the strong spirit from where she sat, but she hadn't noticed it on his breath. Last night's then. Feeling sorry for this abandoned man, Steph found it difficult to believe he was the threat Bella was escaping.

'How can I help you?' Jon looked over at Hale.

'I'm sure Mr Percy will have told you about our latest findings regarding your wife's accident?'

'He said you thought it was started deliberately. Petrol, he said. I can't believe it.' He shook his head. 'I mean... if that is so... How?'

'That's what we'd like to find out. Do you think you can go back to the early afternoon and tell us what happened between yourself and your wife?'

'You may know I work from home, here on my own projects or over in the estate office for Glebe Hall.'

'Doing what exactly?'

'I run my own marketing company from my office next door and also look after the PR side of Glebe Hall, as part of our contribution to living on the estate.'

Steph couldn't resist it. 'It sounds like living in paradise – I mean the arrangement you have here with the Percys.'

A weak smile crept across his face. 'Paradise? Umm... you could say that. Yes, I suppose so. Doesn't feel much like that at the moment. Although I must say I welcome the additional help... Actually, not sure how I'd manage without it.'

'You must be great friends with Esme and Hector after all this time?'

'Yes, they're like a family, but one you've chosen.' Jon made a slight movement, about to reach for the beaker, but appeared to stop himself and instead scratched at the bandage on that hand, then glanced at Hale, presumably to see if he'd noticed.

Hale leaned forward. 'Getting back to the afternoon when your wife died. Did she work from home too?'

'Good heavens, no. She was a primary school teacher, and an excellent one too. She runs the free school in the outbuildings on the edge of the estate. You probably won't have seen them. She has Reception to Year Six—'

'Sorry?' said Hale.

'From four to eleven-year-olds. About fifty children in total. She and Hector set it up about seven years ago. Some of the year groups are taught together as there aren't enough children to have them in separate classes. But even then, they do very well.'

Jon paused, and they waited for him to continue. Talking about the school, his voice was stronger and confident, in presentation mode.

'Their progress data shows they're well ahead of children of similar ability in the local schools and they excel in secondary education. You see, Madeline teaches them to think, gives them skills for learning, doesn't fill them with facts...'

He stopped and sighed, evidently recognising he was

reciting the school's marketing speech as if Madeline was still there. As Steph knew, it took some time to adjust to the past tense after a bereavement.

'So, that afternoon she came back from teaching, then?' Hale prompted him.

'She was upset. Madeline loved her job. That was all she'd ever wanted to do, teach. When Hector suggested setting up a free school, it was a dream come true. She could run it her way, choose her own teachers, design the curriculum. Yes – she lived her dream...' Jon's voice had become quieter as he appeared to be drifting off, lost in his memories. Once again, Steph felt sorry for him and his loss of the beautiful Madeline.

Hale leaned forward into his sight line. 'What had upset her that afternoon?'

'She came in exhausted. Early. Immediately she started drinking – neat whisky—'

'Was this unusual?'

'Yes. She was in a dreadful state and kept saying it had all been for nothing and she needed to drown her sorrows.'

'Why?'

'She wasn't too clear about that... I... er... I left her alone... gave her some space... waited until she wanted to talk, you know. If only I'd stayed with her. She drove off and... Well, you know...' He sniffed into a well-used tissue, stuffed beside him on the chair cushion. They waited, but it appeared Jon had finished.

Hale gave him a few moments before pushing on with his calm questioning. 'Your friend, Hector, told us that Madeline and you had a row and that's why she stormed out.'

'How does he know? He wasn't here.'

'He said you phoned him, and you both went tearing off after her on your quad bikes.'

'Madeline drove into a tree, and we were too late to save her.'

'So Hector told us.'

Obviously upset, Jon walked to the table in the bay to get another tissue from the box on top of a pile of papers. He had problems pulling it out, so Steph got up and fished out a few tissues for him, which he took in the fingers outside his bandaged paws. She sat down again while he remained by the table, a puzzled expression on his face and his voice once again wobbly. 'I'm not sure what Hector's talking about... a row? We loved each other... and... and it was his plan to close the school that made her angry, not me.'

'I see. Closing the school? Why?'

'She wasn't too clear – just upset and angry. I thought I'd leave her to it and come back later. But I left it too late... If only I'd come back sooner, I could have stopped her.' Tears dripped down his cheeks. Noticing them, he wiped his face with the handful of tissues.

Hale spoke at last. 'And do you have any idea where the petrol came from that appears to have been used as an accelerant?'

Jon's head jerked back as if hearing it for the first time. Had he forgotten the conversation when they arrived? His voice was now louder. 'What? Certainly not from me! I loved Madeline and wouldn't dream of harming her.'

Hale sighed. 'Well, someone did and wanted her dead. Did you see anyone else in the wood?'

'No, only the car in flames.'

Jon stepped back against the table, and for a moment, Steph was convinced he would faint. But he steadied himself and stayed upright.

'Moving on to Bella.' Hale gave Jon time to take in his

change of tack. 'Last Friday evening, when I visited you, she said I stopped an almighty row between the two of you and she used my arrival to escape the threat of living here. Can you explain what she meant?'

In slow motion, Jon returned to his seat by the dead fire. 'I don't know what she's talking about. We didn't have a row, not at all. Obviously, Bella's devastated by the death of her mother and upset beyond words. She doesn't know what she's saying, but I can assure you we didn't have a row. We never row.'

'And do you know who's threatening her, so she won't come home?'

'Threatening? She said threatening?'

A sudden drumming on the long window made them all look out at the park, now hidden by a veil of horizontal rain. Thunder rumbled overhead. A branch from a rose bush caught by the wind bashed against the window.

His voice pulled them back inside. 'I'm her father and would never hurt her. Can't think what's got into her head.' Once again, his eyes filled. 'Please tell her to come home. I miss her – I need her.'

After this appeal to Hale, Jon put his head in his hands and drips plopped from the end of his nose onto the floor. He didn't bother using the tissues, and once again, appeared not to notice.

Clearly Hale had decided they would get no more from him on this visit, and after saying goodbye and re-assuring him they would find their own way out, they ran through the rain, alongside the house to their car parked by the main door.

As they drove off towards the gates, Hale put his hand on Steph's thigh and gently squeezed it. 'Fascinating, eh? No rows there at all then. All peace and quiet, apparently. And did you see Hector eyeballing us as we left?'

'Yes. And didn't you think it weird that no one jumped to the obvious conclusion that Madeline may have been murdered?'

'Yeah, I did. I wonder what is going on in that house – we're nowhere near the bottom of it yet.'

CHAPTER FIFTEEN

THE BEACH HUT was a perfect doll's house in an outstanding position beneath Gun Hill. As Steph walked down the hill towards the sea, past the cannon fired on jubilees and state occasions, she spotted the hut, each vertical weather board a different shade of the rainbow. Even on a grey evening the bright colours made her smile – in the summer sunshine it would glitter.

Ensuring that she could suss out the place and check out a potential escape route, Steph had arrived first, then chided herself for her over-reaction. But old habits are hard to break. She gazed at the sea, watching the high tide eating away at the sand and lapping right up to the concrete promenade. As usual, she was hypnotised and calmed by the rhythmic splashes as the waves moved up the beach. She hadn't brought Derek, as dogs weren't welcome on the prom, and anyway, he would have been a distraction in what she assumed might be a difficult meeting.

Voices coming down the steep slope above her heralded the arrival of Caroline and Bella. Predictably, Caroline had dressed for the part; this evening Steph assumed it was her spy suit – her grey curls pushed up under a beige beret, the same shade as her tightly belted mack, with a geometric black and beige scarf tucked into the neckline. An elderly couple strolling along the prom turned to gaze at her. Not great as a spy then? Steph could hear laughter as Bella revelled in her company and the total attention Caroline gave her.

This Bella was very different from the one she had met at Caroline's. Still thin and pale, she appeared stronger and more determined. Caroline had told her that Bella had returned to college to work on her art project, but Steph hadn't bumped into her, despite several trips to the canteen and wandering around Main Quad, the grassy square at the core of the campus.

'Good evening, Steph. Shall we go in?' Caroline smiled at Bella, who pulled out a gigantic iron key, unlocked the beach hut, hooked the doors back and moved to the side so Caroline and Steph could climb up the three steps.

'What a great place!' Looking around, Steph sat beside Caroline on one of the green canvas beach chairs at the back of the hut, in front of a bar that held a Calor Gas hob and a pile of brightly coloured crockery. Admiring the red, blue and green striped material covering the seat on top of the storage box along the side of the hut, Steph laughed. 'This really is a Tardis, isn't it? I've never been inside one before. Didn't realise there'd be so much space.'

'Yes, I've been very lucky to have it all my life. It belongs to the Hall – one of the perks of living there. Spent most summers down here.' Bella sat on top of the storage box, kicked off her flip-flops and, obviously at home, pulled up her long legs beneath her. Now relaxed and smiling, Steph could see that Bella had inherited her mother's beauty, despite her dark hair with its red strands, she had the same enormous blue-grey eyes and cupid bow lips.

They all waited while Bella fiddled with her bag, then made eye contact with Caroline, who turned to Steph. 'Thanks for coming, Steph. Bella wanted us to talk to you away from college, as she needs some help. She wants this to be in confidence.'

Steph jumped in at once, holding her hand up to interrupt Caroline, while looking across at Bella. 'Before you start, depending on what you say, I can't promise confidentiality, but I can promise that we'll decide together who we talk to. Is that, OK?' As she said it, she knew it sounded trite, but it was well rehearsed and well used, as she'd found it stopped any difficulties later.

Bella nodded in agreement, took a deep breath as if she was going to launch into a speech, but then leaned forward and let her hair fall forward to hide her face. At last, when she lifted her head, she swept away two tears that had dribbled down her cheeks and darted a glance at Caroline, who gave her an encouraging smile. It appeared they'd rehearsed what they were going to tell her.

But it must all have been too much for her, as Bella grabbed her backpack and, delving into it, seized a tissue, wiped her eyes and started sobbing. Caroline frowned at Steph, who raised her hand, signalling that they should wait for Bella to calm down. This was going to be really serious.

Sitting side by side on their beach chairs, Steph and Caroline stared out to the sea, now splashing over the top of the concrete prom, the pattering and slaps of the escaped tips of the waves leaving damp patches and puddles on the concrete. A tiny rivulet formed along one of the tar joints and worked its way back to disappear over the edge and return to the sea.

Fascinated, Steph began predicting which of the oncoming waves would tip over onto the prom and which would stop short. Confident she had it sussed and was now becoming an expert wave watcher, she became aware of Bella moving to her right and the girl's blotched face emerging from behind her hair. She appealed to Caroline between her sobs. 'You tell her... please.'

'Right, if that's what you want?' Bella nodded, clearly trying to control her breathing. 'Interrupt if I get it wrong or miss anything, won't you?'

Bella gave Caroline a weak smile, blew her nose and dabbed at her eyes.

'Bella now realises she's been sexually abused since she was a child.'

This horrific announcement made Steph shudder inside, but aware of Bella scrutinising her, she ensured that her expression didn't change while she continued to pay attention to Caroline.

'It started when she was young. Like all of us, they played those games – mummies and daddies, doctors and nurses, you know the sort of thing.'

Steph nodded, suspecting what was coming.

'They spent all their time together, built camps, dens – the usual stuff kids do. Apparently, he was abusing Bella then, and it's carried on until now and she's only recently understood what he did to her.'

With a raised eyebrow and a smile, Caroline checked with Bella that she was telling her story correctly. Bella caught her breath. Her sobs were subsiding and she nodded at Caroline.

'Apparently, he convinced Bella it was her idea and if she said anything, he'd tell her parents, so it appears it has continued.'

Clearly Caroline had finished Bella's story and she turned to Steph, who knew she must now tread really carefully.

'Listen, Bella. What's happened to you wasn't your fault, whatever he's told you. You mustn't blame yourself. You've done the right thing, confronting it, and we can get help from someone who understands and will help you cope with it.'

'But nothing happens when I say something, does it?' Bella sat up straight, challenging Steph and suddenly furious.

'What do you mean?'

'When he... He had a go at me when I was working in the library, late after college. I was so angry, I told my tutor who took me to the Vice Principal—'

'Mr Field?'

'Yes, that's him. I had to sit there telling him all the details.'

'Really?' Caroline leaned forward, clearly taken aback by Bella's latest revelation.

'Didn't your tutor take you to see Mrs Betts?' Steph realised she was opening rather a large can of worms.

'No, who's she?'

'The DSL, she's called – the Designated Safeguarding Lead. Her photo's in Reception and the canteen – she's the teacher in the college who's trained to help with what you're describing. Who's your tutor?'

'Miss Greenhalgh.'

Holding back a sigh, as she didn't want to appear unprofessional, Steph realised poor Bella had confided in two of the college dinosaurs. Poor girl.

'And what happened when you told Mr Field?'

'I felt so filthy and so ashamed going through it all.' Bella stopped, dabbed at her eyes. Her voice reflected her resentment. 'All he said was that sometimes these things happen as we're growing up and we have to put it down to experience – or something like that – and he advised me to take it no further and not to make a fuss. He did nothing about it, even though it happened at college.'

Steph felt Caroline about to explode, so got in quickly. 'Obviously we don't know why Mr Field said that, but I can assure you, Bella, you're not making a fuss. What you've told us is really serious and we want to help you.'

Bella's anger appeared to have made her stronger. 'I want it to stop. Now that Graham and I are... you know... involved...'

'Graham?'

'Graham Andrews – he left last year. You know, he got that award for getting the highest mark in the country for his history A Level.'

Of course, that Graham! Bella had mentioned a Graham when Steph and Hale had met her last Saturday. A picture of a good looking, mature student flashed into Steph's mind. She had enjoyed many lively conversations with him and was pleased that Bella had such a reliable and sensitive boyfriend.

'Oh yes, I remember him. Tall, good looking – and wasn't he the star of the debating team?'

'Yes, that's Graham.' Bella smiled and appeared to be pleased that Graham was so easily recognisable. 'It may sound silly, but since we've been together, I've realised what has been happening to me.'

Steph knew only too well that when girls who have been abused enter loving sexual relationships, they often become suddenly aware of what they have suffered and repressed.

'And the abuse is still going on?'

'Yes, actually it is...' She darted a glance at Caroline, who once again gave her an encouraging smile. 'He keeps saying it was me who started it – it's my fault, and if I tell anyone, he'll tell all my friends what a... what a slag... what a slut I am. He also said he'd tell my parents. I felt so ashamed when I realised what had been happening... The last thing I wanted was for them to know about it. I had to keep it quiet... to keep it a secret from them.'

Bella raised her head and tried to smile at Steph. To admit all this was costing her a great deal.

Steph returned her smile. 'Now you've told us, we can get help from someone who understands what you've been through, a specialist police officer – a woman. I know her – she's good and has helped others who've had experiences like yours. We need to decide if you're willing to be interviewed.'

Bella's head jerked up and panic flashed across her face. 'Oh no! I don't want to involve the police – that's why I came to you. Caroline said you and your friend could sort it out quietly. That's why I'm telling you.'

Steph's stomach tightened. Well done, Caroline – Hale was going to love being dumped in this! The world had moved on and Steph knew only too well that even if Bella didn't want to make a formal complaint of sexual assault, the police would have to record and investigate it. 'Bella, what exactly do you want to happen?'

'I want it to stop, and I want him to know what he did to me was wrong and he shouldn't have been doing it.'

Before Steph could respond, Bella continued. 'I want you and your friend to talk to him and tell him you know about it and if it doesn't stop, I *will* go to the police – the real police.' Suddenly, Bella's voice was strong and confident.

'And who is this?'

'It's Jack, Jack Percy.'

CHAPTER SIXTEEN

'So, you'll find time to talk to Jack?' Steph, standing in front of the mirror, had another go at tying a pale green silk scarf around her neck artfully. She stood back to admire her work. She frowned. The colour went well with her blonde hair, but the woman in the mirror looked as if she was suffering from a toothache or a sore throat. How could Caroline and Esme wear them with such apparent and casual ease? She gave up, pulled the scarf off and threw it over the back of the sofa.

'You don't ask much, do you? Bella accuses him of years of abuse but won't make a formal complaint. Exactly how am I going to do that off the record? And to make it worse, his father's already threatened to call in the big guns.'

'Derek, here boy!' His helicoptering tail showed that Derek knew he was off to see his friends at doggy day care, so he bounced up to her while she fixed his lead. Pulling her coat off the hook by the door, she turned to Hale. 'Have a good day and see what you can do. You usually find a way.' She blew him a kiss and left for work.

Driving through Oakwood to Felicity's, the dog lady, her

thoughts flew to Glebe Hall. How quickly that place had become an enormous problem. She'd hardly known it was there and bam! A fire, apparently set by someone, and now years of child abuse. Talk about appearance and reality!

Arriving at work she was met by Caroline in summer mode – a long floaty grey dress with a contrasting dusty pink scarf draped around her neck. How had she done that? 'You look wonderful! Is everything all right?'

'Fine. Thanks for last night. It's really helped. Bella's much happier, back on track and in college. I bring her in, then Graham will walk her home to mine at the end of the day. He's a lovely boy. She's chosen well, unlike the other...'

She lowered her voice, aware of groups of students chatting and laughing their way past her on their way to lessons. 'Just thought I'd see what Hale has done.'

Irritated, Steph stared at her friend. 'What time was it when I left you last night?'

'About eight o'clock, why—'

'And what did you expect Hale to do overnight? He has to sleep sometimes, you know.'

'I'm only asking.'

For a few moments, Caroline appeared to be chastened, but it didn't take her long to bounce back. 'And have you decided what you'll do about Paul Field? What he did was monstrous and so unprofessional.'

'Me? You were there too!'

'Ah! But you have Peter's ear. We all know if we want something, you're the power behind the throne!'

'Come off it, that's not true.' Steph sighed, embarrassed in front of Caroline's wide grin. She got on well with Peter most of the time and knew she was a good confidant as she didn't frequent the staff room, where most of the politicking and gossiping took place. 'All right, I'll have a word. Paul Field already loathes me and thinks I'm always getting above myself.'

'Rubbish, everyone knows he's a prize twit and thinks you're good news. Right, I'll be off – students to see.'

As Caroline floated off, Steph's phone rang, and she saw Hale's name appear on the screen. 'Hi ... really? ... That's inspired ... I knew you'd think of something. I'll tell Peter ... Of course, he has to know. See you later.'

Tidying the newspapers on the coffee table by the black leather sofas, opening the visitors' book ready for the day and turning on the photocopier behind the screen, she nearly missed Peter as he strode in, chatting to a group of students in bright summer outfits. She followed him into his office.

'Gosh – you made me jump! Good morning.'

'Do you have a moment?'

'What's happened now?' He perched on the edge of his desk, waiting for her to talk. She told him about the conversation in the beach hut with Bella.

His face registered shock at her news, but before he could say anything, she added. 'I've just had a phone call from Hale, who's contacted Mr Percy and asked his permission to talk to Jack here, as part of his investigation into the fire.'

'Oh?'

'While he's at it, he can touch on Jack's relationship with Bella and see if he picks anything up. He'd need a more formal interview later if he finds something, but it may be a start, as Bella doesn't want to make a formal complaint at this stage.'

'Good, I'd have called in the police myself to investigate Bella's accusations.'

'Mr Percy agreed that Hale can see Jack in college, as he's already left home and doesn't want to be present at the interview. Hale also said Mr Percy's agreed for another adult to be present, even though Jack's over eighteen, so if you don't mind...'

'If you being there gets this sorted sooner, then go for it. That's fine. Sounds as if organising a session on consent was exactly the right move. I'll see you and Hale after the interview.' Peter went around his desk and turned on his computer.

'Of course.' She moved a step closer to his desk, a little reluctant to reveal the rest of the story and dreading the inevitable fall-out. 'But there's something else you ought to know.'

Peter looked up.

'Bella said she reported Jack's abuse to her tutor after an incident in our library.'

'Oh? I haven't been told about that.'

Steph took a deep breath. 'Apparently, Bella's tutor took her to see Paul Field, and he told her not to make a fuss and to take it no further.'

Peter leaped up from his chair, came around from behind his desk, and gripping the back of the nearest armchair, scrutinised her face. 'Paul said what? I can't believe it! He wouldn't have said that!'

'Bella sounded convincing, and he wasn't too keen on introducing the consent session, was he?'

Peter's frown deepened as he was evidently thinking through the implications of Steph's news.

'You say Bella told her tutor? Who's that?'

'Anne Greenhalgh.'

Peter rolled his eyes – apparently, he too shared her view of these old-school members of staff.

'Oh no! It would be! Anne knows she should take any such disclosures to Mrs Betts, the DSL. It's made clear in the staff handbook and in the safeguarding training each September. Whatever was she thinking?'

Steph decided it wasn't her place to comment.

Peter rubbed his forehead as if he was getting a headache, his frown deepening. 'Does Mrs Betts know about this yet?'

'No. I heard about it last night and I'm telling you first.'

Peter sighed. 'Indeed. I'd better have a word with Paul – and I want you to be here when I do.'

Steph nodded, her stomach knotting.

Peter moved back behind his desk. 'And remember, whatever Jack has done, and at this stage it's a suspicion as you have no firm evidence, you have a duty to both students to make sure you do nothing to disrupt their A Levels. They'll live with their grades for the rest of their lives and—'

The buzzing of Steph's phone stopped him for a moment. 'Take it.' Peter flapped his hand at her, and she moved towards the door, phone at her ear.

'I'm with him now ... Oh? I see ... Oh ... I'll let him know.'

Ending the call, Steph stood in front of Peter's desk. 'That was Hale. He won't be coming in but has got to go to Glebe Hall as he's received evidence that Madeline Henderson was probably murdered.'

CHAPTER SEVENTEEN

'That Chief Inspector has just left me and I'm not sure what to do – what it all means.'

Jon hovered in the doorway, shaking. Each time she saw him, Esme was shocked at his deterioration since the fire, but he'd been through so much. At least he'd changed his clothes but he hadn't shaved and the dark circles around his eyes were getting deeper. Now what had happened?

Hector frowned, paused, inspected Jon, then continued eating, clearly annoyed at having his breakfast invaded once more by what promised to be a drama.

'We wondered why you'd been delayed.' Esme smiled and gestured to Jon's place, already set at the table, and moved to the large hotplate on the sideboard, which Liz had installed as there were now four of them for most meals. 'The usual?'

He nodded. Esme lifted the silver covers and served out Jon's scrambled eggs and bacon. After she placed the loaded plate in front of him, she poured his coffee and moved the milk jug, toast rack, and butter dish within his reach.

'Thank you so much – you're so kind—'

'Well? Come on then, tell us what that policeman had to say for himself.' Emotional displays were not for Hector, but he could have waited for the poor man to have his breakfast.

Jon, who had manoeuvred a forkful of eggs into his mouth, swallowed it down quickly so he could reply and choked on it, coughing and spluttering over his plate. Hector tutted loudly. Reacting quickly, Esme rushed around the table with her water glass, which she held to Jon's mouth so he could gulp some water. It worked. He stopped coughing and smiled up at Esme. 'Thank you. I don't know what I'd do without you—'

'What did that Hale fellow want? We're all waiting.'

'He said he'd received evidence in the pathologist's report that Madeline's death was suspicious.'

After a moment to allow his words to be translated into meaning, there was silence. Hector stopped eating and frowned. 'What does he mean? Suspicious? We all know what happened. She got drunk, drove her car into a tree, and it burst into flames. A tragedy, but hardly suspicious.'

They both observed Hector and said nothing, aware that he hadn't finished opining. 'Anyway, whatever could a pathologist make of her remains after that inferno? There wouldn't be anything left of her.'

'Hector!' Esme glared at him. Knowing him so well, she could tell he was revving up for an argument. Hector ignored her and threw his knife and fork onto his plate with a clatter that made them all jump.

'I asked him that too – well, not quite like that. He said that the temperature in a car fire is not the same as in a furnace or a – or a – you know – a cremation, so there's more... they can find out more.'

His face drained and deathly pale, Jon looked as if he was going to throw up or faint. Hector could be so heartless at times. Esme rushed around the table and poured more water into the glass, which he dutifully sipped. She dragged a chair beside him so she could catch him if necessary, and Jon leaned against her. She suspected there was worse to come.

'And they have found what, exactly?' Hector ignored Esme's attempt to shut him down with her eye signal.

Jon drooped further. 'It appears her skull was fractured before her body was burnt. Here, on her temple.' He lifted his hand and patted the right side of his head above his eye. 'He said at least we know she didn't die in that inferno.'

Hector's head shot forward, staring at Jon. 'And how on earth can they know that?'

Once again, Esme felt Jon wobble slightly and signalled Hector to stop. He ignored her. 'And the fire itself would have upset her bone structure, so they can't be sure if the fracture occurred before or during the fire.'

Jon sighed. 'The pathologist said the fracture, not the fire, caused her death.' He'd stopped eating and placed his knife and fork on his plate. 'He said the question that now needs to be answered is, how did she drive a car with a fracture large enough to kill her?'

'If the pathologist's right, then she couldn't have driven the car, could she?' Esme realised she had said out loud what she'd been thinking when Hector banged his hand on the table. She jumped.

'So, you're a forensic scientist now, are you?' Hector drilled Esme with his stare. Clearly annoyed, Hector attempted to regain the upper hand; Esme kept her mouth firmly shut. 'This is all pseudo-science. You've only got to watch that rubbish on the box to see how many court cases have failed because these so-called experts are wrong. No, I'm sure we could find a pathologist who would be of the opinion that it could occur in the fire.'

Jon appeared to be confused by Hector's latest pronouncement. 'But where would we—'

'And did he give you a copy of the pathologist's report?'

Jon shook his head. 'I didn't think to ask.'

'It's not up to you to ask. He should have given it to you. Does it exist? Is he making it up?'

Esme couldn't resist it. 'Why would he do that?'

'Isn't it obvious? This is probably the most dramatic case he's had for years. Most of the time, it's speeding motorists. After promotion probably – and he's trying to make something out of nothing here to do it!'

Hector straightened his knife and fork, so they were aligned perfectly on his plate. Esme recognised the signs – he was about to lose it.

'We welcomed that man into our home, cooperated with him, answered his questions, but after this farce, I've had enough!' He picked up *The Telegraph* and slapped it on the table. Esme winced. 'We are a house in mourning, and I will not have him upsetting you in this insensitive way.'

Jon appeared to freeze under Hector's angry stare and clearly didn't know what to say.

'As soon as I've had another coffee,' Hector held his cup up so Esme could collect the coffee pot and re-fill it, 'I'll be on the phone to the Chief Constable and inform him Hale is no longer welcome in this house.'

Esme, who was no longer hungry, picked up her uneaten breakfast, walked over to the sideboard, picked up the coffeepot and re-filled Hector's cup. 'Jon?'

'Please.'

Apparently, Hector was on a roll. 'And I'll make a few calls to the Home Office. I was at school with one of the top chaps there, who'll soon put me in touch with someone who can talk sense. They're mishandling this dreadfully.'

'If he has this evidence from the pathologist, he has a responsibility to investigate it, doesn't he?' Esme poured a top-up into Jon's cup.

'Hmm! Complete and utter rubbish! Hole in her head? It's bad enough coping with what actually happened, without adding more unnecessary drama.'

As she resumed her seat opposite Jon, Esme could see how shocked he was by the news. 'Jon, is there anything we can do?'

'No. You've both been marvellous, thank you. It's just... coping with... Madeline going is bad enough, but to have lost Bella too. Everything feels hopeless.'

'And that's another thing. Why isn't he making that girl come home instead of chasing ridiculous mysteries, like some Sherlock Holmes character? He should keep that girl safe, instead of letting her stay with those lesbians. God knows what they're doing to her.'

'Hector, that's enough. You know that's nonsense. Bella's shocked like the rest of us, and she needs some space. I'm pleased she's with Caroline, who'll look after her.'

Hector threw her a thunderous look, which she ignored. 'Now Jon, do you feel strong enough to visit the undertaker this morning and start making arrangements?'

'Perhaps another day? I can't face it, not yet.'

'Leave the poor man alone, woman.'

'Well, at least let me come home with you to help with some of the admin.'

Jon dragged himself to his feet and sighed. 'Thank you, Esme, that would be helpful.'

CHAPTER EIGHTEEN

PAUL FIELD FLUFFED up the little silk handkerchief that dripped out of his top pocket and checked that his matching claret tie was perfectly aligned, before he made his usual cursory knock on Peter's door and walked in.

Steph felt sick and crossed her fingers, hoping that maybe Peter would get on with it and not involve her. No chance. Her phone rang with his summons, and as she grabbed her notebook and pen, her heart rate went through the roof.

A fuming Paul Field, seated opposite Peter, scowled as he obviously realised she was joining them – and presumably he didn't know about Bella's account yet!

'Please, take a seat.' Peter nodded at the chair between them. Looking to the left, she gave Peter her full attention, trying to cut Paul Field out of her sight line, but it wasn't to be for long.

'Mrs Grant, will you please tell Paul what you told me this morning about Bella Henderson?'

No choice. She had to turn to face Paul, who gave her a look reserved for the muck he'd picked up on the bottom of his shoe. Taking a deep breath, she summarised the account Bella had given of the abuse she'd suffered over many years. Paul Field tried several times to interrupt, his mouth opening fish-like, only to be silenced at each attempt by Peter's warning look and once, his raised hand.

Reaching the end of her report, Steph was aware her voice had risen half an octave. She cleared her throat, lowering the tone of her voice. 'Then Bella said she told her tutor, who brought her to the Vice Principal who, she said, told her not to make a fuss.'

Paul Field shot her a poison look. 'And you believed her, no doubt.' He shook his head and tutted. 'You may have had years in the police, Mrs Grant, but I've had a lifetime's experience with children of this age, and I know they have a tendency to overdramatise events. And, of course, all of it goes on their phones to be sent to goodness knows where.'

Having delivered what she knew, she decided it wasn't her place to interrupt his patronising sermon, and it appeared Peter wasn't going to either. Was he giving him enough rope to hang himself, or did he think Paul Field could be right? Surely not?

She tuned back into Paul Field's whiney voice. 'It's this celebrity culture – they absorb it all, you know, and so much of what they think is happening is actually in their imagination. A minor incident gets blown up out of all proportion and we run around in circles, investigating it like demented detectives, only to find it wasn't worth bothering with in the first place.'

He snatched a breath and waggled his finger at Peter. 'And what's more, I can't believe any such thing would happen in the Percy family, one of the oldest families in the county, you know.'

Peter remained silent and, despite the threatened volcanic eruption she was experiencing inside her at Paul Field's appalling argument, she felt it wasn't her place to protest. Screams of delight and laughter invaded the room from the car park, as apparently some students were celebrating something, or perhaps simply being students.

Paul Field peered out of the window, raised his eyebrows at the interruption, and tutted. 'I mean – really! This *Me Too* and *Welcome Everybody Moan About Your School* site, or whatever it's called, is asking for young people to exaggerate and simply make things up to give them five minutes of fame.'

Out of the corner of her eye she could see Peter listening intently, head on one side, while Paul Field declaimed from his soapbox. He appeared to be getting into his stride. 'No, I wasn't convinced what that girl was telling me had a scintilla of truth in it. It felt like something she'd read about on that social medium place and was repeating. And a Percy? Unthinkable!'

A slight pause for breath. Peter said nothing. Clearly, Paul Field took this as a sign of approval and droned on.

'And what would have happened if I hadn't nipped it in the bud? Eh? It could have damaged the reputation of my – er – our college and the Percys. The Percys would have been outraged and quite right, too. They have great hopes for Jack and the story this girl was propagating would have ruined his life and goodness knows where it would have gone next. I mean, she might even have involved the police!'

He paused, glancing at them both, clearly expecting them to share his horror at calling in the police. 'If they'd become involved, there's no telling where it would have ended up. No, I'm convinced I was right in squashing it at an early stage.'

He slapped his right hand on his thigh. Steph bit her lip to keep her face straight – she had seen the same movement by a principal boy in a pantomime. Still, Peter stayed silent.

'I mean, Mrs Grant, surely you experienced of this sort of thing when you were a young gal?'

'Yes, I did. But that doesn't mean it was right, or that I encouraged or enjoyed it. When I was younger, we simply put up with it – scared of being told we were frigid if we didn't. Now this generation is calling it out and not putting up with behaviour they feel is intrusive, offensive and wrong, and I applaud them for it.'

'Hmmph!' Paul Field responded with a venomous look, then brushed a piece of fluff off his right trouser leg.

At last, Peter spoke, his voice so quiet Paul Field had to lean forward to catch it above the students chatting outside. 'It has been interesting listening to your point of view, Paul, but I must disagree with you. The world has moved on and I agree with Mrs Grant – it is right that this sort of behaviour is no longer tolerated.'

A quick glance at Paul Field's face showed he was clearly taken aback by Peter's reaction to his speech. 'From what I've heard, you were in the wrong not to investigate further or to take her accusations seriously. I gather Bella came to you, trusting you and confiding in you as a sympathetic adult.'

The puzzled frown on Paul Field's face morphed into outrage; presumably he was amazed that Peter could disagree with him. He listened, his lips tight and thin.

'It must have taken a great deal of strength for Bella to disclose what had happened to her, and you failed to take her seriously and accused her of making a fuss. That was wrong.'

Peter paused after emphasising his last words. 'You know our procedures and should have referred it immediately to the DSL, Mrs Betts. You didn't think of going to her?'

Paul Field didn't reply but sat looking inconvenienced and annoyed. Peter continued, 'At the very least you could have discussed it with me, and we'd have found a way forward together involving the DSL. Instead of which you made a judgement call you had no right to make, and it was the wrong one.'

Paul Field's fury was now evident. He opened his mouth, about to protest, only to have Peter raise his hand. 'From now on, Paul, I insist you bring any such complaint to me. This is an extremely serious issue, which should have been handled sensitively and formally, using our safeguarding procedures.'

Steph became fascinated by the pattern on the red Persian rug as she heard Peter draw another deep breath. 'And it's irrelevant if the family involved is privileged or poor – we have a duty to each one of our students. I dread to think what would have happened if Bella had reported your response to Social Services. You may well have lost your job and the resultant bad publicity would have ruined the reputation of the college.'

Peter stopped, clearly wanting Paul Field to let this last point sink in. A quick glance at his puce face, lemon-sucking lips and deep frown confirmed that Peter had hit home. Resuming her examination of a bald patch in the rug, Steph didn't dare to look at either man and felt more and more uncomfortable at witnessing this dressing down.

'I will see Bella and apologise for your mishandling of her complaint and assure her we will do everything to support her in coping with the trauma she's experienced. If it is her wish, I shall also investigate her allegations or hand the matter to the police.'

Shock at this last comment was clear on Paul Field's face; he had obviously not thought it sufficiently serious to count as a crime. He kept his mouth shut.

'At least both students are at the end of their A Level course and will be leaving, but you should have dealt with this as soon as it arose, not brushed it under the carpet hoping it would disappear and certainly not kow-towing to one family because of their status in the local community. Understood?'

'Yes.' A grudging agreement and a bowed head.

'This incident will be recorded as a verbal warning on your file. You understand, Paul?'

Paul Field, horrified, nodded. 'I understand.'

'Thank you, that is all.'

Clearly, Paul Field couldn't wait to escape from Peter's calm disapproval and bustled out of the room, slamming the door behind him. For several moments, they both observed the closed door. Paul Field's overpowering cologne lingered.

Peter stood. 'Thank you for bringing this issue to my attention. If there is any – shall we say – further unpleasantness to you or Bella from that quarter, you are to tell me at once – understand? *At once!'*

'Yes, Peter.'

'Thank you. That's all.'

CHAPTER NINETEEN

IT HAD BEEN a long day at college and Steph's feet were killing her. As Peter had already left, she peeled off her shoes and sighed with relief as her little toes unfolded. She padded over to the coffee table to tidy the newspapers, collect some random cups abandoned there and an empty crisp packet – how did that get there?

'Hi, Steph.'

She jumped as the voice crashed into her fantasy of an early night with Hale. 'Good heavens, Bella. Didn't hear you come in. How are you?'

'Fine, thanks. I'm getting so much work done now I'm with Caroline. She doesn't help me, she's not allowed to, but just being there away from – you know – it's made such a difference.'

'I'm pleased to hear that.'

Bella sat down. Staying with Caroline was obviously doing her good. The colour had returned to her cheeks. She looked as if she was eating again and appeared happier in her own skin.

'I've just left Caroline up in the studio. She said she'll be down in a few minutes to take me home with her.'

'I thought Graham took you to Caroline's?'

'He does when he's not at Glebe Hall.'

'Glebe Hall?'

'His dad's head gardener there and Graham works with him on Saturdays, holidays and some evenings. His dad needed help tonight – cutting the lawns for a wedding tomorrow.'

Did everyone around here have links with Glebe Hall? Once it was the mysterious house behind the crinkley-crankley wall, now it popped up everywhere she turned.

'Right, well, I'll just wash these cups. If you've gone before I get back, have a good evening.'

Returning to her Hale fantasy, Steph went around the screen that divided Reception from the admin team to collect more dirty mugs. In common with most office workers, they were all so protective of their personal mugs, but apparently couldn't find the time to go to the kitchen to wash them up!

A loud scream made her dump the tray and rush out. Bella was being attacked – a boy was trying to strangle her! Steph leaped across the floor, grabbed the back of his hoodie, and hauled the boy off Bella. Her throat freed, Bella gasped for breath, coughed, then fell back. Steph struggled to hold the lad, who was strong and pulling away, but before he could get the zip of his hoodie undone and escape, she seized his arm and pulled it up behind his back, hard.

He yelled, 'Ouch! Fuck off!'

She pulled it up higher. He screamed in pain and tried to kick her out of the way. She jerked it higher still and leaned on his back. 'Move again and I'll break it.'

The boy gasped in pain, then she felt him give in a little, so she pulled him upright. 'Now we're both going into that office and when we're inside, I'll let go. Understand?' The boy grunted but didn't resist her not too gentle shove towards Peter's office. 'Are you OK, Bella?'

'Yeah, fine now, thanks.' Her voice was hoarse.

'Stay there. I'll be back.'

Pushing the open door with her foot, she propelled the boy towards the chair opposite the window. 'Now, sit. Don't you dare move!' Now she could see who it was – Jack Percy.

He shot her a vicious look but remained seated.

Not wanting to stay alone with Jack in the room, but not wanting to lose the moment, she stepped just outside the office door, desperately hoping for someone to pass. She could always phone Peter to return. A swishing made her turn her head to the left. Caroline was floating down the stairs, humming to herself.

Taking a small step further from the office, Steph beckoned her over. 'Miss Jones, will you join me in the Principal's office for a few moments, please?'

Caroline's confusion at this formal tone disappeared when she glanced over Steph's shoulder and saw an aggressive-looking Jack; quickly appraising the situation, she assumed a serious expression and sat on the chair opposite the fireplace.

Steph sat with her back to the window, forcing Jack to face the bright late afternoon sun behind her. Her glare made him lower his eyes. She was aware of Caroline sitting to her right and knew she had to put up a good performance.

'Now, Jack, what made you attack Bella?'

Caroline gasped beside her. Steph's warning look silenced her.

Jack, red faced and furious, stared across at her. 'I didn't attack her.'

'Shall we see?'

Thrilled by the look of alarm that flashed over Jack's face, she went to Peter's computer, typed in a password and loaded the security film for the last fifteen minutes, whizzing on until she found the part where Jack attempted to strangle Bella. She paused it and turned the screen around so he could see it. The image of him lying across Bella with his hands around her throat was dramatic, and he had the grace to look shocked for a moment.

'Well?' She sat, leaving the frozen image behind her head, and met his eyes. He tried to stare her out. She won the match.

He frowned. 'She asked for it.'

'So, it was her fault you assaulted her?'

For the second time that day, she felt she was little more than something the cat had brought in.

'She's behaving like a prize bitch!'

Once again, Caroline gasped beside her. Steph darted a glance, which was enough to prevent her from interrupting. Seething with anger, Jack appeared not to have noticed.

'There's no need for that.'

He took a deep breath. 'You've no idea how much my parents have done for her and her family. Now she betrays them when they need her support most.' His voice rose to a shout at the end.

'That's enough. Let's calm down and talk this through reasonably. What do you mean?'

It appeared as if Jack was preparing for a major speech, but then, deflated, he slumped in his chair, and said in a quiet voice. 'She knows what she's done and how she's made things worse. Let her tell you.' His eyes moved from Steph's face to the floor; he was apparently calmer now, but his jaw remained rigid. She could see little pulsing movements below his ears.

'She will, but now I'm asking you.'

His lips closed in a thin, stubborn line. After a few moments, he appeared to change his mind and took a deep breath. 'I texted her to ask what she thought she was doing, upsetting everyone like this, and she replied she wanted to stay out of danger.'

'Out of danger? What do you think she meant?'

'Ask her. She's gone looney since her mother died in that car.'

'You don't sound very sympathetic.'

'She died in a drink-drive accident. That's stupid of her, but not a danger to Bella. All she ever thinks about is herself.' Jack's voice got louder the longer he spoke, and he lifted himself off his chair slightly. Steph shot him a warning look, and he sat back down.

She felt Caroline desperate to join in, so got in quickly. 'Can you imagine what Bella is going through or what it's like to lose someone you love and in such an appalling way?' Steph challenged him, and she saw Hector glaring back at her. 'She deserves your sympathy and understanding, not to be attacked or assaulted like that.'

'That wasn't an attack or an assault!'

'Well, what would you call it then?' His insolent glare was solid, but he didn't reply. 'I saw you on top of Bella with your hands around her throat. Look at yourself. In my book, that counts as an assault.'

She gestured towards the monitor, paused and again won the staring match. He lowered his eyes. 'In my old job in the police, what I just saw would be defined as Common Assault and Bella could report you for it.'

His quizzical gaze fixed on her. At least he was listening. 'It's a crime, Jack, and you'd get a criminal record.'

The stare continued; he wasn't going to back down this

time. 'I wonder what your mother will say when she has to go to court with you.'

At last, a flicker of concern. 'It wouldn't come to that.'

'Really? You're sure of that, are you? I suggest if you want to avoid it, you explain exactly what's going on.'

He folded his arms, a sullen expression on his face, and compressed his lips. It appeared he wasn't about to admit to anything as, no doubt, he assumed his father would pull some strings and get him off. He sat, stubborn and resentful. She tried another tack.

'OK, if you don't like the words attack or assault, let's try the word abuse.'

At last, he reacted. 'It wasn't abuse! You don't understand...'

'What don't I understand?'

'Our relationship – we're like... er... brother and sister.'

'And is that how brothers and sisters behave?'

'We've lived together all our lives. I got carried away, that's all.'

She waited, head on one side, listening intently. Caroline appeared to be hypnotised by his words and remained statue still.

'It's because... because I care for her.'

'So do you usually strangle people you care for then?'

A puzzled look crossed his face. 'I wouldn't actually *do* anything. It was nothing.'

'It didn't look like nothing from where I was standing.'

No way was this boy going to show remorse or even admit he'd done anything wrong.

'I gather that you've been, how should I describe it, physical with Bella before—'

'Is that what she told you? It's not true! She's lying!' His eyes pierced her, and she knew his temper was close to exploding again.

She held up her hands, trying to damp down his anger. 'OK, OK, Jack.'

'But she's making it up. It's not true!'

'OK. Now, just for a moment, let's imagine Bella *isn't* lying and what she's saying is that she's uncomfortable with the way you behave towards her. You must respect that and stop any physical contact with her. Understand?' Subdued and sullen, he stared at her, but appeared to be taking in what she was saying.

She spoke slowly, lowering her voice so it was just above a whisper, forcing Jack to lean forward to hear what she was saying. 'Listen carefully. I shall insist Bella tells me if anything more – shall we say physical – happens between you and if it doesn't stop, then I shall report it to the police, and you will go to court.' Good, he was listening. She paused. 'You do not touch her ever again. Do you hear me?'

He'd admitted nothing. He wouldn't, would he? But his outraged protests appeared to have stopped and, once again, he lowered his head. She was convinced he had heard her.

'Look at me, Jack.' Taking his time to raise his head, he looked straight at her. 'I mean it. And in college, you are to keep away from Bella. You don't take the same subjects and I'll be keeping an eye on you at break and lunchtime. Do you understand?'

'Yes.' She accepted that mumble was the most she'd get from him, and an apology? No way.

'Right, I suggest we leave together.'

He stood defiant, and while he took ages to zip up his top and make sure his hood was perfectly aligned, she gestured to Caroline that she should stay where she was.

Having made her wait for him, he gave her a withering look and walked out to Reception. What was it about him that made her feel like a servant? He crossed to the door quickly, with his head erect, and appeared not to make eye contact with Bella.

Steph matched him, step for step. Awkwardly, they stood side by side, waiting for the doors to open. At last, they released him and he strode off into the car park towards his car, one of the few left at this time of day.

While her back was turned, Caroline had left Peter's office and stood in the middle of Reception.

'So, what exactly happened with Mr Percy?'

Steph collapsed on the sofa opposite Bella. 'Do you want to tell her?'

Bella moved up so Caroline could join her. 'Jack attacked me – tried to strangle me – said I was betraying everyone, should go home and not be so selfish. You should have heard what he called me!'

'Look at your throat – it's bright red!' Caroline bent down to examine Bella's neck. 'Couldn't you have stopped him earlier, Steph?'

Before Steph could respond with the righteous indignation she felt, Bella jumped in. 'You should have seen her, Caroline. She was magnificent! When he left, he looked as if you'd sorted him out.'

'Yes, she did that all right.' Caroline turned to Steph and grinned. 'Never seen that side of you before. Wouldn't like to be on the receiving end!'

Steph felt the blood rush into her cheeks. Caroline's praise meant such a lot. 'I hope that's stopped it, Bella. He knows that if he comes near you again, I'll report what I witnessed to the police, and he'll go to court for common assault.'

'You certainly told him. But,' Caroline paused, 'he is a

Percy, and the usual rules don't apply to them, as they're the entitled ones.'

'I can promise you, entitled or not, if he comes anywhere near you or threatens you again, Bella, I *will* report him. I'm convinced it will be safe for you to go home now.'

Bella stood and moved closer to Caroline. 'Would it be all right if I stayed just a bit longer, please – just to make sure?'

'You can stay as long as you like, darling. Gosh, look at the time – we should be going. Thank you so much, Steph, for all you've done.'

'Yes, thank you, Steph.' Bella echoed and rushed out after Caroline.

Watching them as they chatted their way to Caroline's car, Steph was convinced Bella still hadn't told them everything about what was going on at Glebe Hall. That place appeared to be full of secrets.

CHAPTER TWENTY

Esme was surprised to see Jack in the kitchen. He usually went straight to his room after college to 'work' (translated as playing on his computer) and he didn't appear until supper. He picked up her phone from the dresser by the door and brought it round to her.

'Thanks. Can't remember leaving it there – oh well.'

'Tea, Mother?'

'Lovely. Thanks.' Slightly surprised at this rare event, she watched him go off to make a pot of tea after placing two coasters on the table, where she was doing the household accounts. Luke did the professional accounts and financial planning for all the Glebe Hall activities, but Hector expected her to produce accounts each month for their day-to-day domestic expenditure.

Her habit was to work in the heavy black ledger going back decades, on the large pine table dominating the kitchen, looking out at the oldest oak tree on the estate. In some strange way, she felt she was contributing to their present and ensuring their future bent over the books, balancing the detailed income and expenditure of their lives. At times, it was pretty hairy when the two columns just about balanced, but that was becoming less frequent with the rising cost of living and the vast running costs. Soon, very soon, they would need new projects to keep the Hall going.

Jack cleared his throat. She had forgotten he was there, as he was such a silent and unexpected presence standing over the kettle, waiting for it to boil. Why did she feel that meant trouble?

'You may get a call from college, Mother.'

Ah! Here it was. 'Really, Jack? About what?'

'Nothing much, honestly.'

He dismissed her stare with a wave of his hand. 'Fuss about nothing.'

'Really? They wouldn't call for nothing, would they? And you obviously think it's sufficiently serious to want to talk about it.'

'You know how cross Father and Jon are about Bella running away to Caroline when she should be here helping her father cope with Madeline's death?'

'Go on.'

'They're right. I think she's being really selfish, not contributing to the Hall and all that you're doing to keep it for us.'

He was a mini-Hector all right. He unhooked two mugs from under the dresser shelf, poured some milk into a jug, not noticing the puddle he made on the table, eyes fixed on her face, searching for approval, as usual.

'What have you done?' He poured the tea and she reached for the mug he'd put beside her on the table. 'Thanks.'

He sat opposite, took a gulp of his tea, clearly thinking how to let her down gently. Esme dreaded what was coming out of his mouth next. Throughout his school career she'd had to go in to talk to heads of year, deputy heads and in one case the head-teacher, usually without Hector's knowledge, to get him out of scrapes. Scrapes? That was a polite word for the messes he'd got in through his temper and she knew he could be violent. Like Hector, he knew what he wanted and would do anything to get it. Unfortunately, unlike Hector, he didn't know how to make sure the bruises didn't show and that no one found out. Jack always got found out.

'This evening as I was leaving college, I saw Bella sitting in Reception, waiting for Caroline, so I joined her and tried to tell her how much she was hurting her father and us.'

He paused, apparently taking an intense interest in the accounts book in front of her.

'And then what happened?'

'At first she listened to me and didn't say anything, and, Mother — I could hardly believe it was Bella – she kicked me! Bella actually kicked me. Can you believe that?'

Her stomach tightened as she knew what was coming. 'You're right, it's difficult to believe that of Bella.'

'After she kicked me once, I thought she would stop, but she didn't and really hurt my leg. So, I got hold of her hands, and held them like this —' He raised both hands, holding up a phantom as if the movement would convince her he'd been gentle. 'And then she started screaming and Steph came out—'

'Steph Grant?'

'Yes. How do you know her?'

'She's been here several times since the fire with that Chief Inspector – she works for the police, you know.'

'But she's at college full time.'

'She also works for them too, apparently. Anyway, then what happened?'

He stared out of the window, clearly trying to put off the dreadful moment. 'She dragged me into the Principal's office—'

'Mr Bryant? What did he say?'

'Oh no, he wasn't there. She took me in his room, told me she knew I abused Bella—'

'What?'

'And then she hit me.'

'Hit you?'

'That Grant woman hit me on my head. I was so shocked, Mother. She told me not to tell anyone, or she'd get me thrown out of college.'

'She hit you? Really hit you?'

Jack looked as if it was the end of the world and he was in need of an immediate cuddle. 'Yes, Mother. She did. She hit me. Right here.' He rubbed the side of his head to show where. 'I don't think that's right or even allowed, is it?'

CHAPTER TWENTY-ONE

DEREK IN TOW, Steph arrived at Oakwood Police Station and waved to her old colleague Joyce, who was working at her computer in the CID room; she felt as if she'd only walked out the day before, not over three years ago. It could do with a re-decorate, as it had back then, as blue tack, banned but used everywhere, had pulled tiny flecks of paint off the walls to reveal the plaster beneath. Desks were piled with files, and many of them had lines of post-it notes decorating the rims of computer monitors. At this time of night, the buzz and noise had disappeared.

Hale had suggested she arrive at seven thirty when most of the troops had left. Not that he had to hide her involvement, he told her, but he didn't want to take her away from her day job and they could go through the interview tapes in peace, avoiding the polite questions about how she was getting on and anecdotes from Mike's time with them.

Sitting waiting for him, she reflected on the case. Hale was frustrated that he didn't have enough to arrest Hector or Jon yet but hoped that these interviews might give him some more leads to follow. Derek gave a low growl as apparently someone had joined Joyce and the chatter from the next-door office exploded into laughter. This building never slept.

The door opened and Hale bounced in; from the look of it, he'd obviously had a good day. After a quick peck on the cheek, he touched her elbow. 'Let's go to my office. I've got the coffee machine fired up and ready.'

'Are we in for a late night? Although after the day I've had, I could do with gallons of it!'

'Oh? What's happened?' He opened his office door for her.

She threw herself in the chair he had set out for her, while he remained standing, a concerned expression on his face. Hale paused while Derek tramped around in circles until he found just the right snooze spot between their chairs. 'OK, Derek?' Derek wagged his tail, ignoring the sarcasm. 'Well?'

'I watched Field being eviscerated by Peter for telling Bella not to make a fuss.'

'Quite right too! I'd have thought you'd have enjoyed it!'

'In theory, yes, but the reality was pretty brutal and now Field hates me.'

'I wouldn't worry about that.'

'And Jack Percy attempted to strangle Bella Henderson. I had to restrain him and then tried to convince him to stop abusing her.'

'Did you succeed?'

'Not sure.'

'Sounds as if you're having an exciting time – more than we did with these interviews.'

'Oh?'

'We're getting nowhere fast.' He came round and kissed the top of her head. 'Are you sure you're happy to go through these now?'

'Absolutely. I feel better already, having thrown up all over you!'

Hale joined her and sat at his desk. 'I want you to see the highlights, not the whole interviews. You know, look at their body language – often says more than their words.'

Two mugs of coffee and his favourite fig biscuits in hand, she settled down on the chair Hale had placed before the monitor and he whizzed through the first interview. He froze it on a picture of Hector. 'I called Hector, then Esme came in with Jon. Talk about singing from the same hymn sheet! Anyway, I'll let you see what I mean.'

He pressed a button and Hector appeared on the screen, sitting opposite Dick Davis, a new face to Steph, who appeared to be the same age as one of her college students, and Bob Johnson, Hale's recently promoted Detective Sergeant. She'd known Bob since he'd first arrived at the station, straight out of training. They'd called him Tigger then, as he was so enthusiastic, up for anything and knowing everything.

She wondered if after five years he'd grown a little worn and weary. His smile lines were deeper, and he had the start of a bald patch on the top of his blonde hair, which had also darkened with age. He now wore a wedding ring on his left hand and spoke and moved with confidence. A good deputy for Hale, who she knew relied on him and trusted him absolutely.

Hector was in his lord of the manor suit – pinky-red trousers, blazer and open-necked white shirt. He assumed a bored expression, as if he was doing them a great favour and must have felt this would be a walk-over as he hadn't brought his solicitor with him. Perhaps he assumed it was a sign of his innocence. His good looks and aristocratic bone structure worked well on TV, as did his erect posture compared to Bob's slight slump.

She tuned in and listened to Bob asking the questions. Presumably, Hale had worked with Bob and Joe to prepare for the interview, and the Hall crowd would benefit from a different approach.

Bob: Thank you for confirming that, Mr Percy. Now, on the day Madeline Henderson died, will you go through your movements please?

Hector: From what time? Breakfast? (He did not try to conceal his impatience with the entire process and adopted a superior, bored expression.)

Bob: The 999 call was made at six thirty-seven pm, so let's start late afternoon when you first became aware there might be problems in the Henderson household.

Hector: As I've said so many times (He paused for a sigh and eye-rolling.) *I received a phone call from Jon Henderson saying he'd had a serious argument with his wife, Madeline. She'd been drinking and had gone off in her car—*

Bob: What time was that?

Hector: I hardly checked my watch, officer. My friend was in distress and needed help. It didn't occur to me to note the time for an occasion such as this. (He looked and sounded cocky.)

Bob: Approximate time would do, Mr Percy.

Hector: I suppose it would be about... yes... about six o'clock. (He gazed into the distance, thoughtfully, frowning). *Yes, I think I could hear a radio on somewhere with what sounded like the news. That do you?*

Bob: Thank you, Mr Percy. Please describe what happened next.

Hector: We both got on our quads—

Bob: Quads?

Hector: Quad bikes. (He looked at Bob Johnson as if he was a total idiot).

Bob: Where were they?

Hector: What do you mean – where were they?

Bob: Simply that. Where were they parked? Where did you go to get them?

Hector: They were outside the front door.

Bob: Is that where they are always kept, outside your front door?

Hector: (He paused slightly and took a sip of water from the plastic beaker in front of him.) *I'm not sure why they were there. Usually in the barn with the rest of the gardening paraphernalia, but that's where they were that day.* (He squirmed in his chair then sat up straight, cleared his throat, raised his hand and slapped the table.) *Of course! That's why! That morning Jon and I had been out on them to review the proposed site of an arbour we are building for wedding photographs beside the rose garden.* (His voice became stronger and his speech faster.) *Wedding parties like to go there for drinks after the ceremony and we thought a rose arbour with seating would make a good feature. One day, when our antediluvian laws change and we can hold wedding ceremonies outside, it will make a super spot. We must have dumped the quads there when we came back for lunch and Andrews hadn't moved them.*

Bob: Andrews?

Hector: Head gardener. Jolly good chap, been at Glebe Hall for as long as I can recall. Can't get them like him nowadays, you know. Loyal chap.

Beside her, Hale ran his fingers through his hair, a sure sign he was getting irritated. Even though he'd seen Hector in this mode before, it still pressed his buttons. Hector's voice had become stronger as he played his role with greater confidence. Role? Yes, that was it. Steph was sure he was playing a role, a performance like the one he'd put on when they'd first seen him at the Open Day. No wonder Hale was becoming impatient.

Bob: Back to that afternoon. Did you go to Jon Henderson's wing and bring him back to your front door, or did he arrive there?
Hector: Good heavens, what does that matter?
(Neither Bob nor Joe said anything, but left the question hanging.)
Hector: Very well. Now what happened exactly? Let me think...
(He closed his eyes, placing his long fingers on his brow as if considering some philosophical point.) *I think I must have had said to Jon on the phone to come round and we'd use the quad bikes.*
Bob: And why not use your car?
Hector: (He sighed, clearly irritated.) *Oh! What difference would that have made?*
Bob: A great difference if Mrs Henderson had gone out onto the road.
Hector: We never thought about details like that. We knew she'd driven off; the quads were to hand, and we went after her.
Bob: So, assuming she was going to drive around the estate, you chased her on the quads.
Dick: Where did you say the cars were parked? (He leaned forward to clarify the point. Bob sat back a little.)
Hector: I didn't. Around the side of the house. Further away than the quads, which happened to be there. Really! This is becoming absurd! (He drummed his fingers on the table.)
Dick: Which way did you go?
Hector: Towards Badgers' Wood.
Dick: Why there?
Hector: Sorry?

Dick: *Why go to that particular spot? You live on a large estate – why go there?*

Hector: *Jon must have told me that's where she was headed.*

Dick: *Do you remember what he said?*

Hector: *No. Look, we were in a panic, wanting to rescue Madeline. We followed her and saw her car in flames. Jon tried to get her out but couldn't. Got badly burnt, as your Chief Inspector witnessed.*

Bob: *Rescue? When did you know she was in trouble?* (Hale nodded at Bob Johnson's smart pick up.)

Hector: (He appeared to be trying to keep his temper, speaking slowly, with precise enunciation of each consonant.) *We didn't when we set off. We thought we were going to stop her driving the car as she was drunk and bring her home, but then we heard the crash and saw the flames. Look, this is all I can tell you and I keep telling you again and again. It won't change what happened, you know.*

Bob: *No, I'm sure it won't.*

Hector: *What does that mean, exactly?* (He pulled himself up straight, his eyes challenging Bob.)

Bob: *Only that we have the conundrum of how Madeline drove with a skull fracture we believe caused her death. How do you account for that?*

Hector: *I don't. All I know is she drove the car. We chased after her and it went up in flames – how many times?*

Bob: *I'm sure you can see from our point of view that what the pathologist has found makes it difficult to imagine her driving.*

Hector: *Perhaps, Sergeant, you need to have a quick search on the internet, and you'll find many cases of people with fractured skulls taking action and once again, I stress that it could have occurred in the car crash. I have someone from the Home Office interested in reviewing your pathologist's findings – an old school chum.*

Bob: You appear to be taking a lot of trouble to refute the pathologist's findings.

Hector: Damn right. (He stood.) *Well, if that's all, may I go now?*

(Bob stood to face him.)

Bob: What will happen to Madeline Henderson's school, now she'd gone?

Hector: We haven't finally decided, but it was haemorrhaging money, so I suspect it'll close. That was on the cards before she died, but now she's gone, it's highly likely.

Bob: And what will happen to the children?

Hector: We'll make sure they're settled in new schools. We're aware of our responsibilities, you know. And that's if we close it, and, as I say, it isn't decided yet.

Hale switched off the interview. 'Well, what do you think?'

Steph swivelled her chair to face him. 'I think that was a performance. I'm not sure I've ever seen the real Hector, but that wasn't him. It was rehearsed, and it was only when pushed over the quad bikes and the last section where anything like the authentic Hector appeared to come through.'

'I agree; the same story was trotted out by Jon Henderson, but there is a part I want you to see.'

CHAPTER TWENTY-TWO

Steph watched as Hale fiddled around with the IT system, swearing under his breath when it didn't do exactly as he wanted. He was getting tired, and this case was becoming frustrating. There had been very few breaks, and they needed one badly.

'Ah! At last – here we are. He'd gone through the preliminaries and seemed to be settled, so Dick started pushing him on the row with Madeline.'

'Not Bob Johnson?'

'No, I thought it was time for Dick to lead for a change. I've only had one real meeting with Jon after the fire and I haven't pissed him off as much as Hector, so I assumed he wouldn't be as antagonistic. Do you think I shouldn't have?'

Smiling at Hale's sudden defensive tone, she shook her head. 'No, not at all. I was thinking how far Bob has come from "I know all the answers" to learning how to listen and pick up on what he hears. He's now a really good interviewer.'

'I'd forgotten you'd looked after him when he arrived. After you left, no one else had much patience with him. You did well – he's grown up all right; no one calls him Tigger now.'

The screen burst into life and magnified the further deterioration in Jon Henderson, now a walking dump of a man. Losing his daughter on top of his wife appeared to be destroying him. Hale nudged her, and she concentrated on the interview.

Dick: Let's go over that again. You came in and found Madeline drinking? What time was that?
Jon: About four o'clock. School ends at three thirty and she usually stays on to prepare her lessons for the next day and, you know, manage the place, but that afternoon she came home early and started drinking.
Dick: What?
Jon: She came home—
Dick: Sorry, I meant what was she drinking?

Steph was impressed by Dick's assured, calm demeanour for such a young officer. His quiet, soothing voice invited confidences and his slight smile was disarming. He looked a little like Brad Pitt with dark brown, intelligent eyes. Yes, he was a good find for Hale's team.

Jon: Scotch.
Dick: Is that what she normally drank?
Jon: No, she drank white wine mostly. It was unusual for her to drink spirits. She was in a state.
Dick: What had upset her?
Jon: Hector had been over at the end of school and told her there we couldn't afford to keep it open. Apparently, Luke had been

looking at the accounts and found the school was making a massive loss, so it was up the fees or close it.

Dick: *That sounds a little extreme. Was she expecting it?*

Jon: *No, it came out of the blue.*

Dick: *You do marketing for the Hall, don't you? Couldn't you do something to save it? It has a great reputation locally.*

Jon: *Yes, Madeline built it up from nothing and made it into an outstanding school.*

Dick: *So, if you both agreed, what did you row about?* (Jon frowned and appeared to be puzzled.)

Jon: *Are you married?*

Dick: *No.*

Jon: *Well, perhaps you won't know how it's possible to argue about nothing. The argument that afternoon was one of those.*

Dick: *Tell me, however inconsequential it was – what did you actually argue about?* (Once again, it was impressive how he could give a gentle push.)

Jon: (He sighed.) *Why I never unload the dishwasher.*

Dick: (He paused, referred to his notes, then put his head on one side.) *And that was why the daughter of an alcoholic, who hardly ever touched alcohol, got very drunk before driving off into the wood?*

Jon: (He looked taken aback, frowned, cleared his throat.) *As crazy as it sounds, yes.*

Dick: *Obviously I never met her, but Mrs Henderson, from what I've heard, was a bright, strong woman. It's difficult to see her getting drunk over a dishwasher, then driving off and crashing the car. And then there's the fractured skull.*

Jon: *But Hector said that could have happened in the fire.*

Dick: *Oh, did he? Do you have any idea how her skull could have been fractured before the fire? It was about here.* (Dick pointed to the right-hand side of his forehead. Jon examined where he was tapping.)

Jon: (He looked Dick in the eye.) *If, as you say, it happened before the fire, I've no idea how.*

Dick: So, you don't know how she fractured her skull, and you were only arguing about who empties the dishwasher?

Jon: (He wiped his sleeve under his nose, Bob pushed a box of tissues close to him and he blew his nose.) *Of course, it wasn't really about the dishwasher; she had to take it out on someone. It was because Hector was going to close the school. That was what was underneath it all, but she wouldn't say that. I know that now. The dishwasher was her way of getting at me. Our marriage had been — shall we say — difficult for some time. I knew if her school went, she would leave Glebe Hall... and me.*

Dick: If you knew it was really about the school, why didn't you talk to her about that?

Jon: Because there was nothing we could do. That was that. If only she'd talked to me like she used to, we could have worked it out together instead of rowing about who empties the fucking dishwasher. Hector speaks, and it is so. Oh, we'd have a long meeting where Luke would present the figures with lots of pie charts and graphs and projections and we'd all spend ages discussing how we could generate more income to avoid closing it, but Hector makes the decisions.

Bob: Thought you all had equal shares.

Jon: We do, but some are more equal than others.

Bob: Going back to her fractured skull – have you any idea how that might have happened?

Jon: None whatsoever. She rushed out of our sitting room, jumped into the car and drove off – as I keep saying, and I rang Hector, and we went after her...

Hale switched it off. 'We move onto the fire, and the story he tells is an exact copy of Hector's. Thoughts?'

'Slightly more authentic than Hector's, but he's not telling you everything and he lied. Previously he said they hadn't been rowing at all, now he says they rowed about the dishwasher. I find that plausible, I mean, partners argue about the most trivial things, but a dishwasher's not enough for someone who doesn't drink much to get smashed and crash their car.'

Hale nodded and turned off the computer. 'Go on.'

'No, he knew it was about the school and she was angry with Hector for his high-handed decision on her life.'

Hale squared off a pile of papers on his desk. 'Yes, Jon said that at the end, so why go on about the dishwasher?'

'I think their marriage must have got to the point where they'd stopped talking about real things and prodded each other about insignificant stuff. But if they argued about the school closing, what's wrong with him telling us? Like Hector, I think he'd rehearsed the dishwasher story – he kept repeating it too much.' Steph buttoned up her coat. She was cold and needed supper. 'Strong comment about Hector at the end.'

'Indeed. I think Hector and Jon's relationship is under pressure. Whatever happened was between the two of them and neither will give in.'

'Jon will be the first to crack.' Steph started walking to the door. Hale followed and switched off the light.

'Yes, I think we'll make another visit to Jon after all the formal interviews are finished.'

'And Esme?'

'Nothing there. Esme was in her studio running a yoga class and knew nothing about the fire until we arrived with Hector, and I believed her. Tomorrow we've got Luke and Zac.

I hope to get some gossip out of them as they don't seem to be so intimately involved in all this'

'But?'

'But, it's proving impossible to get any of the Glebe Hall crowd to deviate from the official version according to Hector.'

CHAPTER TWENTY-THREE

ESME DROPPED Jack off and parked the car in the visitor's space by Reception. She watched as he strode off, joined a group of four boys and went around the corner of the old building, his hand on one of the boy's shoulders, laughing. It was good he was so popular at college. Despite a few hiccups, he seemed to have settled down since he came here, almost two years ago. About to take his A Levels, she hadn't the faintest idea how well he'd do, but feared the worst as study didn't appear to be his number one priority.

Hector and she had come to all the parents' evenings and read all his reports, which she had to admit were detailed, but she was so worried that he hadn't done enough work. He could always go to one of those independent re-sit colleges in Cambridge or London if he failed or didn't get the grades he needed. But needed for what? He didn't know, and all Hector kept saying was that it was a great shame he wasn't going to his old college, Queen's in Oxford or even hers, St Catherine's.

Her empty driving and wing mirrors told her when lessons were beginning, as the cars no longer streamed in and the chatting groups of students disappeared. When an uncanny silence fell on the car park and there appeared to be little movement, she took a deep breath and entered the glass box.

Steph Grant was behind the long desk, counting out some photocopies or papers. Her dark blue dress and jacket were stylish, although hardly designer, but Esme had to admit that the outfit suited her and made her look professional, helped by her good posture, probably the result of years in a police uniform. The doors closed behind her; she moved towards the desk and waited for Steph to notice her.

'Good morning, Mrs Percy. If you've come to see the Principal, I'm afraid he's out at a meeting until this afternoon.'

'No, it's you I've come to see, Mrs Grant.'

'Really?'

She enjoyed the flicker of panic that crossed Steph's face before she regained her practised expression.

'Please sign the visitors' book and we can sit over there.' She gestured at the two black sofas by the front door.

'I would prefer somewhere a little more private, as I'm sure you appreciate.'

As she was filling in the visitors' book and making up half her car number plate, she saw Steph disappear behind a screen and return with a tall, dark-haired woman. 'Jane, Mrs Percy and I will be in the Principal's office if anyone wants me.' Jane nodded and smiled, obviously not minding being in charge, and accepted Steph's quiet authority.

Seeing that Steph woman in her own environment was fascinating. Esme sensed a strength she'd not picked up on her visits to the Hall, but then, that happened to lots of people, as it was a pretty grand place and could be intimidating if you weren't used to such surroundings.

Walking through the oak door into the Principal's office, or 'study', was like stepping back into the nineteen thirties, with a hint of art nouveau on the poppies decorating the copper hood over the fireplace and an oak arts and crafts desk. Whoever had originally furnished this room would have fitted in perfectly at the Hall.

The Steph woman showed her to one of the red leather chairs, its patina created by years of meetings. She sat, deliberately keeping her back straight so her pearls and dove grey cashmere pullover over her dark grey designer trousers could leave the woman opposite in no doubt that this outfit had cost more than she earned in a month. Although it was May, and a little warm, she had decided this outfit would give the right impression rather than linen, which creased so easily.

The woman sat opposite, waiting for her to speak. Esme looked her straight in the eye. 'I think you know why I'm here.'

'I think I can guess, but perhaps you will tell me.'

A good first move, but she refused to lose the advantage her sudden arrival had given her. She breathed in and kept her voice slow and strong. 'It's about yesterday's incident when you accused my son of abusing Bella and then hit him.'

Steph stood up. 'Excuse me, Mrs Percy, but for both our sakes, I would like to bring in a witness to our meeting and for you to repeat the accusation you've just made.'

'A shame you feel the need to do that. I'd hoped we could resolve this woman to woman.'

Steph paused and appeared unsure. Esme was pleased that she'd unnerved this woman, who had up to now appeared to be in charge.

'Very well, but I assume you have no objection to me recording our conversation?'

'I don't think that is necessary.'

'I can assure you it is very necessary as far as I'm

concerned, Mrs Percy. You have made a serious accusation, which could have implications for my job or lead to criminal charges, so I'm not prepared to continue this conversation without a witness or a recording.'

'Very well, record it if you must.'

Steph went back out to Reception and returned a few moments later with her phone, which she put on the table between them. Apparently, she'd switched it on while she was walking back, for she spoke immediately.

'This is Steph Grant; it is nine fifteen, Thursday 13th May and I'm in the Principal's office at Oakwood Sixth Form College, with Mrs Esme Percy. Mrs Percy, would you like to repeat what you have just said for the recording?'

The formal ritual Steph had recited reduced her confidence a little, but Esme refused to be intimidated, as she was convinced she was right and the recording should capture that.

'Yes, I'm happy to repeat what I've just said. I am Esme Percy, mother of Jack Percy, and I have accused Mrs Grant of hitting my son after college last night, when she also accused him of abusing a close friend's daughter, who lives on our estate.' Proud that she'd got out such a long sentence without a second breath or needing to swallow, Esme pulled herself up straighter waiting for a reply, feeling that once again she had the upper hand.

'Perhaps you would like me to tell you what I saw last night?'

Esme nodded. 'Please do.'

'Bella arrived to wait for Caroline Jones, with whom she is staying, as she says she feels in danger at Glebe Hall. She sat on one of the sofas in the Reception, and I was in the main office clearing up for the night when I heard a scream. I came back to see Jack on top of Bella, trying to strangle her, so I pulled him off her and brought him into this room, the Principal's study, which was empty. He sat there.' She pointed to a chair beside Esme and for a moment they both stared at it as if Jack might re-appear.

'I went outside and asked Miss Jones to join us. She sat in your chair and was here throughout the interview. I told Jack his behaviour was unacceptable. In fact, in the eyes of the law, it was common assault. I also told him that if he ever touched her again, I would report what I'd seen to the police, and he could face a court case and possibly receive a criminal record. I informed him that Bella had reported other incidents of abuse but had not gone into the detail and warned him that whatever had gone on had to stop. Then he left.'

'After you hit him.'

'I'm sorry, Mrs Percy, but I'm afraid Jack is lying to you. Yes, I restrained him, to stop him throttling Bella, but after that, I didn't lay a finger on him. I wouldn't.'

'So, it's your word against his, then?'

'Not quite. Caroline Jones was here throughout the interview and saw the red marks on Bella's neck. She followed us out and saw Jack leaving through Reception.'

'That proves nothing. Bella could have made those marks herself; she can be a little drama queen, you know. And as you say yourself, you were alone when you brought Jack into this office when he says you hit him.'

Esme was pleased to see Steph pause and think after her latest point. Finally, she spoke and stood up. 'Mrs Percy, you're right. There is no evidence of what happened in the minute or so we were alone in this room, but we do have CCTV pictures of what happened in Reception, which I can show you now if you'd like to come over to Mr Bryant's desk.'

This was unexpected and Esme had no alternative but to

go along with her suggestion. Taking her time, she stood and moved to the wooden chair Steph had placed beside the one she was sitting in and watched her fiddling with the computer.

The screen flickered and four pictures quartered the screen. Steph zoomed through them until she found the time, which she pointed out on the top of the screen. She indicated the picture on the top right which showed Bella sitting alone in Reception. The pictures were jerky, but clear enough to see Steph collecting something from the table and leaving. After a brief gap, she saw Jack rush in and jump on top of Bella, and there was no mistake – he was holding his hands around her throat and appeared to be hurting her.

Then she saw the back of Steph as she dragged him off Bella and, holding his right arm up his back, marched a struggling Jack out of the picture. He re-appeared on the bottom left quarter as she pushed him into the Principal's office. Then nothing, until Steph stood in the doorway and Caroline came into shot and joined her in the room before shutting the door.

Once again, Steph pointed to the time and fast-forwarded to where Jack came back into view. She could see Bella on the sofa and Caroline behind Steph as Jack walked out of the sliding doors, into the car park. Esme followed him as he moved to the top left quarter on the screen and watched as he drove his car down the drive, far too fast.

Steph turned to her. 'So, you can see what happened before Jack accused me of hitting him and that I was only in this office with Jack for a brief time without Caroline Jones as a witness. I'm not sure what Jack told you, but does it fit with the truth on the screen?'

Her face was now close to Steph's, and she got a whiff of a familiar Yves St Laurent perfume she herself had used some time ago, Rive Gauche?

She sat back. 'Obviously he didn't go into the detail you have on the CCTV but he said he was angry with Bella for all the trouble she is causing at home and I can see that he lost his temper a little.'

'A little? I suspect anyone watching that would say it was a lot!'

'Be that as it may, it doesn't prove that you didn't hit him.'

'No, you're right, Mrs Percy. If you would like to make a formal complaint to the Principal, he should be back this afternoon. Would you like me to make an appointment for you?'

Annoyed at the sudden confidence of this Steph woman, Esme sensed that Jack might have been exaggerating a little, but she couldn't reveal that. 'Thank you, Mrs Grant. I will discuss this incident with my husband before we decide on any further action we plan to take.'

She pushed back the chair, which scraped on the floor, and walked towards the door. She turned the copper handle and, holding her head erect as she'd been taught in her deportment lessons, swept out of the office. Irritatingly, the effect was spoiled a little as she had to wait for the automatic doors to open, but she used the opportunity to open her handbag and find her keys. Released at last, she climbed into her car as elegantly as possible and drove off.

She was aware of the Steph woman watching her and didn't feel her heart slowing down until she'd turned left at the bottom of the drive. Jack had a few questions to answer when he came home.

CHAPTER TWENTY-FOUR

HALE FIDDLED WITH THE COMPUTER. 'Not so dramatic today, but fascinating stuff from another angle...'

Steph was miles away, staring out of the window down the hill into Oakwood High Street. The picture book white clouds zipped along on the evening wind and a tractor was driving across the field in the distance. If only she could be there walking Derek and get away from Glebe Hall. She'd had enough of the Percys and their lies. Could she cope with another load?

'Hale to Steph – are you receiving me?'

'Sorry. Still at college.'

'Why, what's happened?'

'Oh, I'll tell you on the way home. Sorry. Let's watch this.'

It was the wrong time and place to tell Hale about the latest revelation from Glebe Hall. No, get these interviews out of the way first. She sat up and turned to the monitor.

Zac appeared on the screen, looking slightly ill at ease, but that was the reaction of most people when asked to come to a police station. It was a shame that Hector's aggression had forced the interviews to be in these soulless rooms rather than the Hall, as Steph would have been fascinated to see how this creative man had decorated his living space.

'Zac is a lovely man.'

'How do you know that?'

'Caroline says so – he teaches part-time in her department.'

'Maybe I should interview her. She seems to know everyone and everything!'

Zac's Indian-inspired, pale green collarless shirt of rough weave material highlighted his eyes and, apart from his finger pinging his thumbnail, he appeared calm. He was clearly inhibited by the camera, as his eyes constantly darted up to the globe in the corner of the room. Hale whizzed through the interview, stopped, listened for a moment, then went on again until he found the section he wanted. Dick was leading again with his well-spoken, understated authority, helped by his professional appearance – a navy suit and white shirt. No doubt he would find it easy to fit in at the Hall. A picture of Hale when she first knew him flashed into her mind. Of course! He was a younger version of Hale.

Dick: Thank you for that clear account. Now tell me how you and Luke came to live at Glebe Hall.

Zac: I was at Oxford with Hector and Jon—

Dick: Aren't you a textile designer? Didn't know they did degrees in that.

Zac: Went to Ruskin School of Art.

Dick: I see. You were saying you know Hector and Jon.

Zac: Yes, it was after college that they got to know Luke. We came up to the Hall for weekends and loved it. Hector's father was – shall we say – a challenging man, so we didn't visit much

when he was alive. But we came often after Hector inherited
Glebe Hall from William.
Dick: William?
Zac: Hector's older brother.
Dick: And how was it you moved here?
Zac: We lived in Battersea, London – I had a studio down the
road and taught at an art school – St Martin's. Luke worked at
one of the large accountancy firms in the City. One weekend we
were up here, and Hector told us that after paying death duties,
he was having problems keeping Glebe Hall going, and if we
bought in, we'd own a third of it – the west wing.

Steph was struck by the conversational tone of the interview and his straightforward telling of his story. So different to
the others.

Dick: So, you both moved up?
Zac: At first, Luke continued commuting for a few days a week,
but now he's here all the time. He runs his own business from
his office here and does all the Hall accounts. I have a textiles
studio in the grounds, where I run workshops and design fabrics
for places like Liberty, and I teach A Level at Oakwood College.
Dick: Is the extent of your contribution to the Hall the purchase
of the wing?
Zac: No, we all contribute to the running of it through our
activity – teaching, marketing, running workshops and the stuff
we're good at, and share some of the bills for gardening, house-
keeping and so on. It covers the costs, I think, but you'll have to
ask Luke about the detail.
Dick: And where were you the evening Madeline died?
Zac: In my workshop. It's at the far end of the three barns, well
away from Badgers' Wood – I knew nothing about it until later

*that evening, when Esme came round to tell us. Terrible – what
an awful way to die.*

Dick: And Luke?

*Zac: He'd been up to Norwich to visit a client and didn't return
until about eight o'clock, so the first thing he knew was when
Esme arrived.*

Dick: Didn't you hear the sirens?

*Zac: In the distance, but I thought they were on the main road to
Beccles, which runs behind my studio, and it was only later I
realised what they were.*

Dick: How did Madeline and Jon get on?

*Zac: OK, I think. Like all couples they had their moments, but
generally fine.*

Dick: Did you see much of them?

*Zac: From the start we made it a tradition to have a weekly
dinner together in the formal dining room, so we'd catch up with
what we'd all been doing. Esme runs popular yoga and meditation workshops while Madeline had done a fabulous job in
developing her school and Jon worked well with Hector
marketing the Hall.*

*Bob: I gather the Hall is in financial difficulty and the school is
going to close.*

Zac: (He hesitated and frowned before pulling himself up as if
taking on a challenge and facing Bob.) *Oh, not heard that. I
think weddings doubled last summer and mine and Esme's
workshops also increased in number and attendance.* (He
frowned.) *You'll have to ask Luke for the detail.*

Hale pressed a button, and the image froze. 'Well?'

'Interesting. He got a bit twitchy about the finances,
didn't he?'

'Yes. I was interested in the background of the arrangement. Got more about that from Luke. The first bit is the same story as Zac's, but the interesting part is when he gets to the money.'

Derek stood and sniffed loudly at the bottom drawer of Hale's desk, gave a pleading whine, and peered up at Hale, who pulled open the drawer and held out a dog treat to him.

'Have many dogs visiting, do you?' Steph was amused and rather pleased that Hale was making provision for Derek.

'No, just one.' He patted Derek on the head.

Hale moved on to the interview with Luke and zoomed through it until he found the part he wanted; a frozen picture of Luke came on the screen. More traditional than Zac, he wore a dark blue blazer, white shirt and tie and could have passed for a Middle Eastern ambassador or Oxford don. Almost completely bald, he appeared older than the others at the Hall, but the wrinkles around his eyes and mouth suggested a face well used to smiling. His hazel-green eyes, which stood out in his tanned face, were alert and somehow suggested his intelligence. Distinguished – yes, that was the word that described him.

'You decided Bob would do him?'

'Yes. Dick has great interpersonal skills, but Bob has a forensic, mathematical brain, as you know, and can get to the detail when we follow the money. He's getting a lot better at sussing people out, thanks to your training.'

Smiling, Steph felt like a proud mother, flattered by Hale's praise.

Bob: Tell me about the finances of the Hall.
Luke: Our accounts are in the public domain, on Companies House website.

Bob: *I've read the official accounts – what I'd like to know is what is behind them.*

Luke: *I think you'll find there is nothing "behind them" as you suggest.* (He bristled and looked guarded, then he spoke in a slightly more aggressive tone.) *All is perfectly legal and proper.*

Bob: (Riffling through some notes, he stopped and appeared to be examining one of the pages) *Oh? We've been told that the Hall is in some financial difficulty.*

Luke: *I'm not sure who told you that, but I can assure you it isn't true, and if it was, it would be confidential.*

Bob: *I'm afraid there is no such thing as confidential in a murder enquiry.*

Luke: *Murder? But surely, Madeline's death was accidental?*

Bob: *Hector hasn't told you then? We now think she was murdered.*

Luke: *Murdered? That's impossible!*

Bob: *Why?*

Luke: *Well, that just doesn't happen here. Are you sure?*

Bob: *Absolutely. She had a fractured skull before she drove the car, and an accelerant was used to set the fire.*

Luke: *But couldn't the fracture have happened in the crash?*

Bob: *We think not.*

Luke: (He looked puzzled and paused.) *I see.*

Bob: *According to Jon, Madeline was upset before the crash, as apparently the school was making a loss and Hector was going to close it.*

Luke: *Really? That's not—* (He frowned and moved his head to one side as if to concentrate on what he was hearing.) *Are you sure that's what he said?*

Bob: *Yes.*

Luke: *I'd need to have a more detailed examination of the school's accounts, but I'm surprised. It provided a consistent*

income all year, unlike the weddings, which are seasonal, and the intake was growing rapidly as its excellent reputation spread. (He shrugged his shoulders.) *But Hector was more closely involved with it, so maybe he was right.*
Bob: Right. I presume we can visit you and see the accounts?
Luke: Of course.
Dick: Do you and Zac plan to continue living at the Hall?

Hale nudged Steph and grinned. 'They make a good team, don't they?'

'Most impressive.'

Luke: Funny you should ask that. (He shifted in his seat and leaned in closer to Dick. His hands, previously relaxed on his lap, were now clasped tightly in front of him on the table; she could see his knuckles were white.) *I'm now in my early sixties, you know, and planning for our future. The Hall will change when the young ones take over – Jack and Bella will inherit their share of it. We've no one to leave our share to, so we've been talking to Hector and Jon about selling it to them or, if they can't afford it, putting it on the market and moving to Norwich.*
Dick: I see.
Luke: As we get older, we need to be somewhere with more facilities, in walking distance, you know. A car is essential at the Hall – we both feel now is time to move back to a more urban existence before we get too old. Life at the Hall has been good for us, but we now have to construct the next stage of our lives.
Dick: And what's Hector's take on your plans?
Luke: (He paused and once again moved closer as if sharing a confidence, his voice lower.) *Well, he wasn't thrilled, naturally. Our arrangement has worked well for about fifteen years – probably because the three of them were close friends at Oxford and*

we, their partners, got on with each other too. But it looks as if in the long term it won't be viable.

Dick: Really?

Luke: I fear Hector and Jon may not be able to afford to buy us out, so we may have to sell to outsiders. Then Bella and Jack will probably bring new partners in – that's if they want to continue living at the Hall. It has been an exceptionally comfortable way of life, but now, for us, it's time to move on.

Hale switched it off. 'Fascinating hint on the finances, wasn't it?'

'I wonder where the truth lies.'

'We can find out when we have a look at the accounts. He strikes me as straight down the line and very professional. If, as Luke suspects, the school wasn't making a loss, why was Jon so insistent that Hector was closing it?'

Steph reached down and patted Derek. 'That's if he actually said he was planning to close it?'

Hale stood and plucked his jacket off the back of his chair. 'And then there's the future. With Zac and Luke going, Hector's paradise appears to be crumbling.'

'Umm, doesn't it?' She stood and stretched after so long sitting hunched over the screen. Derek immediately stood, tail wagging, ready for a walk. 'Supper? I got a chicken and leek pie out of the freezer before I left for work this morning. I'm starving.'

'What an amazing woman you are! And I'll do the dishwasher!'

CHAPTER TWENTY-FIVE

Esme looked at the outsize clock on the kitchen wall opposite the Aga, where she had sat for far too many nights lately. A quarter to one. This was becoming a habit, no – stronger than that – a way of life. And she was sure he had one of his exam papers tomorrow – or rather today – was it General Studies?

Jack had always wanted to get out of it, and right at the start of his course he'd persuaded Hector to go up to the college, to see Mr Bryant and argue that it was of no value to him and he should be able to drop it to concentrate on proper subjects that mattered.

Esme couldn't help smiling as she recalled the supper following the visit. Hector had sympathised with Jack but explained that these state institutions, all of which were left wing and close to Stalinist Russia, imposed such rules, however absurd. But, he argued, as they were no longer paying this piper, they could not call the tune.

Jack had pleaded to return to his old school or go to another independent sixth form with the 'right people'. Hector pointed out that his previous school would not take him back after his latest expulsion for sending sexually explicit and bullying emails, which he pronounced was a fuss over nothing, but he insisted Jack knuckle down and get on with it, like the Percy he was.

Inside, Esme had cheered Mr Bryant, who had been intransigent – either Jack took General Studies, or he could choose to take his A Levels somewhere else. She'd spent a lifetime supporting Hector and would never dream of arguing with him in public, but this time he was wrong, and although even he knew it, she had to live through the bluster and bluff until he moved onto another issue.

Ten past one. The bass note tick of the clock measured her irritation and emphasised her tiredness. Now it seemed Jack had made his own decision. Silly boy.

She yawned and stretched. It had been a hard few days. Running her yoga and meditation workshops was a full-time job and she could hardly appear in front of her groups looking stressed and coming apart at the edges, could she? On top of that, she'd been helping Jon with so many things he couldn't do because of his hands.

A ping, then a light by the sink attracted her attention. Ah! Her phone. Picking it up, she glanced at the marketing email from the flower company, then she stuffed it into her pocket and returned to her chair. Hector must have been through it again. Now he didn't even bother to pretend to put it back where he'd found it.

The amount of admin following a death was enormous, on top of the organisation of the funeral, but Jon couldn't face doing anything about it. Just as well the police hadn't released Madeline's body yet. Maybe he hoped to have the funeral in the Glebe Hall chapel and for Madeline to be buried in the family plot but was afraid to ask. How would Hector react if that was what Jon wanted? The Percy family had been laid to rest there for generations, and Hector might find it difficult to have an outsider joining their ranks for eternity. But then, Jon was really family, wasn't he?

For the last few weeks, she'd felt excluded from something. Whenever she'd found Hector and Jon together, they'd fallen silent or pretended they were talking about some mundane subject. What were they up to? Her musings were smashed when the back door banged against the wall and Jack stumbled through.

'Hello, Mummy. Key got stuck – then door fell – fell like me.' He laughed loudly, finding it hilarious.

'Shhh! You'll wake your father.'

Jack staggered around the enormous pine table and threw himself on the Windsor chair opposite, almost squashing Middleton, who meowed in panic and fled under the table. The large tapestry cushion, the picture no longer discernible after years of use, fell to the floor, and he rested his feet on it.

'Shhh!' he echoed, louder. 'Mustn't wake Daddy, must we? Mustn't know. Shhhhhh!'

Hand to his lips, she wanted to slap him out of his clownish behaviour. She loved him to bits but couldn't stand him like this.

'Look at the state of you! How could you do this the night before your exam?'

'Doesn't matter. Not a real subject.'

'You've done this deliberately, haven't you?'

Jack grinned. 'Off to bed... Sleepy.' He tried to haul himself up, but his hands slipped off the wooden arms of the chair and he fell back down again. 'Can't get up. Stuck.' Again, his laugh bounced off the walls.

'I went to college today and spoke to Mrs Grant.'

'Good Mummy.' His little boy's voice made her furious.

'She denied hitting you and showed me your attack on Bella.' Her voice was louder, trying to shock him.

'What on earth is going on here? Do you know what time it is?' Filling the doorway, Hector scowled at them both. They froze; neither responded 'Go on. Explain yourselves.'

Even when drunk, some primitive urge for survival made Jack remain silent under his father's piercing stare.

'Well, Esme? What was that about someone in college hitting him?'

Trying to recall what he might have overheard; Esme decided the best way was to tell him all. He'd find out anyway and if he knew she'd been lying... Well, it was better to face it now. Jack fiddled with the loose label on the front of the Aga, apparently occupied with turning it up the right way. Typical. Hector moved closer and stood over them both.

'And my lad, there's no need to tell me what you've been up to. I can smell it from here.'

At last Jack looked up and mumbled, 'Revision group with some friends and we had a few at the end.'

How pathetic he sounded. Revision group! Did he really expect Hector to swallow that?

'Well, at least you started with good intentions.' He patted Jack's shoulder. 'Didn't you say he'd got some exam or other tomorrow?' This was directed at Esme, and she knew once again it was the familiar boys versus girls and somehow it would end up being her fault.

'Yesterday, Jack accused Mrs Grant—'

'That policeman's sidekick, who's always poking her nose in here?'

'That Mrs Grant, yes.' Why did he always do this? Interrupt her so she'd lose her place. 'Jack had accused her of hitting him, so I went to see her—'

'To lodge a formal complaint, I hope?'

Esme could see where this was going. She got up and poured herself a glass of tap water.

'Well, come on, woman, we're waiting. The tension's killing me. Did you or did you not make a formal complaint?'

Esme leaned against the sink. 'No, I didn't. Not after she showed me CCTV footage of your son attacking Bella.'

'Are you sure it was Jack?'

'Absolutely.'

'Where did she hit him?'

'On the head.' Jack joined in, attempting to pat himself on the side of the head, accompanied by a wounded expression.

'No, stupid boy, *where*? Reception?'

'She pulled my arm right up behind my back – still hurts.' He rubbed the top of his arm, 'Sure, it must be bruised – dragged me to the Principal's room and hit me, Daddy.'

Esme felt a wave of nausea as she listened to him attempting to suck up to Hector.

'And there are no cameras in that room, are there, Mummy? So, she couldn't prove she didn't, could she Mummy?'

Once again, it was going to be her fault – she'd got something wrong, failed again. Both of the Percy men were ganging up on her now. It wasn't fair. She stood up as tall as possible.

'No, Jack, you're right, there are no cameras in the Principal's study, but to see you attack Bella in Reception was horrible.'

'Will you stop saying "attack", woman? I'm sure it was horseplay, eh?'

'Horseplay – exactly that, Daddy – horseplay without the

horse!' Jack collapsed into fits of giggles until his father swiped him around the head.

'Enough!'

'Ow! That hurt.'

'Now you get to bed, and I'll take you in for your exam tomorrow and visit that Principal to make an official complaint against that nosey woman. Who does she think she is?'

After two attempts at getting out of the chair, Jack stumbled to his feet and tottered out of the kitchen; as he reached the door, he turned and smiled at Esme – a sickly smile of victory that made her want to throw up.

Hector's hand snaked from her shoulder and down the length of her spine. He leaned into her; his low voice in her ear made her feel nauseous. 'Now, after all that drama, let's be off to bed.'

Esme couldn't trust herself to reply but, head down, walked through the door Hector held open for her.

'Boys will be boys, my dear, and they do these madcap things. And now, as we are wide awake...' His pointy fingers caressed her bottom.

CHAPTER TWENTY-SIX

STEPH SHUDDERED, feeling as if someone was walking over her grave before she saw who it was. Hector loomed over her desk, and she breathed in Jo Malone's Lime Basil and Mandarin; however, the expensive perfume did not reduce the distaste she felt towards him. His voice rang out across Reception, although he was only a few feet away from her.

'I'm here to see Mr Bryant.'

'Do you have an appointment, Mr Percy?'

'I think you'll find I don't need one.'

'Please wait over there and I'll see if the Principal is free, Mr Percy.'

Waiting until he'd left her desk and gone over to the waiting area, she knocked and walked into Peter's office.

'Well, he's arrived.'

'As we thought.' Peter shoved the papers for the Suffolk Local Authority meeting back inside a folder and swivelled to his computer. 'Give me a moment so I can get that CCTV footage cued up.'

When Steph had told Peter about the incident with Jack and Esme's visit, he'd put odds on Hector coming in to make a fuss.

'When you bring him in, pick up the papers I've sent to the printer, will you?'

She went out to find Hector riffling through the visitors' book. 'May I help you?' Steph took the book from him and replaced it on the desk, realising he was checking the day when Esme had signed in. He glared at her as if she was the one in the wrong. 'Mr Bryant, will see you now.'

Head raised, he pushed past her, not quite touching her but closer than necessary, opened the door to Peter's room, then shut it. As she lifted the papers from the printer tray, she smiled, anticipating Hector's annoyance when she arrived.

Without knocking, she walked in and handed the papers, now in a folder, to Peter. Hector stopped speaking as the door opened, then waited for her to leave. She took her time sitting down on one of the chairs between them, flipped open her notebook and sat, pen ready.

'I didn't realise Mrs Grant was going to join us.'

'As my PA, she attends all such meetings.'

'And if it concerns her?'

'Even more reason she should be here.'

Peter's tone was unequivocal. He was not going to be cowed by Hector. Clearly, Hector had also picked up Peter's tone and capitulated. 'As I was saying, I would like to make a formal complaint against Mrs Grant for assaulting my son.'

'You have evidence of that, naturally?'

'Evidence? Surely the word of my son is sufficient. He said Mrs Grant hit him and I believe him.'

'Really? Perhaps you will tell me what Jack said. Unfortunately, we can't ask him as he should be in his General Studies exam.'

Hector sat up straighter. 'It appears there was some silly horseplay between Jack and Bella Henderson out there in your entrance hall and Mrs Grant over-reacted, dragged him into your office, using a method of restraint routinely used in her previous role in the police force, then hit him around the head.'

Getting up to go to his desk, where he turned the monitor round so Hector could see it from his seat, Peter pressed the play button and the CCTV picture flashed on the screen. Peter had managed to get a full screen instead of the quarter segments she'd shown Esme, and it was now indisputable that Jack's attack on Bella was vicious. Hector watched, his face frozen, hiding any reaction.

'Hardly horseplay, is it? Would you like to see it again?' Peter's voice was the epitome of politeness.

'Not very clear, is it? Can't actually see who it is. Could be anyone.'

Peter re-wound to the part where Steph pushed Jack into his office and pressed pause. 'I think this might help you identify Jack. That is him in this shot, isn't it?'

He frowned, then his eyes met Peter's, as if he'd thought of something. 'All that shows is the start of Mrs Grant's assault on my son, which was uncalled for and was painful and humiliating.'

'I'd say the restraint she used was absolutely necessary to stop the assault on Bella Henderson, and in my professional opinion, Mrs Grant used reasonable force to stop your son from hurting her further. I thoroughly approve of all Mrs Grant's actions.'

'I disagree. You don't have any evidence of what happened in this room, do you?'

'Neither do you. Or perhaps you have a photograph of Jack's injuries caused by this alleged assault?'

'I assumed my word would be sufficient.'

Peter resumed his seat. 'With an accusation as serious as this, we need more than your word to support it, as Mrs Grant's job could be at stake.'

'Quite right, too. Such an unstable person should not be allowed near children, even if they're over sixteen.'

Steph struggled to keep her mouth shut as the anger bubbled up inside her. Compressing her lips tight together, she fought the desire to scream her protest at him. Anyway, Peter was doing a great job defending her, and an emotional outburst from her at this stage could only support Hector's claim that she was unstable.

'And Jack?'

'What about him?' Clearly Hector was getting irritated.

'With the evidence we have, we could report him to the police for his assault on Bella Henderson.'

'She would never press charges against Jack; they're great pals. Played together since they were babies.'

'So I understand.' There was a pause while Peter opened the file of papers Steph had brought in. 'I think you will be aware Jack has a record of not always, shall we say, telling the entire story as others might see it.'

For once, Hector appeared confused.

'Sorry?'

'I have here accounts of three...' Peter riffled through the folder, making a meal of scanning the reports. 'No, four incidents over the last two years where Jack has been in trouble for bullying and, not to put too fine a point on it, he lied. Twice to his Senior Tutor, once to the Vice Principal and, in the last case, to me.'

Apparently taken aback, Hector, for once, appeared as if he had no words left to defend his son. 'Boys behaving like boys, surely?'

Peter closed the folder before looking across at Hector. 'I presume you received the letters we sent in each case?'

'Of course.'

'I was a little concerned that you didn't reply to them or come to college to discuss the incidents, but... ah... I see that his mother did. Maybe you didn't think them sufficiently serious?' Steph could see Peter relishing this slow torment of the entitled Hector, who was doing his best to save his face. 'You're welcome to have copies of the letters if you'd like to read them again?'

'Thank you.'

Extracting several sheets of paper from the file, Peter passed them over to Hector, who, despite appearing desperate to read them, folded them and tucked them in his jacket pocket.

'Now, Mr Percy. If you wish to make a formal complaint against Mrs Grant, I will need to institute an internal investigation into the matter before taking any action.'

Clearly containing his fury and struggling to maintain his dignity, Hector stood. 'No need for that, Principal. I am sure, as a result of this incident, Mrs Grant will moderate her behaviour. That will be all.'

'And would you like me to send you a copy of the CCTV pictures of Jack's attack on Bella in case she or we decide to take action?'

'I don't think that will be necessary. Thank you for your time, Principal.' He turned and opened the door. Steph let him leave without seeing him to the sliding doors, as she couldn't trust herself to keep her mouth shut.

She shut the door and collapsed into her chair. 'Oh, thank you so much Peter, you were amazing!'

'Oh, I did enjoy that.' Peter grinned.

CHAPTER TWENTY-SEVEN

Esme knew she was in for it as soon as the front door smashed shut and she heard her name screamed out. 'Esme! Where are you? I need you here, *now*!'

Another door crashed shut as he looked for her in the kitchen, then stormed off into his study beside the dining room. Quaking, she walked through the open door and faced Hector, sitting at his desk, his back to the long window, and waited for the explosion.

'And what do you know about these?'

He flung some sheets of paper at her across his desk. Two pages landed on the floor at her feet. Picking them up, she felt dizzy, and a knot tightened in her stomach. She knew exactly what they were. Without looking, she backed into the chair in front of his desk and pretended to read the four letters, working out how much he might know and what she might say in her defence.

'Well?'

'Oh, these letters... I didn't want to bother you with them. You're so busy managing everything here for us; Jack and I sorted it all out without bothering you. Pretty trivial, don't you think?'

'No, I don't think! I know these "trivial events", as you call them, needed me to deal with them, not you. What gives you the right—'

Another door smashed. Jack had landed after his exam, and she couldn't get to him first.

'Jack? Come in here!' Hector's voice bellowed down the hall.

Poking his head around the door, Jack peered in, and from his expression, he knew something was up.

'Sit.'

Jack edged into the other low armchair opposite Hector's desk. Esme knew this was a deliberate ploy to ensure Hector was well above anyone who sat in these low chairs. It was impossible to signal a warning to Jack, with Hector observing both of them from his perch behind the desk.

'And how was General Studies?'

'Waste of time.'

'Let's hope you do better with the subjects that matter. Even second-rate places want top grades now.'

'You mean second to Oxford?'

'Precisely. Now I understand from the Principal that you have muddied our reputation. And you,' he scowled, his pointy finger aimed at Esme, 'had no right going behind my back protecting this little rat. I should have been informed. Those letters were addressed to me.'

'Also to me.'

'Yes, of course they were, you stupid woman, because you're married to me and are the mother of that lazy child.' He paused, giving black looks to both. 'Now, tell me, Jack, what have you done?'

'Nothing, Father.'

'Come off it! It's me you're talking to, not one of your teachers. I saw that CCTV footage and what you did to Bella. I haven't felt so ashamed in my life.' He paused, skewering Jack with his stare. 'She didn't hit you, did she?'

'Sort of she—'

'*Sort of? Sort of! Either she did or she didn't. Which was it?*' His voice drilled into their heads; Esme winced. Jack stared at the sepia print on the wall of Glebe Hall, apparently trying to look cool. It didn't work.

'And don't you dare look at that picture, boy! You don't deserve to inherit this... this house and land, where your ancestors have lived with honour. You have let down the Percy name. Our reputation is now in the gutter because of what you've done and said.'

Jack glanced up at him. 'It's not that bad. There are others who're much worse than me.'

'I don't care about the others. They are not Percys. We have standards to maintain.'

'I think you're going a bit over the top.'

'*Over the top?* You have no idea, do you? That college Principal can ruin your future with one stroke of his pen. One sentence in your reference and you won't get a place anywhere worth going to or a job afterwards.'

Esme knew it was useless to say anything when he was in this mood and spouting this script. Better to let him get it all out and wait until she could leave and find some quiet place somewhere. She slowed her breathing and concentrated on tracing a large grey streak on the marble fireplace, examining its shape, its route around a mountain range and a lake – the dark colour dissolving as it dribbled down to the hearth. His voice pulled her back into the room and shattered her calm.

'No, the real crime here, boy, is getting found out. You don't get found out in the first place, then you don't have to lie. Lie if you have to – that doesn't matter if in the long run you win. But you're not winning, are you?'

'I wouldn't say that.'

'I would. Look at Bella. A bright girl with an independent spirit like her mother and almost as beautiful. Your job is to court her, not to attack her, boy. She needs to be wooed, touched gently, not strangled.'

'But she's going out with that Graham.'

'Graham?'

'You know, Graham Andrews—'

'Not that grubby little gardener who trails around after Andrews?'

'That's him.'

Esme sank into the world of grey veins once again. How much longer could she tolerate his bluster? She looked across at Jack and saw him as a happy four-year-old, free and exploring life. Now he was being shaped into a mini-Hector. If only she could stop it somehow.

'A gardener? What the fuck is that girl doing, going after a gardener? Who does she think she is – Lady Chatterley?'

Jack sniggered, prompting a smug expression on Hector's face and urging him to take action. 'I can see I need to tell that Graham his fortune. Leave him to me.' As usual, Hector thought he could control everything, while Jack sucked up to him.

'I bet you will, Father.'

Desperate to puncture their snobbish arrogance, Esme interrupted, and they both stared at her, no doubt shocked by her impertinence. 'If either of you had bothered to talk to him, you'd know Graham Andrews is taking a year out to earn money before he goes up to Cambridge to read history. He may have dirty fingernails, but he's got a great brain – earned him a scholarship.' Pulling herself up and out of the chair, she walked to the door, hoping her shaking legs didn't show.

'Come back, woman! I've not finished yet!'

She carried on walking into the hall, murmuring under her breath, 'But I have.'

CHAPTER TWENTY-EIGHT

Steph's stomach churned as Hale drove them to Glebe Hall. He'd phoned late in the afternoon and told her Luke had agreed to meet them in his office at five o'clock, after work. Immediately Steph expressed her reluctance to go to the Hall so soon after all the fuss with Jack, but Hale assured her she was in the right and it was the Percys who should be feeling ashamed of their son's lies. Somehow, she thought they wouldn't.

They skirted the Hall and went beyond the barns to a small cottage which Luke had told Hale was the office. Estate agents would describe it as 'bijou'. It was thatched, with wonky ancient grey beams cutting through the Suffolk pink walls and encircling the tiny leaded glass windows. The solid front door, fractured over centuries, held an iron circular knocker which had worn a crevice in the wood, now filled in with a modern piece of metal. As Hale reached out for it, the door opened and Luke stood to the side, gesturing that they should step down into the dark room.

The uneven floor was covered in old terracotta pamments,

typical of East Anglia, and led to the inglenook brick fireplace, complete with a hook over the fire basket. In contrast, the furniture was definitely not hundreds of years old but modern Ikea-style light wood office furniture with sharp lines, lit by LED lamps. A row of three computer screens on the table beneath the window was sandwiched between floor to ceiling bookshelves loaded with files, all in a dark blue shade. Here was someone who organised life down to the last full stop, or perhaps it should be the last pound sign?

Luke pulled two chairs in front of the screens on either side of his office chair and invited them to join him. Steph's original assessment of him as an ambassador was reinforced. Polite – no – courteous and elegant in his ivory shirt and navy chinos; everything about him was understated, and she could see how the flamboyant Zac complemented him.

Patiently, he took them through the accounts he'd submitted to Companies House, which showed a profit. Not an enormous one, but a solid profit many small businesses would envy.

'May we see the accounts for the individual activities, please?' asked Hale.

'Of course. I'll put them on the screens in front of you, so you can get hold of the detail.'

Luke took them through the various enterprises run at the Hall. Open Days, weddings, yoga and textiles workshops all 'wiped their face', as Luke put it.

'And the school?'

Another set of figures whizzed on the screens. 'There you are. Thought so. Probably the most profitable business – almost makes as much as all the others put together – does extremely well for a small school. As I said, it's popular and grows each year.'

They watched as Hale perused the columns of figures. 'Since we met at the station, have you thought of any reason why Hector would want to close it?'

'None. As you can see, the financials work and, I understand, the education is outstanding.'

Steph's head was beginning to ache with the endless screens of figures and the dull explanations. Leaving Hale to continue scanning the columns of income and expenditure, she caught Luke's eye and moved onto more personal ground. 'What will happen to the Hall when you and Zac leave?'

Oops! Would he realise she'd watched his interview? Luke's face didn't change – he must have thought he'd mentioned it. Hale didn't appear to have noticed it either, as she felt him relax and lean back, apparently letting her probe.

Luke smiled and assumed his professional expression. 'It will continue as it has for hundreds of years.'

It was difficult to engage him beyond spreadsheets, but it was worth a go. 'But won't they miss your contribution?'

'I've told Hector I'll carry on with the financial management. Much of it can be done online from wherever we end up living.'

'Do you think they'll be able to buy your share, or will you have to sell it?'

Had she gone too far? For the first time, Luke looked uncomfortable and once again she noted the hand clasping, and again could see that his knuckles were white. 'I don't have access to... er... personal accounts, you understand, so cannot answer that.'

'But your hunch?' Steph smiled at him.

Luke paused for a moment – apparently unhappy with expressing an opinion rather than working with cast iron figures. Steph waited, knowing that silence often worked. He lifted his head up; he'd decided. 'From what Hector has said, socially, you know, I suspect they may... er... have some difficulty.'

Steph felt he was starting to open up, so pushed. 'You've been such a tight-knit group of friends. It sounds like a perfect arrangement.'

Luke smiled in agreement. 'Indeed. It has worked for fifteen years and was an inspired move when Hector was in... umm... difficulty in the early days.'

'An ideal solution – you all benefitted.'

'Indeed, it has worked so well, but I think he grasped a solution at that time, not thinking of potential problems so far in the future.'

'Fifteen years seems an age away when we're young, isn't it?' Steph felt she was getting through to Luke at last as he visibly relaxed, wheeled over a chair and joined them at the desk.

'Indeed.' He smiled at her. 'I hope Hector can buy us out. If we have to sell our wing, it will dilute the philosophy he established and make it a... a more commercial arrangement, naturally.'

'And do you think Jon will stay?'

'Well, after all he's been through, he may want to move from the memories, but then, Esme and Hector have been so supportive.' His furrowed brow suggested he was reflecting on the possibility of Jon's future for the first time. 'Basically, I'm not sure.'

Steph was aware of Hale moving back further, leaving her to continue. 'Over the last fifteen years or so, the relationships between you must have changed?'

'Yes and no. Like all groups, we've had periods where we'd work closer together or at other times become more distanced. I think Zac and I have always been... a little on the edge... not having children, for example.'

'Oh?'

'They shared a daily nanny – went on trips – holidays together and, especially when the children were younger, spent much of their time together. We always went to the weekly dinners but favoured our independent existence and kept up our London friends.'

'And was it just the mothers who became closer or the men too?'

'What a strange question!' He was clearly trying to recall the evidence he needed to support his response but appeared to be happy to continue chatting. His voice had become softer, and his shoulders relaxed. 'Neither Jon nor Hector got as involved in child rearing to the extent fathers do today – but they often enjoyed trips out together during that period.'

'Oh?'

'You know, cricket, rugby matches... horse racing – Newmarket and Yarmouth mostly, but also the London tracks. They enjoyed a day out and a flutter.'

'And you and Zac didn't?'

'Good heavens, no! Gambling on horses is hardly a prudent financial investment, to say the least. No, we'd rather make use of London's theatres and concert halls.' Moving into the financial world made him sit up straight once again and assume his more professional stance. She suspected she'd got as much out of him as possible.

Hale rolled his chair over the wobbly floor towards them. 'Going back to the school. From memory, you said that Hector was behind it originally.'

'He saw what a brilliant teacher Madeline was – she worked in the local primary school at that stage – and they both realised there was an opportunity in the local market, and indeed the outbuildings, for another school.'

'Really?' Steph prompted him.

'There was a sudden growth in young families moving up here from London, which has continued. But they were well ahead of the curve.'

'Right. Sharp of Hector and Madeline to seize on that.'

'Indeed. For years they worked closely together – they were obsessed with it – always became the main topic of conversation at our dinners. We'd often go through for coffee, leaving the two of them arguing or plotting some innovation or other.'

'They were close?' Steph smiled, inviting him to confide once more.

'I suppose you could say that... Professionally, they worked well together. The school prospered because of their enthusiasm and hard work.'

Had they touched on something? Luke appeared to have retreated and become more guarded again.

'And did Jon resent it?'

'Good heavens! No way! Too busy debating form and likely winners at the next race meeting with Hector.'

'And Esme?'

'Esme? Esme always supports Hector.'

Hale stood. 'Thank you so much for taking us through the accounts, Mr Roy; it has been most helpful. Oh, before we go, do you have any idea how Madeline may have fractured her skull before the car fire?'

'Hector mentioned that... but, sorry, no.'

CHAPTER TWENTY-NINE

STEPH GESTURED to Hale that he should wait on one of the sofas in Reception until Peter arrived and she'd completed her routine morning tasks.

About ten minutes later, Peter breezed in. 'Morning, Steph.'

'Morning, Peter. Hale wondered if you could give him a few minutes?' She nodded over to the sofas and Peter turned to meet Hale, who put his phone in his pocket. 'Good to see you. Of course, come in. You too, Steph.'

When Peter had dumped his briefcase behind his desk, he joined them around the low coffee table. 'Now, what have our students been up to?'

'No, it's not the students, I want to ask you a favour.'

'Oh?'

'Naturally, I've heard about the assault on Bella Henderson by Jack Percy.'

'Naturally.' Peter raised his eyebrow and darted a piercing glance at Steph, who lowered her eyes, not wanting to resurrect the antipathy that had grown up between the two men when they'd been involved in trying to stop drug dealing in the college. 'Well, what about it?'

'If it was as serious as I suspect it was, I wonder if you'd like us to investigate it?'

Peter laughed. 'Not the usual story I hear about the police. Normally you're overworked and yet here you are, touting for business. Why?'

'It links to a case we're working on.'

Clearly, Peter was not going to make this easy. 'So, let me get this right. You're not concerned about the welfare of one of our students but making progress on one of your cases?'

'I wouldn't put it like that.'

'How would you put it then?'

Instead of responding to Peter's challenge, Hale took out his notebook and turned over a few pages until apparently he found the one he wanted. Steph could see the page and it had nothing to do with the case but had given him time to re-set his approach.

'Sorry Peter. Gone at this from the wrong angle. Let me start again.'

He looked up at Peter, who said nothing.

'As you know, we found Madeline Henderson's body in a car fire. At first, we thought that was how she died, until the pathologist found that Madeline had a rather large fracture on her temple, which we now think caused her death.'

'So, the fire was a way of disposing of her body, then?'

'Precisely. We're now conducting a murder investigation. But to say we're stuck would be an understatement.'

'And this is where I come in?'

Clearly, Peter was taking the bait. Steph hoped that this wouldn't lead to another period of mistrust between them.

'The residents at Glebe Hall are united in their version of

events and we can find no firm evidence to arrest anyone or even to continue questioning them.'

'I see.'

Hale's voice became stronger as he developed his argument. 'We are convinced that one or more of them is involved in her death but can't prove it.'

He paused and fixed Peter with a firm look. 'If you would ask me to investigate the attack on Bella Henderson, which you might very well do in such a case, then I can go in with something concrete to work with. It would mean I could investigate a crime with the people we suspect of committing a murder.'

Peter fiddled with a loose button on the arm of his chair before replying. 'But what if I don't want to press charges? I know Bella doesn't.'

'It won't get that far. I can always agree with Jack and his parents that this time we'll let it go with a warning and no further action.'

'You can do that?'

'Yes, if you ask us to investigate. You don't have to insist on us pressing charges.'

Peter tried to push the button back into the hole in the chair arm. 'You are aware that Hector Percy has the ear of the great and good of Suffolk?'

'The Chief Constable's been in touch.'

'I see.'

'He informed me that he'd been contacted but said it made no difference to my investigation, only to ensure the paperwork provides clear audit trails.'

Peter frowned. 'That must be stressful and create more paperwork?'

Hale nodded. Steph could feel Peter warming to Hale, as clearly, he too had been warned from above. She'd put through a call from the Education Officer a few hours after Hector Percy's first visit to the college to complain about Bella staying at Caroline's.

Peter got up, sat behind his desk and fiddled with his computer. 'Well, in that case, you'd better come over here to see the attack I'd like you to investigate.'

CHAPTER THIRTY

Her heart racing, Esme opened the front door as Hale approached it.

'Do come in, Chief Inspector. You know the way. Jack is in there waiting for you. I assume I may join you?'

He waited while she shut the door behind him and for her to lead the way. He had some manners then. 'Yes, if that is Jack's wish. He is over eighteen, I understand?'

'Just.'

'Then it's up to him.'

They opened the door to the sitting room, and she saw Jack on the far Chesterfield reading a book. She had to stop herself from laughing out loud. The picture he'd created of the studious young man didn't suit him at all, but well done for trying. He was so like Hector. She loved him lots, but he was difficult to like sometimes.

'Jack, I believe you've met Chief Inspector Hale?' Jack stood and politely reached across the space in front of the fireplace to shake Hale's hand.

'Chief Inspector.' Jack inclined his head so low it was

almost a bow. Esme winced. Maybe he was taking it a bit too far?

She intervened before he could. 'As you know, the Chief Inspector is here to talk with you about the incident with Bella at college. He said I can stay, but it's up to you. Would you like that or prefer to see him alone?'

'I'd prefer you to stay, please, Mummy.'

Wow! He really was going for the impression of the perfect son, wasn't he? Hale sat on the opposite Chesterfield to Jack, while she chose the one between the two, facing the fireplace. Her mouth dry, she sat back and waited for Hale to begin.

'Jack, I have been asked by Mr Bryant, the Principal of Oakwood Sixth Form College, to investigate the assault on Bella Henderson at the college last Wednesday.'

'Not Bella then?' Jack already had the cocky tone of voice he used when challenged. 'It has nothing to do with him, does it?'

'Actually, it does. The assault took place at his college, and he has a duty to safeguard his students and report such serious incidents to the police. Now, if I may ask you a few questions?'

Jack sat to attention, his head slightly on one side as he listened to the Chief Inspector explaining that he was being interviewed as a suspect in an offence and, although he gave him that official scary sounding caution, assured him he wasn't under arrest. Jack was frozen in a pose that reminded her of one of Hector's hunting spaniels waiting for instruction, and he didn't appear to be as worried as she felt.

'You've seen the CCTV of the incident?'

Jack nodded. 'Yes.'

'Have you, Mrs Percy?'

'Yes.' Her neck felt hot, and she suspected a red rash was creeping above her silk scarf.

Hale turned back to Jack. 'So, would you like to tell me what made you do it?'

Esme became aware of Jack staring at her before he turned to Hale. 'I'm not quite sure how to say this... but Bella and I were, how do I put this? We became more than friends and we enjoyed a... a friendship with benefits.'

'What's that?' Esme couldn't help herself.

'Such relationships didn't exist when you and Daddy were young. It's a friendship where you also have sex with no strings. Bella likes her men to be... er... strong, if you understand me, Chief Inspector?'

Did he wink at Hale? Esme was shocked. How could Jack act like this?

Hale wrote in the notebook that had appeared from somewhere. 'You mean she likes it rough?'

Esme felt the bile erupt from her stomach. She clenched her lips tight and swallowed.

'Precisely. I saw her on the sofa and, not realising there were cameras there, I simply behaved as I might in her home or mine. Not in front of our parents, you understand? Nothing to it. Just foreplay – it turns her on.'

'And if I ask Bella, will she confirm this?'

'I shouldn't think so. Girls don't like to present themselves as sluts — I mean promiscuous, do they? So, no, I'd say she'll probably deny it.'

Esme wasn't invited to speak, but she doubted she could, anyway. Was he telling the truth? He appeared to be sincere, but you could never tell with Jack. Bella and Jack behaving like that? Why hadn't she guessed or noticed?

'Did you know she had a boyfriend?'

'No.'

Esme did her best to keep her face fixed. Oh, Jack! How stupid telling such a silly lie – bound to get found out.

'Apparently, she's been going out with Graham Andrews for some time. Do you know him?'

'No, I don't think I do.'

'He was in the year above you at college and works as a gardener here in Glebe Hall, before going up to Cambridge.'

Jack frowned and looked as if he was trying to puzzle something out.

Hale prompted him. 'Surely you know the people who work here?'

'You have to understand, Chief Inspector, that we have lots of people coming and going on this estate. I don't get to know all of them – often don't notice them.'

Esme wanted this to be over before she saw any more of this Jack who oozed entitlement – she didn't know how to stop it.

'Well, Bella says that since she has developed a loving relationship with Graham, she realises you've been sexually abusing her for years.'

Esme felt faint. She gripped onto the arms of the chair. Surely this couldn't be true? Jack? Sexual abuse?

Jack cleared his throat. 'That's what she's saying, is it? She would, wouldn't she?'

The look he gave Hale was of the man-to-man variety she'd seen Hector use so many times when he wanted his own way. She was impressed that Hale didn't appear to respond to this appeal for matey-ness. Jack had obviously underestimated this man and needed to convince him further.

'See? Exactly what I said. She's covering up our relationship as something vile. Now she's got a boyfriend and is scared he might find out what a good fuck she is.'

'Jack! That's enough!' Esme could stand it no longer.

The door flew open. 'What's enough?'

Hector stormed in. 'What's going on here? Chief Inspector, why are you talking to my wife and son behind my back?'

Hale stood. He was a few inches taller than Hector, and he pulled himself up a little more. Hector, clearly not used to being challenged by a taller man, took two steps back.

'Good afternoon, Mr Percy. I made an appointment to see your son, Jack, about an assault on Bella Henderson at the college. I've been asked by the Principal to investigate.'

Hector appeared to be taken aback for a moment, before he re-gained his composure. 'Appointment? I wasn't aware of an appointment.'

Esme also stood. 'I was here when the Chief Inspector phoned and agreed the time for his visit.'

'Agreed a time when I wasn't here?' Hector's aggression oozed out of every pore and Esme felt ashamed of the impression the policeman must be forming of them, based on this afternoon's performance. At least Jack was keeping his mouth shut now.

'I have been informed of the incident, which I consider trivial, and I'm surprised that the Principal wants you to follow it up. Strikes me as a total waste of police time.'

Was he really going to get away with this bluster?

'You've seen the CCTV footage?'

'Yes. Proves my point. A lot of fuss over nothing. I'm sure Bella won't want to take further action.' Hector leaned closer to Hale, speaking man to man. 'Between us, the girl's a bolter! Won't stay and support her father when he needs her but goes running off to that pair of dykes who—'

'Hector, that's enough!' Esme didn't know where to look – her red-faced husband or the smug Jack. She chose the unperturbed Hale. 'I must apologise, Chief Inspector; this family is under a great deal of stress, as I'm sure you can see. If you've finished with Jack, I'll see you out.' Esme was desperate to finish this embarrassing interview, but Hale didn't move.

'Thank you, Mrs Percy, but I haven't finished interviewing Jack.' He turned to Hector. 'Mr Percy, may I suggest you leave while Jack and I continue with the interview?'

Evidently outraged at being ordered around in his own home, Hector stepped towards Hale. 'I think you may have finished here, Chief Inspector.'

Hale's voice was just above a whisper. 'Very well, Mr Percy, you leave me no alternative but to arrest Jack and take him to the station to conclude the interview.'

Esme stood between Hale and Jack. 'There's no need, Chief Inspector. Please finish the interview here. Hector, I suggest you leave and let the Chief Inspector do his job.'

As a thunderous Hector moved towards her, she flinched. She glanced at Hale – he had seen it too. Defeated, Hector turned on his heel, head high, and barged out of the room, slamming the door behind him.

She resumed her seat and Hale also sat, calmly finding his place in his notebook, and returning to question Jack about the attack on Bella and her accusations of his abuse, then he issued warnings of the serious crimes with which Jack could be charged. She was amazed at Jack's stubborn refusal to accept he'd done anything wrong, and his insistence that Bella had been the one who had asked for it and he'd obliged. He was so convincing she began to believe him, but surely Bella wouldn't have done that, would she?

Eventually, Hale closed his notebook and said that he would interview Bella to hear her side of the story and could well be back with further questions. Jack didn't appear at all bothered and didn't get up as Hale stood to leave. She showed Hale to the door and followed him out into the hall and safely through the front door before returning to a red-faced Hector, prowling outside the sitting room door. His pointy finger prodded her back into the room. She obeyed.

'Sit.' Hector's voice had that soft, menacing tone he used when he would accept no argument. 'I said, *sit*.' Hector stared at Jack, who was now standing, no doubt assuming he could escape. She got ready to step between them. Jack assumed a sulky expression and slowly, very slowly, resumed his seat. Hector positioned himself in front of the fireplace, where he could eyeball them both.

'Now, listen, and listen carefully. I do *not* want that policeman to put a foot in this house again without my knowledge. If he contacts either of you again, I expect you to refer him to me, understand? *Understand?*'

His eyes flashed at them.

Esme mumbled, 'Yes, Hector.' Jack grunted something that sounded like an agreement.

'Good, now if you'll excuse me, I have a phone call to make to the Chief Constable.'

CHAPTER THIRTY-ONE

THE BRASS LION-HEAD knocker made a rat-tat-tat sound, which echoed down the hall while Esme waited for the front door to open. At last Caroline flung it open and stood back, visibly shaken to see her standing on the doorstep.

'Caroline, good evening. May I come in?'

'Esme. Lovely to see you; it's been too long.' Having done the ritual two-cheeked air kisses, Esme could see the big question in Caroline's face – why is she here?

'Go through to the kitchen. Margaret and Bella are there, clearing away supper.'

Esme's high-heeled shoes tapped down the black and white tiled hallway through to the kitchen, where she found them clearing up the supper plates.

'Margaret, Bella, so sorry. I didn't mean to intrude on your supper.'

Margaret, in her usual sensible tweed skirt and fawn pullover, was stacking the dishwasher. 'No problem, Esme. We've finished. Will you join us for coffee? I was about to make a pot.'

'That would be lovely. May I?' Esme gestured to the chair opposite Bella, who looked up at her from beneath her eyelashes – a mixture of sheepish and scared. The last time she had seen Bella was when she'd told her about Madeline's death, which was one of the most difficult things she'd ever had to do. She had stayed with Bella that evening until she fell asleep, sitting beside her on the sofa then taking her up to her bed, holding her and rocking her as she had when she was a baby, the girl's sobs tearing her apart.

Caroline sat beside Bella and they both looked at her expectantly. 'I'd like to have a word with Bella if that would be all right – Bella?'

Bella's dark hair fell into a curtain, shielding her face from Esme, who realised that arriving unannounced when this girl was feeling so fragile could have been a big mistake. But she'd done it on instinct, and as she'd grown older, she'd learned to trust her instinct more. Now she was here, she had no choice, and she needed to know.

No one said anything, and the silence began to feel heavy. 'Bella, would you mind talking with me for a few minutes, please?'

'Only if Caroline's here.'

'That's fine.'

'Right, if you'll excuse me, I've got practice to do. College concert next week.' Margaret, who had been standing by the door watching the exchange, bustled around the table, picked up her coffee mug, then disappeared somewhere up the hall, from where they soon could hear her playing a piece on her piano – was it Haydn? Certainly something from about that period.

Esme had come here to talk to Bella, so she took a deep breath and got on with it.

'Bella, I'm so, so sorry about Madeline. You've been having a terrible time, haven't you?'

Bella's eyes filled and for a moment Esme wished she hadn't dived in so quickly, but having started, she had no choice but to carry on. Suddenly she was thrown back in time to when her father had died. She'd been so close to him, and it was fine until someone was kind to her – that was when she fell apart.

Caroline intervened. 'I'm sure you can understand that Bella is still in a state of shock following her mother's death, but I'd say she's doing well, managing to stay upright.' In a quieter voice, she turned to Esme. 'Are you sure you want to do this, Esme?'

Two tears dribbled down Bella's cheeks, and faced with it for the first time, Esme really appreciated the horror this girl was experiencing.

'You're right. I shouldn't have come. It was wrong of me. I came to talk to you about Jack, but I see now that I was being selfish and not thinking about you at all. So sorry, Bella, I'll go.'

Bella retreated further behind her hair. Esme shuddered to think she was the cause of further misery. The question was how to get out, now she was here. She'd come to deliver a message and was taken by surprise when she heard herself saying it. 'Jack is so distressed by what has happened, Bella. He's really sorry for what happened at college and hopes you'll take it no further.'

'And he couldn't come himself and tell me that?' Bella's voice was strangled by her grief and anger. Esme had the same thought after the words had left her mouth. It wasn't easy excusing or even lying for her son. Jack wasn't distressed. He didn't seem to care about any of it. But she felt compelled to reach out to this poor girl to stop things going further.

'I'm afraid you know Jack only too well. It appears I didn't.' Esme paused, not sure how to carry on or what she really wanted or how to get out of it. It had been such a mistake coming. She stood. 'I'm sorry I shouldn't have come – shouldn't have disturbed you. Sorry Bella.'

Bella's eyes moved up Esme's face until their eyes met. Esme could see the pain behind them and Bella's face, ravaged by grief, reminded her of that Munch painting *The Scream* – the enormous mouth in an agonising scream below blood-red clouds. She could bear the girl's unflinching stare no longer and lowered her eyes first.

'You came here wanting to know what he'd done to me – *if* he'd done it – didn't you?'

Esme froze, not daring to move but not desperate to hear what Bella had to say.

'I'm not making it up. Jack has abused me from when we were children and blackmailed me to keep quiet as we got older. Now I know how he did it and I've stopped believing it was my fault. He did all you can imagine he did. Is that what you wanted?'

That defiant, exhausted face would stay with Esme forever. 'I'm sorry I shouldn't have come. I know your father misses you.' Why did she say that? Using emotional blackmail was appalling. Hurriedly, she added, 'You don't need to worry about him. We're looking after him and he's fine – doing well in the circumstances. No, please stay here as long as you need to. You must put yourself first and look after yourself. Sorry.' Bella's eyes bored into hers.

Esme pulled her coat around her, left the kitchen and walked to the front door, with Caroline behind her. Stepping into the tiny front garden, Esme turned to find Caroline shutting the door.

'Please!' Esme held onto the edge of the door. Caroline stopped halfway and peered out at her. 'You're right, I shouldn't have come. I wanted to find out if—'

'If it was true?'

Esme nodded, unable to speak.

'I can assure you, having heard rather too much of this in my job, I'd say Bella is convincing. A pity you didn't come to me first.'

'Sorry. Should have. Thank you.'

CHAPTER THIRTY-TWO

THE DOOR SHUT with a firm click. Transfixed, Esme stared at the lion knocker for a few seconds, then climbed into her car. Less public. She didn't want to go back to the Hall. Her hands were shaking, so she didn't want to risk driving.

It started raining, hard. The windscreen became filled with little rivers, chasing down the glass, merging and re-routing when they met. Fascinated, she became hypnotised as the torrents created a constantly changing image – a natural art installation.

Did she need any shopping? Should she go down to the beach or find a pub for a while? No, she hadn't the energy to move. All sorts of potential distractions pushed their way into her mind. Anything but Jack. She mustn't think about Jack. But inevitably, he sneaked his way in. She shuddered.

Caroline was right. The truth had been clear in Bella's face – her eyes. Never could she recall that girl looking so lost and exhausted and angry all at the same time. But all children did that sort of thing, didn't they? Desperate to find a defence for her Jack, she tried to postpone the thought that other children stopped, but he hadn't. It didn't work.

She loved him – perhaps too much. Could you love someone too much? True, she'd never liked him when he was drunk, which happened more frequently lately. When he was drunk, he became like Hector – charming and bullying and only listening to his own voice, all at the same time. Wanting exactly what he wanted *now*. She'd hoped that as he grew up the charming, gentle side of him she'd seen so often as a child would dominate, but somehow lately it had dissolved—

Bang! She squealed and her heart jumped as a black shape battered the passenger window. She wasn't on a double yellow, was she? She pressed the button, and the window dropped a little, enough to see the top of Caroline's face peering in. 'Thought you might like company.'

That was the last thing she needed right now, but politeness always ruled, so she leaned across and opened the door to allow the PVC mack and Caroline to squeak in beside her.

'Are you OK?' Caroline was being nice to her. She felt her eyes brimming over.

'What do you think?' Surprised by her aggressive tone of voice, Esme put her arm on Caroline's slippery sleeve. 'Sorry. A lot to take in.'

'I bet.'

'I can see she's telling the truth. I don't know – don't want to know – but it sounds grim and you know the worst part?'

'What?'

'I shouldn't be saying it out loud but... but I fear Jack couldn't give a damn.'

She felt herself unable to stop herself welling up, swallowed and tried to force it down. She failed. Tears coursed down her cheeks and dripped onto her trousers. She found some old tissues in the side pocket of the door and blew her nose. 'Sorry.'

'Don't be silly. You don't need to apologise. It wasn't your fault.'

'Wasn't it?' Blowing her nose appeared to help control it, so she found a less grubby tissue and tried again. 'If I'd been a proper mother, I'd have noticed and could have stopped it.'

'What Jack did was wrong, very wrong, but whatever he's done isn't your fault. You can't blame yourself. Working with kids all my life, I know if they're going to do something, they go and do it. That's that.'

'Do you think she'll press charges?'

'No, I don't think she wants all the fuss. Would you?'

A tiny splinter of hope arrived. 'Suppose I wouldn't.' At least they might be spared that.

They watched the rivers for a while before Esme glanced at Caroline. 'Sorry, I shouldn't have come.'

'No, you shouldn't.' A pause. 'But I can understand why you did.'

'Will you tell Bella how sorry I am about Jack, her mother and... and for upsetting her even more?' They observed the rivulets drying up as the rain appeared to be stopping and no longer battering the roof of the car. 'Saying it out loud like that, it's quite a list. What a mess!'

'Sure is.' Caroline opened the door and swivelled so her feet were on the kerb. Before climbing out, she twisted back towards Esme. 'Whatever's been going on in your house, you need to sort it. If you know anything, I'd tell someone. Steph Grant would listen and help.'

Esme felt conflicted. 'What! That "nosy woman", as Hector calls her, who always comes with that Chief Inspector?'

'That's her. And Hector doesn't need to know, does he?

Strikes me you may be in a mess I suspect isn't of your making, and you need to get out of it somehow.'

'But I know nothing to tell her.'

'Whatever. Take care driving home.'

'Thanks Caroline, and sorry.'

Caroline pulled herself out of the seat, and just when Esme thought she'd climbed out, she fell back down into the seat again and grinned at her. 'Steph's our blood group, you know.'

How long was it since she'd heard those words? It took Esme back to her twenties when she'd first arrived in Suffolk. The three of them – she, Madeline and Caroline – had been the closest of friends. The sort of friends you only find a few times in your life, and Caroline had just used one of their codes to decide if someone was worth bothering with. What had happened? Why had she let Caroline go? But then, she didn't see many of her old friends now. Hector hadn't got on with them, had he?

'Our blood group, eh? Is that right?' She grinned at Caroline, who appeared to be on the edge of forgiving her.

'Yes, you ought to give her a chance.' Caroline had resumed her seat in the car properly and both faced out of the front windscreen.

'Only seen her with that man from the police. Not much to her, I thought...' Not wanting to alienate Caroline's attempt at re-establishing contact, she added. 'But she could well be different by herself and... if you approve of her...'

'That's because he's the boss when they're on police work, but get her alone and she's like us.'

'Like we were, you mean? I'm not sure what happened to the woman you knew.'

'We've all changed, had to... We've grown up.'

'You haven't, though, have you?'

Caroline said nothing. Esme said nothing. They sat and reflected on the years that saw them drift apart.

'It wasn't really Hector, you know.'

'No?'

'It all became so serious and not such fun any more. There was more to do at the Hall to keep things going. We always seemed to chase more and more income to pay for the roof, the boiler – the basics.'

'Really?'

'I suppose when I wasn't with Hector or Jack, my yoga and meditation training and classes took over my life. The Hall became the centre. I didn't have time for anything or anyone else.'

Shifting in her seat, Caroline glanced at her. 'Hector seems to have preserved his own life rather well, though, hasn't he?'

Esme felt the need to defend Hector but stopped herself. Recognising there was some truth in what Caroline had said, she said nothing. She'd been the one who'd lost her group of friends, lost touch with her family, while he'd kept his younger life somehow. She'd assumed that was the price of marriage and motherhood.

'Madeline kept her life, despite Bella and her teaching.' Where was Caroline going with this? 'Did you see much of her?'

Esme thought. 'Naturally, at the weekly dinners – but she was so busy with that school – she and Hector were always discussing some strategy or other. He spent hours with her.' There, she'd said it. 'Did you see much of Madeline, then?'

'We'd meet regularly for coffee at The Two Magpies or for a walk along Blackshore or Dunwich beach. I suppose once a month or so.'

'I didn't know that.' Esme let this sink in. A shot of jealousy ran through her. How come she'd been excluded? 'Did she talk about the Hall?'

'Sometimes.'

'Me?'

'Sometimes... But you know... I wasn't shocked to hear she'd died. I think she saw it coming.'

CHAPTER THIRTY-THREE

Esme parked her car, although she couldn't remember driving it to the Hall from Caroline's and sat re-playing the conversations for about thirty minutes. She couldn't face Jack or Hector after what Bella and Caroline had told her.

Caroline, as usual, had worked her spell, and she wondered why they'd drifted apart. They'd been such firm friends, the three of them revelling in each other's company and making the most ordinary things extraordinary. She remembered feeling her best self when she was with them both. Why had it stopped? It wasn't a sudden decision, or even a decision at all – perhaps it was when she'd had Jack and her social life shrank. But then, Madeline had Bella and still maintained her friendship with Caroline.

Of course, Hector had never got on well with Caroline and she'd stopped coming to parties and dinners. Again, it wasn't as fixed as that, but now, thinking back, that's what had happened. It had happened slowly – opportunities to see Caroline had simply disappeared, hadn't they?

No. Hector hadn't wanted her to see Caroline, and always

found something else they had to do or somewhere they had to be whenever she tried to arrange a visit. Why hadn't she seen Caroline by herself? Hector organised their social diary, and they had so many demands on their time, didn't they?

She shivered. She couldn't sit out here all night, could she? Oh, if only the heat of that first week in May would return. It had been grey and rainy for days. Taking a deep breath, she entered the Hall and made it to the kitchen without meeting anyone.

Warm in her seat by the Aga, Middleton purring on her lap and a chamomile tea calming her down, she shuffled off her shoes and concentrated on taking slow breaths. The cat's rhythmic purr soothed her as she thought about what to do next. Nothing, and see what happened? Somewhere she'd read that the fluttering of a butterfly's wing on one continent could start a hurricane on another. Maybe now was the time to—The door crashed open as usual and Jack stood in the doorway holding onto the door frame.

'Oops! It slipped.'

He hesitated before stepping into the kitchen, as if each step had to be planned and risk-assessed before taking it. Her mind switched back to when he was a toddler and made similar jerky attempts at walking. Happier, lighter times when she and Hector would claim, '*Your* son needs his nappy changing' or 'Now look what *your* son is doing'. Then they had shared him and delighted in each new stage of his development. Now a young adult, he was a mini-Hector all right.

Jack stumbled towards her, juddering her chair and scaring Middleton off her lap. His claws scratched her leg through her grey linen trousers. 'Ouch!'

'Mumsy, make me a cup, will you?'

'And the magic word?'

'Abracadabra?'

Once, that was charming. Now it got up her nose. 'Try please?'

Jack frowned, clearly confused by her curt tone. 'Right then... er... please.'

Middleton jumped up and re-settled himself on her lap. About to push him off again, she changed her mind and sat back as Jack plonked himself in the chair opposite.

'Well? Per-lease, Mumsie... Per-lease darling Mumsie.' His mocking tone was really starting to make her angry.

'Jack, the kettle is over there. Press the red switch on the back. Tea bags in the red tin. Mugs on the shelf above.'

Taken aback, he frowned, then staggered towards the kettle to do it himself, making as much clatter and fuss as he could. She closed her eyes to shut him out.

Aware of him returning to his seat when he nudged her foot, she opened her eyes and breathed in solid alcohol. No way would he be sober for his history exam tomorrow.

'What's wrong?'

'What do you think is wrong?'

He shook his head and shrugged his shoulders, which made his tea slurp over the edge of the mug and onto his jeans. He didn't notice.

'Earlier this evening I saw Bella – how was it you described her? Your friend with benefits?'

'Well done, Mums, now you're sounding really cool.' He grinned at her, then burped. More boozy breath – how disgusting.

'And who got the benefits exactly? You or her?'

'Both, of course.'

She stared at him, feeling only disgust – how had he got

here?' 'It would appear, Jack, that was not how it worked. Bella feels she's been abused by you for most of her life.'

His head was buried in the wide brim of the mug, avoiding her penetrating stare.

'Well?'

'Well, what? She's lying.'

A dark shadow moved across the hearth. 'Who's lying?'

Looming above them both, Hector waited for one of them to give him an answer. Not again! Why did he always have to slink in at the worst moments? Jack responded to the challenge first.

'That Steph Grant woman who spies on us for the police. You know she lies. We all know she lies. You said so, Father.' Jack was such a creep. She was ashamed of him for not standing up to Hector, but then, she wasn't much better, was she?

About to open her mouth, a warning shot from Hector made her remain silent. 'That's enough. We must all move on from that unfortunate incident. I do not want it mentioned again – understood?'

'Yes, Father. Well, I should be off to blanket fair. Exam tomorrow, you know.'

His little boy voice made Esme nauseous.

'I think it's time we were all tucked up in our beds, don't you?' Hector lifted the cat off her lap and dumped it on the floor, ignoring its cross meow, then took Esme's mug and placed it on the table. 'Come along, my darling.'

Grasping her elbow, he urged her out of her chair and, putting his arm around her shoulders, led her out of the kitchen door, up the stairs and into their bedroom. Esme shuddered.

CHAPTER THIRTY-FOUR

STEPH WAS LOOKING FORWARD to their first supper outside on her new garden furniture. The terrace, sunny most of the day, also captured the last of the sun's rays and was perfect for late suppers. She'd bought salmon steaks on the way home and was preparing a salad and boiling some local new potatoes to go with them when Hale arrived looking as shattered as she felt.

'What a day!'

'Ditto!'

'I've been looking forward to a cold beer, supper and a long, long chat with you!' He strode across, put his arms around her and kissed her lips passionately. Was he suggesting they should postpone supper for a while? As he released her and went to the fridge for a beer, his phone rang. They both knew what was coming and stared at it resentfully, willing it to stop.

Hale picked it up. 'Yes... of course.... Be right over. About ten minutes.' He put his arm around her shoulders, and she stopped dressing the salad. 'It's OK. You don't need to come.'

'Where?'

'Glebe Hall. Another incident.'

'What! What is going on at that place? Wait, no, I'll come.' She stacked supper in the fridge, out of Derek's reach, and pulled her jacket off the hook by the door as she dashed out after Hale.

'Apparently it's a young man – tried to hang himself.' He started the car.

'Oh no! Don't say that! Did they say who? Surely not Jack?' Now really concerned in case they'd had something to do with it, she panicked, horrified. Surely it couldn't be? He seemed to have an ironclad ego, but you never knew with kids that age. One minute they were invincible, the next collapsed in a heap.

With Steph gripping the door handle and her brake foot firmly on the floor, Hale threw the car around corners as they drove through Oakwood High Street towards Southwold. He overtook a large four-by-four, narrowly missing a tractor on the other side of the road.

'That was close!' Steph heard herself squeaking.

'Not at all – we had masses of space.' Despite his apparent confidence, he slowed as they got close to the thirty miles an hour zone.

Passing the crinkley-crankley wall at speed, they reached the gates to find they had joined the end of a procession, comprising two police cars. Once again, a man stood at the gate, directing them, but this time not the gardener, but Jon Henderson flapping his hand towards the barns beyond the house. They sped around the house and drew up beside an ambulance slewed across the entrance of a large shed.

They entered a barn full of garden machinery, tools and bags of compost. Two sit-on mowers, a small tractor and trailers for spraying pesticide, were tidily parked and surrounded by walls of tools, neatly hung inside their painted shapes on the wall. All appeared ordered and well-cared for.

Then at the far end of the barn, she saw him, a young lad laid out on the earth floor, two paramedics administrating CPR to revive him. A rope, cut above the knot, had been removed and lay on the floor bedside him; the rest of the rope dangled from a beam and was tied around the stout legs of a workbench. Eerily, it swung a little in the breeze. There was no kicked away stool or chair, and she assumed he must have jumped from the trailer beside him. She could see his face – it wasn't Jack, but Graham.

The man doubled up, crying and being comforted by Hector must be Graham's father, the gardener she recognised from the gates when they first came to the fire. Picking up a stool from beneath the workbench, she pushed it behind him and helped him to sit.

He leaned against her, and she put her arm around him to offer him physical and emotional support. Hardly blinking, his eyes stuck on his son, being given CPR by the paramedics. The tall one shook his head towards his partner, and they stood back. It had been too late.

'No! No!' Graham's father howled.

For the first time since they'd arrived, there was no noise, no movement as everyone froze and stared at the empty body on the dirt floor. She'd hardly known Graham but felt anger and deep sadness at the loss of this young life. Whatever could have affected him so much that he had to stop living? This was dreadful. He appeared thoughtful and loving towards Bella... Oh! Bella! That poor girl. As if losing her mother wasn't bad enough, now to lose Graham too...

A fluttering on the edge of her vision was Esme arriving with a mug of something, which she handed to the horrified man beside her. At first, he appeared not to know what to do with it and stared up at her, puzzled. She stroked his arm. 'Tea, Dan. Try to drink it if you can.'

He sipped it as Esme watched and standing in front of him, took it from his shaking hands between mouthfuls. Clearly, she hoped to block his view of his son's body, but he peered around her, his eyes transfixed by the appalling sight. Once he finished his tea, Esme moved to his side and, putting her hand under his elbow, gently helped him to stand.

'Come on, Dan, let's go to the house. You don't want to see this. Graham wouldn't have wanted you to.'

Too weak and shocked to protest, he allowed Esme to lead him from the barn. Through the wide barn doors, Steph watched Dan and Esme's slow progress back to the house and turned to see Hector deep in conversation with Hale, who was insisting they move further away from the body.

Hale signalled she should join them as they ducked beneath the blue and white plastic police incident tape, now fixed around the entrance to the barn, which was guarded by a police officer with a clipboard. It would be a couple of hours before the SOCOs arrived.

They headed to the house and once again sat on the Chesterfields, this time with a shocked Dan Andrews clinging to Esme's hand. Hector sat opposite, so Hale joined him while Steph perched at the other side of the square.

'Mr Andrews, I'm so very sorry, but I need to ask you a few questions. Can you tell me what happened here today?'

'I say! Can't you leave the poor man alone for a while? He's just found his son hanging from a beam in his workshop. This is not appropriate or acceptable.'

'Mr Percy, I know it appears hard, but I have my job to do and I suggest that you and Mrs Percy leave and let me get on with it. And a member of my team will be along to take DNA samples from all of your residents and staff for elimination purposes.'

For once, Hector didn't answer, but huffily stood and bustled out of the room as noisily as possible. Esme, following, stopped and spoke to Steph. 'I shall be in the kitchen. Please let me know if Dan needs anything.'

Steph acknowledged her offer with a smile, then turned to Hale and Dan. As the door clicked shut, she heard Dan whisper, 'Graham didn't do it – I know it – he wouldn't. Someone did it to him.'

CHAPTER THIRTY-FIVE

HALE PERSUADED Dan Andrews that he would be more comfortable in his own home and drove him there. In shock, Dan was not aware what was going on, and when they arrived at his traditional fisherman's cottage in Southwold, he automatically took them into the sitting room where they sat in silence, facing the grey man as he slumped in his gardening clothes and muddy boots by the unlit wood burner. It had been a warm day, but Dan was shaking, his lips blue.

Steph found the kitchen and made them all tea, bringing back a sheepskin coat she found on a hook by the back door, which she laid over Dan's legs. He didn't appear to notice. While he was sipping his tea and staring at nothing, Hale phoned the Family Liaison Co-ordinator to arrange for a Family Liaison Officer to come to the cottage.

'Do you have anyone we could call for you?' Steph took the mug off him as he'd gestured he'd had enough.

'My daughter, Graham's sister, Zoe, lives in Halesworth. She'll come. Number on the list by the phone.'

Steph went out to the kitchen again, where she'd seen the

phone stuck on the wall with a list of numbers beside it. She found a Zoe Finch on the list and dialled the number. Luckily, the phone was answered quickly, and Steph explained as briefly as possible that her brother had been involved in an incident and her father had asked for her. Steph didn't mention suicide and was as vague as possible, trying not to alarm her.

When she returned to the sitting room, she heard Dan repeating what he'd said at Glebe Hall. 'He wouldn't have... you know...'

Graham's father made little rocking movements as he sat by the hearth, shaking his head, evidently not yet sure how he'd got there or what had happened. Hale sat on the sofa to his right; being there, but not intruding. Steph knew he would wait until the initial shock had retreated a little before trying to get clues as to what had happened.

'More tea? Anything else?' Steph held out the mug towards Dan, ready to make more if he would drink it.

'No thanks, pet.'

Northern then. His accent had all but disappeared until that word, 'pet'.

'Yorkshire?'

A slight smile, as he moved back into his life for a moment and out of this nightmare. 'Newcastle, born and bred.'

'Newcastle to Glebe Hall – I bet there's a story there.'

'There is that. The wife came from Suffolk. Met on a gardening course down here and I never went back.' His eyes focused on a point in the distance, apparently drifting off, far away into his memories.

'She was a gardener too, then?'

'That she was. Both got jobs at the Hall and loved it. She died two years back, cancer. Gardens there have never regained their colour since she left.'

'Sorry to hear that.'

'Thank you... and now Graham...' He closed his eyes. Hale and Steph sat on the sofa, but he had retreated from them. They let him sit.

The doorbell rang, and Hale leaped up to answer it. Dan didn't appear to hear it, or didn't want to, as he remained still, eyes closed. Steph could hear Hale explaining all to Zoe, going into more of the details, now she was here and safe.

Steph knew that for Dan, this room and everything else would never look quite the same again. Yes, the colour would return eventually, but it would always be muted without the person who made it special for him. Dan appeared to have lived the days without his wife, as the cared-for house witnessed, but losing his son would push him down so much further.

Zoe rushed over to her father and threw herself on the floor before him, wrapping her arms around his knees and looking up intently into his face. 'Dad... Dad... it's me, I'm here. Dad?' The last word, louder, made him open his eyes, and his face softened.

'Zoe, pet... Graham... dreadful... So dreadful.'

'I know, Dad, I'm so sorry.'

'He was in the barn. Went to get some hedge loppers to trim that box hedge – you know the one by the steps where they take the photos? Wedding tomorrow, you see.'

'Yes?' Zoe reached out, took his hand and held it, stroking it softly.

'He didn't come back... I was vexed, so vexed. Thought he'd sloped off for a tea or met that Jack and they were gassing. All that time he was... If I'd gone sooner, I could have... If only I'd gone...'

'You can't know that, Dad.'

'By the time I got there, I was so angry and there he was... on that rope... the rope we used to keep people off the grass when we've seeded it... you know.'

Zoe held his hand tight as the awfulness of Graham's death seeped into her brain and she, too, allowed the tears to dribble down her face, unnoticed.

'Why, Zoe? He had everything to live for, a place at that Cambridge college, a lovely girl – oh no! Bella! I must tell her!' Struggling to take action, he tried to stand, but fell back down. 'Oh! Bella!'

'Don't worry. I know her well and we'll tell her and make sure she's looked after.' Steph's words appeared to settle him.

'Thanks, pet.' He placed his hand on top of Zoe's. 'Graham wasn't depressed, was he?'

Zoe shook her head. 'No, Dad, he wasn't.'

'Had everything to live for... Great future... so why?'

'Don't know, Dad. The police will find out.' Squirming round, she looked at Hale, who nodded.

'We'll leave you in peace, but before we go, a couple of questions. Mr Andrews, did you see anyone else near the barn when you went back?'

'No.'

'Has Graham acted strangely over the last few weeks?'

'No, he's been himself... just himself.'

'Thanks. Would you mind if we went up to his room, please? I'll need to take his computer and his phone. What's on them may answer some of your questions.'

Always difficult this one, Steph knew. Zoe started to get up. Hale held up his hand to stop her. 'No, don't you worry. Just tell us where it is; you stay with your father.'

'Top of the stairs, door to the right.'

'Thank you.'

Steph followed Hale out of the sitting room, into the hall and up the steep stairs to Graham's room. The steps were so narrow – the fishermen must have had tiny feet when the cottage was built. As they opened the door, they were hit by an unexpected smell; not the usual smelly socks typical of boys' rooms, but the heady perfume of lilies. Steph chided herself for her stereotyping, but immediately justified it in the light of her experience of so many of these searches.

A carefully made bed, with spotless white duvet and pillows, beside a pine bedside table on which was a black angle poise lamp above a small pile of novels – Conrad, Hemingway, a Japanese author she didn't recognise. The bookcase continued the classics as well as some modern novels and a line of poetry books. Steph knew he'd been a star at history, but it looked as if Graham had also been into literature. A tidy desk held a MacBook Air and charger, which they unplugged and picked up.

'Thoughtful, organised chap from this room. Not someone to take reckless action, I'd have thought.' Hale opened a desk draw with stationery supplies arranged in strict lines inside.

Steph nodded. 'And look at those lilies' She pointed to the side of the desk. 'Green fingers too. I can never get them to look like that.' The pot of lilies was magnificent – vibrant pale pink trumpets all at the same stage and height, in a perfectly matched pale pink planter, giving off a deep musky perfume.

'I remember him from college. A lovely boy. He didn't say much, but was always polite, calm and reflective. As you say, not erratic, but thoughtful.' She bent down to breathe in the powerful perfume of the flowers. 'Unusual candidate for a suicide... but then, is there a usual?'

They paused, making a final scan of the room. 'Hang on a moment, there's something there.' Steph returned to the desk and picked up the plant pot; underneath the plate was a copy of *Rough Guide to South America* with the corner of a piece of paper poking out. She pulled it out and opened it.

'What is it?'

'Dramatic stuff! Look at this.' Hale peered over her shoulder. 'It's a print-out of an e-ticket for him and Bella. It appears they were going to South America together immediately after Bella's A Levels!'

CHAPTER THIRTY-SIX

STEPH BROUGHT a bottle of Pinot Noir and glasses to the table, where Hale was opening a file of papers. She had recently found a local vineyard and bought several bottles of the delicious red and some exquisite pink fizz.

'Whatever's going on at that place?' She opened the bottle to let it breathe.

Hale raised his eyebrows. 'If only we could find out! Anyway, this stuff may give us more background.'

He pulled out a few sheets of paper.

'Right. I've had the tech chaps get a production order and they've got into Graham's phone and printed off WhatsApps between him and Bella. Let's see what they tell us. They're still working on getting into his computer.'

He slid the papers between them so Steph could see. 'OK. Off we go. At least with WhatsApp it's shorter and quicker.' He pointed to the top of the page. 'They've added the names, although they're all between Bella and Graham. And they've given us the relevant ones – they start just after that Open Day.'

'Hang on – he wants to go out.' Steph opened the door, and Derek dashed out to chase some invader or other.

Tuesday 4 May

From: Bella Henderson 22.05
Sorry. Didn't mean to go weird. Can't tell you what's wrong.
Stuff going on at GH is tough. Don't know what to do. Will tell
all soon. XXX

From: Graham Andrews 22.08.
Must be grim. Talk to your mum or dad? Anyone at GH?

From Bella 22.12.
No. Rows all the time. Without you I'd be lost. Did the history
revision!!

From Graham 22.15
See you tomorrow

From Bella 22.40.
Can't sleep. Rowing downstairs too noisy. Turned up iPod – no
good. Wish I could stay with you?????? XXXXXXXXX

From Graham 22.43.
Sorry. NO way Dad would allow

From Bella 22.51.
Have to get away – cant stand it much longer. Why wont he
fuck off? XXX

From Graham 23.01.
I'll come to college and sort him

From Bella 23.05.
Don't!!!! Make it worse. PLEASE DONT xxx

From Graham 23.07.
Needs to be stopped

From Bella 23.11
Dont know how. Impossible. Feel trapped. But dont do anything PLEASE xxx

From Graham 23.15.
Only a few weeks til after exams

From Bella 23.17.
Can't wait XXXXX

From Graham 23.18.
Hold on

From Bella 23.24.
Can we do like we said?

From Graham 23.29.
You need to sort it. Tell police?

From Bella 23.35.
Wouldn't believe me.

From Graham 23.38
Dont know that

From Bella 23.45.
Hes clever. Never gets caught

Wednesday 5 May

From Bella 19.49
Need to talk. Desperate. Mum had accident. Where are you?
Need you.

From Graham 20.50
No battery. Sorry. Will phone 5 mins

Friday 7 May

From Bella 19.50
Theyre covering something up. Horrific. Have gone to stay with
Caroline xxx

Hale replaced the sheet in the file and shut it.

'Is that it?' Steph picked up the last page and turned it over to check there were no more messages.

'Yes, I'm afraid so. They stop after that. Either he deleted them, or they relied on meeting, phone calls or emails. Won't know until they get to them.'

'Well, all this shows is that they were close, and she must have told him everything – shame we still don't know what that was.'

'If they were planning to go to Peru, they'd have to be careful.' Steph reached for the bottle, sniffed it and confirming her initial judgement at the tasting, filled their glasses with the deep blackcurrant-coloured wine.

Taking a sip, Hale examined his glass against the light, 'Umm. Good stuff... and it's local, you say?'

'Pleased you like it.'

Hale took another sip. 'I think we'll visit Bella again; tell her we've got these and see if she'll open up.'

'Not much to go on. I wonder if she's told Caroline? Perhaps we could—'

Hale's phone pinged, and he glared at it. 'Now what? Seems as if someone else is working late.' In a moment, his face was transformed. 'Great! Dave's got into Graham's computer and sent me a folder, he says here.'

'That's dedication.'

'One of the good ones. Gets into the computer and then sorts through the emails and folders – mint!'

The adrenaline rush energised Hale, as he pulled his laptop out of its bag and set it up on the table. 'Typical Dave. Let's see what he's found. Plug this in, will you?'

Steph plugged in the laptop on her side of the table, moved her chair, and joined him in front of the screen. Hale was now in dynamic mode once again. It was incredible how the hope of a clue motivated him.

'Amazing guy, Dave. He'll work on trying to crack a code or password until late at night or the early hours of the morning. Says he can't sleep when he's trying to do it, so may as well stay up and keep working on it.' Opening his emails, he clicked on the latest. 'Right, let's hope we have something here that helps.'

Hale clicked on the attached folder, and a sound file appeared. 'Ah! At last. Now, just hope this is what we need.'

After some buzzing and some breathing, they could hear Bella's voice, a little above a whisper.

'Graham? Sorry... about this evening. I shouldn't have lost it but I ... I couldn't tell you about it... not while... while you were there. Not sure I can even now... (long pause, sniffling, blowing nose, deep breath) *It's just that, since we've – you know – I've realised what's been... been going on. Not sure where to start.* (pause) *He and I've always been together and... well, you know... but it sort of continued and he told me it was our secret and no-one else must know. I told him to stop, but he turned nasty and said that if I said anything he'd tell Mum and Dad, it was me who wanted it and he'd tell everyone I was a... you know... It wasn't me, honestly... honestly it wasn't. It was him all the time, and I want it to stop. Sorry about tonight... sorry. If you don't want to see me again, I'll understand.* (noise of her blowing her nose then sighing) *This is rubbish. I'll try an email.*

Steph sat back, stretching her elbows back behind her after crouching over the computer screen. 'Is that all? Is it dated?'

'Yes. 28th April.'

'Doesn't give us much to go on.'

'But even this tells us she told Graham and he knew about Jack's abuse.' Hale looked back at the WhatsApp messages in the light of the sound file.

Steph got up, tipped some peanuts in a bowl and brought them over to the table. 'That explains some of Graham's comments on the WhatsApp messages and why he wants to come into college to sort Jack.'

Hale opened another file. 'Another email by the look of it – maybe this will be the one telling him about the abuse.'

From: Bella Henderson
Sent: Friday 7th May 19.05 pm
To: Graham Andrews
Subject: GH

Graham – something dreadful has happened. Can't stay here now, I can't – nothing I can do to stop all this. I've got to get out.

Hector was here with Dad when I got home from college, and I could hear them shouting. After he left, Dad came to my room. Think he'd been crying. Told me to save him, to save our home, I had to agree to marry Jack!!!! He said there was no other way. Said we'd been friends since we were children and we'd be good together.

He's gone mad. Been in a dreadful state since Mum. Told him I'd go to uni and he could move out and we didn't need to live there any more. Whatever, I wouldn't marry that little shit. He wouldn't shut up – said it was the best thing for both of us and Mum would have wanted it.

I lost it and told him no way would I marry that fucking bastard. He shouted – he's never shouted like that before. He slapped me. Slapped me across the face. How could my Dad do that? He was so angry. Couldn't believe what he'd done – he hit me.

I'm going to Caroline's — she'll help — not staying here. Will phone you from hers. Don't want to talk yet and need to get stuff together. I'll send a WhatsApp in case you're out.
Bella XXXXXXXXXXXXXXXXXX

From: Graham Andrews
Sent: 7th May 20.08
To: Bella Henderson
Subject: GH

What?????!!! That's medieval!!! They can't force you to marry anyone. It's the twentieth, not the twelfth century!!!!! THINK BELLA. How would they do it? No way could they force you to go through it. Get real. It won't happen. Don't panic. We'll work something out. I've got an idea. I'll talk to Hector and your Dad. I'll sort it out.

Graham
XXXXXXX

Steph sat back and pushed the peanuts over to Hale

Hale picked up a handful. 'That's it for this file. There's a note at the bottom from Dave to say they're the relevant ones. I can see the rest tomorrow – he says they're the usual teenage stuff – nothing to do with what's happened at the Hall.'

'At least we know why she's at Caroline's.' Derek was pawing at the back door; she got up to let him in and save the paint on her back door from his impatient scratching.

'Do you think Caroline knows—'

'About the forced marriage? Shouldn't think so. She'd have said.' Steph shut the door and returned to her seat, moving her chair so she could face Hale.

'Caroline's not always told us everything though, has she?' Hale winced and lifted his hands in front of his face, clearly protecting himself from a potential attack.

'OK. I'll ask her tomorrow. But more important is that final line where Graham says he's got an idea. I wonder if he did anything?'

Hale wiggled the mouse and returned to Dave's email. 'Hang on, there's another file here. Maybe that will tell us more.'

CHAPTER THIRTY-SEVEN

CLICKING on the file brought up a series of emails. 'Strange – thought these would be Bella and Graham. They're not – they're between Luke and Graham.'

Steph leaned towards the screen again. 'What? Why would they be exchanging emails?'

'Let's see, shall we?' Hale enlarged the page. 'Obviously, Dave thought they were worth sending, and he's got a good eye.'

They scanned the first page, which comprised one liners making appointments for meeting up.

'What would they need to meet about?' Steph pointed to the top of the screen. 'If Dave has included them all, it seems they started last September. Before we read them all, let's see how far they go.'

Hale whizzed through about ten pages of the small font until he reached the final email from Luke to Graham. 'That's dated the day before he died and... in the last one – here – see? They planned to meet about the time he died.'

'Whatever was going on?'

Hale scrolled back to the start of the emails. As he did, they noticed there was a pattern. Luke initiated an exchange. His emails were long and got longer as the months passed, while Graham's were short – often only a couple of lines agreeing the time to meet.

From: Luke Roy
Sent: 4th September
To: Graham Andrews
Subject: Meeting

Dear Graham,

I enjoyed our chat in the rose garden the other day – you know an awful lot about roses – much more than I do. Would you be able to pop over and look at the roses outside the office door, please? I'd value your opinion as I suspect they may be dying – some bug seems to have turned their leaves a bronze colour. I shall be there at the end of play– 5.30 tomorrow?

Best wishes,

Luke

From: Graham Andrews
Sent 4th September
To: Luke Roy
Subject: Meeting

Dear Luke,

No problem. See you then.

Graham

From: Luke Roy
Sent: 4th September
To: Graham Andrews
Subject: Meeting

Dear Graham,

Thank you so much for your advice. Do you think you could get the chemical you mentioned earlier and come over and treat them tomorrow, same time? I'd be so grateful.

Best wishes

Luke

From: Graham Andrews
Sent 4th September
To: Luke Roy
Subject: Meeting

That's fine – see you tomorrow, Luke

BW

Graham

'Do they go on for ten pages about Graham visiting the roses? Surely not in the winter?'

'I'll move on a bit.' Hale wiggled the mouse.

'And why did he keep asking Graham to help? It's his

father who is the horticultural expert. Graham's just the muscle, isn't he?'

'You said it!'

He moved to page three, and they scanned the emails in which Luke continued to arrange visits for the problems with the garden around the office.

Steph threw a bone-shaped treat to a restless Derek and returned to scan the screen. 'Interesting that it's the office rather than the flower beds around his home!'

Hale pointed to an email that had moved up the screen. 'There – now it looks as if Luke has moved on from roses to giving him coaching sessions.'

'Coaching? On what?'

'Economics, I think. Graham says here that Luke's explanation of some economic theory in a book on his Cambridge reading list has been really helpful, and if he brought over one of the other ones, please could he explain it?'

Steph was puzzled. 'But he was a star at history. I thought he was going to do that.'

'From these emails, it appears a part of his course is economic history and he wants to get ahead.'

'How often did they meet?'

Hale whizzed through a couple of screens of emails. 'Looks like once – sometimes twice a week from these in December to January and always in the office, not the west wing.'

'It feels a little like something's going on here – or is that my suspicious mind?'

'Not at all. I was thinking precisely the same thing. Look.' Hale pointed to the longer emails at the end of the series and scanned them. Steph peered over his shoulder as he pointed to the screen. 'Luke's emails get longer with each month and flatter Graham's intellect and his ability to pick up difficult concepts quickly.'

Steph moved her finger down to a message at the bottom of Hale's screen. 'And in this one, he even suggests popping over to Cambridge when Graham starts his course to help him if he gets stuck on anything.'

Hale read the email at which Steph was pointing. 'Really? How can Graham be involved with Luke one minute and planning to go to South America with Bella the next?'

Amazed and a little disappointed at this latest revelation, Steph sighed and picked at the peanuts. 'I find it difficult to believe it of either of them. From what I've seen, Luke is committed to Zac and Graham was obviously crazy about Bella. Maybe there was nothing more to it than the economics coaching?'

Hale pointed again to the screen. 'Whatever was going on I think it was one sided. Look at Graham's responses. They're transactional – time and the topic and thank you so much for helping in a couple of lines, while Luke becomes more fulsome and makes more personal comments about Graham.'

Steph sat back, reflecting on what Hale had said and the emails she'd read. 'So, do you think Luke was grooming Graham while Graham was saving Bella from being abused by Jack? What a mess!'

'From the tone of these emails, it certainly looks like it.'

Hale's phone cut into their conversation, and he dashed to his coat pocket to fish it out.

'Hale here... You're working late... I see... Are you sure? I'll come in... Yes, thanks.'

Placing the phone on the table, Hale sighed. 'That was the pathologist. It doesn't look as if Graham's death was suicide – it appears he'd been in a fight and had a whopping bump on the head.'

'Not another one!'

'Not enough to kill him, but to knock him unconscious. There are also signs of a ligature mark around his neck – not made by the rope. They think he was hanged to make it look like suicide, but they're sure he was murdered.'

'You going in?'

'Yes. Need to get the ball rolling.'

Steph looked at his almost full glass of wine. 'You OK to drive?'

'Luckily, yes.' Hale pushed the wine glass away from him.

Steph checked her watch. Nine forty. She went over to the fire and fiddled with a brass tap beside the hearth and turned it on. The gas flames flickered from green to orange as they heated up the pretend logs. Replacing the cork back in the bottle, she picked up her glass and moved to the armchair by the fire, where Derek immediately joined her, stretching out at her feet. 'Umm, that's better. I'm cold. Mad country this. We go from salad to soup in a day.'

Hale stepped over Derek, checked the mantelpiece and scanned the room as if he'd lost something. 'If the pathologist's right, who on earth would want to kill Graham?'

'Suppose he talked to Jon or Hector or even Zac? That could give any of them a motive.' Steph found a dog treat in her pocket and threw it to Derek – he caught it in his mouth.

'Maybe.' Hale frowned, swivelling on his feet and looking around the room.

'Or perhaps Graham knew something about how Madeline died and Jon needed to silence him... Or found out that Bella was going to run away with Graham, so killed him to stop them going?'

'Second idea's more plausible. Hector?' Hale frowned.

'More difficult to find a motive for him, however much I don't like him. But there's the suggestion of him getting in the way of the forced marriage, or if Graham had found out about Madeline's death, he could have done it for the same reason... Not too helpful...'

The gentle hissing of the gas fire punctuated their silence. Steph turned down the flames a little, while Hale prowled around the room searching for something.

'Lost something?'

'Keys. I thought I'd put them in that bowl.' He pointed to the turquoise bowl on the table inside the door where they usually left their keys. Only her set was visible.

He checked the desk in the bay window. 'Esme's not strong enough, but I'm sure she'd do anything to protect Jack.'

'Jack – what about Jack?' Steph pulled herself out of her chair and went into the kitchen, picked up the missing keys from beside the hob and threw them across the room.

'Thanks.' Having caught his keys, he checked he'd got his phone and went to the door. 'Jack's in trouble and may be scared about more coming out about his abuse of Bella, or he may be insanely jealous and want to get rid of his rival.'

'Possible. Don't think he's got the bottle.' As she was by the dog food cupboard, she gave Derek another bone-shaped biscuit, which he inhaled, then sat at her feet in adoration and hope. 'And now we have those emails from Luke. Maybe he groomed Graham, and all was well until he made a move and Graham rejected him, so Luke needed him out of the way. Nothing about Zac in those emails – maybe Graham threatened to tell him. That would give Luke a motive, wouldn't it?'

'Perhaps. Must go.' He didn't move but stared into the flames. Clearly, Hale would rather sit by the fire.

He sighed. He looked exhausted. 'No easy answer to any of this, is there? We don't know what happened to Madeline and now we don't know who had a motive to kill Graham.'

'And of course, as strange as it may seem, Madeline's and Graham's murders may not be linked. Just coincidental – happening in the same house.'

Hale ran his hand through his hair. 'Great! Not sure where to go next. The team's working so hard but getting nowhere fast.'

He walked to the door, stopped, and turned back. 'You said it earlier. Let's talk to Caroline and Bella – I want to hear what they have to say myself and find out if Bella knew about Graham's meetings with Luke.'

'And then we visit the urbane Luke again?'

'We certainly do!' He came across the room and kissed her, caressing her back. 'Don't wait up.'

Looking up into his eyes, her hands on his shoulders, she grinned. 'Perhaps there'll be something worth waiting up for!'

CHAPTER THIRTY-EIGHT

Esme woke to silence. A rare silence. Hector was no longer snoring beside her, and she felt a chilly draft where he'd thrown the covers back. It was she who was the light sleeper and wandered to the kitchen during the night, never him. Maybe he was ill.

Shuddering as her feet touched the cold wooden floor, she grabbed her dressing gown from the end of the bed and peeped through the thick floor-to-ceiling blue brocade curtains, which were interlined with blankets to keep what little heat there was inside the bedroom.

A full moon straight out of a children's book glittered in a black sky but, as she scanned the garden, a cloud blotted it out. A flash startled her, as the security light outside the barn was triggered and she saw a black shape open its doors. Convinced that the shape wasn't a burglar after their garden implements, but Hector, she pushed her feet into her Ugg boots and padded downstairs and out to the barn.

Inside the barn, a row of hanging light bulbs threw circles

of light along the centre, leaving grey patches between them. In one of them, Hector was on his knees, his hands extended as he crawled along, feeling for something. He knelt back, dusting off his hands as he moved into a pool of light. His face was thunder, and his frown lines were deeply etched into his forehead.

Esme stepped back, thinking she'd sneak out again, but she dislodged a rake, which clattered to the floor.

'So, it's you. I felt someone spying on me.'

'I wasn't spying, I was worried about you.'

'And why's that?'

He struggled up to his feet, his knees cracking, and he winced as the effort made them ache. They were both getting old.

'I said, what are you doing here?' Striding towards her, he put his hands on her shoulders, giving her a rough shake. His fingers pinched her skin.

'Ouch! That hurts.'

'And it'll hurt more if you don't tell me what you're up to!'

She dodged out of his hold and turned towards the door as if to go. Once again, he seized her shoulder, pulling her round to face him and tightening his grip.

'I woke and you weren't there, then the light went on outside the barn, so I came out and saw you on your hands and knees looking for something.' She looked up at the beam. 'That was where Graham was found, wasn't it?'

He shoved her away. 'Get back to bed. It doesn't concern you. This is none of your business.'

'What are you looking for?'

He grabbed her arm, swung her round so his face was up against hers and hissed. 'If you must know, one of Father's gold cuff links with his monogram – must have come off when I was out here giving Andrews his orders about the lawn for that last wedding.'

Roughly pushing her aside, he cleared his throat. 'Grass was too long last time and stained the bride's train. It needs to be cut shorter.'

'I see. I hope you find it.' Esme moved out of his reach and walked swiftly out of the barn. He let her go.

The security light cast a long beam across the lawn and the full moon had emerged from the clouds and showed her the way through the rose beds. She had chosen them for their scent. The palest pink St Ethelburga, with its musky scent, calmed her as she breathed in deep and closed her eyes, revelling in the perfume. She opened her eyes to touch one of the old-fashioned roses, its silk petals making delicate cushions of a rose that went back hundreds of years, maybe as far as Shakespeare or the Tudors who built the Hall. Her heartbeat slowed.

She knew he was lying. What was he doing there? Going into the barn to talk to Andrews was beneath him. Hector never ventured among the mud and tools of the workmen but would phone and give Andrews his orders from his study, his domain.

Taking the left-hand door, she went through to the kitchen. Sleep would evade her, she was sure – a chamomile tea might help. The clock on the wall showed three thirty-five. Too early to get up, but she didn't want to return to his bed. He was angry with her for following him and would need to make a point – she knew what was coming.

Breathing in chamomile tea steam, she sat by the comfort of the Aga, warming her hands on the mug. Middleton appeared from nowhere and jumped up on her lap, purring and kneading her, obviously thrilled at this unexpected visit.

Sighing, she knew she would make the perfect picture if someone took a photograph now – a woman relaxed in the gentle light, warm in the ancient kitchen, secure in her home. Photographs can lie too.

CHAPTER THIRTY-NINE

In the car once again, driving across town to talk to Bella, Steph glanced at Hale, whose dark bags and sunken eyes revealed his exhaustion and frustration with making so little progress. They'd taken Derek, rather than leaving him in the flat, as Steph had only had time for a brisk walk around the block and at Caroline's he could chase Marlene around the garden and get exhausted.

In the car, Hale summarised the content and outcomes they hoped for from the meeting. 'Bella needs to know what we've seen on Graham's computer and his phone – that he knew about the abuse, and we know about the forced marriage and them planning to go away to South America.'

'And we need to find out if anyone else knew or if she suspected they did.' Steph checked her phone, which had just beeped. No one important. 'Also, if she knew about his meetings with Luke.'

Hale stopped at some traffic lights, tutting at the driver in front, who zoomed through the red. 'Now we know it wasn't suicide, we can ask her if she thinks anyone would have reason to kill Graham, suggest Hector and her father and see her reaction.'

'Don't forget Luke's in the frame and possibly Jack too.'

'Who isn't?' Hale drew up outside Caroline's.

Concerned that Bella would be too grief stricken to talk to them, Steph hesitated a few moments before she knocked on the door, but knew that if they were to get Graham's murderer, they had to speak to her. Caroline had agreed to the meeting but warned them that Bella was fragile.

Derek and Marlene completed the ritual sniffing with enthusiasm and bounded out to the garden. When she saw Steph and Hale, Margaret raised an eyebrow, said she felt some practice coming on, then disappeared. They all agreed that Caroline should stay and sat down in their usual places in the conservatory at the back of the house – Steph and Hale on the basket-weave armchairs and Bella beside Caroline on the sofa.

It was a sensational evening with a clear blue sky, so Caroline left the door to the garden open so that they could hear the bird song and smell the stocks that grew just outside. It also meant that they didn't have to jump up every few minutes whenever one of the dogs wanted to come in.

Although they had expected Bella to be in the depths of further grief, the reality of seeing her come in and sit opposite them was a shock and Steph asked herself whether it was fair they should be there at all. Exhausted, her eyes swollen and sunk deep in dark shadows, her hair hanging limply around her face and huddled in a blanket over her PJs, the elegant Bella had disappeared. How long would it take her to come back?

Steph, as agreed, kicked off, expressing their deep sympathy to Bella on losing Graham and promising her they would find out what had happened. Although it was painful to have to go through this when she must be feeling so low, Steph explained that they needed to ask some questions about what they'd found on Graham's computer and phone. A flush crept up from Bella's neck to her face – was she angry or embarrassed? Probably both. It was never easy when all your most intimate secrets were revealed to the police – it was like undressing in public.

'If this is all too much for you, just tell us to stop. OK?'

Bella nodded and looked up at them.

Steph pressed on quickly. 'We know you told Graham in a voice mail about the abuse by Jack. Did you ever speak to Graham about it face to face?'

'Yes... Eventually.'

'Do you know how he responded? Would he have confronted Jack?'

'I don't think so. I asked him not to. Unless it was that evening before he...' Bella's head went down, and her voice tailed off.

'We'll ask Jack about that, don't worry,' Hale intervened.

He nodded at Steph to continue. 'In one of the emails, you mentioned you felt you were being forced to marry Jack. Will you tell us about that please?' Caroline, who sat opposite Steph, stiffened and looked horrified. So, she didn't know about the forced marriage either.

'Well, you've read the emails, what else do you want to know?' Bella's voice quivered with anger. She took a deep breath. 'Hector is obsessed with Glebe Hall and his inheritance. I assume he wants to make sure that after inheritance tax, there's enough left for Jack to take over.'

'By you two marrying?'

'Exactly. If we married, it would add mine and Jack's portions of the house together and if he buys back Luke and Zac's wing, it will make sure a Percy is in total control again.'

'And your father?'

A tear overflowed and rolled down her cheek, she brushed it away and sniffed. 'I couldn't believe he'd go along with it. I could see he was upset, and his words sounded wrong – you know, like they were somebody else's. He didn't seem like my dad any more.' Bella shut her eyes and wiped her tears away with her hand.

'But he wanted you to go along with it?' Steph prompted Bella, echoing her words

Bella sighed. 'That's what he said. Told me Jack and I had always been close friends and that we'd said when we grew up we'd marry, even played at weddings. The most hurtful thing he said was that Jack and me reminded him of how he and Mum were when they were young – best friends more than anything else, which is so important in a marriage.'

'And were they?'

'Best friends? Yes.' Bella twisted her hair around her fingers, clearly thinking something through before pulling a scrunchy off her wrist and using it to pull her hair back into a ponytail. 'Well, they were best friends until... until recently when they had lots of rows – no, they weren't rows exactly, more like... like squabbles. Dad always gave in to Mum; he wasn't weak or anything, but I think he wanted things to be smooth and calm. Does that sound silly?'

'No. But you think he wanted you to marry Jack?'

'That's what he said, probably because Hector wanted it. But I heard them shouting before he came to talk to me, so maybe he stood up to him for a bit, then gave in.'

'Did he always give in to Hector?'

'I suppose he did – but then we all did. Hector has a way of persuading you he's right about everything and gets you to see his side of the argument, so you find yourself agreeing.'

What this girl had been through was beyond belief, and once again Steph felt so sorry for her. Caroline had been looking after her and making sure she was eating, but Bella was pale and thin, and her bright blue pyjamas glimpsed below the grey blankets contrasted with her exhausted face. So much to cope with at the same time as taking her A Levels, but despite Graham's tragic death, she appeared to be ready to talk more this time.

Bella looked away, up the garden, at the dogs running around a tree. 'The day before I left, I heard them talking about Luke and Zac leaving. Hector wanted Dad to join him in using Mum's life insurance to buy their share.'

Tears dribbled down her face again and she dabbed them with some tissues Caroline handed to her. Derek and Marlene exhausted from chasing each other, stood at the door, panting, and while Steph filled their water bowls, Bella had time to compose herself.

Steph sat down. 'I'm not sure how to ask this, Bella, but is there any way you'd go along with their plans?'

'No way. Never. That's why I ran to Caroline's. You read it. Graham said it. It's medieval.'

Another pause – they said nothing but waited.

'There's no way I'm ever going back there, now Dad's on Hector's side.'

'So, the plan was to go to South America with Graham?' Steph was aware of Caroline making a little gasping noise – another piece of news she was delivering then.

'How did you... We were so careful... We never said, even on email...' Frowning, Bella paused, clearly trying to recall what was in the emails and texts they'd sent. 'But you searched Graham's room and found the tickets, didn't you?' She scrutinised Hale, looking for confirmation, which he gave with an acquiescent incline of his head.

In the silence that followed, Bella appeared to move to a different place. The calm, reasonable young adult who had answered their questions disappeared. Hollowed out, her voice was little more than a whisper. 'Without Mum, without Graham, I don't have a future.'

Caroline leaned over, put her arms around Bella and hugged her. 'Now I know it all feels utterly hopeless after all you've been through, my love. But let's get you through those exams and see where we go next. One step at a time. Margaret and I will always be here for you.'

Bella tried a weak smile, but it failed to reach her eyes. Hale's eyes darted towards Steph. Tough though it was, if they were to get anywhere at all, they had to hope that Bella was strong enough to carry on.

'Bella, I know it's grim, and this is going to be difficult to hear, but we now believe both Graham and your mother were murdered.'

Any slight colour that Bella had in her face drained away. Steph moved a little closer, ready to catch Bella if she fainted. 'You were right about your mother. It wasn't an accident. She wasn't drunk. We think she was dead before the car fire, and the same with Graham — someone killed him but made it look like suicide.'

On the sofa, Caroline reached for Bella's hand and stroked it gently, while Bella leaned against her for support. To give her time for this pronouncement to sink in, Steph made coffee for them all and only when she'd handed round the mugs and gone through the ritual of offering milk and sugar did she feel she stood a chance of getting Bella to answer some more questions.

CHAPTER FORTY

'HALE HAS a large team of police officers and forensic scientists working hard to find who was involved in Graham's and your mother's deaths.' Steph sipped her coffee, giving Bella some space to let it sink in. 'But it's difficult, as they're trying to piece together what happened from the end all the way back to the beginning. It's like...' She knew what she wanted to say but found it difficult to find a way to say it. 'I don't know... Like finding a pulled thread in a piece of material and tracing it back to where it got pulled, to see what happened at the beginning. We need help from someone there at the beginning. Do you understand what I'm saying?'

Bella nodded, keeping her eyes fixed on Steph.

'Let's start with your mother. Was there anything odd that you noticed in the days or weeks before she died?'

'She was worried about something and also angry, I think. She snapped a lot at Dad, and I heard them rowing when I went to bed.'

'About what?'

'Just heard their voices screaming at each other, but not the words.'

'You're doing great – anything else?'

Steph had to admire the courage of this girl. In her place she'd have gone to bed and pulled the duvet over her head. Bella sat with her eyes closed, a deep frown on her forehead as if trying to think of something. She opened her eyes.

'She often sat in the car when she came home from school, around the back of the house where she thought we couldn't see her and talk on her phone.'

'Why there?'

'Poor reception in lots of other places on the estate – there it's strong.'

'Any idea what it was all about?'

'No.'

'Right—'

Bella interrupted. 'Hang on, there was something else strange with Hector. He always came round to talk about the school with her, Luke and Dad before supper every Tuesday – you know the bills and how it should be marketed, but he stopped a few weeks before...' Her voice faded away.

'Do you know why? Did she say anything?' Steph had got into her stride, and she was aware of Hale listening intently, making the occasional note in the book balanced on his lap.

Bella paused for a moment; her eyes closed again, and she was clearly trying to think back. 'No, but it was weird. Luke arrived one Tuesday a few weeks ago and said Hector wasn't coming as he was busy and he'd send them emails.'

'That's so helpful, Bella. Anything else?'

Hale scribbled a few lines in his notebook. Bella observed him, then suddenly recalled something else.

'She also stopped her weekly visits to The Crown with you, didn't she, Caroline?'

Caroline picked up the mug from the floor and, making sure Bella couldn't see, pulled a face at Steph, suggesting she knew nothing about it.

'When did she stop?' Steph hurriedly asked as Caroline took the mugs through to the kitchen.

'About the same time. It was as if all the old routines that had gone on for ages stopped. Is this the sort of thing you want?'

'Absolutely. That's so helpful.' Hale was adding more notes to the list he was making.

'Did she ever go out regularly anywhere else?' said Steph.

'I think she went to Pilates on another evening... er... Monday, I think.'

'Didn't she go to Esme's yoga class ever?'

Bella smiled, this time for real. 'No, they agreed she wouldn't. They used to giggle a lot – she and Esme – like kids sometimes when they were together.'

Somehow Steph couldn't see Esme as a giggly girl but she said nothing.

'Mum tried to behave, but when Esme got them to lie with their bottoms against the skirting board with their legs up the wall in a V shape, she couldn't stop laughing, and that would set Esme off, so they agreed she wouldn't come, and she went to Pilates on those evenings instead.'

'Where? Do you know?'

'Southwold, somewhere I think.'

Hale made some more notes. 'This is all so helpful, Bella.'

'Is it?'

'Yes, it helps us to build a pattern and when that changes, we try to see why.' Hale smiled at her. 'Anything else?'

Bella frowned and she closed her eyes as she appeared to be delving into her memory. She shook her head, opened her eyes and looked across at Hale. 'No, I don't think so.'

Caroline returned from the kitchen and sat beside Bella once more. 'Well done! You're doing so well!'

As she passed, Hale prompted Steph by moving his hand across his notebook, suggesting she should move on. Or at least that was what she thought he meant. As she asked the next question, she knew she'd been right.

'Now, if you feel you can cope, let's move onto Graham. Did you tell anyone about your plans to go to South America?'

Taking a deep breath, Bella squeezed the hand Caroline held out to her. 'No one. That's why we never wrote about it in the emails.'

'Did he tell anyone – his father? His sister?'

A few moments' thought before she answered. 'No, I don't think so... No, I'm sure he didn't because he'd planned to write letters to post from Heathrow so they'd know but couldn't stop us.'

'And you don't think he changed his mind?'

'No. I'm sure he told no one.'

'In the messages, he said he would sort Jack out – do you think he did?'

'I don't know. After he said it, I tried to phone him, but he never answered.'

'And is there anyone you can think of who might have wanted to hurt him?'

'Jack, I suppose and, after the row with my dad, possibly him and Hector. They might have thought he was getting in the way of their plans for Glebe Hall... Well, he was, wasn't he? We were going to leave together, and I wasn't going to marry Jack.'

'But no one knew that?'

'No one.'

In the silence they could hear the end of a Mozart sonata and, after a brief pause and a riffling of sheet music, the opening of the Rachmaninov No 2 Piano Concerto, one of Steph's favourites. No wonder she gave recitals at Glebe Hall; Margaret was a superb pianist, and the students were lucky to have her. It would be such a shame when her Parkinson's stole this talent.

Hale, who'd been scribbling away during this musical inter-lude, stopped making notes and frowned. 'Tell me Bella, did your mother know about the suggested marriage between you and Jack?'

'I don't think so... Actually, I don't know. She never said anything and I'm sure she would have... No, she'd have put a stop to it.'

'So, it was your father who broached the subject, was it?'

'Yes, it was after Mum... The way he spoke made it sound normal – like let's talk about plans for your holiday or Christmas – and he sat there and told me marrying Jack would be the best solution.'

'Solution? Did he say what the problem was?' Hale wrote something down.

Puzzled, Bella suddenly appeared to get it. 'No, he didn't, but he said that – "solution". You're right, he had to think there was a problem for him to say that didn't he?'

Steph grabbed Derek away from the biscuit tin Caroline had left on the floor, pushed the lid down hard, and put it on the table beside her. 'So, did you think that was what he wanted?'

'Rather than pleasing Hector, you mean?'

'Yes.'

'Not sure.' She pulled the bright green cushion from her side and hugged it in front of her.

'Dad wouldn't shut up. He went on and on about all the advantages and how the Hall had always been an important part of my life and it would ensure my future there and how Jack and I were destined to be together.'

She hugged the cushion closer to her. 'I told him I wasn't in love with Jack and never would be but loved Graham and if I was to think of marrying or living with anyone, which I wasn't, it would be him.'

'What happened then?'

'Dad shouted at me like a kid. He told me it was about time I did as I was told and thought of the family instead of being selfish and only thinking of me. Then he hit me. He's never hit me before. I was terrified. And then you came,' Bella nodded at Hale.

Hale closed his notebook and smiled across at Bella. 'You've been so brave, answering all our questions. Just one more before we go. How was Graham's relationship with the rest of the adults? Luke and Zac, for instance?'

'Well, he worked on the estate with his father and knew them all. Did odd jobs for them, but that was all.'

'Do you know if Luke helped him to prepare for Cambridge?'

'Don't think so.' She shook her head. 'Hang on, you're right. I remember now. Graham told me Luke had explained some economic theory once. But apart from that, he didn't have much to do with them.'

A look from Hale prompted Steph, and she caught Bella's eye. 'Bella, we need to find as much evidence as possible if we're to catch whoever killed Graham, so we'd like your permission to tell your father what's been going on.' Bella pulled off the scrunchy and let her hair loose, hiding behind it. This was a tough ask. 'You haven't told him, have you?'

'Of course not.' Suddenly alert, she searched Steph's face for clues. 'You think Jack had something to do with it, don't you?'

'We don't know yet. But it would help us find whoever did this if your father understands what's been going on with Jack. Would you rather we wait until you've told him?'

Her eyes filled once again, but she blinked her tears away. 'No. You tell him. He ought to know what the bastard has done.'

CHAPTER FORTY-ONE

THEY ABANDONED the supper Steph had left in the fridge, and despite Derek's frolic with Marlene, they took him for a short walk followed by supper at The Harbour Inn – they could just make it in time for the last serving. After the drama of the early evening, Steph felt like being around normal people, doing routine things, far away from death.

After a short walk along Blackshore, they found a table in the bar, placed their order and sipped their Adnams beer, able to relax at last. Inside, Steph quietly vowed not to mention suicide, the fire or anything to do with Glebe Hall and quickly added the college to the list. What was left?

'How about planning a holiday? You could do with one.'

Clearly surprised, Hale took a gulp of his beer. Was he avoiding it? Had she gone too far? They'd been together for almost two years and, although he spent most nights at hers, he'd kept his flat. They'd simply got on with a shared life together and not discussed commitment or even joint finances. It just worked out, and she didn't want to disrupt it. Was suggesting a holiday together somehow a step towards... towards what?

Hale put his glass down on the scrubbed pine table. 'That sounds like a plan. Always fancied the far reaches of Scotland or – and don't laugh at me – a cruise along the Danube!'

Somehow, Hale-cruise felt like an oxymoron. What a surprising man he was!

'The Danube? Why that river?'

'Well, it goes through the centre of Europe, and I don't know much about that – never been there, and a cruise means no decisions about what to do each day.' He paused. 'Does that make me sound like an old man?'

'Perhaps...' she laughed. 'But actually, it makes all the problems somebody else's – only unpacking once and lots of different places to see. But...'

'But?'

'What about all those boring people we could get stuck with?'

'Quite simple – we ignore them!'

'And who are you ignoring now, Hale?' The new voice made them jump. Derek crawled out from under their table and sniffed the jeans of a tall man who had blocked out the light. Hale stood, so he could see who it was.

'Andy! It's you. What are you doing here?'

'Like you – having a drink.' Andy held his pint mug in his hand and put it down on their table.

'Come and join us.' The man pulled out a chair and plonked himself opposite. 'Steph, you remember Andy Cutler? Or maybe he'd retired before you arrived? Steph Grant, Andy Cutler.'

'Good to meet you, Steph.' His warm voice and brown

wrinkled skin hinted at an outdoor life, and he reeked of pipe tobacco – a rare smell nowadays. 'You're looking good, Hale. She must suit you.'

Hale grinned. 'You look well, too. What have you been up to, Andy?'

'I run the ferry here. Spend my life crossing the Blyth between Blackshore and Walberswick and when I'm not doing that, I'm fishing. Sea fishing mostly. Keeps me out of mischief.'

For the next ten minutes, they swapped information about ex-colleagues, only a few of whom Steph knew. From the range of people they discussed, she realised Andy went back a long way and had kept up with loads of officers who'd moved else-where, retired or died. She wondered what he said about Hale when he met other ex-colleagues.

His type of policeman – and they were men, not officers – took her back to over thirty years ago when she'd joined the Met. Either she was patronised as a delicate maiden, who shouldn't be paddling her fingers in the grubby world of crime, or she was only there to make the tea and take notes in meetings.

'We've just been talking about Glebe Hall, what a coinci-dence!' Hale gave her a subtle nudge under the table and Steph tuned back in.

'Knew the family when Hector's parents lived there, you know.'

'Really?' Hale was after more. They all knew it and Andy made himself comfortable, downing another slurp of beer to help him tell all. If they were allowed to smoke in pubs, she could see him lighting his pipe and settling in for a long tale.

'Hector's dad was a gambler, you know, old Arthur. Not too posh to owe the bookies shed loads and wherever he went –

pubs, restaurants, the bookies – he had the same line, "put it on the account, my good man", in that cut glass voice of his.'

He did a rather good impression of Hector. Steph sat back, enjoying his performance.

Andy took a gulp from his pint. 'I can hear him now! And the stupid sods did! Never paid up. And he got away with it. And as for Glebe Hall,' he leaned in, having looked around to check no one could listen to the next gobbet of scandal he was giving them, 'Arthur let Glebe Hall go to rack and ruin. There were rumours he'd re-mortgaged it up to the hilt.'

'Really? What did he gamble on?'

'You name it, he'd bet on it. Horses were where he lost most money, but he'd look at two flies on a window and offer odds on which one flew away first. No, William was lucky to hang onto the Hall after the death duties.'

'William?'

'Hector's older brother. Terrible tragedy. He was a lovely lad. Always cheerful and spoke to everyone. Never played lord of the manor like his father or that brother of his.'

'Really?'

'Didn't fall far from the tree, that Hector. Spitting image of his father and just as arrogant.'

'What happened to William?' Hale prompted him.

'Lovely lad he was. Very athletic, you know. Good sailor and loved skiing. Was in one of those trendy ski places and on something called... What was it? Ah, yes, a black run. Anyway, hit ice apparently and fell. Just like that. His life smashed in an instant.'

'How dreadful.' Steph felt she could participate at last. 'Did he die?'

'Not then, my dear. They brought him back, and he spent

over a year in one of those specialist hospitals down south. They patched him up, but he couldn't walk. Paraplegic, I think they call it. They all said he'd been lucky to survive, but I often wondered if he thought that.'

'How awful for him.'

He nodded at her. 'It meant that Hector had to get off his arse and do something for a change. He had to wait on his brother hand and foot – well, I suppose he didn't do it all himself; they have maids and such like to do that, haven't they, those people?'

'What happened?'

'He died, my dear... Must've been... let me see... yes, 2001.'

'Oh! How sad.'

Again, Andy leaned in and his voice became a whisper. 'Strange circumstances. We could never get to the bottom of it, but we had our suspicions, my dear.' Yep, he'd be a founder member of the dainty maiden brigade and expect endless cups of tea!

Steph, intrigued but also amused by him, was waiting for him to tap the side of his nose like they did in old black and white films. Keeping her lips tightly controlled, she felt Hale nudge her under the table and struggled further to freeze them. He took over.

'Go on, Andy. Tell us all.'

'Well, William could move about in a wheelchair – good upper arm strength, you know. Had one of those chairs with motors and zipped round the estate. Also had a small car adapted with hand controls – you know the sort of thing. Saw him about town sometimes; had lovely manners, always spoke. So different to his father, he was.'

'And what happened?' said Hale.

'One night William went out in that car of his, smashed into a tree – burst into flames it did. By the time the fire engine arrived, it was all over. A wreck and just his bones. Maybe he'd had enough – you know – and – well, there it is.' He paused, presumably for dramatic effect. 'We wondered what had gone on, as it seemed peculiar at the time, but we found no evidence of anything.'

'Really?' Hale, now alert, pushed him. 'What were you suspicious about?'

'You know, perhaps he wanted to end it all or... someone else did.'

'Someone? Hector, you mean?'

Andy wriggled around in his chair, apparently uncomfortable. 'I'm not saying nothing mind, but it cropped up more than once. But Hector had a cast-iron alibi. A mason, he was, and at a Lodge meeting the evening it happened. Whole room of witnesses, including the Chief Constable. Only that nice wife of his at the Hall when it happened.'

'Did she call it in?' Hale finished his beer and waved the glass at Andy, who shook his head.

Scratching his head, Andy frowned. 'Thanks, but no thanks. Had enough for one night. Now, what was that you asked?'

'Did Esme Percy call it in?'

Andy sat ruminating for a moment. 'I could be wrong, but I think it was Hector – yes, it was him. He drove back, saw a glow in the dark and that was that. Should all be in the files in the store. Why? You interested?'

'Just copper's curiosity, that's all—'

'Two fish pies and peas?' The barman placed the plates on the table in front of them.

'Thanks, they look great.'

'Anything else I can get for you?'

'No, thanks.' The barman walked back behind the bar.

'Right good, that looks. I'll leave you two to get on with it, then. Good to see you, Hale, and to meet you again, Sheila.'

Steph didn't react as he muddled her with Hale's ex-wife. She felt Hale's hand squeeze her thigh under the table in an apology before he stood up. 'Good to see you, Andy. Next time, you'll have to join us.'

'Thanks. See you later.' With that, he walked off and climbed the three steps out of the bar, up to the riverbank.

Famished, they ate the scrumptious fish pies with relish. It had been so long since they'd been able to come out here and have supper together and they'd even got their favourite table. Full, Steph sat back and sighed contentedly while Hale helped himself to the small pile of mashed potato and peas she'd left on the side of her plate.

'Well, that was an interesting snippet Andy gave us.' Steph smiled at Hale.

'Quite the coincidence, wasn't it?' Hale cleaned her plate. 'I wonder how many evenings he just happened to be here waiting for us.'

'I wonder why he didn't come to the station.'

'Not his style. He finds out all he needs to know outside but still wants to be involved. But give him his due, what he had to say could be relevant – more than that – possibly crucial to the investigation. Tomorrow Johnson will be mining the depths of the archives for that paperwork from... He didn't say when, did he?'

For a moment, they sat re-playing his story. Steph fed a treat from her pocket to a waggy-tailed Derek, then sat up suddenly, making Hale jump. 'We can look in the Land

Registry. If Glebe Hall was transferred from William to Hector, there will be a record of the change of ownership.'

'What would I do without you? That's what I call quick thinking!' He leaned, pecked her on her left cheek and held up his glass. 'Now, another? And then we can talk about this holiday.'

CHAPTER FORTY-TWO

'Now you're sober, we need to have a talk.' Having made sure that Hector would be out for several hours checking the fences around the estate, Esme closed Jack's bedroom door with a sharp click and sat on the side of his bed.

He appeared to have been awake for some time as he was sitting up, leaning on his pillows, absorbed in some beat'em up video game. Wrinkling her nose at the overwhelming sock smell, she opened the curtains as wide as they would go, pushed up the sash window, and breathed in the cold air.

'Oy! That's cold.' He blinked at the intrusion of sunshine, which illuminated the piles of clothes scattered across the floor. Reaching for the games' controller, she was relieved that he let her take it without a fight and resumed her seat on the side of his bed.

'You should be revising—' She interrupted herself. This had to be a one topic conversation and not a litany of moans. Revision would have to wait. 'But that isn't what I want to talk to you about. I want to know what's been going on with Bella.'

He slid down the bed, pulling up his duvet to his neck as if to protect himself from her. 'Oh, not that again. I told you she's lying.'

'Come on Jack. It's me, not your father. I've spoken to Bella, and she has told Caroline. Now I'd like to hear your side.'

His lips appeared to be welded together, and he had the sulky look of a three-year-old caught stealing the biscuits.

'Well, come on. I'm waiting.'

Irritated, he sighed. 'Look, she's a slut and one with a big mouth, too! It was all her fault.'

'Really? It's been going on for some time, hasn't it?'

'Is that what she says? I'm not sure what she thinks was "going on" but nothing happened that she didn't want to happen. She's making it up.'

Some long-remembered quote about protesting too much entered her head.

'But you told me you were "friends with benefits" – tell me exactly what that means.'

He had the grace to blush. After all, the one thing you don't want to discuss or even think about is the sexual activities of your parents or your children, and she was tramping through both taboos. Fixing him with the 'I'm not going anywhere look', she tapped the side of the bed. 'Well?'

'Oh,' he tutted. 'She suggested it, Mummy. Honestly, I wasn't sure what it meant at first. She said we were both over sixteen – that's the legal thing, you know – and we were chums. Why not?'

Esme said nothing but waited for more. Eventually, he obliged.

'She said I was her perfect man and she'd rather lose it to me than anyone else.'

Jack obviously thought that was it. He'd finished and

moved his legs under the covers as if he was about to get up. But he was not getting away with it that easily.

'And did you use protection, or was she on the pill?'

A horrified look flashed across his face; he was evidently shocked at where she was going.

'I did.'

'So if, as you say, she was a slut, and it was what she wanted, why wasn't she on the pill?'

'Don't know – she just wasn't.'

'And each time she wanted your "friendship with benefits", she asked you, did she?'

'Well... not exactly like that. She'd sort of make it... you know... known... and we'd... you know.'

'No, I don't think I do know.'

He was getting redder by the minute and there was a definite sheen developing on his forehead; she found she was enjoying watching him squirm, convinced that his vague comments hid the awful truth.

'And where did these benefits take place?'

'Mostly the sofa in the old summerhouse.' A mumble.

'I presume you agreed not to tell anyone?'

'Oh, she threatened me that if I said anything she'd tell Jon and Father that I'd... umm... raped her, so I had no choice, did I?'

Trying to look sympathetic, Esme shook her head. 'What a dreadful position to be in, Jack.'

He sat up, moving towards her. 'Yes, it was. I'm so relieved to tell you, Mummy. It has been dreadful, keeping it a secret.'

'I can imagine. You've been a sex slave to a nymphomaniac, by the sound of it!'

Apparently shocked, again he lay back, considering her comment. 'I wouldn't put it like that.'

'Well, how would you put it? You say she was insistent that you... serviced her – or do we say fucked – and blackmailed you into keeping your sex services secret?'

At last, a slight wince at her crudity.

'And did she also go with other young men during this time?'

He grinned and looked at her through his eyelashes. 'She didn't need to, Mummy.'

His smug arrogance sickened her. She'd had enough.

'Well, it's been fascinating to hear your side of this mess, Jack.' She stood up, distancing herself from her son. 'I think Bella is going to make a formal complaint about you to the police. She insists it was you who abused her for years and blackmailed her into keeping quiet.'

'It'll be her word against mine then.' His aggressive tone did nothing to reassure her or influence her judgement.

'Yes, it will, unless you start telling the truth.'

'But I've just told you the truth!'

'Really? Perhaps you should think again.'

'I bet Father will believe me.'

'He may well – and I'm sure he'll find friends in high places to support you, but even if you talk your way out of this mess, you'll have to live with yourself, Jack.'

His pointy fingers reached for the games console once again. Disappointed and shocked at the son she no longer knew but recognised only too well, and feeling a failure as a mother, she left his bedroom.

CHAPTER FORTY-THREE

Apparently taken by surprise at seeing Steph and Hale when he answered their knock on the ancient, weathered door, Luke composed himself and stepped back, welcoming them into the office.

'Do come in. How may I help you?'

Stepping out of the sunshine into the gloom of the Tudor cottage, Steph blinked several times to accommodate to the shadows, checking there was no one else in the office. Arriving unannounced gave them the advantage of surprise, but didn't guarantee privacy, or even that he'd be there. Their luck was in.

Hale came through the door behind her and she stopped to let him pass. 'May we have a few minutes of your time, please? We have some more questions for you.'

With a frown, Luke faced Hale. 'Shall we go through to the computer station? I assume it's something on the accounts?'

'No, not the accounts. May we sit here, please?' Hale's tone, although quiet, did not invite debate. He moved to one of the modern black leather steel-framed chairs beside the red brick inglenook fireplace.

'Of course.' Luke took the chair opposite, while Steph sat on a matching two seater between them. It was a bold move to place the Scandinavian style furniture in the sixteenth-century cottage and she wasn't sure it worked, but then, it was an office. Luke sat erect and paying attention, waiting for Hale to start and she was reminded of Derek, waiting for his dinner.

Luke eventually broke the silence, clearly not comfortable away from his spreadsheets. 'Now, how may I help you?'

His immaculate ivory shirt and navy trousers were perfectly co-ordinated and, with his smooth, unlined face and intelligent dark brown eyes, reinforced her view of him as an eminent diplomat or a high-ranking government official. She suspected it would take a great deal to puncture his calm self-confidence and wondered if Hale's questions might achieve that or if Luke would brush them away, as he did the minuscule piece of fluff he'd spotted on his trouser leg.

Hale opened the buff folder on his lap, taking his time to flip through the ten or so pages fixed inside it. Apparently curious, Luke concentrated on the pages as Hale riffled through them. He closed the file and looked up at Luke.

'In our investigation into Graham Andrews' death, we have discovered a series of emails on his computer between you and him over the last nine months and we'd like to discuss them with you.'

'Aren't they self-evident? If you have them all, you will see that I was assisting Graham with his preparation for going up to Cambridge to read history.'

'But you're not a historian?'

'No, I'm an economist, and a module on his course is economic history, for which he's expected to have a grasp of basic economic concepts. He has never studied economics and was finding the texts rather a struggle. I spent about an hour with him each week helping him to understand his reading and giving him a grounding in economic theory. Anything else?' Luke placed his hands on the arms of his chair as if he was planning to push himself up.

After a few moments, he removed them again and let them fall on his lap, assuming a consciously relaxed position; he sat back, waiting for Hale to continue. Here was a man used to asking the questions and controlling the conversation; he clearly felt uncomfortable with this role reversal and appeared to be struggling hard to disguise it. From her seat, Steph noted his jaw tightening and his eyes blinked more frequently, common signs of stress.

'Yes, there is something else. You always met here in the office and not in your home? Why was that?'

A puzzled look crossed Luke's face. 'Why on earth does that matter?'

'Perhaps you didn't want your meetings to be known by your partner?'

'I will not dignify that with an answer!' Luke frowned but then appeared to relent. 'When Graham worked here, he was based in the barn and the office is closer than the house.'

Steph glanced at Hale, who did not seem convinced. Luke was looking more uncomfortable with each question, and a light sheen now covered his forehead.

Hale scanned the emails once again, while Luke watched him, an anxious expression on his face. At last Hale appeared to find what he was searching for. 'In your emails there are several comments about your – shall we say – your admiration or appreciation of Graham's intellect.'

'So? He was a bright boy. Why not tell him?'

'He was also good looking, wasn't he?' A slight edge in Hale's voice prompted Luke to sit up, more alert.

'I hope you aren't suggesting what I think you're suggesting, Chief Inspector?'

'And what would that be, Mr Roy?'

Luke clasped his hands tighter in his lap. 'That I was trying to seduce Graham Andrews.'

'Were you?'

'Don't be ridiculous, man, of course not! As you will know,' he turned to Steph, 'Zac and I are happily married, and I have no need for dalliances with young men.'

Hale opened the file and spent some time looking for something. It appeared to be making Luke uncomfortable, as he squirmed a little on the leather seat and the squeak he made shot through the silence. 'Throughout the emails you are fulsome in your praise of Graham's intellect, and on one occasion, after he appeared to have had a problem understanding a topic, you comment that "with your good looks and IQ you should have no problems making new friends as you have done here" – what did you mean by that?'

'What it says. He is – was – a good-looking, bright boy who was also charming and unassuming and had a great future.'

'Did you think he might be interested in you?'

'Look, I've told you – I'm perfectly happy with Zac and not looking elsewhere.'

Hale patted the folder. 'You're a bright man. Look at it from our point of view. We now know Graham did not commit suicide, but we have evidence he was murdered—'

'No! That's dreadful! Whoever would do that?' Luke appeared to be genuinely shocked, but Steph had seen some good performances in her time and continued to observe him.

'That's what we're trying to find out.'

Luke lowered his head into his hands, rubbed his forehead as if relieving a headache, and stared across at Hale. 'You can't think I had anything to do with this! I appreciated the talent and potential of that boy and was nurturing it – I'd never do anything to harm him. I can't believe it – what a loss! And how hateful to make that insinuation!'

'As I was saying, looked at it from our point of view, we have a folder of emails sent by you, admiring him and obviously valuing the time you spent together. Let's suppose you made a – shall we say – a request to become closer, and he rejected you, threatened to tell his father or Bella about your approach – wouldn't that give you a motive to silence him to retain your reputation and relationship with Zac?'

Luke shot out of his chair and stood over Hale. Steph tensed, ready to tackle him if he made a further move, while Hale gazed up at him, his face in neutral.

'You have to admit, that could be a possibility.'

'And so could lots of things, *but it wasn't me!*'

Instead of moving further towards Hale, he collapsed back into his chair; Steph also sat back – panic over.

'Believe me, those meetings and emails were innocent. I enjoyed helping Graham and spending time with him, but that was as far as it went and no further.' He ran his right hand over his face. 'I am horrified that anyone would want to take the life of that young man, but *it wasn't me.*'

Hale stood, took a card from his pocket and walked in front of the fireplace to Luke, who slumped, exhausted. As Hale blocked his light, Luke raised his head and saw the card at eye level.

'If you do think you can help us further or there is anything you want to tell us, here is my mobile number.'

Luke took the card but didn't move.

'We'll see ourselves out. Thank you for your help, Mr Roy.'

Hale stood back, so Steph could open the door, then

followed her through and shut it with a sharp click. As they walked along the path, with red and white Tudor roses on either side, she looked back and whispered, 'Well?'

Hale shook his head. 'Convincing, but I'm not taking him off my list yet.'

CHAPTER FORTY-FOUR

STEPH HEARD A MUFFLED attempt at knocking on the door and, pulling back a growling Derek, opened it to see Hale balancing a large cardboard box of files against the wall with one hand while knocking with the other. He couldn't reach the bell.

'Took your time – this is heavy!'

'Why didn't you phone me from the car and you could have walked straight in?'

'Hadn't thought of that.'

Dumping the heavy box on the table, he pulled off his coat, laid it over the back of one of the chairs and started unloading the files.

'Supper in an hour?'

'Sounds about right. Give me time to sort through this box and then we can go through the important bits in detail.'

Steph knew that at this stage he had his own system of organising what he wanted to explore and left him to it, to concentrate on making supper. Although it was his turn, she assembled the parts of the shepherd's pie from bags she'd defrosted from the freezer. She watched as he sorted in the way he always did; head down, intensely concentrating on the piles in front of him. A quick scan of each sheet of paper, followed by a decision to put it on one of three piles – not important, could be worth looking at and vital.

At last, the box had been divided into the three piles, and she joined him while the pie was in the oven. 'May I help?'

'Please. That lot can go back in the box, but this pile needs another look.' He pointed at the 'worth looking at' pile. 'See if you pick up anything that we should follow up on while I go through this one.'

He had the witness statements that he'd thought important and the path lab reports, and he'd given her the newspaper reports and some photocopies of the officers' notes. Apparently, these confirmed what Andy had told them in the pub.

William had been depressed and, according to one report of the inquest in the local rag, he had seen his doctor for anti-depressants as he tried to come to terms with the fact that he had improved as much as he was going to and all he had to look forward to was a slow deterioration. He'd been getting physio to improve his muscle tone, and apparently at this stage could still drive his adapted car with his hands, but he feared it wouldn't be long before he lost his independence totally.

On the night he'd died, Hector was out at a Lodge meeting. It was summertime and apparently William had asked Hector to postpone putting him to bed until he came home. William wanted to stay on the terrace, watching the sunset, and finish his book. As he was able to control his motorised wheelchair himself, Hector left him with a bottle of wine and his book while he went to his meeting.

It appeared that William had taken himself to the car and at this stage could manoeuvre himself into it. No one had seen the crash, but he had driven across the estate and apparently hit a tree, and the car had burst into flames.

Hector saw the glow as he arrived home and drove over to investigate. When he saw the car he rushed back to the Hall, woke Esme and phoned for help. By the time the fire engine arrived, it was too late. The car was incinerated, along with William.

Steph was struck by the carbon copy of Madeline's death — no wonder Andy had wanted to tell them about it. The pathologist's report claimed William must have died in the fire, as there was little left of the body to examine.

She finished reading and handed the report back to Hale. 'It's only when reading something like this, you realise how far pathology has come over the last fifteen years. A couple of sentences and that's it.'

Hale handed her a few more pages. 'These notes and witness statements are interesting, especially Andy's. He recorded several meetings with Hector and Esme, exploring William's mobility and how easy it was for him to get from his chair to the car.'

Steph read through the statements. Hector was robust in claiming William had no problem and insisted on being as independent as possible, while Andy, at least she assumed it was him, had highlighted a line in Hector's statement where he said he thought William was starting to need more help.

In the middle of the pile, she fished out a newspaper cutting, which she unfolded and smoothed out on the table. After over fifteen years, it had faded, and the creases made it difficult to read some of the words, but it was good enough. It was a long article from the East Anglian Daily Times, complete with photographs of the burnt-out car and one of Glebe Hall at a flattering angle – the garden appeared to be a little less mani-cured but otherwise it looked the same.

June 2001
LOCAL OLYMPIC HERO KILLED IN CAR CRASH

William Percy (30) of Glebe Hall, Southwold, died in a horrific car crash late on Friday night when his adapted Volkswagen Golf smashed into a tree and burst into flames.

He had been a popular member of the GB team at the 1994 Olympic Winter Games, known as Lillehammer'94, and competed in the Alpine Ski event, finishing in the top ten, the highest ranking for a GB skier. He later became a familiar face on the BBC commentary team.

In 1999, when skiing at Verbiers with a party of family and friends, he suffered a devastating and life-changing accident when he hit some ice and fell down the mountain onto a ledge. Despite becoming a paraplegic, he remained active, running the Glebe Hall estate, setting up a charity giving young people from inner cities outward bound holidays and continuing as a regular commentator on winter sports for the BBC.

His younger brother, Hector Percy, who now inherits Glebe Hall, discovered the car fire when he returned to the Hall after attending a meeting in Southwold. On Friday night, William climbed into his car unaided and drove across the estate and it is thought he hit a tree. It was not possible to rescue him from the ferocious fire and his body was recovered by the local Fire Service, comprising volunteers from the local area.

A statement made on behalf of the Percy family was issued this morning by his brother. 'We are horrified by the death of my brother, William, who was loved by all who knew him. He was a force of nature and, even after his accident, insisted on living his life to the full. He fought every day to be as independent as possible and found it difficult when his injuries became a barrier to his indomitable spirit. This has been a devastating tragedy for our family, and I appeal that our privacy is respected during this difficult time.'

The police spokesman, Sergeant Andrew Cutler, appealed for any witnesses who were driving past the Hall between nine and ten o'clock on Friday night and saw any other cars or signs of the fire to contact him at Southwold Police Station. In a tribute to William Percy, he commented, 'William Percy was a good man and played an active role in the local community, even after his skiing accident. He did the Percy name proud and will be missed.'

Members of staff at Glebe Hall were devastated by news of his death. 'He was one of the best. A really good boss – he cared for the people who worked for him,' said the gardener, Mr Dan Andrews of Southwold. 'He was always cheerful, despite all he had to put up with, and made a good fist of running the estate. He'd set up a charity to help less privileged youngsters and had been making plans to build a ski slope to the east of the estate to train them to take up the sport.'

One of the oldest families in the county, the Percys have lived at the palatial Glebe Hall since the sixteenth century, but their lives have often been touched by tragedy. Arthur Percy, William's father, was killed in a shooting accident, and a few months later his wife, Constance, suffered a heart attack and her body was found at the bottom of the grand staircase. His grandfather never returned from the First World War, after being shot the day after the Armistice was declared.

A memorial service will be held at St Edmund's Church in Southwold, following which William Percy will be interred in a private ceremony on the Glebe Hall estate.

. . .

There were another three articles re-cycling the same content by the same journalist, describing progress into the investigation and the inquest, which recorded the death as accidental, despite three accounts of his increasing depression with his deteriorating condition and the strong suspicion that he committed suicide. Carefully re-folding the cuttings, Steph placed them on the table and wrapped her arm around Hale's shoulders; he leaned back and kissed her.

He threw the last sheet of paper onto the pile and sighed. 'Andy and the team appear to have done a solid job, but they didn't have anywhere near the science we have, and a couple of times I can feel his doubts creeping in. As he said in the pub, his instinct was murder, but from these statements and the evidence they gathered, there is no way it could be proved.'

'And the only actual evidence we have in Madeline's death is the fractured skull, and I bet a really good barrister could convince a jury that it could have happened in the fire.' Steph brought over a glass of beer and handed it to a grateful Hale.

As she walked towards the oven to check on the shepherd's pie, a thought struck her. 'Maybe it's worth talking to that reporter.'

'Which reporter?'

'The one who wrote up the inquest and some of the other articles on the fire. There are hints in the sub-text—'

'Sub-text? A bit flash, isn't it?'

'Stop taking the piss.' She threw the oven gloves at him. He ducked.

As she walked past him to pick them up, he pulled her towards him and, holding her close, smiled up at her. 'I think you're quite magnificent when you spot things we miss. Now, tell me about – what was it – sub-text?'

She stifled a giggle and tried to ignore his hands stroking her thighs as she launched into her explanation. 'Sub-text is the meaning below the text – we were talking about it in our book group.'

'You're so sexy when you talk like that!' His hands moved up to stroke her bottom.

'Are you going to listen or not?' She tried to wriggle away from his clasping hand, then decided she rather liked it.

'Sorry. You were saying.' He undid his grin, winked, and adopted a serious expression.

'Throughout the articles you've given me, it feels as if he's holding back – you know – wanting to say something but can't – presumably because he didn't have the evidence. A bit like your hunches.'

'Good call. Fifteen years? Probably moved on but might live locally or we could try to find him. What's his name?'

'Chris Stevens, I think.'

CHAPTER FORTY-FIVE

STEPH ALWAYS ENJOYED HAVING a drink in The Nelson and even more when they stayed for their fish and chips. The Adnams Broadside batter melted in the mouth and the chips tasted like the ones she remembered from her childhood – crunchy and thick. Savouring the anticipation, they waited for Chris Stevens to arrive. They spotted the tall, skinny man as soon as he ducked under the low door, and he must have recognised Hale, as he nodded towards them and moved to the back bar, through the standing groups sipping their pints.

Chris Stevens, retired journalist, had moved to Southwold via Fleet Street and Wapping and now ran the local community news for fun. It took him some time to reach the back bar, as he was greeted with shoulder slaps and handshakes from men in at least three different groups.

Every day The Nelson resembled most pubs on Christmas Eve – crammed and full of excited chatter – if you wanted one of the worn, scrubbed pine tables, you had to get there at noon for lunch. The uneven floor bore witness to the thousands of feet that had re-shaped the stone, and the ceiling didn't appear to have a decent piece of joinery in it.

It was the most popular pub in Southwold, with tourists and locals alike, who relished its unique atmosphere. The narrow back bar, the walls lined with sailing boat pictures and Nelson memorabilia, was the only place where the floor didn't have standing room, so it was quieter.

As Chris approached their table, Hale stood and leaned across to shake his hand. 'Popular man!'

'Need to know what's going on. Good to see you again.' Chris gave Steph a firm handshake with a wide grin and she warmed to him immediately. He squeezed into the seat opposite, trying not to disturb the family on the table behind, concentrating on their supper.

'We're about to order fish and chips and a pint – same for you?'

'Please.'

Hale squirmed along the bench and joined the queue at the hatch to place their order. Steph had asked Hale why Chris had chosen such a popular pub to have the sensitive conversation. Apparently, Chris never went anywhere else – no other pub stored the beer correctly – and amid that noise level, no one would hear them anyway. He smiled at Steph. 'Aren't you Mike Grant's wife?'

'I am – I mean I was. He died almost five years ago.'

'I'm sorry. I knew him when I used to do the court reporting in Ipswich and saw you two several times at a pub in Tuddenham, I think it was.'

'The Tuddenham Fountain – great pub.'

'Yes, he was one of the good ones all right.'

'Thanks.'

'And now I see you've found another good'un. Long time since I supped a pint with Hale. He looks well, considering.'

'Considering?'

'How hard they make those poor sods work. Ah! And here he is!' He reached over, took the pint glass and immediately lifted it to his lips. 'Umm! Good, that. Perfectly kept.' He held it up to the light and nodded, appreciating its golden shades, then took another large gulp and smacked his lips.

'Right. You didn't get hold of me to natter about beer. How can I help you?'

After Hale had given him a summary of what they'd read in the archives about William's accident, Chris grinned once again. 'You took your time, lad.' His slight northern accent crept in. 'I expected you a good few days ago – a couple of weeks back.'

'Really?'

'As soon as I heard about Madeline Henderson's accident, I knew you'd be looking fifteen years back.'

'Oh?'

'Come on, Hale. We both know that was no accident, the same as William's wasn't.'

'That didn't appear in any of your reporting.'

'It couldn't, could it? No evidence. But Andy and I both had a hunch, and, as it turns out now, that hunch was right.'

He grinned at Steph and she returned it, knowing that the efficient grapevine had done its stuff as usual. She could see Chris and Andy sitting here late into the evening, raking over the past case and their suspicions.

'You too, eh?' Clearly, Hale wanted to show that he wasn't a young ignoramus plod.

'It seems that anyone who gets close to our lord of the manor risks a hot car ride. We couldn't prove it as there

278

wasn't a scrap of evidence, but it felt wrong. That wife of his, Ella?'

'Esme.'

'That's right, Esme – I think she suspected something too. It wasn't easy for that William to get himself into the car on his own, but of course Hector had a cast-iron alibi. Spent the evening with the Chief Constable at one of them Lodge meetings. All masons then, you know.'

'Did Esme say anything?'

'Nothing on record. It was her face when Hector recited his story. One glance said it all. I knew she wasn't convinced William got in the car himself. And there was Hector's story. Recited, yes, recited was the word. Sounded rehearsed. Funny how you can hear voices back when you first heard them years ago, and now I can't remember if I locked the front door!'

'So, what was your theory, then?'

'Andy and I thought Hector could've drugged him or even killed him...' Steph leaned in closer to catch his words as he'd lowered his voice to a whisper and the group at the table opposite, having ploughed their way through their meal, was now screaming with laughter over something. 'He could've put him in the car, driven it into the tree and left him until he came back from the Lodge and set the fire then. Waited for a bit, then called it in. The car was in the middle of the estate with no witnesses to say when they first saw it, and by the time the firemen arrived, it was almost over.'

Hale was all ears. 'Did you and Andy tell anyone your suspicions?'

'I couldn't write a word without evidence and Andy tried, but again had nothing tangible, so it was dismissed. You'll have more from this latest death, I'll wager?'

Clearly, Hale wasn't going to be drawn in to give anything

away – once a journalist, always a journalist. 'What did you mean by getting "close" to him? Was there someone else?'

The gigantic plates were placed in front of them by the barman. 'Anything else?' He reached behind him to the hatch and picked up the tomato ketchup, vinegar, salt and pepper with a practised move.

'No, thanks. Looks great.' Steph felt slightly overwhelmed by the enormous battered fish that covered most of her plate. 'More of a whale, isn't it?'

'Funny you should say that – they used to put whale and chips on their menu until some thick Londoner thought it really was whale!'

For several mouthfuls, no one spoke.

Chris balanced his knife and fork on the edge of his plate. 'Now what was it you asked? Oh yeah, who else was close to Hector? There was Madeline, of course.'

'Well, she and Jon lived at the Hall from the start, and they were friends at Oxford – at least, Jon was.' Hale bent down to pick a bone out of his fish, wiping it on the side of his plate.

'They were close... close... You know.'

Steph grinned at Chris' sudden coy embarrassment. 'You mean an affair?'

Chris looked relieved. 'Word was it started just before she opened that school of hers and has gone on ever since.'

'Really? How do you know?' Steph shunted a small mountain of chips to the side of her plate. She'd not lost all that weight to blow it now.

'You just do. The rumours ran through the town, and you only had to see them together to know.'

'Did Esme and Jon know?'

'Shouldn't think so. Husbands and wives are usually the last to find out in my experience.'

Hale appeared to have the whale with extra bones as he extracted another one from his teeth. 'So, you reckon it was still going on, then?'

'Up until the so-called accident? Yes, I do. Hector has always been one for the ladies and put himself around. Always got what he wanted, that one. And as for William – well, he was the only thing stood between Hector and the Hall, wasn't he?'

Chris held up his empty glass to Hale, who immediately took it. 'Think you've earned this one, Chris.'

CHAPTER FORTY-SIX

STEPH AND HALE had arranged to call in to see Jon Henderson on their way to walk Derek on Southwold beach. They'd phoned ahead to make sure he'd be there, and as they drew up outside his front door, he was standing in the open doorway to greet them. The boxing glove bandages had been removed and his hands were now covered in sticking plaster, which apparently made it easier for him to use his hands.

The dressings might have been reduced, but the bags under his eyes hadn't – they'd grown deeper and darker since they'd last seen him. He was wearing the same pale blue shirt as last time, with the same coffee stain just above the waistline of his jeans. Did he never look in the mirror or take his clothes off? He waved towards the car at Derek, who was standing up, staring out of the window.

'Please, bring him in with you.'

Steph opened the hatchback, and Derek jumped out of the car, tail wagging. By the time Steph arrived in the sitting room, Hale and Jon were seated in armchairs on either side of the enormous stone fireplace, so she led Derek to the sofa between them, where he settled down at her feet.

'Thank you so much for seeing us. We have some additional information we would like to share with you.'

'News on Madeline?'

'No, I'm afraid not. This concerns Bella.'

His face reflected the alarm he appeared to feel. 'What's happened to her? What's she done?'

'Nothing, as far as I know, but we're investigating some allegations she's made about Jack Percy.'

'Oh? Jack? What about him?'

Hale opened his notebook. 'Following his attack on Bella at college—'

'Sorry! What attack?'

'Surely you know about it?'

'No, tell me.'

Steph responded to Hale's nod in her direction. 'Perhaps I can help as I was involved. The Wednesday before last, at the end of college when Bella was waiting in Reception for Caroline to collect her, Jack assaulted her and attempted to strangle her.'

'What! Why wasn't I informed?' He turned to Hale.

'Because at that stage, Bella asked us not to tell you, as she didn't want to worry you. However, the college Principal has asked me to investigate, as the assault occurred on college premises, so I have discussed it with Jack and his parents and Bella has agreed that we may tell you.' Once again, Hale nodded to Steph to continue.

'I witnessed Jack assaulting Bella, restrained him, then took him into the Principal's office and made it clear that his behaviour was unacceptable, in fact a crime. The assault was

283

recorded by the CCTV camera in Reception. Jack and his parents have seen it.'

'Really! Why haven't they said anything about this? I mean... I've eaten with them every day since... Well... since the accident. And Bella, you say, didn't want me to know anything about it?'

'No, she didn't want to worry you.'

Jon turned his head from Hale to Steph and then back again. 'If that's so, why are you here now?'

'I'm afraid we have come to tell you that Bella is also accusing Jack of sexual abuse, which has taken place over some time.'

'Are you sure it isn't Graham you're talking about? Have you got it wrong? I wondered if something had been going on there to make him take his own life – maybe that was why.'

Steph shook her head. 'No, it's Jack she accuses. No doubt about that. It was the strength of her relationship with Graham that gave her the courage to confront what had been happening and talk about it.'

Jon struggled to his feet, then fell back into his chair again. 'I'm flabbergasted – no, horrified at what you've said. Bella and Jack were brought up like brother and sister, and I'm sure Jack would never be capable of doing anything so vile.'

'According to Bella, that's exactly what he was doing, and from what you say, you didn't know what was going on?'

His horrified expression gave her his answer.

'Bella felt threatened and trapped by Jack and it was only because his attack was witnessed that she felt able to make public what was happening.'

'I can't believe it of Jack. Are you sure Bella's got this right?'

'Does Bella often make things up?'

Jon frowned. 'No, she's always been a truthful girl.'

Hale joined in. 'We certainly found her story convincing and felt she was telling the truth. Following Graham's death, we discovered that she and Graham were planning to fly to South America to escape Jack. I presume you knew nothing about that?'

Jon's jaw dropped. 'South America! Of course not. South America! I can't believe this is happening.'

'I can assure you we have evidence to back up everything we're telling you.' Hale closed his notebook. 'I'm sorry this has been such a distressing visit for you.'

Jon sighed. 'You can say that again! Madeline and now all this about Bella.' He stared out of the window. 'Suddenly, my life is turned upside down. Had no idea... No idea at all.'

Hale and Steph held the silence, while the realisation of what they'd told Jon filtered down through the layers. The scream of a peacock punctured the peace, making Derek growl and stand to attention, ready to attack. Steph shushed him and patted him on the head. He sank to the ground, alert for any peacock invasion.

At last, Jon looked up. 'You say Hector knew about all this?'

Hale nodded.

Jon's voice was cold and louder. 'Right, thank you for telling me. If you see Bella, please send her my love and tell her I will support her in anything she wants to do. I shall send her a text to that effect.' He stood with greater energy than when they arrived. 'I'll see you out.'

Hand on the door, Hale stopped and turned to Jon. 'Oh, one last thing, were you here when William died?'

'William? Oh, William! No, I was there when he had the skiing accident... tragic... but not here when he died.'

'And did you think it was suicide?'

285

'Suicide? No, it was an accident, wasn't it? There were a few rumours at the time, but those died down after the inquest.'

'Right. Thank you.'

As they drove around the Hall, Steph nudged Hale. 'You didn't want to push him?'

'No, just a nudge to get him thinking.'

Once again, she admired the glow of the Tudor bricks in the evening sunshine. 'Quick! There, at the window. Did you see him?'

'I did indeed. I'm sure Hector will now be off to find out what we wanted to talk to Jon about, and I think this time, he may get his fortune told!'

CHAPTER FORTY-SEVEN

Esme closed her eyes, letting the stresses of the difficult day float away, basking in the last rays of the sun on the west terrace and breathing in the faint perfume of the rose garden. Middleton had found his way to her lap and his purr was almost as loud as the slight breeze drifting through the silver-leafed poplar trees along the drive.

She recalled sitting here beside the handsome, charming Hector the first time he'd brought her to the Hall, when she adored him and tingled whenever he came close to her. Lucky did not describe how she felt when he proposed to her with his grandmother's emerald and diamond ring, which was a perfect fit. Opening her eyes, she absorbed the stunning panorama and knew she should appreciate living in such a beautiful place, but perhaps now—

'Where's Hector?' Jon barrelled along the terrace, almost tripping over the edge of one of the uneven stone flags by the window.

'In his study, I think.' Raising her hands to shield her eyes from the sun, Esme was surprised to see the agitated Jon. So unlike him; he was usually so calm.

'Will you get him, please?'

'Jon, is everything all right?' What was wrong with him? Why wouldn't he go indoors to see Hector?

'I need to talk to you both and I'd prefer to do it out here, not in his study.'

'Oh. Right. I'll get Hector.'

Jon sat in the chair opposite and placed his phone on the table in front of him, as if he'd come for a formal meeting. Not like him at all. As instructed, she hurried to fetch Hector, who, when he heard of Jon's mood, picked up a decent bottle of claret and three glasses on his way outside.

They emerged together to find Jon sitting erect, checking his phone. His pale blue shirt could do with an iron and a wash too, but he'd shaved off the straggly beard he'd allowed to grow since the fire. It hadn't suited this man, who had always taken such pride in his appearance. She must have a word with Liz and ask her to check on his wash box and ironing pile.

Hector opened the bottle and handed a glass to Esme, then Jon. 'Needs time to open up, but I think it's rather good. Such a beautiful evening and so warm. Cheers.'

They clinked their glasses and sipped the dark ruby wine – at least Esme and Hector did, but Jon placed his glass on the table north of his phone, apparently resisting the temptation.

'Lovely to see you, old man.' Hector, charming as ever, patted Jon's arm just beneath his shoulder, letting his hand remain there for a few moments before he breathed out and relaxed. 'Nothing like it, is there? Sitting at the end of the day with friends and a decent claret.' Jon didn't reply or react but appeared hypnotised by the untouched glass of wine. 'So lucky with the weather, too. Wonderful day.'

Jon remained silent. Hector raised his right eyebrow and frowned – a silent question to Esme asking what he should do. Confused by the unusual behaviour of both men – Hector was never at a loss, Jon always polite – Esme concluded it was safer to say nothing.

'You knew all the time, didn't you?' Jon turned from his glass to stare Hector down. He didn't succeed.

'Know what, old chap?'

'About Jack and Bella.'

'What about them? They make a wonderful couple.'

'That's what I thought until I heard he'd been abusing her.'

For a moment, shock flashed across Hector's face and he frowned, clearly working out what Jon might have found out. He took a sip of wine, and by the time he'd replaced it on the table, he'd resumed his urbane confidence. 'Abuse? If you're talking about that ridiculous horseplay at college, I'd hardly call that abuse. More robust courting.'

'Would you? Not what the police or the Principal are saying. Apparently, the Principal has asked the police to investigate what was described to me as "an attack". I understand there's video footage of Jack trying the strangle Bella, which I gather you've both seen.'

Hector took a measured sip of wine. Esme daren't say anything in case she said the wrong thing, so also resorted to the wine. Taking great care to place his glass in the centre of a flower pattern on the green metal table, Hector smiled at Jon. 'You're not drinking, old chap. Would appreciate your opinion on this.'

Jon swept his arm across the table and whacked his glass with a powerful backhand. The glass soared through the air, smashing on the flagstones, and the wine appeared to form a perfect slow motion arc before splashing Hector's beige trouser legs and Esme's bare feet. Although aware, both refused to acknowledge the fall-out.

'I say, old chap. Rather dramatic! Pretty good stuff too! Now, let's talk this through calmly.'

'Perhaps you'd like to include Jack's long term sexual abuse of Bella as an item on our agenda and don't you dare "old chap" me!'

Hector paused to top up his glass. 'Right, let's start off by hearing your side of it.'

Typical of Hector not to give anything away, but Jon knew him well and clearly wasn't going to be conned by that approach.

'No, let's start with the attack and what *you* know about Jack's abuse.' Jon placed his plastered hands on the table where they appeared to grow cartoon-like and remind them of the misery he was already enduring.

Hector took another mouthful, savouring the wine as if at a tasting, clearly composing how he was going to respond. Esme had to admire his self-possession, even under fire.

'I'm afraid Jack is a typical boy. You've been lucky with Bella, a fine and sensible girl, but boys will be boys and they do stupid things without considering the consequences. That's what all this is about, old chap.'

Hector looked at Jon, clearly assessing how well he was doing so far. Jon appeared not to be impressed but said nothing, so Hector continued his attempt at damage limitation.

'It's quite clear; Jack's in love with Bella, always has been – knows what a wonderful girl she is. Doesn't know how to express it, stupid boy. He sees her recent dalliance with the gardener's son as a way of provoking him, of making him jealous, so he over-reacts and behaves like a boor and the video caught him. That's all.'

'That's all! I gather she was bruised for days from his boorish behaviour. Hid it from us – I mean me – as she did the years of his sexual predation.'

'Oh, come on – hardy predation! Children's games, that's all. She'll come round and realise all this is Jack being immature and not being able to express his love for her.'

'And if she doesn't "come round", but takes him to court, what then?'

'It will hardly come to that, will it? She'd never want to make a fuss or go through the public humiliation of a trial.' Hector lowered his voice. 'And anyway, it would be her word against his, wouldn't it?'

Jon leaped up – was he about to up-end the table? No, he stood furious, glaring down on Hector. 'Are you saying Bella would lie about being sexually abused?'

'No, not at all, old man,' Hector took another sip, apparently trying to appear unruffled. 'Sometimes people get the wrong end of the stick, that's all. When Bella deigns to come home, let's listen to what she has to say and see where we go from there. If Jack has done wrong, he will be severely punished, I assure you.'

Jon's anger appeared to subside a little but he continued to frown at Hector, who tapped him on the upper arm and placed his hand on Jon's shoulder. 'No need for us to quarrel, old chap. Let's wait to see what Bella has to say. We're almost family, after all, and owe each other so much.'

Jon slumped a little in his chair and seemed to lose all energy. He fiddled with the plaster on his right hand, smoothing down a curled-up edge, and said nothing.

Hector observed him for a moment, then grinned at Esme. 'Now, Esme, fetch Jon another glass and let's enjoy this magnificent sunset together.'

Hardly believing that Hector had got away with it again, Esme did as she was told and fetched another glass for Jon and a brush and dustpan for the broken glass.

When she returned, they were sitting side-by-side chatting about the cricket score as if nothing had happened. How did Hector charm his way out of these messes? How could Jon let it go? She felt angry on Bella's behalf, convinced she was telling the truth. It was appalling how these men shrugged it off with the 'boys will be boys' stuff.

Reaching for her glass, she looked across at Jon and sensed that all wasn't well there. There was a distance that she hadn't felt before. Why wasn't he angry? Why had he given in so easily?

CHAPTER FORTY-EIGHT

'I NEED to talk to you *now!*' Hector's voice echoed along the marble hall from where he stood, a tall shadow in his study door.

Esme responded, her heart racing, dreading what was to come, and took her time getting there. 'Coming.'

She sighed as she entered his study and, as she was lowering herself into her usual chair before his desk, he barked, 'The door, woman! Won't close itself.'

Hauling herself up, she trudged to the door; as she closed it, a draught caught it and slammed it shut.

'No need for drama, is there?' Frowning, Hector waved her to her seat. Why did he always have to take control, even over the little things? She fixed her face in neutral, not sure what was coming next.

He had drunk most of the bottle of claret, as neither she nor Jon wanted more than a glass, and he was in action mode. Although Jon had given in and accepted the wine when she returned with the replacement glass, she wasn't sure he was totally satisfied but apparently knew he couldn't fight Hector and win. She was surprised after his initial, strong reaction that he hadn't persevered, as she was certain Jon was in the right and Jack was guilty of Bella's accusations.

'I need to talk to you about what has been going on and ask for your support – your active involvement in resolving this mess and getting the police off this estate, once and for all.' Hector paused, apparently waiting for her agreement. He was not to be argued with. 'Well, do I have your support?'

'Of course.' Agreeing was the best way of getting out of there as soon as possible.

'First of all, there's Bella and Jack. You've been siding with Bella—'

About to protest, Esme opened her mouth, only to have Hector tap on the desk. 'No! That will not do. You are to support Jack; do you hear me? You contributed nothing out there, did you? Nothing.' He slammed his hand on the desk. She jumped and closed her eyes.

'Now listen!' He slapped his hand down again. She winced, then opened her eyes and looked up at him. 'That's better. I expect you to visit that busy-body woman, Caroline, and insist that Bella is telling a pack of lies. Girls can get hysterical, especially at that age – hormones and all that sort of thing, so it's quite plausible she has mistaken what is actually extremely trivial and blown it up out of all proportion.'

Saying nothing was the best thing to do.

'She's an attractive young lady who made overtures to Graham Andrews to make Jack jealous. It is, after all, a well-known ploy you women use to get us men... umm... how can I put it... fascinated and involved in the hunt.'

He frowned and scanned the sky outside the window, apparently searching for inspiration. The last pink trailing clouds were now becoming grey as the light dissolved beneath them. If only she could be out there, breathing the gentle perfume of the roses and walking out beyond to the silver birches and oaks where she could find peace from this battering monotone. She jumped as his voice forced her back into the room.

'Ah-ha! That's the quote; "A man chases a woman, until she catches him". Precisely what has been going on here.'

The nursery rhymes picture book image of Jack Horner popped into her head, plum pulled from the pie balanced on top of his thumb, wearing the same smug expression she saw on Hector's face.

'Don't you agree, Esme? Don't you think this is what has really been going on all this time?'

'If you say so, Hector.' Returning to the room, the grey veins on the fireplace pulled her in once again. Get absorbed in the mountain and lakes until he was done. From somewhere, she stirred. No, it wasn't all right.

'If what you are saying is true, why did he assault her in the college?'

Taken aback by her question, Hector fixed her with a 'how dare you' look. 'Whatever do you mean by that?'

She tried to keep her voice strong and not letting it wobble. 'What I say, Hector. We all saw that film footage and there was no doubt that Jack attacked Bella. That wasn't affection or love, it was anger and aggression.'

'You are wrong. It was horseplay.'

'No, it was serious. Serious enough for Mrs Grant and the Principal to think about making a formal complaint to the police on Bella's behalf.'

'Come off it. That was part of her strategy. Bella wouldn't make a complaint because she welcomed Jack's attention.'

'Attention? She was hurt in that attack—'

'Will you stop saying "attack"!'

'She wasn't enjoying it as sexual foreplay, or whatever you think it might have been. We have to be realistic; Jack is a bully and I believe he's been abusing Bella for some time.'

Hector swooped around the desk and stood over her, his hand gripping her shoulder. It hurt.

'Let's get something straight, Esme. There is no debate about this. Jack and Bella are meant for each other, and this is a slight tussle in their story. Jack may not always be the most subtle, but he is sincere – he cares for Bella and wouldn't hurt her, however much she provokes him or leads him on.'

His grasp on her shoulder became sharp, his pointy fingers exerting their power as he squeezed just beneath the bone. She squirmed, trying to wriggle out, but he tightened his hold. It was useless to argue, and only worse would follow if she did.

'Do you agree with me?'

'Yes, Hector.'

At last, he let go. A burning sensation remained, but she supposed it would go – if not, there were always the painkillers. He returned to his seat and placed his hands on the desk in front of him, posing like the lord of the manor he was. Clearly, this session wasn't finished yet.

'Well, I'm pleased we've cleared that up. When you've spoken to Caroline and Bella, I expect you to report back to me. Is that clear?'

She nodded.

'Now, moving on to Jon. I've noticed you've become closer to him since the accident and for some strange reason he has become... what shall I say... rather stiff and distant where I'm concerned and his behaviour this evening was appalling. Not him at all. Actually, I suspect his mind has been turned by that interfering police couple. We need him back on side, Esme, and this is where you will help.'

Her eyes shut, she took deep breaths to slow her heart rate and stop the panic from spreading. Now what did he expect her to do?

'I'd like you to invite Jon, Luke and Zac to dinner – one evening this week, when they're all free. And I mean dinner, not one of those kitchen suppers everyone goes in for nowadays. Five courses – I'll leave the menu to you. Let me know what you plan tomorrow morning at the latest so I can select the wine and – yes – come to think it, I have a rather fine bottle of vintage port that will go down well.'

Esme wasn't convinced that a resurrection of their old-style dinners would mend the rift with Jon that had appeared since Madeline's death and the revelation of Jack's abuse, nor convince Luke and Zac that their future was to remain at the Hall.

'Well, don't just sit there, woman. Off you go. Masses to do.'

Dismissed, she went straight to the kitchen to see if she could persuade Liz to rustle up a full dinner party at such short notice. What Hector wanted, Hector got.

CHAPTER FORTY-NINE

STEPH HAD BEEN SURPRISED to receive a phone call from Esme asking if they could have a chat away from college and the Hall, and she suggested meeting in the harbour car park and a walk along the beach.

The sun was out and the sandblasting wind had disappeared as Steph stood with Derek beside her stepping on the spot with his front paws, clearly anxious about the delay in being allowed to jump into the sea. Looking out over the river to Walberswick, she was always puzzled that the sea swept in a lot further up that beach than it did on the Southwold side. Once again, she was mulling over this geographical oddity, when Esme's car pulled up beside hers.

Smiling, Steph went to the driver's side to greet Esme, who was sporting large sunglasses, a scarf tied Audrey Hepburn-like over her hair, and a tightly belted raincoat. It made Steph feel under-dressed in her scruffy dog walking suit of jeans and old Barbour, but she realised Esme didn't want to be recognised. At this time, there were few people walking their dogs, so they should be safe.

Derek ran to pounce on the first ball throw, taking him to the edge of the waves, which were moving up the beach with the in-coming tide. At least she didn't have to worry about Derek getting swept out on the riptide and could concentrate on listening to Esme.

They started with the usual 'dancing round the handbags' chat – the weather, the difficulty of parking in Southwold during the bank holiday and their plans for the summer holiday. By that time, they were halfway to the brightly coloured beach huts – the point at which dogs had to be put on their leads and Steph usually made an about-turn. She spotted a large piece of driftwood – half a tree – up by the Maran grassed dunes and suggested they sit on it.

'How may I help you?' Steph decided to go for it.

'I wanted to talk to you about all that has been going at the Hall – away from the Hall, if you understand what I mean. This isn't being recorded or anything is it?' Esme had obviously seen too many cop shows on TV – but then Steph recalled their meeting in Peter's room where she had insisted she recorded their conversation, so reprimanded herself.

'No, of course not. This is between us, but I do need to warn you that although I'm not a full-time police officer, I do work with them, and if you tell me anything that I consider to be criminal activity, I will have to report it.'

'Naturally. I wouldn't expect anything else, and I wouldn't dream of putting you in a difficult position.' She paused. Steph wondered if her comments had made Esme have second thoughts about the meeting, as she must now realise that once she'd said something, it would be difficult to take it back.

The silence grew between them, punctuated by the slapping of the waves as the tide pushed the sea rapidly up the beach. They were well above the tide line, but the rhythmic swooshing helped to reduce the tension.

Esme took a deep breath. 'I need to make it clear that I'm not involved in anything that has been going on at the Hall. You know – the deaths of Madeline and Graham. I'm not sure what's going on, but I want to talk to you as I'm worried in case something else happens. You can decide how much you want to tell your... er... friend.'

'Right.' Steph smiled at her, hoping she would be re-assured and continue; though in her experience, those who protested they weren't involved were often in it up to their neck.

'Madeline and Hector were having an affair...' She sneaked a glance at Steph, who made sure her face didn't change. 'I'm sure I knew exactly when it all started. Hector thinks he's able to hide everything from me, but I knew. He became, how shall I describe it? More solicitous – gentle, you know.'

Steph nodded. Interesting word, that – gentle.

'And then there were the presents. He'd always asked what to get for my birthdays or Christmas or he'd get me to leave a wish list on Amazon or John Lewis and he'd go there. Suddenly presents just appeared – he even remembered several wedding anniversaries. And they were thoughtful – you know – more like the presents women who know each other well give to each other. Does that make me sound terribly sexist?'

'Not at all. I think you're probably right – about the presents, I mean.'

'And then, there were the additional Lodge meetings and golf played at strange times, as apparently the course was fully booked. Anyway, I knew, and I think Madeline knew that I knew. That was when Hector helped her start the school on the estate. Pumped money into it.'

Esme frowned and stopped, apparently re-playing what she'd just said. 'I don't want you to think that Madeline only got involved for the money – I'm sure she didn't. I could see that she and Jon were drifting apart, and Hector was there, as Hector's always there. She never spoke to me about it but went out of her way to be nice to me.'

'You sound as if you didn't mind.'

Esme smiled, her head on one side. 'I don't think I did. They were both careful to make sure I didn't see anything, and life appeared to be going on as it always had, and Hector was fully occupied – if you know what I mean?'

Steph thought she did and nodded.

'He made a greater effort to involve Jon in the estate – he'd stopped commuting to London for work four days a week. I always wondered if Jon had done that because he suspected, but I don't know. He gave no sign that he knew.'

'Really?'

'And Hector spent more time with Jon. You know, trips to the pub and visits to races – Newmarket, Great Yarmouth, occasionally even to London. Jon has always worshipped Hector – is that cruel?'

'Not really, if that's how you saw it.'

'Hector can be so charming when he wants, and everything he does is planned. He's good at the detail and always thinking of new schemes for Glebe Hall. That's his life, and he's made sure it survived.'

'Didn't he inherit it from his brother?'

Esme frowned. 'Yes. William was a lovely man, and it was tragic what happened to him.'

'You mean the skiing accident?'

Esme stiffened up. 'You know a lot. That was ages ago.' She

paused, scrutinising Steph, who wished she'd kept her mouth firmly shut.

The frothy edge of the sea was getting closer. It wouldn't reach them, but Steph wondered if Esme would use it as an excuse to move and stop confiding in her. Esme stared unblinking at the waves eating up the sand, apparently hypnotised by their rhythm. Steph waited patiently, her lips closed tight, to stop herself from saying anything.

'As I was saying, there has been too much death at the Hall, and I want it to stop. Madeline and then that poor boy, Graham. I'm not sure what is going on, but I do know how you might find out.'

CHAPTER FIFTY

It was cold in the barn. Steph, Hale, Bob and Dick were spread around its edge in the darkest spots, hunched down behind large lawn mowers, bags of compost and rusty old implements. The traditional old mud and lath walls might appear romantic on postcards, but at this time of night, the draughts let in through the gaps peppered around the walls made sitting on piles of damp old sacks uncomfortable. A needle stab made Steph jump, and she scratched at what she was sure was a flea bite on her arm. Why had she agreed to come?

They had parked their cars on the grass verge outside the pedestrian gate at about eleven, after the sun had gone down, and crept along the wall, behind the tall beech hedge, to the barn. Esme had told Steph about Hector's nightly forays searching for a cuff link, a story she didn't believe and she feared Hector was searching for something connected to Graham's death.

According to Esme, if Hector turned up tonight, it would be his third attempt to find whatever might be incriminating, and Hale hoped they'd be able to confront him and shock him into admitting something. Although the forensic team had combed the barn and surrounding area following Graham's death, they hadn't found any significant evidence.

In the gloom she could make out the shape of Hale opposite, behind enormous barrels of chemical weedkiller; Dick was crouched below the side of the truck where they'd found Graham, while Bob sat on a stool behind the workbench. They had been there about an hour and Steph was starting to stiffen as the cold penetrated her bones. She was flexing her right leg, as she could feel it cramping when she heard something. The tension was solid, and she felt the others hold their breath to listen to a noise that came from the right of the open barn door. Had she imagined it?

No, there it was again. The nearly full moon moved from behind a cloud and lit up the path outside. There it was again. Then she saw it – a rat – ugh! It skittered around the door and into the barn. Oh, no! Please don't let it come towards her. Would she be able to hold her nerve and not scream?

A shadow moved in the silver moon path. A figure, a man, crept towards the barn, holding a phone torch to light his way. He held it down low so that the light was directed in a tight beam in front of his feet. The others had seen it too – she was aware of them moving a little, tensing, ready to act.

The light entered the barn and with slow but deliberate movements it swept the floor as the figure above it searched the ground just inside the door, to the left. It stopped. The man's foot scuffed at the ground and kicked a stone away, then he moved forward. He crouched down. Fingers appeared in the beam and dug around in the tyre track of dried mud left by the truck or mower. The hand moved along the track, sieving the grains, stopped, dug deeper and picked up something hidden deep inside the pile of soil at the very edge of the barn. She knew Hale would go mad if he'd found something the SOCO team had missed.

A startling white LED light flashed into life opposite, followed by two others from the other sides of the barn, spot-lighting the figure who knelt on the floor. A loud scream echoed around the walls and cut through the silence. The three lights moved in and illuminated the figure, who held up his arms to protect himself from the onslaught. As he moved his right arm to shade his eyes, she caught sight of his face – no, it wasn't Hector but Jon Henderson.

Holding his elbow, Hale helped him to his feet, and his hands could be seen in the light. His plasters were frayed and grubby from the search and he tried to brush off the grit that stuck to them. 'What are you doing here?' Jon's grey face was shocked and scared; his voice wavered.

The beams from the three torches moved from Jon's face and created a circle of light around him. 'I could ask you the same question.' Hale stood implacable in front of him. 'What were you looking for?'

'Something that was lost here.'

The absurdity of the situation struck Steph, but obviously hadn't got through to Jon, who answered Hale's questions as if it was quite normal to have a conversation after midnight in a dark barn by torchlight. If it had been Hector, she doubted they'd have got away with it so easily.

'And what would that be?'

'One of Hector's cuff links. He dropped it when he was out here, talking to Andrews and Hector's been so good to me, I thought I would help him by coming out to look.'

'At night? Wouldn't it be easier to find it in daylight?'

'Probably – but I couldn't sleep, and we'd been talking about it over supper, so I thought I'd come out and have a look.'

'And is that what you've got in your left hand?' Hale held out his hand, waiting for Jon to give him whatever he was holding.

Jon hesitated and evidently considered refusing, then with a sigh dropped something into Hale's open palm.

One light beam slid across to light up the gold that glinted in Hale's palm. It wasn't a cuff link but a signet ring. What was going on here?

CHAPTER FIFTY-ONE

THE NEXT MORNING, Steph and Hale arrived at the Hall as the church clock was coming up to eight o'clock. Steph had left a message for Peter explaining she would be about an hour late for college and they'd brought Derek with them before dropping him off at the dog lady's house. They could give him a quick run in the park and a dog magically appeared to lower the threat level and helped people relax.

Hale didn't have enough evidence to arrest anybody for anything yet but hoped his relentless visits and questioning would lead to a breakthrough soon. He had a shed load of suspicions, but no actual proof of who had murdered Madeline or Graham. He had sympathy with Andy Cutler, who must have felt the same all those years ago when investigating William's death.

After pulling the metal ring three times, they were greeted by Jack in his boxers and were forced to breathe in his saturated alcohol breath. Peering through the narrow crack of the open door, he scowled when he saw who it was.

'Yes?'

'We'd like to speak to your parents, please. May we come in?' Reacting to Hale's strong formal tone, Jack took a step back and opened the door a little further.

'You could, but they're not here. I think Mummy said she was going over to see Daddy in the hunting lodge. He often goes there to shoot vermin when he needs to calm down.'

Calm down? Had there been enough time for Jon to tell Hector about being caught in the barn? Surely, Jon had just got back from the police station? Hale only had time to grab a quick coffee and a change of shirt before they'd rushed out again.

'And precisely where is the hunting lodge?' Again, Hale's voice pierced Jack's hangover and made him wince. He must have had a skinful, as breathing in his fumes made her feel dizzy. Steph didn't envy his headache.

Making a great effort, Jack ventured out onto the steps beside them, gripping the wall to steady himself, ignoring, or not feeling the tiny stones that must be cutting into his bare feet. He waved his hand to the right. 'Past the lake, at the far end of Badgers' Wood.' He took another step to peer around to the front and side of the Hall. 'Erm... Sure the quads were here when I got home this morning. Now gone. They must have taken them. Sorry.' Jack burped more concentrated alcohol breath in their direction before turning round and staggering back into the house.

'Good job we've got the four-wheel drive then.' Hale spoke to the closed door.

Hale had returned from the station at dawn, where he'd learned little new information from Jon, who claimed he must have misheard Hector when he spoke of a cuff link – he must have meant his signet ring. They must understand he hadn't been sleeping well since the accident and hardly knew what day it was. Hale found his confused state convincing but didn't believe a word he said about the muddle over the ring and the cuff link.

When pushed on why he'd been searching for Hector's property, Jon mumbled a long and confused explanation about owing Hector and Esme so much and wanting to help after they'd done so much for him.

'Look, all the curtains are shut tight. Jon must be in bed.' Steph gestured towards Jon's wing of the Hall.

'Lucky old Jon. All right for some.' Hale turned off the road and headed over the grass towards Badgers' Wood.

Having passed the blackened patch where the car fire had been, they drove on along the rutted track for another half mile or so until they spotted a building the size of a detached house, which they guessed was the hunting lodge and climbed out of the car.

For many people, not graced with living in a Tudor mansion, it would make a large home with its mullioned windows, thatched roof and lime-washed walls, punctuated with grey, weather-aged oak beams supporting the structure. This perfect country home even had a pale pink rambling rose growing around the door.

As they stumbled towards it over the rough ground at the edge of the wood, trying to keep up with Derek, Steph took in the stunning views of the flowing Suffolk landscape, far away from the constant traffic buzz of the A12. The silence was fractured by a shot that reverberated around the trees; the sound seemed to come from behind them.

A figure emerged from the far side of the hunting lodge,

silhouetted against the sun, aiming a gun across the field, re-creating a Victorian etching she'd seen in the sitting room. The figure froze, concentrating on following his prey, his gun sweeping from left to right. It promised to be a bright summer's day with the dew already drying, a heat haze distorting the view and the sky deepening to a rich azure blue.

As they got closer, Hector evolved from a silhouette to a man dressed in a traditional green and brown shooting outfit, resembling the generations of his family who had shot there before him. He broke his gun and let it lie across his arm as he turned, shouting at someone hidden by the house. They couldn't hear the words, but from his angry tone, it was clear he was losing it.

From behind a tree, Steph saw Esme appear, moving towards Hector, waving her arms as if trying to explain something. In contrast to Hector's shooting camouflage, she wore bright colours – red top, blue jeans and a floaty red and white spotted scarf. Obviously, she didn't plan to join him in tracking and shooting rabbits or whatever he was after.

Derek growled, but not loud enough for them to hear him.

'Shh!' For once, he did. It appeared Esme and Hector were in the middle of a row, and she was getting the worst of it. His voice dominated and echoed across the wood as he yelled at her. Esme's shorter replies were high pitched and sounded desperate. Hale raised his eyebrows towards the couple, and they crept across the tussocky grass towards them, Steph keeping Derek tight and close to her legs on his short lead.

A slight breeze carried Hector's words towards them. 'You don't know what you're saying, woman. Think for once in your life, will you? Think of the consequences of what you're suggesting.'

'I am – I have thought it through. Why don't you listen to me for once?'

'I'll tell you why – because you're a total waste of space. I need you to shut the fuck up and let me get on with it.'

'Like you did with Madeline, you mean?'

'That's enough. Leave Madeline out of this.'

'I knew all the time what was going on. You think you're so clever, but I knew from day one.'

'Don't lie.'

'Lie? Me? You lie every time you open your mouth. You can't help yourself.'

They were so involved in shouting at each other, they failed to see Steph, Hale and Derek in the shadow of the house, creeping closer. Steph noticed that Hale kept his eyes on the gun, not Hector. It was a twelve bore, a Boss – a valuable gun passed down through families like Hector's. He'd fired it once, so there was a second cartridge in the chamber.

'I know you killed Madeline. Got bored with you, did she? Didn't dance attendance on you any more, or did you kill her because she stopped submitting to you?' Esme appeared taller as she ripped into Hector and, head jutted out, pushed towards him, a woman driven by fury.

He took a step back.

'Refused to submit to your big man act, did she? Resisted the ropes, the whips, the droit de seigneur? Did she tell you role playing can't make up for your flaccid, tiny—'

Rage flashed across his face, and cracking up his gun, he pointed it at Esme. Derek, standing tense throughout the shouting, the fur on the scruff of his neck erect, tore his lead out of Steph's hand and flew across the space towards Hector. Hale and Steph shouted as one, 'Derek!'

Distracted, Hector swung his gun at the snarling shadow as

Derek leaped at him. Hale followed, desperate to save the dog. The gun went off; the explosion drowned out Esme's scream and Hector yelled as he fell to the ground, Derek and Hale on top of him. For a moment the world stopped; the pile on the ground froze – apart from a pool of blood seeping into the grass.

CHAPTER FIFTY-TWO

ESME STORMED across the room from her desk below the window, slammed the door so no one could hear them and shoved Jack back onto the sofa. Standing over him, glaring down into his face, she froze as she pictured herself adopting a Hector pose, so she unwound and sat on the Chesterfield opposite.

'Now, tell me again slowly. What exactly have you done?'

Jack picked up an olive-green velvet cushion, held it in front of him and cuddled it for a few moments before arranging it with care on the seat beside him. Irritated by his attempt at creating drama and forcing her to wait, she squirmed and leaned forward. 'Well?'

A melodramatic sigh was followed by a rueful expression. 'I had to do it. You know that, don't you? It was my duty.'

'What did you do? What are you talking about?' She wanted to slap him into telling her.

'Well, after Father tried to shoot you, I went down to the police station this morning.'

'But I thought you said you were going to the hospital to

visit him? I told him you'd go after college when I saw him last night.'

'On the way, I changed my mind. He's hardly at death's door, is he? I can always go later.'

'Jack! Tell me what you've done!' Her voice became shrill with frustration and fear.

'As I was saying, I thought it was better to get it off my chest.'

'Get what off your chest?'

'I'll tell you if you'll listen.' Clearly waiting for her response, head on one side, he stared her out. She remained silent, biting the inside of her lip to stop herself from speaking.

'Anyway, I spoke to a man called Sergeant Johnson, who assured me he was working on our case with the Hale man. I didn't know we were "a case". I signed a statement as I wanted to go on the record before Father came out of hospital and told them something false.' He paused again. Apparently, he was enjoying spinning it out. She decided not to play, and bit harder – she tasted blood.

'I told him about Bella making false accusations against me and Mrs Grant hurting me after I was messing around in college Reception and how Bella was only going out with Graham Andrews to make me jealous.'

He paused again. Esme waited.

'I told him about that afternoon in the barn when I went there to see Graham to tell him to leave her alone.'

'Sorry? What afternoon?'

Jack picked up the cushion again, moulded it into a more comfortable shape and hugged it to him. Adopting a patronising tone, he spelt it out as if she was a total idiot.

'I went out to the barn to talk to Graham Andrews about Bella the afternoon he died. Understand?'

'Yes, thank you.'

'When I went there, I thought he'd listen and that would be that. But he shouted at me and told me to fuck off and leave Bella alone. That he was her boyfriend, that she loathed me, that every time I went near her, I made her flesh creep, and if I didn't stop, he would make me.'

Esme's stomach tightened as she suspected and dreaded what was coming next.

'Suddenly he flew at me, like the thug he is – was. We hit each other and rolled around on the ground until I grabbed a spade leaning against the truck and hit him with it on the side of the head. I had to do it, understand? It was self-defence. I think the police officer understood.'

Esme, horrified, froze, waiting for the next appalling instalment.

'He fell to the floor and lay there. I thought I'd killed him, but he was still breathing, I swear it. He was breathing. I hadn't killed him. I had to hit him in self-defence, or he might have killed me.'

'Jack...' His whispered name came out in her breath as she released it. Scared of him telling her more, yet knowing she had to know.

'It was then I realised I'd lost my signet ring, and although I looked around by the truck where we'd been, I couldn't find it. And that was it.'

'What do you mean? That was it!'

'What I say. I came back here. The next thing I heard was that Graham was dead.'

Esme felt nauseous. Surely, she couldn't have heard what Jack had just told her? The fight, then... it was too awful to think about. Yet, Jack appeared to be serious and calm. After this, the police were bound to think he'd murdered Graham, and Hector would be furious when he heard Jack had been to the police.

'And that's what you told the police?'

'Yes. That's what I told the police. Thought it was best before they found out.'

'Why?'

'I suppose they'll arrest Father for trying to kill you at the lodge and I wanted to make sure they knew it wasn't me who killed Graham by admitting to what I had done.'

Horrified, Esme wasn't sure what on earth was going on. Surely Jack would now be a suspect as he'd admitted responsibility for injuring Graham so he was unconscious and couldn't resist? She felt faint. Could Jack have killed him?

Jack placed the cushion carefully beside him on the Chesterfield and looked up at her through his eyelashes, Now what?

'You see, I know, Mums, I've not always been good or what you or Father hoped I'd be, and this was a way of putting it right. I felt uncomfortable knowing what I'd done to Graham.'

Jack checked on her appreciation of his words by glancing at her through his eyelashes again. She had no intention of making it easy for him, so she kept her face straight and sat silent, waiting for him to talk his way through his explanation.

'I never intended to hurt him but to scare him away from Bella and I knew it was wrong to hit him with a – to knock him unconscious. It was cheating, wasn't it?'

Once again, he gave her what he obviously thought was a winning glance. As she said nothing, he continued. 'But I wanted them to know I hadn't killed him and I was sorry. I felt it was time to tell the truth. I don't want to be like Father—'

Further revelations were interrupted by the landline ringing. Esme made it out to the hall table before the answerphone kicked in. 'Yes ... Hello ... Of course, that's fine ... Ten minutes? ... Yes, see you then.'

Her leg muscles appeared to have dissolved, and Esme found it difficult to walk back into the sitting room. Holding onto the edge of the door, she stared across at Jack. 'That was Steph Grant. She's coming over to collect her coat. She laid it over Hector, while we waited for the ambulance after the shooting, and she said she also wants to check how I'm doing.' Her robotic recitation of the conversation appeared to have little impact on Jack, who looked as cool and innocent as ever.

'I'll be in my room if you want me. Don't want to see that woman after what she did to me.'

Esme wasn't sure what to say or do after Jack's revelation. Madeline's death had started it all, hadn't it? And now here was Jack telling her he'd been involved in Graham's death. Could Jack have murdered him? What a nightmare! The door-bell rang and Jack swept past her up the stairs as she went to the front door.

CHAPTER FIFTY-THREE

As THE DOOR was thrown open, Steph rushed in, pushing past an amazed Esme, who stood back to let her in.

'How do I get to the roof?'

'Up there, why?' Esme pointed to the main staircase to the side of the marble hall.

'He's on the roof! Show me!'

'Who is?'

'Jon. Quick!'

Steph pushed Esme in front so she could show the way up the flights of stairs, which became narrower as they climbed each floor. Her lungs burned with the climb of three, or was it four floors? She'd lost count. At last, they ran down what must have been the servants' quarters. Bare floorboards, doors down both sides of the narrow corridor, led to an ancient door at the end with an ornate iron key in the lock. It swung open easily in the strong wind from the roof.

The steps to the roof were more like rungs on a ladder rather than stairs. Steph clambered her way up to the top and, catching her breath, pushed the two wooden flaps open so they fell on the roof; she peered through the open hatch. Esme was behind her. She could feel the stair ladder wobbling as the vibrations loosened the metal loops holding it into the wall – would it bear their weight?

Gripping the rotting frame, blood pounding in her ears and panting, she tried to climb out without alarming him. She knew any sharp movement could push him over the edge, literally. Looking down behind her, she saw the top of Esme's head and bent down to whisper, 'Go back and call the lot – police, ambulance, fire service – we'll need them all.'

The ladder juddered again as Esme climbed down and Steph, with a slightly slower heartbeat, clambered up the last few rungs and emerged onto the roof. It was flat, thank heavens. Slates, many of them worn, chipped and split, ran to the small brick battlement wall at the edge of the Hall roof, on which sat, or rather swayed, Jon Henderson.

The roof was edged by a lead-lined, deep gutter, presumably to carry away the rain, in front of the crenelated brick parapet – the top sections about four bricks high and four across, with a lower gap between each one. Jon sat in one of the brick indentations, his back to her, his legs dangling over the edge of the roof, a three-quarter full bottle of brandy balanced on the next brick hump. As she crept towards him, one slate cracked and he turned. 'No! No further or I'll jump!'

'Ok. I'll stay here, Jon.' She moved her weight to spread it across both feet – the slate under her left foot shattered and fell into a black space below. The wooden slats beneath were thin and nibbled in places; many showed cracks, and some had jagged edges where they were already broken. It wasn't a good plan to stay here for much longer. She could see herself falling through the fragile roof to somewhere below – but how far?

'Look, Jon, I just want to talk, but these old slates won't

319

hold me. Is it OK if I come to sit up there beside you – there – to your right – but not too close? Just for a few minutes?'

Jon appeared to be thinking about it and counting the top sections to his right. 'You can go to that one there, the third one, the one in front of you. There—'

As he pointed, he wobbled a little and gripped the top brick with his left hand. If the brandy had started off as a fresh bottle, he must be almost out of it. As if reading her mind, he took another gulp, wiping his mouth with the back of his hand. Every movement made him less stable. Steph had to keep him talking until help arrived.

On tip toe, she gingerly placed each foot, trying to select the most stable parts of a slate before she transferred her weight. She was doing well when a resounding crack made her pull her foot back. Another slate disintegrated and clattered into the void below. She didn't hear it land. How far down would she drop? Stop thinking about it, she told herself, and scoured the nearest slates to identify the strongest.

At last, she made it to the brick battlement and sat down sideways on to Jon, but with her feet firmly on the roof side in the gutter. While she'd been picking her way across the roof, Jon had taken another gulp. He'd be totally wrecked soon. Was it already too late?

Peeping over the edge of the wall, she estimated it was – it was far too high to survive a fall. No bushes or canopies to break the fall like in films, but a sheer drop onto the stone flags of the terrace.

Feeling dizzy, she closed her eyes, took a deep breath and sat up, concentrating on Jon. The strong wind nudged her towards the drop but she clung on to the edge of the bricks. If it was like this now, whatever was it like in the winter?

Jon faced forwards, apparently hypnotised by Badgers'

Wood with the most sensational sunset beyond it. A smear of grey-pink cloud above the tree line highlighted the searing orange pink of the setting sun, transforming the wood into a magical image of black, lacy silhouettes.

'Stunning, isn't it?'

'Umm.' His grunt was accompanied by another gulp.

Bizarre sitting here watching the magnificent sunset with a man about to commit suicide – she'd be discussing the weather next!

'Look, Jon, this isn't the way. This isn't the way to sort this mess out.'

'No way out.'

'There's always a way out. We can work through this.'

'Too late for me.'

'Think of Bella then. She's lost her mother – she needs you.'

'She's gone.'

'Not really, she hasn't. She's shocked and scared and had to run away. She'll come back to you.'

'Won't be here.'

'You can't do that to her, Jon. You'll ruin her life.'

'Like I've ruined mine, you mean?' Another gulp. 'It's all over for me. Best way.'

'I'm sure you haven't ruined your life and Bella loves you. She's confused and upset, but when she comes back, she'll need you.'

He moved forward and appeared to be looking down at the ground below.

'Look at me, Jon. I know; I've spoken to her. She loves you, she needs you. You can't leave her too.'

As he turned to face her, he wobbled a little and had to grab the top of the bricks to steady himself. She had to get him down as soon as possible, before he lost his balance. He appeared to be thinking through what she'd said, then shook his head, looking hopeless.

'What? With all my debts?'

'I'm sure whatever they are, they're not worth this. They can be sorted—'

'You don't know.'

'Tell me then.'

'I owe thousands – thousands, hundreds of thousands.'

'I'm sure—'

He leaned forward, about to launch himself, then reconsidered and grabbed the bottle once more. Steph felt a little more optimistic – he wasn't sure, was he?

'You don't know. I've gambled thousands. All our savings, our pensions. Bella has nothing. I've left her nothing. The house – it's gone too.'

Another sway, as he turned his head to look at her. 'I promised Madeline I'd stop, but I couldn't.' Another glug. 'I could have got back all the money I'd lost. If only she'd had a little more patience, I know I could have won it back.'

'Is that what you argued about that day?'

'Of course, that's what we always rowed about. That and Hector.'

'Hector?'

'We both owed Hector. Me – I owed thousands – hundreds of thousands – he bailed me out – I'll never be able to pay him back – and then there's the house. That's gone too. Nothing left for Bella. Only way is to marry Jack. Only future.'

'I'm sure—'

'Stop saying you're sure!' Jon screamed and wobbled closer to the edge.

'Sorry.' She held up her hands in surrender, trying to re-assure him, then felt herself pushed by a gust of wind, so she gripped the bricks on either side again. 'You're right. I don't know what you must be feeling, but why don't you come down and we'll talk about it and find a way out of it? There must be a way, Jon.'

'No, this is the best way after what I did to Madeline.'

'Madeline?'

'She came home screaming at me. Hector had been at the school and told her exactly how much he'd lent me, and she was furious. She wanted to finish with him – everyone knew about them.' He scrutinised her, clearly testing whether it was news or if she knew too. She kept her face straight. 'But she said she couldn't finish it because of me. I owed him. She couldn't leave him. We were both trapped. He blackmailed us both.'

Wiping his tears away with his sleeve, his voice got louder as he punished himself. 'I owe him. Thousands. She screamed and screamed – I'd ruined her life and she wouldn't let me ruin Bella's – told me I was a failure – a useless husband and father and she'd wished she'd never married me. I hit her – I hit her, I hit her hard, and she fell – fell on the coffee table – the metal edge caught her head.'

He lifted his hand to his head and touched his right temple. His sobs echoed in the wind and Steph understood the depth of the pit he was in.

'I'm so sorry. I loved her – I hit her. She lay there, bleeding, not breathing. I'd killed her. I deserve to die.' He placed both hands on the top of the bricks either side of him.

'Stop! Jon, you don't! It was an accident. You didn't mean to hurt her. We can explain it to them. It was an accident, Bella will—'

'Bella will what? Forgive the father who killed her mother?'

he shouted and almost lost his balance. 'Forgive? No, she'll hate me, like Madeline did.'

Head down, shoulders slumped, he sobbed, then looked up again at Badgers' Wood. The sun had almost sunk below the line of trees, a burning crescent, signalling the end of the day. Above it, the clouds had darkened to a shade of deep lead. It would be dark soon.

Where the hell were they? No sign of firemen waiting below in case or blue lights along the road. How much longer could she go on? How much longer could she keep him talking?

'Why the car fire, Jon? Why didn't you call the police and tell them the truth?'

He howled an animal howl, again, dashing his tears away with this sleeve. 'You don't think I've asked myself that every moment since?' He fought for breath through his sobs. 'I phoned Hector – he said he'd make it go away – make it look like she'd done it, not me.' He fought his breath. 'We put her in the car, drove it over there—'

He waved his arm towards the wood and got close to over-balancing. Steph held her breath, tensed, ready to grab hold of him, to stop him from going over. She had to save him.

'Set it on fire – I couldn't bear it, seeing her burning. I knew she'd gone, but it was so cruel to burn my Madeline.'

A scraping on the slates behind her made her turn her head. Hale skidded on the ground to her left as he grabbed her. At last! She turned to re-assure Jon and panicked. There was a space where Jon had been. He had gone.

CHAPTER FIFTY-FOUR

ONCE AGAIN, they waited patiently on the steps of Glebe Hall, trusting that the bell pull would summon someone from wherever it rang deep in the house. At last Esme opened the door.

Steph took a step forward into the entrance hall. 'Sorry it's so early, but we've just come from the hospital and thought you'd like the latest news.'

'Thank you. That's kind – do come in. You know the way.' As Steph passed her, an exhausted-looking Esme touched her arm, smiled and mouthed, 'Thank you.'

They sat in what had become their usual seats, and both women looked at Hale, waiting for him to speak.

'Jon had a peaceful night, sedated, of course, which had quite an impact on top of the amount of brandy he'd drunk, but at least he's in safe hands with no injuries. They'll assess him later today when he comes round. I assume you heard what he said to Steph on the roof – she did a magnificent job, by the way.'

Steph blushed, flattered at his praise in front of Esme.

'Yes, I agree.' Esme smiled at Steph. 'I thought you were amazing! How you kept your nerve and stopped him jumping was amazing. I thought he was going over so many times.' Esme re-adjusted her silk scarf, which had slipped down to her lap. Even in the middle of an emergency, Esme looked so elegant, while Steph had caught sight of herself in the hall mirror and knew she resembled someone who'd spent the night under a hedge!

Both looked at her with what she realised was admiration. 'I think I'm supposed to say it was nothing, but I was really terrified up there. Not only that he'd jump but also the height – not great at heights, and the fall was – ugh – makes my legs turn to jelly just thinking of it! And that dreadful moment when I was convinced he'd gone. That was so grim.'

'All thanks to your quick thinking.' Hale turned to Esme.

'Well, I knew there was another hatch, but I've never bothered to go up there. Incidentally, now it's open I can't shut it – the wood must have grown or changed shape or something. I must get Andrews to have a look when he comes back. Can't have the rain coming in. Was your man all right? He must have hurt his leg when Jon fell on him. I'm sure I heard it crack.'

'He'll be fine. It got the full force of Jon's weight when he pulled him off the wall — twisted under him. A Beckham boot for a few weeks and he'll be as good as new.'

Steph had missed the final rescue, as both she and Jon had been distracted by Hale and didn't see Bob Johnson drag Jon into the deep gutter and pull him to safety, despite his injured leg. It was amazing what could be achieved with a massive dose of adrenaline.

'You heard what Jon said about Madeline's death?' Hale, opposite Esme, observed her reaction.

'Yes. It sounded plausible.' Esme sighed. 'Jon was in financial difficulty. I'd known it for some time. Hector said nothing, and hadn't told me how much he'd lent him, but Madeline talked. It started with horse racing, which stopped being fun when it became an addiction, not only at the tracks but online. He found one of those betting sites and that was it – he was hooked. Madeline tried everything – took his phone, locked the computer, but he always found a way round it.'

'But that wasn't the reason they argued, was it?' Steph heard herself ask.

Esme fiddled with the knot on her bright blue scarf and needlessly re-tied it, clearly considering how to go on under Hale's penetrating gaze. She responded, looking at him. 'No. I'm sure it wasn't. As I told Steph, I've known for some time about Madeline and Hector, and I suspected she wanted out. I'm afraid it's typical of Hector to want to keep what he can't have.' She paused. 'Madeline and Jon are – were – both calm, lovely people, but they were at the edge and that's when you do desperate things—'

Hale's phone rang. He fished it out of his pocket, examined the screen, and walked towards the door. 'Excuse me, must take this.' He was gone.

For a moment they sat, listening to the murmur outside, then Esme broke the silence. 'Does Bella know about her father?'

'Yes, I phoned Caroline on my way back from the hospital. She'll take Bella to see him later.'

Hale returned and stood by Esme, his voice serious. 'Is Jack upstairs?'

'Yes. Why? Is it about his visit to the police station yesterday?'

'Could you ask him to join us, please?'

Esme hurried out of the room and soon returned with a

tousled Jack, who'd obviously been roused from his bed. An inside-out tee shirt over shorts that didn't match provided evidence of the speed at which he'd dressed. He scanned the room and when he saw Hale and then Steph waiting for him, he halted, making Esme bump into his back. She nudged him into the room, and he sat on the sofa opposite with her beside him.

'Good morning. What can I do for you?'

Steph admired his composure and confidence. Few eighteen-year-olds would be able to open a conversation when at such a disadvantage.

'We need to talk to you about Graham Andrews' murder.'

CHAPTER FIFTY-FIVE

FOR A FEW MOMENTS, the silence was ear shattering. The ticking clock measured the tension and the whirr of a lawn mower outside reminded them of a normal life beyond the grand windows.

'What the fuck are you going on about?'

'Jack!' Esme held on to the back of his tee shirt, apparently concerned he was about to dart across to Hale.

'But I came to the police station yesterday and told that sergeant everything that happened!'

'But you didn't tell him the whole truth, did you?'

Jack aimed a poison glare at Hale. 'I didn't have to say anything at all, did I? But I thought it would help, and this is what happens when you're a good citizen, is it?'

Cocky was the only word to describe his arrogant confidence. He was wrong if he thought he could take Hale on and win. Hale took a step towards Jack and stood between him and the door.

'Oh, I believe you and Graham fought in the barn, and we have your signet ring to prove it. We know Graham received a powerful blow to his head, as you described, which would have rendered him unconscious, but after that, I think you may have, shall we say, misremembered,'

Hale tensed up, ready to leap into action if necessary. 'Right. Perhaps then, you could explain how we've found traces of your DNA on a piece of wire that you tried to strangle Graham with and then, when that failed, the rope that hanged him?'

Disbelief, replaced at once by anger. 'That could have got there at any time, couldn't it? I might have picked up the wire or the rope when I was in the barn.'

'And you often go into the barn, do you?'

'Sometimes.' Jack's confidence was returning.

'But how do you explain why we found it on the outside, and indeed the inside of the knot and in several other places that tie in —'

Jack groaned at Hale's unintended pun. For a moment, Hale hadn't realised what he'd said. When it clicked, Steph could see he was fuming.

'Very funny, son. This is no joke, but the murder of an innocent lad we're talking about here, and a cold-blooded murder at that.' Hale stood in front of Jack. 'Jack Percy, I'm arresting you on suspicion of the murder of Graham Andrews. You don't have to say anything...'

Esme, mouth open, horrified, listened to the rest of the arrest mantra, while Jack sat looking petrified. Steph knew they'd found DNA from two people on the rope – obviously one of them was Jack. It wasn't looking good for Jack, but after his abuse of Bella and his attack on Graham she found it difficult to feel sorry for him.

When he'd finished, Hale reached for Jack's elbow. 'We need to go to the station now, Jack.'

Jack resisted Hale's hand. 'But it wasn't me! Father could have done it, like he murdered his brother, Uncle William!'

Even Hale was shocked by this latest revelation and let his arm drop as he frowned down at Jack. Esme stared at him. 'You don't know what you're talking about, Jack. William died in a car fire.'

'Just like Madeline.' Jack said what they were all thinking. 'It worked for him, so why not for her? Father's good at sorting things out and making them go away, isn't he?'

'You don't know that, Jack.'

'I didn't, but now I do. I thought they were dreams I was having after Madeline died, but then I realised it wasn't a dream but a memory.'

'Oh Jack, you're talking nonsense.' Was Esme hiding something?

'No, I remembered. Every morning I used to visit Uncle William in his bed for stories – he told great adventure stories. You and Father told me not to go in and disturb him, but he said I wasn't disturbing him, so I carried on. One day I heard someone coming, so I hid under the bed.'

'What?' Esme looked incredulous at his story.

'And someone, who I now know was Father, came in and smothered Uncle William, then later pretended he died in a car accident.'

'How on earth did you know it was Hector? You say you were under the bed?' Esme had taken over the interrogation; Hale let her.

'I saw his shoes, those blue deck shoes he always wears with jeans. It was only after Madeline and the car fire it started coming back in bits until they all joined together. It was him. I know it was.'

'Oh, Jack. What are you saying? First of all, he murders

William, then Graham? The police haven't evidence that he did either.' She glanced at Hale. 'Have you?' A challenge or a search for information?

'As far as William's death is concerned, we have circumstantial evidence and the suspicions of the officers who investigated at the time, but no forensic evidence or witness testimony.'

Esme paused and frowned. 'And if you got some?'

'What?'

'Witness testimony.'

'Then we'd re-open the case.'

'I see.' Esme bit her lip. 'And what happens now?'

Hale moved towards Jack. 'Jack is under arrest, and I'll take him down to the station. We've also arrested Jon and Hector – they'll be interviewed when they're released from hospital and may be charged.'

'Charged? With what?' Esme appeared to be calm, as if she was fishing for information rather than being shocked.

'Difficult to say until we've had their statements and investigated further. But from what we've heard in the last couple of days, we've quite a list – unlawful disposal of a body, perverting the course of justice, blackmail, attempted murder, manslaughter and murder. I'm unable to say what the CPS will decide until we have their statements and identify the DNA.'

'But Hector won't be accused of murder?'

'Too early to say.' Hale waited for Esme to respond. When she didn't, he turned towards Jack. 'Right, Jack, I'll come upstairs while you get changed into more appropriate clothes, as you may be with us for a long time.'

He put his hand on Jack's shoulder while looking over his head at Esme. 'I assume you have a lawyer you can call, or would you like us to provide a duty solicitor?'

'I'll phone our solicitor.'

Steph was fascinated by the birds landing on the lake while Esme, head bowed, fiddled with her wedding and engagement rings as they endured a few minutes of awkward silence, waiting for Hale and Jack to re-appear.

Relieved when they did, the women followed them out to the police car waiting outside. Esme embraced a defeated and subdued Jack before he was ushered into the back of the police car which drove around the side of the house. Esme stood transfixed until the car was out of sight, then bowed her head and walked into the house, shutting the door behind her.

Steph and Hale climbed into her car and sat for a moment, staring out of the windscreen at nothing in particular.

'Well, that was all unexpected, wasn't it?'

Hale patted her thigh. 'If it wasn't so early, I'd suggest we went for a strong drink!'

She started the engine and drove around the Hall. 'You must be pleased that you and the team are getting somewhere at last.'

'Not there yet. This family has a way of worming its way out of problems – started in the sixteenth century, you know!'

'Stop it!' They drove out of the gates that were now so familiar. 'I wonder if Esme will come forward and make a statement?'

'We'll have to wait and see, won't we?'

CHAPTER FIFTY-SIX

Esme stretched over to the kitchen table and switched on the radio; for the second night running, she felt the suffocating silence of knowing no one else was in the house. The pizzicato movement from Ravel's string quartet pinged across the kitchen – she smiled, re-assured and comforted by the random playing of one of her favourite pieces of music.

She could cope; of course she could. After all, she'd lived alone before she met Hector and could do it again. But how did she feel about losing both Jack and Hector?

Closing her eyes, she imagined neither would return. Pausing, she let the thought settle and 'tried on the clothes' as she called it when thinking through a new idea. Umm. It didn't feel so bad. In fact, turning that negative to a positive, she found she felt lighter and relieved.

At once, a shot of guilt went through her, as she disposed of her son and husband and considered a future alone, without them. Of course, she would miss them, but she wouldn't miss the constant compromises and responding to their needs and the sheer exhaustion of living with them.

With Jon, if he came back, on one side of the house and Luke and Zac on the other, she might even develop some new projects. They'd always been easy to work with, and maybe they could develop the workshop side of the business to keep the house going. Hector had always called their suggestions 'arty-farty' but now she'd be able to—

The door slammed against the wall. 'Jack!'

When would he learn? Switching on the light, a figure loomed out of the glare.

'No, not Jack. Disappointed?'

Did that show on her face? He towered over her. Startled, Middleton jumped off her lap and sought refuge under her chair.

'No – no, of course not.' She heard her voice tight, high and stammering like a schoolgirl caught in the act. 'It's just – it's just that Jack always opens the door like that – just like that, so it hits the wall when he comes in and – er – you don't usually.'

Saying nothing, he glared at her, smashed the button on the top of the radio and threw himself in the chair opposite. 'Well, get me a drink, woman. I need one.' A deep frown cut into his forehead, his lips were tight and tension came off him in waves. Now was not the time to ask questions, but to wait until he talked. Esme poured him a large whisky from the bottle in the top cupboard and handed it to him. He grunted.

Middleton leaped up on her lap the second she sat down.

'Bloody cat. Should wring its neck. No use nor ornament. Selfish animals, cats.' He gulped the deep golden drink in one and held out the empty glass to her. Reaching out for it, she dislodged the cat and went to get him a second, larger measure. Once again, he sank it and held out the glass. Esme dreaded him drunk, but his thunderous look warned her not to challenge him.

How had he got here? Was he free of all charges? What had happened to Jack? He would know that she was desperate to ask the questions – that's why he hadn't said anything – but she knew what would happen if she asked, so she bit the inside of her cheek to stop the questions escaping.

Giving him the bottle, hoping he drank himself into a stupor by the Aga, then creeping off to bed was her best plan. Sloshing another large whisky into the glass and placing the bottle on the table within his reach, she turned away, but his iron grip seized her wrist and forced her to her knees beside him. He grabbed a handful of hair and pulled hard so her head was face down on his lap. Please, not that!

'Now where do you think you're off to? Not yet, you don't. Sit.' He shoved her so she fell back, her head hitting the seat of her chair. Biting her cheek hard, she knew not to complain but to do as she was told. Not daring to rub the back of her head, she hauled herself into her chair.

'Now listen and listen hard.' His voice was getting louder each time he spoke. 'They've let me go as they've got no evidence I was involved in that boy's murder, despite your son's attempt to frame me. They—'

'What's happened to Jack?' It came out.

'Ow!' His glass smashed into her head, bounced to the floor, and shattered into tiny shards. The whisky stung her eyes, and the kitchen blurred. Should she sit and blink it out or get up and rinse it?

'Don't dare interrupt me! Get me another!'

Through the stinging mist, holding onto the edge of the table, she pulled her way over to the cupboard, squinted and reached up for a fresh glass, which she held out to him.

'Now shut the fuck up, sit down and listen.' He glugged

another three fingers of Scotch into the glass. Surely, he would collapse soon? 'Your son is in custody but should be out soon, according to that useless solicitor, but he suspects they'll keep Jon for further investigation.'

'Jon? Why?'

'His DNA was on the rope, as I knew it would be.'

'But Jack said *you* sorted it for him.'

A kick aimed at her leg found its target and she winced, trying not to scream out loud.

'Of course I sorted it for him, as I've sorted everything in his useless life. And as for Jon, he owes me.'

Silence was the only way to get out of this. His face contorted into a massive smile. 'And I've saved the house for us.' He leaned forward and caressed her knee, then squeezed it, hard. 'Paid off Jon's debts, got him to take the blame and he's signed over his wing to me.'

Esme couldn't help it. 'What?'

'That's right. We now own two-thirds of this house for a few hundred thousand, which, sadly for Jon, he didn't have.' Hands behind his head, he stretched his elbows back and grinned – his Jack Horner look.

'So that's what he meant when he said he'd ruined Bella's future?'

'Not stupid as you look, are you? As usual, I grasped the opportunity presented to me.' He poured himself another few fingers and gulped it down. Soon he'd be out of it, and she could escape.

'But Jon isn't capable of hanging anyone.'

'No. You're right, he doesn't have the spunk. But he fetched me the rope from the store before he left.'

'Left?' Her erupting anger gave her courage.

'Yes, left – left me to clear up your son's mess.'

'But your DNA—'

'Didn't show up because I grabbed some gardening gloves. Woman, how stupid do you think I am? Anyway, Jon agreed to help when I said I'd let Bella live there until she leaves. Clever move that. And we won't have to worry about buying new furniture for it, will we? Madeline always had excellent taste.'

Bile rose from her stomach. She swallowed, not daring to let him see, and struggled to set her face in a neutral expression.

'And Jack?'

'He'll be fine. He assaulted that boy, knocked him unconscious and may have thought about it and tied the knot, but he left. I saw him leave. I told the police I saw Jon going into the barn after Jack had left, so he must have come along and hanged him later.'

'You told the police that? But why would Jon kill Graham? What reason would he have?'

Frowning, Hector sought deep in his befuddled brain for a motive. She waited, dreading the next pack of lies to flow out of his mouth.

'Funny, the police asked me that too.' He frowned as he was clearly trying to recall what he'd said. 'I told them he didn't approve of Bella being with that oik – that's what I told them, and they sucked it up.'

Hector was starting to slur his words, was slumped in his seat and had problems holding his head up. Soon she'd be free to go. Staring at him, she forced down the anger and disgust that flowed up from deep inside her. Even in this state, he'd spot it.

'Anyway, he deserves what's coming to him for killing

Madeline. That cock and bull story about an accident and hitting her head. He did it – he killed her. Took her away from me – he deserves everything that's coming to him. He took my Maddy away from me. But now, in return, I'm getting the house back.'

An eruption she couldn't control spread through her. She stood over him. 'You've lied and manipulated that man, ruined his marriage and his life just to get his share of the house, haven't you? That was behind all this – this mess. All this tragedy for a house!'

'Shut it, woman!' He grabbed the chair arms, levered himself up a little, but fell back down.

'You killed Graham, that poor boy – he'd done nothing to you. You took his life away for what? A house?'

'A house, yes, *my house*. My family house – centuries of my family – you don't know or care, do you? Now I'm getting it back.'

'Getting it back? Through murder? That's how you got it in the first place, didn't you? You even killed your own brother to get your filthy hands on it. He was a real Percy, a real man, not like you, a bully and a coward and a murderer—'

From nowhere, he launched himself up. His body smashed into her, his hands around her throat, knocking her to the floor and he fell on top of her, squashing the air out of her lungs. Gasping in his boozy breath, she felt sick and turned her head, desperate for clean air. She tried to squirm out from underneath him, but he seized a handful of hair and pulled her back, knelt on her arms, tightening his grip around her throat, and pushed down hard.

Fighting to snatch a breath as his grip became stronger, she tried to kick at him, but his weight was too great; she couldn't move. She must hold on. Usually, he let go before this. Her lungs were exploding, desperate for breath, and her heart raced. She was going. Stars whirled when she closed her eye; there was agonising pain in her throat. She needed air – then everything went black.

CHAPTER FIFTY-SEVEN

STEPH TENTATIVELY LIFTED the latch and peeped round the door. She'd been reluctant to come around the back to the kitchen, but despite several pulls on the bell, she was surprised no one had opened the front door. After all, Esme was expecting her and had agreed it would be a good time for her to collect her coat at last.

Coming in from the bright security light into the gloomy kitchen, she couldn't see much, but heard scuffling behind the far side of the kitchen table. Derek growled, pulling on the lead and standing on his back legs as he strained to be let off. With a tug, he was free; he ran around the table, barked, then whimpered in pain.

'Fuck off!' Hector kicked out again, but Derek bit into his left leg and this time, held on, snarling.

Horrified, she saw Hector kneeling on top of Esme, his hands around her throat. She wasn't moving.

'Hector!'

He ignored her. Had he heard her?

'Hector! Stop!' Screaming, she seized his shoulders and

tried to pull him off. His left elbow jabbed her in the stomach; she gasped and stepped back onto Derek's foot. His squeal made her jump.

She shoved at Hector's back, trying to move him off Esme, but he pushed against her. She kicked his back as hard as she could, but that made him move further forward, leaning on Esme's throat. Desperate, she looked around, and grabbing an iron frying pan from the top of the Aga, she swiped it at him. It hit his head with a crunch, and he crumpled to the floor beside Esme.

Was she dead? She wasn't moving, but neither was Hector. Had she killed him? No, he was breathing. A snore-like snort. She'd knocked him out. There was a gasp, as Esme fought for breath – at least she was alive.

Steph turned her on her side. 'Stay there until you get your breath.' Kneeling beside Esme, she pulled her phone out of her jacket pocket and dialled.

'I need an ambulance, a police car and you to get in here quick!' She hung up.

Esme's gasps were less desperate, and some colour had come back into her face.

'Thank you. He tried – to kill me.' Esme's croaking whisper was punctuated by the snores from the other side of the table.

Light smashed in as Hale threw the door open and dashed over to Steph.

'What's going on?'

'Hector's down there, by the Aga. I knocked him out. He was strangling Esme.'

As she spoke, Hale knelt beside Hector, checked his pulse, and lifted one eyelid.

'Totally out of it. We'll need to get him to hospital. Ambulance on its way.' Returning to Esme, he knelt beside her, examining her neck. 'And you need to get that looked at. Did you lose consciousness?'

At first Esme gave a nod, then shook her head. She tried to sit up but once again didn't appear to have the strength and lay down again.

Steph knelt beside Esme and stroked her arm. 'You should stay there until the paramedics have seen you.' She pulled the cushion down from the chair and gently slid it under Esme's head.

A groan from the floor on the other side of the table alerted them to Hector returning to life. He sat up and held his head in his hands.

'Where am I? What happened?' Holding onto the edge of the table, he pulled himself up a little, then plonked down again. 'Oh! My head hurts.' His fingers explored the lump growing on the right side of his head. Hale stood beside him and helped him to his feet.

'Hector Percy, I am arresting you for the attempted murder of Esme Percy. You do not have to say anything but—'

Hale's calm voice was drowned out by Hector's yell. 'No! Nothing happened. She fell. She won't press charges.'

'I will.' Although a whisper, Esme's words seemed to hit Hector as if she'd slapped him. Defeated and puzzled, he frowned across at her as if he didn't know who she was.

Hale finished arresting Hector for attempted murder as two male paramedics rushed in, followed by two uniformed police officers.

'You need to have a look at both of them. He was unconscious for a while after he hit his head.' Hale nodded at Hector, who probably didn't know what had hit him, the frying pan having been replaced on the Aga.

One paramedic undertook an initial analysis of Hector

while the other checked on Esme. With Steph's help, he got Esme into her chair and continued examining the marks on her throat. He turned to Steph. 'Could you get her some water, please?'

Steph returned with the glass, which she handed to Esme.

'That's right, Esme, just sip it, don't rush.' The paramedic's calm voice was re-assuring and although he was smiling and appeared relaxed, Steph could see that he was observing Esme's every move.

At last, he walked around the table to his partner and, after a quick chat between them, the older man reported to Hale. 'We'll need to take him to hospital to be observed. Although she's badly bruised, she'll be fine here, as long as someone's with her.'

'Thanks. He's under arrest, so I'll have one of my officers accompany him to the hospital.' Hale nodded at the male officer, who walked out beside Hector to the ambulance. As Hector passed Esme, his eyes bored through her, but she lifted her chin to meet his poison glare.

The noise of the ambulance and police car driving away echoed off the Tudor bricks and silence surrounded them.

'I'll call Caroline and Bella. I'm sure they'll come and look after you.'

Esme smiled up at Steph and croaked. 'Please.'

'And while we wait,' said Hale. 'I'll put the kettle on.'

Steph grinned at Hale. She was so glad he was there.

CHAPTER FIFTY-EIGHT

STEPH SAT OUTSIDE, content and soaking in the last rays of the gentle evening sunshine, dreaming with the drifting clouds as the blue dissolved to a pink blush and listening to the cows as they munched along the grass.

After the drama at Glebe Hall, it had been a frantic couple of days for Hale and his team getting the paperwork ready for the CPS. He'd phoned earlier to say he hoped he'd be back for supper and, having lived on sandwiches and crisps for two days, was desperate for some real food.

Caroline had also phoned her to confirm that she and Bella had taken Esme to the police station to make a statement and press charges against Hector. Caroline didn't know what she'd said, and Steph was dying for Hale to appear to tell her all.

At last, the sun dropped behind the silver birch trees in the wood beyond the field, but the evening was still warm. The flat door opened and, after throwing his coat over the usual chair, Hale strode into the garden and leaned over to give Steph the most delicious kiss.

She started to pull herself up. 'I've got one of those quiches you like and a selection of salads in the fridge for us. Hope that's OK?'

He lifted his hand, gesturing she should stay where she was. 'No, I'm fine. G&T?'

'Please.' Derek followed him into the kitchen. 'Don't believe him. He's been fed!'

'That's not what he's telling me.'

'He's lying!'

The clink of ice cubes against the glass announced Hale's return, with a tray of drinks and their plates of salads and quiche she'd picked up from his favourite deli on the way home from work. He let out a deep breath as he relaxed and shared her view across the field towards the black trees, silhouetted against the dark red sky, the cows now wading through the ribbons of mist as the earth cooled. It had been a hot day.

'Oh! That's better!' After a few mouthfuls to assuage his hunger, he reached out to take her hand and squeezed it.

'Good day?'

'Certainly a result – but a lot of work to do before we go to the CPS.' He took another sip and let his breath out slowly, turning towards the final moments of the sunset. 'We are so lucky to have this, aren't we?'

'Yes.' She paused, revelling in the "we". She glanced across; he was busy eating, and she controlled her impatience until he'd finished. 'Well?'

He took a few bone-shaped biscuits from his pocket and threw them across the flagstones for Derek to fetch. 'Esme's statement was gold dust – we've charged Hector with Graham's murder and blackmailing Jon – oh, and the attacks on her.'

'Do you have the evidence?'

'We've got Esme's and Jack's witness statements and now

Jon's account. Hector wasn't as clever as he thought – they found his DNA inside the gardening gloves shoved behind the workbench and a trace on the rope.'

'And William?'

'Apart from Esme's suspicions and Jack's childhood memories, we can't prove it. Unfortunately, William may be a step too far, but we're re-opening the case.'

'And Jon?'

'Jon – what a mess! Manslaughter or maybe accidental death if he's lucky.' He placed his empty glass on the table. Steph noticed and went inside to make him another drink. He looked as he needed it. 'Thanks.'

Wrapping a pashmina around her shoulders against the cool evening air, Steph joined him, observing the cows paddling through the swirling mist. 'Poor Jon. Such a lovely man, but totally manipulated by Hector. Will they take the blackmail into account?'

'Possibly, but he had a choice, didn't he? He could have phoned the police. He didn't have to put Madeline in the car or fetch the rope for Hector. You could argue that through his gambling debts he allowed himself to become Hector's victim.'

'That's a bit unfair. Hector's a powerful man who manipulated everyone, even his wife and son.'

'Especially them. You're right. I hope they recover when he's out of their lives.'

The pale wall lights behind them pushed away the darkness. It was magical sitting out at night, as the moon emerged, and the first stars pierced the dark. She breathed in the peppery scent of a white-flowered plant in one of the pots – she didn't know its name but adored its late evening smell.

'Will they, do you think?'

'What?'

'Recover?'

Hale was silent for a few moments. 'Esme appeared to be strong when she was at the station and gave us all the details we needed to support the case. Not too sure about Jack, though.'

'What will happen to him?'

'He's admitted assaulting Graham and he'll get off the abuse, as Bella said she didn't want to follow it up. What a mixed-up lad!' Hale took a large sip of his drink. 'But in the long run, he's as much a victim of Hector as Jon, Esme or Madeline. Maybe this has really scared him, and when he gets home, he'll find a purpose, apart from being lord of the manor.'

'You're convinced he didn't murder Graham?'

'No, Jon saw him leave the barn before Graham died, and we have evidence he was in his room on social media when Graham was killed. It was interesting spending time with Jack at the station... I felt he was truly remorseful and regretted everything that had happened.'

'Really?' Steph wasn't convinced.

'Yes, really. A few times he said he didn't want to be like his father, and he was so sorry for all he'd done. There seems to have been – what's that word when you suddenly see the light?'

'An epiphany?'

'Oh, I do love an intelligent woman!'

'While all Hector wanted was to question any evidence against him and threaten us with who he would contact to get him off.'

Steph slapped the side of her neck as a mosquito landed for its supper. 'Ouch! We need to go in or get some mozzie spray.'

'It seems a shame to go in.'

Steph fetched the can from the kitchen windowsill, and

after they had sprayed themselves liberally, she lit the yellow citronella candle in the centre of the table as additional protection. The flickering light emphasised the dark bags underneath Hale's eyes. He needed to catch up on some sleep.

Steph patted Derek as he curled down at her feet. 'You might be interested to know what Caroline told me.'

'Caroline? What a surprise!' His grin was ghostly in the candlelight.

Steph leaned over and flicked his arm.

'Go on. What did Caroline say?' He reached for her hand and stroked it.

'Apparently, last night they spent some time going through Hector's desk and, in the obligatory secret drawer, they found the paper Jon had signed returning the east wing to Hector—'

'But SOCO did a search! Don't tell me they messed up again! First the ring and now this!' Hale frowned, clearly annoyed at having to recall their failure.

Not wanting to ruin the mood, she moved on. 'Oh, come on – it was a secret drawer.'

'Anyway, what happened?'

'Esme shredded it, apparently.'

'So, Bella keeps her home?'

'Yeah, great news for Bella. Caroline told me she'll need it when she comes back.'

'Comes back?'

'From New York.' Steph grinned, pleased at her slow reveal of Caroline's news.

'New York?'

'She's taking a gap year working with a friend of Caroline's at the Guggenheim Museum.'

'Lucky girl!'

Hale fished his phone out of his pocket and tapped in a few

words. Steph peered over his shoulder but couldn't make out what he was typing. Aware of her leaning towards him, he looked up and frowned again. 'I'm not sure what's happening with that SOCO team. I'll be having a few words with them tomorrow about secret compartments in antique desks. Making sure I remember.' He slipped his phone back in his pocket.

There was a moment of silence, as the last light in the sky drained away and the glimmering candle gained strength, its light flickering over the table, illuminating Hale's face.

Steph stroked Hale's arm. 'That's that then. Amazing to think we'd no idea what was going on behind the crinkley-crankley wall until a few weeks ago. Since then, we've never been out of the place!' A bat swooped across the courtyard and merged into the grey. 'And how the mighty Hector has fallen!'

'Talk about entitled! He got what he deserved. Only taken four centuries for that family to get its comeuppance! Now, about this holiday...'

ACKNOWLEDGMENTS

Thank you

Rebecca Collins and Adrian Hobart – the talented, tireless power-couple behind Hobeck publishing, for their excellent feedback, inspiration, and encouragement.

Sue Davison, for an outstanding edit and spotting details I missed.

Jayne Mapp, for a creative, evocative and sensational cover design.

Graham Bartlett, for his advice on police procedure and suggesting great solutions to the problems I'd created. Any remaining mistakes are mine.

Brian Price for sharing his extensive knowledge of dead bodies.

Toby Miller for his advice on safeguarding.

Jo Barry, for her constant encouragement and for asking the right questions.

Gerry Wakelin for finding the holes I needed to fill.

Debby Hurst, Freda Noble and Bob Noble – my first readers for their enthusiasm and critical appreciation.

All my friends, for continuing to put up with me banging on about being published!

ABOUT THE AUTHOR

Lin Le Versha has drawn on her experience in London and Surrey schools and colleges as the inspiration for the Steph Grant crime series which now includes two books and a novella.

Lin has written over twenty plays exploring issues faced by secondary school and sixth form students. Commissioned to work with Anne Fine on *The Granny Project*, she created English and drama lesson activities for students aged 11 to 14.

While at a sixth form college, she became the major author for *Teaching at Post 16*, a handbook for trainee and newly qualified teachers. In her role as a Local Authority Consultant, she became a School Improvement Partner, working alongside secondary headteachers, work she continued after moving to the Suffolk coast. She is the Director of the Southwold Arts Festival, comprising over thirty events in an eight-day celebration of the Arts.

Creative writing courses at the Arvon Foundation and *Ways with Words* in Italy, encouraged her to enrol at the UEA MA in Creative Writing and her debut novel was submitted as the final assessment for this excellent course. The first book in this series, *Blood Notes*, was based on her final assessment piece.

Lin is now working on the fourth title in the series.

THE STEPH GRANT MURDER MYSTERIES

Blood Notes

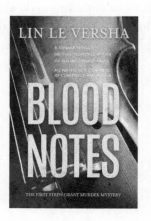

'A wonderful, witty, colourful, debut 'Whodunnit', with a gripping modern twist set in the dark shadows of a Suffolk town.' EMMA FREUD

Edmund Fitzgerald is different.

Sheltered by an over-protective mother, he's a musical prodigy.

Now, against his mother's wishes, he's about to enter formal education for the first time aged sixteen.

Everything is alien to Edmund: teenage style, language and relationships are impossible to understand.

Then there's the searing jealousy his talent inspires, especially when the sixth form college's Head of Music, turns her back on her other students and begins to teach Edmund exclusively.

Observing events is Steph, a former police detective who is rebuilding her life following a bereavement as the college's receptionist. When a student is found dead in the music block, Steph's sleuthing skills help to unravel the dark events engulfing the college community.

Blood Lines

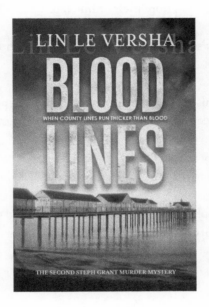

'**This wonderfully fresh take on a crime fighting duo, expertly explores dark, contemporary themes brought to life by a fabulous cast of characters who will stay with you long after the last page.' GRAHAM BARTLETT, AUTHOR OF *BAD FOR GOOD***

Eighteen year-old Darcy Woodard appears to have it all – intelligence, good looks and artistic gifts. His teachers adore him, as does former policewoman Steph Grant, who is now the receptionist at Darcy's college.

But beneath the surface – all is not as it seems.

Darcy is convinced he doesn't fit in with his peers and tries to ignore their online taunts.

There's Darcy's dysfunctional mother Esther who is trapped in a literary time warp.

Then there's his sister Marianne, who Darcy desperately wants to protect from the dark forces that surround her.

Then tragedy rocks Darcy's life when a drugs gang forces its way into his life and all the people he cares for.

What can Steph and her former boss DI Hale do to protect the local community? And can they really trust Darcy to help them defeat the county lines gang?

HOBECK BOOKS – THE HOME OF GREAT STORIES

We hope you've enjoyed reading the second book in Lin Le Versha's crime series. Lin has written a short story prequel to this novel, *A Defining Moment*.

Hobeck Books offers a number of short stories and novellas, including *A Defining Moment* by Lin Le Versha, free for subscribers in the compilation *Crime Bites*.

- *Echo Rock* by Robert Daws
- *Old Dogs, Old Tricks* by AB Morgan
- *The Silence of the Rabbit* by Wendy Turbin
- *Never Mind the Baubles: An Anthology of Twisted Winter Tales* by the Hobeck Team (including many of the Hobeck authors and Hobeck's two publishers)
- *The Clarice Cliff Vase* by Linda Huber
- *Here She Lies* by Kerena Swan
- *The Macnab Principle* by R.D. Nixon
- *Fatal Beginnings* by Brian Price
- *A Defining Moment* by Lin Le Versha
- *Saviour* by Jennie Ensor
- *You Can't Trust Anyone These Days* by Maureen Myant

Also please visit the Hobeck Books website for details of our other superb authors and their books, and if you would like to get in touch, we would love to hear from you.

Hobeck Books also presents a weekly podcast, the Hobcast, where founders Adrian Hobart and Rebecca Collins discuss all things book related, key issues from each week, including the ups and downs of running a creative business. Each episode includes an interview with one of the people who make Hobeck possible: the editors, the authors, the cover designers. These are the people who help Hobeck bring great stories to life. Without them, Hobeck wouldn't exist. The Hobcast can be listened to from all the usual platforms but it can also be found on the Hobeck website: **www.hobeck.net/hobcast**.

Other Hobeck Books to Explore

Silenced

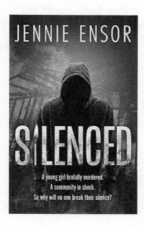

A teenage girl is murdered on her way home from school, stabbed through the heart. Her North London community is shocked, but no-one has the courage to help the police, not even her mother. DI Callum Waverley, in his first job as senior investigating officer, tries to break through the code of silence that shrouds the case.

This is a world where the notorious Skull Crew rules through fear. Everyone knows you keep your mouth shut or you'll be silenced – permanently.

This is Luke's world. Reeling from the loss of his mother to cancer, his step-father distant at best, violent at worst, he slides into the Skull Crew's grip.

This is Jez's world too. Her alcoholic mother neither knows nor cares that her 16-year-old daughter is being exploited by V, all-powerful leader of the gang.

Luke and Jez form a bond. Can Callum win their trust, or will his own demons sabotage his investigation? And can anyone stop the Skull Crew ensuring all witnesses are silenced?

Her Deadly Friend

The Suspect
Bullied by Steph Lewis at school, then betrayed by her lover, Amy Ashby still seethes with fury. Despite the decades-old resentment, she's on the hunt for a new man and a fresh start. This time for keeps.

The Stalker
When both women are stalked by a figure from their shared past, danger threatens.

The Detective
Now Detective Inspector, Steph follows a tip-off to her old rival. After quarrels exploded and changed lives forever, she vowed never to see Amy again. But that was then.

The Deaths

Murder rocks the city. The body count reaches five, and all Steph's leads point to Amy. But is Steph obsessed with a schoolgirl vendetta or closing in on a deadly killer?

Pact of Silence

A fresh start for a new life

Newly pregnant, Emma is startled when her husband Luke announces they're swapping homes with his parents, but the rural idyll where Luke grew up is a great place to start their family. Yet Luke's manner suggests something odd is afoot, something that Emma can't quite fathom.

Too many secrets, not enough truths

Emma works hard to settle into her new life in the Yorkshire countryside, but a chance discovery increases her suspicions. She decides to dig a little deeper...

Be careful what you uncover

Will Emma find out why the locals are behaving so oddly? Can she discover the truth behind Luke's disturbing behaviour? Will the pact of silence ever be broken?

Be Sure Your Sins

Six people
Six events
Six lives destroyed
What is the connection?

Detective **Melissa (Mel) Cooper** has two major investigations on the go. The first involves six apparently unrelated individuals who all suffer inexplicable life-altering events.

Mel is also pursuing a serial blackmailer but just as she's about to prove the link between this man and the six bizarre events, she's ordered to back off.

So why are her bosses interfering with her investigations? Who are they trying to protect? And how far will they go to stop her?

The answers come from a totally unexpected source.

CPSIA information can be obtained
at www.ICGtesting.com
Printed in the USA
BVHW070921310123
657438BV00002B/200